AMANTINE'S SONG

Barbara Morgan

Ghostly Whisper

Website: http://www.ghostlywhisper.com

Facebook: https://www.facebook.com/ghostlywhisperltd

Instagram: https://www.instagram.com/ghostlywhisperltd

Twitter: https://twitter.com/GW_BooksEtc

Whisper of the Heart

Shall I compare thee to a summer's day?
Thou art more lovely and more temperate.
Rough winds do shake the darling buds of May,
And summer's lease hath all too short a date.
Sometime too hot the eye of heaven shines,
And often is his gold complexion dimmed,
And every fair from fair sometime declines,
By chance or nature's changing course untrimmed;
But thy eternal summer shall not fade,
Nor lose possession of that fair thou owest;
Nor shall Death brag thou wand'rest in his shade,
When in eternal lines to time thou grow'st:

> *So long as men can breathe or eyes can see,*
> *So long lives this and this gives life to thee.*

(William Shakespeare)

PROLOGUE

15th March 2014

I'm here. I almost don't understand why. I look at you from a distance. My presence here doesn't make sense. Yet I'm here, on this late winter's day, still very cold. In front of you, you who caused me nothing but pain. One of the greatest agonies of my life. One of those that cannot be forgiven, and dragged over the years takes on exaggerated, exasperating proportions. And maybe I will never really forgive you. With this, I'm not trying to deny my faults, which are many and serious. But you took everything from me. Including what I didn't think I wanted so much, at that time.

They have showered you with flowers. What hypocrisy. I'm sure that most of those who yearn for you now have never really tolerated you. I'm not like that. I won't suddenly turn you into good and holy. And I won't pray for your soul. You can forget about it. I never pray, on principle. Growing up I didn't soften. They say that with the years the character defects are amplified. I am proof of this; I'm even more dried up, colder. All the words you had from me, I would repeat to you, one after the other. I'm not sorry.

I'm angry. You caused me extreme pain and I'm furious. But I repeat, the fault was also mine. I let myself be dragged, I didn't fight. I was what the others had always forced me to be. But now,

7

above all, I have clarity and I face all my responsibilities. I have been the one I committed myself to be.

They leave, finally. They glance at you compassionately for the last time and walk away slowly, then gradually faster. I bet when they reach the iron gate their thoughts, their emotions, will be even further away from you than their bodies. You lost everything, including the memories of those around you.

I can come out of hiding now, detach myself from the tree that kept me sheltered from prying eyes. Better not raise doubts and misunderstandings. I'm only an unimportant shadow in your presence. I carefully observe what is still visible of you. Your name stands out in gold lettering, well highlighted, you would have appreciated it.

I stand. Motionless, dejected. Now I remain the only responsible one. I should step away. Maybe I came here to make sure that it really happened. I had to see with my own eyes. Now I can leave. I feel an overwhelming anger, I can't deny it. And this time, it's not in my power to change the circumstances to my advantage. Curse you!

I hear a rustling behind me. Maybe someone is hiding as I did, waiting for me to get out of here? No. I feel a soft touch on my shoulder. I recognize it even without turning. In my mind's eye I picture his image. I wait for a moment before turning around to confirm my feelings.

Yes, it's really him. I nod, briefly, and then I smile slightly. I look down. It's like my past, my story slipped before my eyes. All of it, without selecting the best, without mercy for the dark moments. The beautiful moments meanwhile caress me, touch me. Some say happiness is never happiness while you're living it. It's just in memory, and I remember right now. A part of me still manages to feel happy. It's like a shiver, a gentle breath sighing from the soul to warm up this day, so grey and cold.

That song that was mine without me being aware of it, for years. Yet I had hummed it myself and listened to it repeatedly. I wanted it, requested it. Without imagining how much it belonged to me. I thought I was a pretext, but I was much more. I was the reason. This, too, I have hidden from my heart. This, too, I will have to begin to atone. The lover's song. *Amantine's Song.*

November 1991

CHAPTER 1

All I really cared about was building my world. And my world had to have very solid foundations. I had a clear perception of my life and my desires, as if I already knew my destiny, the reason why I was born.

In twenty-seven years of life I had never been the victim of hesitations or indecisions. My way was painted in front of me, well defined, like in those paintings where you can see the background and beyond, beyond, even beyond. I had planned my existence as a straight, perfect, incorruptible line. Until I reached old age, I would dare to say. My story. I wouldn't allow anyone to bribe or break it. No one, ever. For any reason. For no curious synchronicity of destiny.

Literature was my life. I've never looked for a real reason. I only knew it was like that. I had chosen it. Whether the choice was mutual or not did not concern me, even if probably it should have. Study, specialization in English, PhD. Mine was a sort of vocation. My mentor was Professor Hermann Frey. I was striving to become his assistant more than anything else in the world, learning from him everything he knew and then one day taking his place. In a purely platonic sense, he was the man of my life.

I lived in a luxury apartment in the Notting Hill area. Not mine. I had settled in the home of family friends, Doris and

Rupert Parker, with the agreement of occasionally taking care of their little daughter, little Jinny. The truth was another. I endured in situations that were not entirely satisfying to avoid more compromising ones, in order not to be forced to give up my freedom. I wasn't ready yet and inside I knew that maybe I would never be.

I wanted to reach my goals alone and my obstinacy wouldn't allow compromises. I intended to build my world without depending on my parents' one. I was myself, Amantine Delamar, completely self-governed and independent from the rest of the world. All I would achieve would be mine only, from the beginning and forever.

What I enthusiastically accepted from my parents, also because I wouldn't have had the chance to reject it, was a good dose of cosmopolitanism that would favour me wherever I decided to live. I was a concentrate of cultures. My father was a French-English diplomat with Spanish ancestry, my mother an Italian-Swiss astrophysicist. Perhaps they should have thought about it before getting married and bringing children into the world. My brother Alain and I belonged to many places and none, with all the advantages and disadvantages of people who had no roots. No bonding, no attachment, no pain. Just ourselves.

CHAPTER 2

Every Sunday morning I used to leave home early. Even earlier than the other days. I used to spend the day with some friends and with Geoffrey, my pseudo boyfriend, or put more accurately... my regular boyfriend.

I had been thinking for some time about leaving the Parkers' house and making myself completely independent, but that would have meant moving to live with Geoffrey and intensifying the level of our relationship, which I did not feel ready for and was not sure I wanted.

Geoffrey Carter, nice guy, serious, motivated, brilliant. He understood me and supported me in my studies. A common destiny, almost. And my parents liked him. His father had been in high school with mine. We were basically made for each other. But to live with him, that would be rushing into things. No, I wasn't ready yet to turn our thing into a serious relationship that would easily point us towards marriage, children and all the rest. I needed intellectual depth but emotional lightness.

I still needed personal freedom. I fought not to fall into that trap like many others. Twenty-seven years were too many or too few, depending on the point of view. Too many, according to someone, to still be sentimentally unresolved, to have no idea about what it meant to truly love. Few, in my opinion, to make a lifetime commitment. Few for a yes, few for a forever, few for a trap from which I would have tried to free myself at all costs, if by chance or by mistake I had ended up in one.

I had learned from experience that it was convenient for me to go out early on Sunday mornings. Not having to go to kindergarten, Jinny had the habit of sticking to me and preventing me from leaving her alone with her mostly absent and distracted parents, during the week. So I tried to sneak out before she woke up, begging me to make up a story on the spot.

I walked quickly to Notting Hill tube station, intending to get to Geoffrey's apartment on Edgware Road. We had started a kind of literary circle with some friends, although by Sunday after a fairly heavy week, most of the time we ended up drinking, smoking, and talking about our tragic and boring lives of assimilated Londoners. The prospects for serious and highly cultural conversations were all there, though. At least they were.

However, on that day, I was firmly determined to show Geoff and the others my notes on Lord Byron's letters. I had found some I had never read before and I felt particularly enthusiastic about it. They showed how the poet was cynical and even a little cruel, especially in love. But maybe he wasn't completely wrong; he was allowed to be like that.

Then I couldn't get it out of my mind the dispute over the non-existence of Shakespeare. I had witnessed a debate in which it was claimed that his was only a fictitious name and that in reality his works had been written by several people. It seemed unacceptable to me as a hypothesis.

'No, no, I can't even think about it. It's crazy and anyone who believes that is crazy!'

I stopped in front of the tube station, shaking my head firmly. The cold was bitter that morning. Too much for my taste. And it wasn't even seven. I let down my brown hair, which I had tied in a ponytail, so that it warmed my neck a little and slipped the hair band around my wrist, like a bracelet. I wrapped myself tightly in my woollen coat. I absolutely needed a hot coffee. Maybe I should stop at a coffee shop. Geoff almost never drank it and always forgot to buy it, so there was little hope of finding it at his place.

There wasn't a soul around at that time on a Sunday morning. Of course, they were not entirely wrong to lie in bed, lounging. I looked around to see if I was in the right place and realized I was wrong. There was a soul around. Two, actually. They stood at the corner, between two streets. I turned to avoid making eye contact but not fast enough. The younger of the two souls looked straight in my direction with an expression of mockery. He had an absolute and perfect punchable face and a look that made me feel inadequate and out of place, as if I had a face full of cream or had gone out, forgetting to put on my underwear.

'Hello, sweetheart. Going somewhere nice at this time?' Punchable face waved his hand to beckon me towards them. He was standing, leaning against the wall. He wore torn jeans and jacket, a black wool hat and fingerless gloves of the same colour. I looked over at the other, an old man sitting on the ground, dressed even worse. Both homeless, of course. Against my will I went back to staring at the young man. His green eyes looked me up and down, sly and restless. He seemed calm but at the same time without peace. I couldn't understand what attracted me in that look or even why I didn't decide to walk down the tube stairs and disappear forever from their path.

I had to reach my friends, soon. We had so much to discuss. I just wanted to stop for a moment to get a coffee. It wasn't my intention to disrupt my life forever. Absolutely not.

CHAPTER 3

Better forget coffee and get away immediately from those two early morning time-wasters. Tube, direction Edgware Road. I could have coffee there, before going to Geoff.

'You don't want to tell us where you're going, my dear?' The old man was also interested in my destination. I remained nailed there, without a real reason except curiosity about those particular, devastated and rather sad forms of humanity. 'Could you go get me another coffee, my dear?' The old man raised the paper cup towards me. Did he read my mind? It was exactly what I wanted as well. 'The coffee shop is across the street, if you don't mind.'

He pointed at it and I turned automatically to look at it. I would have gladly gone, but if I went I would have to get coffee for him too. Then come back to deliver it to him, get closer... interact.

'I can pay for it, girl. Don't worry about it, I'm not begging you for charity.' The old man pointed his placid light eyes at me and rummaged in his worn jacket. He took out some coins and handed them to me.

'Oh no, don't worry about it.' I sighed, pointing at the coffee shop with my head. 'I just wonder why you don't send the lazy one who is standing next to you. Too busy holding up the wall?'

I threw a mocking look at the young punchable face. I was dying to do it, it was my turn. I didn't give him time to reply but set off towards the coffee shop.

For a moment the thought of getting coffee for punchable face crossed my mind, then I told myself no, I shouldn't have to. I was not a waitress! He could fend for himself. After drinking my coffee in the coffee shop, I returned to the corner of the street and found them where I had left them. I handed the paper cup to the old man, feigning a smile.

'Thank you, my dear.' The old man grabbed the cup with a pleased smile. 'I couldn't send the boy there... it is beginning to get busier, too many people around, he would draw attention.'

I shrugged carelessly. The old man was talking in riddles, but it wasn't my problem after all. 'All right, have a good day.'

I was ready to fade away once and for all. I carefully avoided making eye contact again with punchable face, I'd had enough of him and of that situation. I wanted to disappear inside the tube. I wanted to reach my destination.

'What do you do in your life?' The old man, savouring his coffee with exaggerated taste, stopped me again.

What do you do in your life? What kind of question was that for a stranger who had just offered him a coffee? And anyway, I didn't want to answer. I realized that it wasn't a question requiring an answer, it was just something to say. Of course, undoubtedly for many it was. But it was "the question". The essence of a person. Who could answer with one word, or one thousand.

I decided that, for this occasion, one would be enough.

'Literature.'

'Literature?' The old man smiled at me and nodded with exaggerated enthusiasm. 'Me too, lots of literature. The romantics, above all. Keats, Shelley, Wordsworth, Byron, Coleridge... all that gang.'

I looked at him, disbelieving. He looked back at me, frowning, and showing more wrinkles than I had noticed so far.

'How did you spend this month? Who did you smile with? You don't feel what I feel, you don't know what love means, maybe one day you'll know it, but it's not your time yet.'

I was puzzled, the old man caught me by surprise. It was a feeling that I didn't like at all. Meanwhile, the old man continued reciting, undaunted.

'Bright star, would I were stedfast as thou art

Not in lone splendour hung aloft the night
And watching, with eternal lids apart...'

'John Keats, my dear,' he informed me, leaning his back against the wall and squinting. He seemed to have lost himself inside an unknown, recondite, distant world.

He knew poetry. How did he end up there? Perhaps precisely because he knew poetry and not the logic of the world. I had no desire to delve deeper. I just wanted to leave, step away, forget those moments of life, take my train finally and disappear forever in another part of the city.

I tried to avoid it, to resist. But I couldn't help giving a last look at punchable face. What did I care, after all? I would never see him again! He looked back at me but this time he didn't grin. He was serious, it seemed he was thinking. I hoped he didn't begin to recite poetry as well. It would have been too much in one day.

'Anyway... have a good day. And goodbye.' Better for me to fade away immediately.

In the meantime, the old man had opened his light, slightly vacant eyes, pointing them at me again. I didn't want to be held back and I ran away before he tried to, with any excuse. Above all, before being tempted to stop myself again, wasting time with those two individuals. I didn't have a moment of my life to waste. I always devoted it some way. Even the time spent sleeping I considered wasted, but unfortunately necessary. I hated the time-wasters. And I wouldn't turn myself into one of them, not even for a minute more than necessary.

CHAPTER 4

I was trying to delete that strange meeting from my mind getting off at Edgware Road stop. But my steps in the direction of Geoff's apartment were getting heavier.

The truth was that part of me yearned for freedom, both personal and mental. Do nothing. Think nothing. At least for a while. Perhaps for that reason I had stopped to talk to those two layabouts. They led a lifestyle that I secretly felt like experiencing. I would never confess it, not even to myself. But it was undeniably true.

With Geoff and the others, I had to always talk about something clever, express meaningful concepts. After all, they were right, because I was like that too. I had built a world in which the reason controlled the instinct, even if we were talking about literature, poetry, art. I couldn't change it now, it was too late. Everything was managed in a serious and professional way. By insiders, not by beauty contemplators.

About one thing, the old man, through Keats's words, was right. I didn't know what it meant to love. I didn't love Geoffrey Carter. Admitting it or trying to establish it was out of the question. I didn't even ask myself. I didn't care. He belonged to my world, that was enough for me. He was a handsome boy, with blond hair and a sweet smile. More than enough. He didn't bother me, he gave me my space. This made him the ideal man in my eyes. He understood me and I had known him for so long that I was not obliged to explain myself or try to make myself interesting in his eyes. In my own way, however, I loved him. But it seemed silly to me to say it, it seemed useless, superfluous. He knew I wasn't an overly warm or loving type of person and that was fine with him. He wouldn't have asked for more. Perhaps it was for this reason I had chosen him.

I returned his kiss without passion as soon as I entered the house. I mostly wanted to take off my coat and shoes and get comfortable on the sofa, hugging my knees. In a few minutes, I would have to regain my consciousness and start talking about something clever, interesting. About my research, about Frey. I rubbed my temples with my fingertips as if to put my thoughts in order, all lined up in their place.

'Have the others arrived already?' There was nobody in the living room except me and Geoff, who sat beside me. I was hoping there was someone in the kitchen or the bathroom. I didn't want to be alone with him.

'No...' He drew me to him and I leaned my head on his shoulder. I pulled back as he leaned down to pull my hair aside and kiss my neck. 'They'll come later, we have time.'

I kissed him quickly on his lips and moved away, leaning with my elbow on the back of the sofa. 'I'm not in the mood, I'm sorry.' I frowned, looking for a believable excuse. 'Problems at the department.'

'The usual guerrilla wars to win Frey over?' Geoff stroked my cheek with a sympathetic expression. By now he knew everything about me. All that he needed to know.

'He seems unreachable. Whatever I do is never enough, he goes further and further, always wanting more.'

It was true. The competition to become Hermann Frey's assistant was probably beyond my abilities and possibilities. But I didn't want to give up, not yet. My pride kept me in that sort of madhouse, up for anything, that was the department of English literature. My pride demanded that I begin my academic career with one of the greatest intellectuals in the country, maybe even the world.

'I could mention that to my father, you know he was...'

'Absolutely not!' I didn't allow him to finish the sentence. Of course I knew it. Frey and Geoff's father had been college mates and good friends. But what was the point of getting something thanks to his intervention? I would rather have given up, left the challenge. What credit would I have otherwise? I crossed my arms, annoyed, tearing myself definitively away from Geoff. The very thought offended me.

'Not that you need it, Amy. You're still very good. But you could accept a little help, like everyone else does.'

Geoff had always been restrained in pronouncing my whole name. As if in itself it contained something forbidden. Forbidden in the sense of too sensual, lustful, provocative, which embarrassed him. I knew it and I was delighted by this power that only my name had on him.

I remained silent in the face of his suggestion, absorbed in my not so chaste thoughts. I remembered punchable face, in fact. I didn't understand how, nor why. Indeed, yes, actually. Because to the word *provocative* I had connected him, his expression, his almost irreverent way of staring at me.

'You should move in with me instead of babysitting for those friends of yours. Here you would be more peaceful...' Geoff took the opportunity to continue with his indecent proposals. Every now and then he returned to the attack with the idea of making me move to his apartment.

I stroked his blond hair and coaxed him towards me with the precise purpose of distracting him from his intent. Moving in with him was absolutely not part of my plans. It would mean a real commitment and for me it was too much. How long had I been with Geoffrey Carter? I had lost track. It had never been a serious and profound relationship. Much less passionate or romantic. It wasn't down to him. It was me and I had never done anything to hide it. Love, the real one, was not part of my life. I only lived the love of paper, poetry, literature, words. And those had the priority over any human being. But Geoff was fine with it, anyway. Other guys might not have accepted it, maybe. For that reason, Geoff, and no one else, had been with me for so many years.

CHAPTER 5

University, research and life at the Parkers. Little space for anything else. The truth was that I didn't want to compromise myself too much with Geoff. I had reached an age whereby I was at an easy to compromise age, I was the first to realize that. Geoff's intentions were too serious for me. I understood that. But in the end, what could I do? Maybe leave him would be the most sensible and right thing for him. I couldn't go and live with him. I wasn't ready. And I didn't even know if and when I would be.

'Then, Jinny... it's me and you this afternoon!' The little girl had her dark eyes fixed on me and gave me a toothless smile, full of dimples, as I knelt down to secure her in the stroller and placed the little pink woollen hat on her head. 'And we're going for a nice walk, so maybe Amantine will take a nice cup of coffee and for you she will buy a nice biscuit and...'

And nothing! I was shameless and definitely a naughty girl. Because I knew what I was looking for, heading at full speed from Holland Park Avenue to Notting Hill Gate. Above all, stopping at that precise point where I thought I could find him, he who wasn't there now. I used to take the underground at Holland Park, closer to home. Only when I went to Geoff on Sunday mornings, I preferred to reach Notting Hill station so I didn't have to change the line going to Edgware Road.

'We don't care at all if he's not here... they're not here...' I snorted sullenly. 'We're going to get a wonderful coffee and a great bickie!'

'Bic... kie!' Jinny repeated enthusiastically, beating her little hands. Every now and then she pointed at something, murmuring a few words and I, lost in my thoughts, pretended to indulge her.

I did what I could but didn't shine with maternal instinct and active conversation with such a small child. Maybe I had never really been a child myself. I had never claimed anyone's attention. I was born already old, introvert, surly and slightly hysterical.

I took the coffee and the biscuits, one for me as well, not caring about my shape, and we headed to Holland Park. The park had swings for children and we could take advantage of the sunny day that was not so cold. I placed Jinny on the swing and pushed her gently for a while. Shortly thereafter she managed to push herself by swinging her little legs. She was a child of few aspirations, luckily for me. She would swing for a while, easily pleased, she loved the swing.

I went to sit on the bench not far away and took from my bag the book on Byron's life I was reading. I held it on my knees without opening it and looked around. Not many people around, just some other kids in the playground.

I felt like I was being watched. Or maybe I felt lost. Intimidated, scared of a life that wasn't going anywhere. Or maybe, yes, somewhere, it was going somewhere, but... was it really what I wanted? Or just what I thought I wanted?

I had always known exactly what to do with myself. All my life, a well-defined line, without smudges. But what if... I was wrong? If that wasn't the right life for me? If I was stubbornly trying to reach and become part of a world that wasn't and would never be really mine?

No way. I had fought too hard for that world. I was not going to lose it. I wouldn't let it go. It belonged to me. Because in addition to being born already old, introvert, surly and slightly hysterical, I was also born disgustingly and irretrievably coherent.

CHAPTER 6

I felt like I wasn't taken seriously. Even worse, teased. It was horrible. I even thought of giving up my project. It was clear that Hermann Frey didn't consider me worthy enough since he had been paying his full attention to that ass licker Gregor Jackman, lately. A part of me was ready to leave and search for better luck elsewhere. That same part almost felt relieved at the idea. But the truth was that I wouldn't have known what else I could do with my life, or where to go. It was the one that held me back and pushed me, or perhaps forced me, to keep going.

I just hoped that being a woman wouldn't put me at a disadvantage. No, Professor Frey didn't seem like the type. However, I was already psychologically committed to work double or even triple to show him how good I was. And how better I could be than that sleazy little opportunist Gregor.

'What are you working on?'

My attempts to avoid him were useless, and I hated that he inquired about my work. I wasn't jealous about it, on the contrary, I would have gladly talked to anyone else. It could be useful for me to hear some disinterested opinion. Too bad that his wasn't. He was retrieving information to fight back, it was obvious!

'Nothing new.' I remained vague. That then was true, that I hadn't found much exciting lately, it wasn't a lie. But it annoyed me that he knew it. Also because he kept it very confidential, the information about his own work.

'Are you still investigating Byron? Are you sure there is still something to discover?' He gave me a wry, malicious smile. Here was another one that inspired me to punch him in the face. But while the provocative expression contributed to increase the charm of punchable face, Gregor gave the idea of a mocking and at the same time cruel demon. One for whom I wouldn't have shown any mercy and I would willingly have sent to hell. He could also be a handsome man, if he wanted to. If one likes the contrast between dark brown hair and red beard.

Suddenly the old man's words came back to me. Those verses of Keats's poetry. Maybe I could start a parallel research, keeping everyone in the dark. Even Frey, at the moment. They would continue to believe that I was concentrating on my dear beloved Byron, meanwhile...

I wasn't sure though, it seemed like I was going to lose too much time. In fact, I would lose twice as much of it and all the work I had already done would be useless. Follow the instinct or continue on the path of reason even if more and more unsatisfactory? I didn't know. I only knew that each passing day I felt more and more useless, demotivated and above all replaceable.

CHAPTER 7

Another Sunday. Another day in which I would have to make up excuses and look inside me for a foothold, an expedient to keep going. I had taken some time before deciding to go to Geoff, like every Sunday.

I got up at dawn, had a nice shower, applied body cream with exaggerated care, and made a cucumber face mask. Then I applied my makeup to accentuate the green specks in my brown eyes as I was taught by a makeup artist, a friend of my mother... all bullshit! But for once I did it, or at least tried to. I also had to force myself not to bite my lips and eat my lipstick three minutes after I put it on.

I almost hoped that Jinny would hold me back, so I had an excuse. That morning, instead, Jinny decided to sleep blissfully. Maybe it wasn't meant to be. Or maybe it was.

A part of me had completely removed the previous Sunday's meeting. Another side, however, was well aware and couldn't wait for something else like it. Inside me there was a rejection and an expectation at the same time. Of course, at that time I wouldn't have confessed it, not even to myself under torture. But it was true.

I walked fast to Notting Hill Underground, almost breaking into a run. I had no reason to run. I felt my heart thumping in my chest. I didn't dare confess the reasons, not even to myself. I calmed down as soon as I saw them appearing in the distance. None of my physical reactions to that sight made sense as I no longer had to worry about a loss, a lack of which I didn't understand the meaning. Perhaps it was the old man's words, perhaps the young man's look, even though I wasn't able to admit it yet.

They were on the same section of the street, in front of the Underground's staircase, at the corner of two streets. I wouldn't have wanted to, but I suddenly stopped in front of them. Although the road was almost empty, they didn't notice me, as they were busy talking to each other. I felt stupid, stuck there watching them. And I hated feeling stupid or giving the impression of being like that.

'Morning, all right sweetheart?'

The voice of punchable face reached me as soon as I decided to go down the first steps. I turned my face slightly with the most indifferent expression I was able to produce. I could ignore him and keep going downstairs, towards my destination. But the truth was another and I knew it. I had been looking for them all week. Was my life so boring and predictable, then? So much, that I'd to look for a distraction in two strangers I met on the street on a random Sunday morning?

While punchable face's green eyes lingered on my face, I remained motionless. Besides, I was looking at him too. I didn't feel attracted to him, not in the ordinary way at least. Yet there was something that kept me from detaching myself from his face, from his eyes. Something I couldn't identify, translate into words.

'Come closer, my dear. Why do you stand there?' The old man waved to me with a slow hand gesture. He sat quietly on the ground, just like the previous Sunday.

I obeyed him in silence, without finding a reasonable motivation for my compliant attitude.

I held myself in front of them, shifting my look to the old man.

'So you like my friend, as I can see.'

What did he see? I didn't understand. Because there was no way of seeing it. There wasn't because it wasn't true. I didn't know if I should have felt offended and humiliated by his unfounded statement.

'I'm completely indifferent to him, actually.' I decided to show myself cold, as if his words hadn't touched me at all. I turned my eyes fleetingly towards punchable face. 'In fact, he's not my type.'

'Why, who would be your type?' punchable face inquired. He giggled carelessly with the same mocking and defiant expression that seemed embedded on his face.

Good question, anyway! Who was my type? The most logical answer should have been Geoffrey. He was my boyfriend, after all. So I should have answered, to silence them. But why on earth was I discussing my private life with them? What nonsense!

'I don't want to answer, and it's late, I have to go!'

'It's seven-thirty in the morning, sweetheart. It can't be that late.' It seemed that every word of mine aroused the hilarity in punchable face. He had an unbearable attitude. So much that I found myself compelled to measure my words, so that he couldn't use them to return-fire against me.

'I have no reason to stop.' Meanwhile, I was still stuck there, like an idiot. 'And it's cold!'

So why didn't I decide to move and go down the stairs towards the warm and comfortable Underground that would take me to my boyfriend's warm and comfortable apartment?

'If we go to my place, we can find a way to get warm.' I didn't expect this. He caught me off guard, again. But such an audacity was too much for me.

While punchable face was looking at me seriously, the old man laughed, watching the scene and my horrified expression. Probably seeing the smoke coming from my nostrils and ears.

'How dare you! You're a... a...'

'I was thinking about a hot chocolate or maybe a stiff drink.' Punchable face shrugged and his green eyes became almost angelic like, innocent. 'Why... what did you think?'

Cursed. Asshole. Despicable bastard. He knew well what I had thought. So I decided to hate him, and I hated myself too for having thought it and letting him know I thought it. But no, actually. I hadn't only thought about it. I had also pictured the scene. That's my problem!

'I haven't become an alcoholic yet, having a drink early in the morning. And anyway, it was obvious that your proposal had a double meaning, I'm certainly not so stupid to accept it!' Instead, yes, I was. 'However, no, I'm not interested.'

'Many others wouldn't be so fussy!' The old man winced in the vague attempt to imitate me, I think. I tried to pull myself together. 'All the others, I would say. Considering who the proposal came from.'

'And who does it come from?' I didn't want to, but the question came out spontaneously. I snorted, shrugging, glancing almost furiously at the boy. 'From an ignoble scoundrel with...' With a punchable face. I stopped before saying it. But then how the hell was I talking? *Ignoble scoundrel*? For sure he would laugh at me!

The old man burst out laughing even louder, quite coarsely. He didn't try to make a good impression, this was now a fact. Not even punchable face mattered. And, at this point, not even to me.

I was gradually turning into an outcast, abandoned on a street corner, just like them. As the world kept going, I stood there discussing nothing with two strangers, not giving a damn about anything else, including my real life that was waiting for me to be in sound mind again, to resume playing a role, in a sense.

'I'm Jacob,' the old man said, without me asking. 'What's your name, my dear?'

Why would I ever have to tell them my name? And wasn't it punchable face we were talking about just before?

'Amantine.' Now they would tell me it was the strangest name they had ever heard in their miserable and sad existence. I knew it. It was a script known to me.

'Amantine... nice sound. I like it.' The boy frowned thoughtfully. He was strangely serious, as if lost in some controversial reflection.

I was preparing myself to give the usual explanations on the origin and the motivation of my name and to secretly curse my parents for having given it to me, but this time it wasn't necessary. The old man merely nodded, then stretched, yawning and leaned against the wall with his back and head.

'Anyway, I have to go. Goodbye.'

Perhaps it was appropriate to take the advantage and drag myself out of that absurd situation. In a moment I found myself inside the underground. I had climbed the stairs before giving them the chance to reply and hold me again. I tried to push away the thought, but I couldn't ignore the inner derangement that they both caused in me, even if in different ways. As if they lived, without feeling obliged to give explanations to anybody. A part of me envied them. Another rejected them and didn't want to have anything to do with them. Then there was a part I couldn't understand, so deep and intimate, that found in them something familiar, true, intrinsic in me.

I had built a world and forced it to be identified and defined as mine. But did this world really define me, who I was? Who did I want to become? I didn't know. I was starting to wonder if I would ever know. I began to suspect and perhaps even to fear the cry of freedom that exploded inside my chest for a few days now or forever. Living in the moment, living without projects, living outside a world that I had planned at the drawing board for myself and in which I tried in every way to force myself, to push beyond my limits. Living like someone who saw the world going round without struggling to possess it, without trying to rip it away from others. Living on instinct and sensations, not on mind and reason. Accept the punchable face's proposal, whatever it was, simply because I felt like it, without worrying about the consequences. In short, take a vacation from myself, from the world I had built and called mine.

CHAPTER 8

I had to compose and return to myself on the way to Geoff's apartment. Maybe my concern was the sign of something changing inside me. Maybe I should have seriously considered the idea of straightening out, moving in with Geoff and dealing with all that would follow from it.

Finding Rachel and Trevor there as well that Sunday comforted me. I wouldn't have known how to behave alone with Geoff. I felt guilty and uncomfortable. I felt as if I had betrayed him, even if only in my thoughts.

While Geoff was arguing with Trevor on a dissertation about Hegel and the phenomenology of spirit, I took the chance to get out on the balcony. Rachel promptly joined me.

'Soon they will get from Hegel to the sport.' Rachel sighed, shaking her head and letting her bobbed blonde hair swing. Trevor was doing a PhD in philosophy and in his subject he was even more motivated and stubborn than me, if that's possible.

'We're a nice bunch of failed intellectuals, in short.' I stretched my neck in a vain attempt to relax.

'Don't look at me, I don't care about an academic career at all!' Rachel, graduated in medieval history, was very good at teaching at high school. She didn't ask for anything better.

I nodded without excessive participation. Maybe I should have stopped being so reluctant and selfish. Rachel and Trevor had been living together for two years. They were fine. Perhaps it was time for me to give in and please Geoff. At this point I understood that it would only be a matter of time. The alternative was to split up, once and for all.

'Do you think I should move and live with Geoff?' Saying it aloud, I felt suffocating with anxiety.

'I know he would like you to, Amy.' Rachel turned her back to the view, turning to me and resting her hands on the railing. 'But it must be your choice, you shouldn't feel forced.'

'He will leave me if I keep refusing.' I ran my hands over my face and held them to the sides of my neck. I didn't want to move in with him. But I didn't want him to leave me. What would I do then, alone? I would force my friends to make a choice between me and Geoff. And most likely they wouldn't choose me, the one responsible for the break up.

'I don't think so. After all, if you're not ready yet...' Rachel left the sentence deliberately pending, maybe believing that I would continue it. But the truth was that I didn't know how to finish it.

I decided to speak. The real question was not whether and when I was ready or not. 'What if I never am? If I never want to be ready?'

'It would mean Geoff is not the right man for you, Amantine.' Rachel was always very logical. She went straight to the point.

But how could I admit that Geoff was not the right man for me when he had been part of my life all along? When he was part of my world, of the world I had chosen from the first years of my life? That straight and unequivocal line, that fate I couldn't ever change now. It would be too risky. I feared the unknown more than anything else. How could I land in a world that was not mine? What would I do? What would happen to me?

'I've made my choices, now. And Geoff is somehow part of these choices. It's my world, Rachel. What can I do if I lose my world?'

My life and Geoffrey Carter's were somehow inextricably intertwined. We came from the same environment, we had the same studies behind us, the same knowledge, the same ambitions. Nobody could understand me as much as he did. With nobody else could I confide and confront myself in the same way. All the rest was of secondary importance. No, I wouldn't give up my world. The cost was moving in with Geoff, even if I wasn't feeling ready. I would never allow my world to crumble to the point of collapsing and destroying everything I had worked for all my life.

CHAPTER 9

There are moments in life when it seems that the whole world is turning against us. That moment had arrived for me. I had felt it for a while now. I felt targeted everywhere. Geoff's requests about our relationship were becoming pressing, little Jinny was inexplicably more spoiled every day, and that filthy slimy Gregor Jackman shifted all the responsibilities to me. When things went well it was thanks to him. When something went wrong, it was obviously my fault.

The thing that went completely wrong that day was the arrival of an American professor, a great friend and colleague of Hermann Frey, whom we had both forgotten at the airport. I remembered perfectly Gregor said in front of Frey, looking like an arrogant cockerel, that he would take care of it. But then magically it turned into my task. I'd had enough. Of him, of the department, and also of the man of my life, my platonic love Hermann Frey who never took my side!

'You can all go to hell...' I grumbled to myself, obviously not in front of Frey who had left me and Gregor to amiably slaughter each other. I was collecting my notes and my folders in a bag, looking like someone leaving for a long journey.

'Where do you think you're going now?' Gregor was standing in front of me with the expression of a pissed off ferret and that didn't impress me either.

'I'll leave you alone with Frey and our guest, aren't you happy?' No, of course he wasn't. Because, without me, he should also serve as a handyman errand boy and not just as a professional licker. 'I don't feel well, I'm done for today.'

I didn't rise to any of his further provocations. I left the office and then the university without wasting another breath. Maybe it was really the end. Or just the beginning of the end.

Where could I go? It wasn't my shift to take care of Jinny that afternoon and besides, I didn't want to have too many people around. Maybe I could go and lie down in the park, or... No, I should go home instead! I needed to sleep, an almost desperate need to sleep and not think about anything for hours. A long and wonderful sleep would regenerate my body and my mind.

Calling Geoff and lashing out my frustration on him wasn't convenient. He was no longer an external and disinterested confidant. He had become part of the problem.

To get into my room, once inside, I had to walk through the living room. There I found Doris, blissfully sitting on the couch, enjoying a cup of tea. I envied her lately. She always had little to do, to conquer, to fight for. A placid and peaceful life, a wealthy husband, a bit tasteless but unpretentious, a cute little girl to keep in pretty dresses, little ribbons and hairpins. By now everything was accomplished for her, she could resign for the days to come or tell her friends how pleased she was with her situation.

'Do you want some tea? I've made a lot.' Doris smiled at me, brushing her brown hair away from her forehead. 'Keep me company, Jinny just fell asleep.'

'All right.' Well, talking a little about everything and nothing could help me. I diverted towards the kitchen to get the tea. 'Do you want some more?'

'Yes, please,' Doris sighed in a bored voice. Returning to the living room with the teacups I noticed she was rhythmically changing channels on the television. Even having nothing to do was frustrating. Perhaps even more than having too many commitments.

I sat next to her. I didn't know what to say, what to talk about. I didn't even know Doris Parker's real interests besides her daughter, her husband and the dinners she organized with his colleagues and friends. Maybe she really was a woman without a life of her own. But if she was okay with that who was I to criticize her?

I sipped my tea as she explained her Christmas holiday plans in detail. They would leave, go to visit her parents in Leeds and then she and Rupert would take a second honeymoon in Hawaii, leaving the little girl with her grandparents. Great plan! I, on the contrary, didn't even know my fate for the next few hours.

Between the two of us I was the poor frustrated one, I had to admit. I didn't want to tell her about my academic misadventures, so I reluctantly admitted that everything was fine, as usual. I stared at the television screen, to be able to lie better.

No, it couldn't be! I was going crazy. I hallucinated. Perhaps it was the tiredness, or the constant pissed off state I was in. The guy who was fidgeting in front of a microphone in a television studio looked in a freaky way like punchable face. I couldn't hear because Doris had turned the volume down to talk to me. I stared, waiting for something to tell me it was really him, or rather, something that convinced me it wasn't him at all.

'Do you like Darkest Storm?' Doris, probably noticing my cathartic state, turned up the volume. The voice of the guy who looked like punchable face mingled with the others and also with Doris who was asking me the question.

'No, I mean...' Darkest Storm? Yes, I knew them, I heard about them. Well, I was aware of their existence on the face of the earth, but they had never been of any interest to me. 'One of those there...' I pointed. 'Here, that one... looks like a homeless guy I met in Notting Hill.'

'But that's exactly where Peter Wiles lives!' Doris widened her blue, disbelieving eyes on me and put the cup down on the glass table in front of us, with such a blow that if it didn't fall into pieces, it was only by chance. Was she crazy?

I tried to stay calm, at least. It seemed impossible, even if the resemblance was very pronounced. Same eyes, same expression. I waited for them to finish strumming. Then I waited patiently until they framed just him as the talk-show host interviewed them.

Those green eyes, that grin a little disdainful, the sneer when he wrinkled his nose. Yes, it was him. Definitely him. If it wasn't, he had a twin brother or a perfectly equal double. 'What did you say his name is?'

'Peter Wiles!' Doris twisted her hands, still too excited. 'You mean you really met Peter Wiles?'

'No... now I look at him well, I would say no. He was just someone who looked vaguely like him.' By the enthusiasm she showed, I was afraid Doris would follow me on Sunday morning just to see the one who seemed to be some sort of pop star. Maybe she would finally shake up her life of perfect housewife, wife and mother, but I didn't want to be the one to drag her to the path of perdition. I tried to change the subject and looked for a practical moment to withdraw to my room. 'I'm going to rest for a while, I have a bad headache today.'

I finally managed to lie down on my bed. I had his face in my mind. No, not Peter Wiles's face. I couldn't connect that name and that man who appeared on television to the one I identified as punchable face. Although it was indisputably him. But how could it be? Then the old man's words came back to me. The fact he didn't want to go and get him coffee.

No, that wasn't fair for me. I didn't want it to be him. It made him less authentic. I could no longer frame him in the character in which I had delimited him. And, I had to confess it to myself, I couldn't long for him as I wanted anymore.

I tried to remove him from my thoughts, striving to sleep. But my mind went on its own in inappropriate directions. Even hiding my head under the pillow, I couldn't stop the thoughts that I wasn't inclined to indulge.

'Amy... your father is on the phone...' Doris's voice, across the room's door, called me back to reality. Too bad, just a few minutes more and with a little luck I would have sunk into sleep. Or maybe into nightmares.

I went to the living room to take the call. I would say that everything was fine, even to him. No problem, then.

'Amantine, I've talked to Geoffrey's father.' My father's baritone voice didn't permit replies this time. From the start, it was bad. I already expected I wouldn't agree on anything. 'He could easily help you at the department.'

'The real problem, Dad, is I don't want anyone's help. And if Geoffrey, his father or anyone else asked you to call me and convince me he made a big mistake.'

Geoff, it couldn't have been anyone other than him. He knew I didn't agree to that. I had been clear about it and more than once. He shouldn't have done this, put his father, and mine too, into a matter that concerned just me. I wouldn't forgive him. Maybe our relationship had come to an end. Or maybe, but I dared not to admit it, not even to myself, I was desperately looking for an excuse to leave him, to put an end to our relationship and this time I had found it.

CHAPTER 10

Another Sunday. And no desire at all to go to Geoff. In the end I had avoided discussing his interference in my life over the phone, and made up excuses not to see him, not even in the evening. I was too irritated and had to calm down. Why did my words mean nothing to him? Why didn't he respect my will, and not bring his father into this?

However, I went out anyway. I didn't know where I would go but I knew I didn't want to stay indoors. Maybe freezing at the park, maybe visiting the city, maybe shopping. Maybe... In short, I hated the idea of being cornered!

Sunday morning implied only one direction, despite everything. I couldn't lie to myself, this time. I wanted to see if he was still there, still in the same place, for the third time. But this one would be different. I knew who he was. I hated the idea. I preferred him to be an ordinary lout, someone not so defined, so well known. I felt betrayed, teased. A bit like someone had broken my favourite toy and later mercilessly showed me the pieces.

As if he had read my mind, he wasn't there. Jacob was sitting at the usual place, but alone. I slowed down for a moment, determined, however, to continue my journey towards an unknown destination. Maybe in the end I would be better off to go to Geoffrey, as every Sunday, and maybe try to talk to him, to explain to him my reasons.

'Good morning, my dear.'

But the unvarnished truth was that I was just waiting for an excuse to get closer. I raised a faint smile at Jacob. Maybe I could offer him a coffee, just to be nice.

'The boy had one of his commitments...' Jacob disclosed it, before I could talk.

'Oh, I see...' What did I see? Nothing, better not get further into the subject and change it decisively. 'Coffee?' I glanced towards the coffee shop. It wasn't clear to me if I really wanted to offer him a coffee or I was looking for an excuse for myself.

'No, thank you, my dear. Already had it.' Jacob frowned, however, rummaging through his wrinkled, creased jacket pocket and ignoring my presence. I shrugged and decided I had nothing left to do but to make my way down to the tube. 'Wait... here it is, I found it!'

'What is it?' I could see what it was. A folded piece of paper that Jacob was handing out to me. My heart made a curious and unusual leap. A message? What else?

'He left it for you.' There was no need to specify who.

I stood in front of Jacob, who handed me the note that at that moment was no longer a piece of paper. It was my Passport to hell. Whatever was written there would lead me to something that was not part of me, of my environment, of what I had always been. But I couldn't resist.

'Tell him I'm not interested when you see him.' See him? I saw his expression change at my words, the lip slightly bent upward, the mockery that livened my senses and got on my nerves at the same time. I flushed, trying to keep my breathing steady.

'Take it and do whatever you want.' Jacob insisted on delivering the note. 'I always carry out my tasks, girl.'

I grabbed it almost angrily, tearing it from Jacob's hand. 'I'm not...' I opened it and read an address. Notting Hill, of course. Peter Wiles, of course. I closed it. 'I didn't understand it was him,' I finally confessed, resigned. 'I'm not interested in Peter Wiles.'

Jacob shrugged and sighed, running his hand over his head. He took off his grey woollen hat, almost as grey as the strands of hair that fell on either side of his face and then he put it back, covering his ears well. 'Everyone is the way they is. You're not perfect either, my dear.'

I had just said that I wasn't interested in Peter Wiles. Because I wasn't. But... I tightened the note in my hand, tormented it with my nails as if I could destroy it, annihilate it. It didn't matter, I had memorized the name of the street, parallel to the one I was walking, and the number.

'I'm not interested in Peter Wiles,' I repeated, maybe more to myself than to Jacob. Because in the meantime my steps, first oriented towards the staircase that led to the Underground, were instead moving right in the direction of Peter Wiles's house.

CHAPTER 11

Crazy. Crazy, wicked and shameless. But I couldn't stop myself. I couldn't bend my will to reason. I felt, in that precise moment, a bit like one of the characters of *The Betrothed* by Alessandro Manzoni. The nun of Monza, to be exact. I had found the novel years ago in my mother's library. Here, precisely the quote "The poor wretched answered" seemed written just for me.

I walked with my eyes down, as if I didn't even want to look at the road that would lead me to him. I lifted them only when I realized I had arrived right in front of his gate. That was the number, Peter Wiles's house.

A large, multi-storey white house with blue shutters, surrounded by a dark grating. The upper floor was taken up by an immense terrace and a large window. The Parkers' home paled in comparison. So, being a low-key pop star and strumming little songs paid more than an accountant's job. As an aspiring academic, I didn't even try to compete, they would have torn me apart.

I stood there, arms crossed on my chest. How stupid! What did I think I was doing? No, no, it wasn't the right situation for me. I had to get back on track as soon as possible, go to Geoffrey, argue with him, fight over the story of his father and Frey too. Peter Wiles was a distraction that threatened to compromise my career in addition to my private life. I could hold onto the curiosity of what might have happened.

Go away, Amantine, go away immediately! I turned my back on the big white house with blue shutters. I couldn't keep myself from imagining him inside there. But I wouldn't go beyond imagination. And mine would be an affair without a sequel, an adventure on which I would only fantasize in the moments of boredom.

'Where do you think you're going, sweetheart?'

I felt myself held by my wrist. It was the first time he touched me. Without letting me go, I found myself in front of him.

'I was just walking around, I'm leaving now.' I felt like I was burning even though it was November, as his hand slipped from my wrist to my hand.

In my mind there was a repeated symphony that reminded me that he was Peter Wiles and had nothing to do with me and my world, my environment. Another idea, more shameless and daring, reminded me that it wasn't necessary for him to understand the intensity and the depth of my soul and my intellect, to do what I really wanted to do with him, whether he was Peter Wiles or any other.

'What do you want?' He tilted his face slightly, narrowing his eyes so that they looked even greener and animated by a light that seemed intriguing but a little perfidious.

'Nothing. I mean, I just want to get away from here.' I feared his look on me. Even more than his gestures, his touch.

'You must want something if you've come over here.' He suddenly let my hand go, almost sharply, and unexpectedly, I missed it. Yet I had never been very predisposed to physical contact, far from it.

'You're wrong. I had the note from Jacob and... I just wanted to take a walk this morning, so...' I didn't want to justify myself. I just wanted to leave, to get away from him once and for all. 'If you think I'm here for a particular reason, you're wrong!'

'So, let's see if I understand correctly, Amantine...' He remembered my name? Yes, he had just said it. So he remembered it. Why didn't it sound the same from others' lips? Why did it seem sweeter and more intense at the same time coming from him? 'You got my message and you thought about walking up here and then going back.'

'You see, I might have time to waste. A bit like you who spend early Sunday mornings at the corner of a street pretending to be a vagrant!' Well done me, I thought, deserving my self-compliment. Why should I ever be the only one to justify my actions?

'What's wrong with your life? Because I can see you're looking for something. Probably I am not what you are looking for, I grant you this. But it's from the first time I saw you that...'

'My life isn't going anywhere. And anyway, you have no right to interpret it, whoever you are!' He bothered me. This kind of investigation bothered me and forced me to get defensive. 'Maybe your life is perfect! Maybe nobody gets in the way of what you do, nobody trips you or complicates your existence. Nobody expects anything, nobody torments you every day so that everything is done in a certain way, according to the rules and...'

I tried to breathe deeply to calm myself. I wanted to scream. And to take it out on him because I didn't know who else to take it out on. My parents? The Parkers? Frey? Gregor? Geoffrey? No. They were no use. They would have tried to calm me, talk some sense into me and bring me back on my straight and narrow road. And I didn't want to. I wanted to get angry. I wanted to provoke, react and create havoc!

'Amantine, Amantine...' He put both hands on my shoulders. I didn't understand whether he realized the physical and emotional reactions he was rousing inside me. He couldn't be so naïve as not to notice it. For a moment I wondered if it was the same for him too. Then I struggled to remove the question from my mind. I didn't want to know. I was just a girl passing by. What did he want from me? Surely not much more than what I had wanted from him, from the first moment. He wasn't Geoffrey. I didn't have to force myself to be a good girlfriend, clever, beautiful, sweet and kind. It was a great relief.

'Peter, Peter...' I repeated, imitating his tone a bit, and a bit the Shakespearean tragedy in which Juliet invokes her Romeo. 'Why the hell did you leave me that note, Peter Wiles?'

'You didn't recognize me...' He chuckled, pulling me towards him to whisper in my ear, 'You're really in another world, Amantine.'

I pulled away from him, pushing him back. In order to do this, I had to put my hands on his chest, and I noticed that his denim shirt was half open. It wasn't a great image for my fleeting emotional state.

'However, nothing changes. You remain a vagrant I met on the street, from my point of view. And let's say your world doesn't exactly coincide with mine. I don't feel obliged to recognize you.'

'You mean your incredibly self-centred, snobbish little intellectual world, Amantine?'

No way, that was too much. I wasn't a little... I mean, I wasn't really!

'You dare calling me egocentric?' I should have been long gone. Instead I was still there arguing, as if his eyes and all his body had nailed me to the ground in front of his house.

'Let's say I notice someone who tends to compete with me...' He smiled. Suddenly. I hadn't seen him smile like that before. It was a spontaneous smile, almost sweet. Seductive. So much that I wasn't able to resist and I returned it, I smiled too.

He took my hand again and held it in his. The contact with his skin caused me an unwanted chill, especially because I was sure he had noticed it. He said nothing, but with a nod he pointed to the entrance to his house. My resistances were now broken down, collapsed. I did not want to object. I just wanted to live a bit. I just wanted to try to be another version of myself. Freer, bolder. Perhaps even more eccentric, unrestrained, uninhibited. I had no idea what would happen inside Peter Wiles's home. But I was ready to experiment with him whatever he offered me. Even what my education and my composure had always forbidden me. However, there was a certainty in me, perhaps wrong but undeniable. I could reach a completeness with him, a part of me that I still didn't know. But he wouldn't hurt me. Not physically, at least. About it, I was confident.

CHAPTER 12

As soon as we went through the door Peter turned to me. I still had to convince myself I was there. He simply put his hand on my side. His expression became serious, almost composed, as he caressed me with an unexpected gentleness.

I didn't get it. In a few moments he had switched from sarcasm, to harshness, to sweetness. Even his expression had changed from the grin, to seriousness, to a smile. I didn't know from which demon or which angel he was animating. I only knew that I was irresistibly attracted to him, not just physically.

He left me there at the door and tore himself away from me. I watched him as he crossed the living room, big, bright but rather unadorned, to go and sit on the huge light sofa. He took his shoes off, crossed his legs and leaned to grab a guitar placed sideways. I stood in the atrium with my arms on my hips as Peter strummed something, nodding in time. After a few minutes, he seemed to remember my presence.

'I'm a miserable host... do you want something to drink?'

I didn't dare to confess I expected more from him. He was in a phase that I would learn to define as "angelic innocence". It crossed his light eyes as if he was the most innocent and pure being that had ever appeared before me.

'Can I make a phone call?' Maybe I should have taken this opportunity to leave. But I didn't want to. I preferred to persist in that sort of incompleteness existing between us, between innocence and desire.

'Sure, if you can find the phone around, it's all yours, Amantine.' He looked up at me and the ironic, mocking grimace appeared.

'I'm leaving for the treasure hunt, then.' I smiled, biting my lips. I turned to be invisible in his eyes; the guitar was winning this battle and I wasn't a worthy rival.

I found the phone on a small cupboard in the corner of the living room. The corridor led to another room. I glanced, but refrained from going through it to look around. I grabbed the phone and looked at it, uncertain. Would I really do it? Yes. I needed it. I quickly dialled the number of Geoffrey's apartment.

'Geoff... hi, it's me...' I closed my eyes, trying to identify myself and keep a low and suffering tone of voice. 'Unfortunately, I don't feel well today. I also think... I have a slight fever, so...'

So I was a bitch. Hearing him worrying about me and my health hurt me. I felt bad, unfair, treacherous. For sure I was a good liar, Geoffrey believed me without suspecting I was lying to him.

When I hung up the guilt was devouring me. I leaned my back against the wall. What was I doing? And above all, why? But now it was done. I picked up the bag I had left on the floor while I was calling and went to sit on the sofa, next to Peter who continued to seem more interested in his guitar and in the notes he was writing on a notebook that he held balanced on his knee.

All right then! If things were like that... I took off my coat, rummaged in my bag and took out my folders and my notes. I began to reread what I had written during the week.

Every now and then I looked up to see Peter, totally involved in a world that wasn't mine. He occasionally stopped to look at me too, I felt his eyes on me. We didn't touch each other, but I felt his closeness passing through and caressing me. Our worlds ran parallel without colliding, without forcing, without breaking into each others. And I had lost track of time. Was it still morning? I wasn't wearing a watch and I looked around to try to find out what time it was.

Peter stood up suddenly, put down the guitar where he had taken it from and stretched, yawning.

'I'm going to sleep, I haven't slept since yesterday. You make yourself at home... unless you're sleepy too.'

For sure he was making me feel very attractive! Was I so horrible then? I inspired him to go to bed, yes. But to sleep! I hated him. Yet I followed him, like a desperate fool. Yes, desperate and frustrated. If he wasn't interested in me in that way, what was I doing there in his house? I climbed the stairs behind him, walked down a corridor. Peter opened a door to a room and let me in before closing it behind him. It was his bedroom, mostly empty and bare just like the living room and with a large untouched bed in the middle.

Peter leaned over and placed the pillow behind his head. I reached the other side, the right one, and sat down, taking off my shoes and gathering my knees to my chest. I watched him drifting into sleep.

I lay down on my side, facing towards him. He hadn't asked me anything. He hadn't demanded anything from me. No explanation, no question. He wasn't trying to impress me, either with gestures or words. I fell asleep. Waking up I didn't remember where I was. Nor did I find Peter Wiles lying next to me.

I left the room and went down to the living room. By now it was clear to me that he didn't find me attractive. I had slept in his bed and nothing happened.

'I ordered something to eat,' he informed me, stretching on the sofa. 'Pizza, fries, burgers... you do eat high-calorie junk food, don't you little egocentric intellectual?'

'Asshole!' I grabbed a pillow from a small armchair and threw it at him. 'Anyway, I'll leave then.'

'Sure... otherwise you risk your fever getting up and you'll have to stay here with me.'

Of course he had eavesdropped my call to Geoff. But it was his home, at the end of the day. I didn't reply. Peter Wiles confused me. The truth was that I didn't want to go. I was not used to someone who stayed close to me without demanding anything from me. Not my words, not my mind, not my thoughts. And not even my body.

'I'll go eventually, don't worry. But not before having devoured pizza, fries and hamburger. The little egocentric intellectual is greedy for high-calorie junk food, Peter Wiles. Very greedy.'

CHAPTER 13

I came home and rushed into my room, trying to avoid the Parkers as much as possible. We had eaten, then Peter walked me to the door and let me go without excessive ceremony. For sure I wouldn't see him again. Better this way! It would be easier to go back to my everyday life. Better not having overly intimate memories of my absurd crush. Maybe I just needed a day's break from everything else, from everyone else.

I placed myself in front of the mirror of my room. I looked numb and a bit tired. It was clear that I wasn't pretty enough for him. Yet everyone had always found me pretty, since I was a young girl. I had never lacked suitors, on the contrary... He had treated me with indifference, instead. So why did he leave me that note? His intention seemed unequivocal to me.

I had to admit, it was a feeling that irritated me deeply. Maybe he felt lonely. Maybe he just wanted some company. But didn't he have friends or relatives for that?

I ran my fingertips under my somewhat puffy eyes. I didn't wear enough makeup, my mother's friend was right. I had to enhance the green specks of my eyes, maybe even the lips and the cheekbones. And I was wearing clothes that were definitely too large, they didn't highlight my figure. But I had never seriously thought about dressing sexier and more provocatively. I had never really needed to.

I heard a knock on the door. 'Come in...' I answered wearily.

Doris opened the door looking at me with an incomprehensible expression, on the edge between accusatory and curious.

'Geoffrey called a couple of hours ago to check on you, he wanted to know if you still had a fever. I told him you were sleeping. He recommended not to let you work too much, not even on your research. And he said to drink a nice orange juice, you need vitamins.'

'Thank you, Doris.' Yes, thank you, Doris. I already felt like a horrible person. There was no need for her to stare at me like I was a wretched manipulative and an unrepentant traitor. And then I didn't betray Geoff! Sure, I didn't betray him because of Peter's lack of interest, but... 'I needed to stay a bit on my own today.' That's it, my need to justify myself reappearing, as usual.

'I think he believed me.' Doris nodded, shrugging her shoulders, unperturbed. 'After all, it can happen to anyone to want something different from time to time. You did well to get a little distraction.'

Of course, I did well. Too bad that I didn't distract at all. Not as I wanted, at least.

CHAPTER 14

I didn't go back to my usual life the next day. It wasn't an ordinary Monday. The day spent with Peter had not broken my routine and my usual thoughts. Indeed, the opposite seemed to have happened. It was the usual life that broke the persistent thought I had, that was focused on him from the day before. I made an effort not to dwell too much on Peter's image while he was playing, writing or lying in bed ignoring me.

At the university, not even Gregor Jackman's presence, as always wagging his tail behind Frey, could irritate me. I didn't care about him and for once it was a pleasant feeling to not care about all his scams, all his tricks to make me look useless and scrappy. It was funny to see him work hard and incessantly get busy. Maybe because for the first time in my life the doubt had crept inside me that I didn't really want what I had struggled so hard for.

Was it worthwhile to turn myself into a copy of Gregor to please a university professor, even if he was an internationally acclaimed genius of contemporary literature? I wasn't convinced anymore. I wasn't going to give up or withdraw but I didn't intend to compromise, not yet.

Leaving the university, my mind, whether I wanted it or not, was more focused than ever on Peter Wiles and on definitely un-platonic and not very chaste thoughts about him. I would never see him again, I knew that. He hadn't said anything about it, he hadn't invited me to come back and he hadn't asked to see me again. But I would look for him anyway. Without him being aware of it, I would look for him.

Instead of taking my way home or to the library I used to attend occasionally, I went to the centre. I needed Piccadilly Circus. And when I got there, I needed a record store, any one.

Darkest Storm. CDs in alphabetical order. Darkest Storm. If they were so popular, I would find them easily. I moved my fingers on the well-ordered CDs, getting to letter D. Yes, here they were. Perhaps they were popular. And there were not even that many copies of the same album, but there were five different ones. I selected them in order of release. Doing a quick check, I estimated that they had been around for about seven years.

Peter had to be very young when they started. In the picture with the others on the first CD he was. His hair was a little longer, a lock falling over his forehead, the expression of a lost but mischievous child, even if he was at the same time sweeter, more innocent. The expression I rediscovered when he stopped playing and looked up at me.

I also reviewed the other CDs and analysed the covers. More mature, more serious, smarter, more sensual. I put them down, holding the first one, and set off to the cash desk. Why was I buying one of their CDs? And why did I choose the one in which Peter was little more than an adolescent? Human mind mysteries, even mine. But I had no doubts about the choice. Maybe I wanted to go back to when it all started, at the beginning. Maybe it was part of my academic research path, to go back to the first sources and then continue in chronological order. It had to be like that. No mystery, no recondite explanation still buried at the bottom of my soul.

I came back home. I knew the Parkers were not there and Jinny was having a snack with a little friend that afternoon. The girl's mother would take her back home in the evening. So I was theoretically free. I ripped off the transparent coating, opened the CD and flipped through the inside pages. Other photos of them. Peter appeared with a raised eyebrow and his tongue out. The other members of the band were portrayed in more common poses, cute but composed.

'What an idiot...' I sighed to myself as I put the CD in the Parkers' unused stereo. I reviewed the songs' titles. "Winners for love", "Everything for you", "Say my name", "Love forever", "Cry and swear"...

I sat on the sofa with the case in my hands as the first song's notes spread. I closed my eyes and concentrated on searching for his voice that mingled with that of the others. Here it was, yes. I recognized him among the others. It was him.

I jumped at the ring of the telephone and, before answering, I ran to switch everything off, as if I risked being caught red handed in an equivocal attitude. I recognized Geoff's voice as he said my name. When he showed concern for my health the sense of guilt filled me after a few moments, although I tried to shake it off.

'Yes, I'm a little better. Thanks, Geoff.'

I refused his offer to come and see me, offering as an excuse that soon Jinny would return and I would have to deal with her. And later I would work on my research and my PhD thesis. Then there was also a little task that Frey assigned me, and I was forced to complete. I didn't want to argue about his, or his father's interference in my academic career, so I dropped the issue. I would go to bed early, as a good girl. I needed to rest because I couldn't afford relapses considering that fortunately the fever had passed quickly.

I hung up and approached the window. No, I hadn't betrayed him. I had only tricked him a little. For mere necessity, I needed at least a moment of peace. No questions, no requests. I went back to the stereo, pulled out the CD and put it back in the case. I went up to my room and threw it on the bed. Peter's face stared ironically at me from the cover. I undressed calmly, went into the bathroom and then in the shower. It was crazy. Yes, I was planning a craziness, a headshot.

In my bedroom, in my bathrobe, I went through my wardrobe. I hadn't been pretty enough. The bad mood caused me a bite in the pit of my stomach. I didn't want to commit myself, but at the same time I wanted to experiment with something new. I took down a black dress with pink flounces from the closet. No. No, I couldn't wear that stuff. Better my trousers or the frustrated intellectual's long skirts. Or jeans, indeed. Jeans were "neutral territory". Yes, jeans and a sweater, dark blue, not too large. A white t-shirt underneath. Maybe I could accentuate my make-up. Eyes, lips, cheekbones. My brown hair loose, without a hairpin or ponytail to hold it back.

A purely random walk to Notting Hill. Just to have a coffee. A completely innocent thing. As soon as I reached the staircase that led to the Underground I noticed that Jacob wasn't in the usual place. After all, it wasn't seven o'clock on Sunday morning. I stopped at that point, as if I was waiting for something. An inspiration, a voice that guided me towards my destiny.

'Damn...' The voice was leading me towards Peter's street. Then towards Peter's house. But I would just walk by, without stopping. After all, it was a street like many others, it wasn't entirely Peter Wiles's private property.

I glanced at the bell on the gate. His name wasn't there. Maybe it didn't even work. I passed over it with my finger and pressed lightly. I'd better leave. Nobody appeared. And anyway, I could always pretend I was wrong. He might not be there, maybe he was in some recording studio strumming, travelling, on holiday. Away.

At the door appeared a very tall, thin and slightly curved man. He wore a square black jacket that reached his thighs, black trousers and white shirt. His grizzled sideburns came almost to his lips. He had a creepy, gravedigger's look. He stood staring and looking at me like I was an insect, or rather a bacterium harmful to humanity. Better run.

Instead, I didn't run anywhere. The desire to satisfy my curiosity was stronger. 'Peter Wiles...' I said his name in a timid, absorbed little voice.

'I'm sorry, miss. No Peter Wiles lives here.'

'Oh, forget it.' I snorted, turning my back to him. 'Stuffed dummy without balls... I was in bed yesterday with Peter Wiles, right in that house.' Just to sleep. But I had been there!

'Where are you escaping to, little egocentric intellectual?' I recognized his voice, but I continued to move away indifferently, pretending not to have heard. 'Amantine!' He raised his tone considerably. Turning, I saw him on the terrace, in jeans and black tank top. 'Let her in, Gordon, she's harmless. Or at least I hope so...'

'But what a...' I lifted my face and stood looking at him, before the guy named Gordon allowed me in with an obsequious and solemn gesture. I gave him a wicked look. 'You shouldn't tell lies, Gordon. Do you want to go to hell?'

Gordon remained serious and unperturbed at my joke. 'Mr. Wiles is upstairs, miss.'

Climbing the stairs I already knew, I found myself in front of Peter's bedroom. I waited. Then I decided to knock.

'Well, come in. I'm not doing anything that might shock you.'

'How do I know...' I opened the door and looked around the room. 'You could have been naked. Or...'

'Yes, sure. After seeing you from the terrace, I undressed to welcome you!' He looked at me, frowning. 'You look different today. Have you plastered your face for a special occasion?'

That's it, forget it. Hateful. He enjoyed himself, embarrassing me and my efforts. 'Who is that lanky gentleman downstairs? Do you have a butler?'

'Yup. I usually need him to keep away the eager little girls who find out where I live.'

'Oh, he certainly does his job. Maybe the ones you leave notes on the street with your address written on...' I nodded seriously. I didn't understand what I was doing there. He was teasing me again. And I was feeling even more stupid and duller than the day before. Perhaps he was a sadist, a perverse, malicious one. Intrinsically he enjoyed undermining women's self-esteem. He was succeeding with me. 'Anyway... I'm going. Goodbye, Peter.'

'You came here to tell me... *Goodbye, Peter.*' He even tried to imitate my resentful tone, the bastard!

'Yes, I... I really think so.' My voice was trembling. I was furious. If I was a wolf I would have bitten his throat.

'Why, are you leaving? Going somewhere nice?' He pointed those naïve green eyes at me, those he had in his teenager photograph on the CD. He drove me crazy. Regardless of who he was. He drove me crazy.

'To my place. I mean, not mine...' The Parkers' place, I meant. It was useless to get lost in explanations. 'Anyway, goodbye, Peter.' I raised my hand too, this time, to be more incisive.

'Why don't you express clearly what you want and why you're here, Amantine? The reason you looked for me yesterday, too.'

At this point, as if I hadn't hated him enough already for his attitude, my contempt for him touched bottom. He wanted to humiliate me to the end. Maybe... maybe he wasn't even interested in women, maybe...

I remained silent, tilting my face. It had to be like that. For him I was just a game and maybe I wasn't even the first one.

'What are you thinking about now, Amantine? You have a really funny expression.' A few steps and he was facing me, narrowing his eyes as if he was trying to investigate me, to decipher me. He continually repeated my name. And I felt electrified and crossed by a shiver, every time.

'You don't like girls...' I replied simply, before thinking about how to express the concept in a more acceptable way.

'Humm...' he nodded, bending his lips down. 'So, from the fact that I don't jump on you, ripping off your clothes and throwing you on my bed, you assume I don't like girls. Didn't it cross your mind, the thought that the problem could be you?'

'All right!' Had I really thought I couldn't despise him more? I deceived myself! I gave him a shove back with rage, exasperation. I was about to burst into tears. Nobody had ever humiliated me like that.

As I pushed him, Peter grabbed me by the arms and held me against his chest. I felt my legs trembling, as if I was about to fall to the ground. 'What do you want from me, Amantine? That I take you to bed? Because I assure you that I have no problem doing it and forgetting you tomorrow or even in a few hours when I throw you out of my house...'

'No, I... I'm not like that. I...' I wasn't like that. I had never been like that. In twenty-seven years of life, never. 'I don't know why I'm here. I mean, I thought...'

His breath on my face was making me lose track of time and space. It wasn't me. I wasn't myself. I had had Geoffrey for years. And some flirting at high school. It had never been like that. I was the one handling the situation, the emotions. To establish where, how, when. Always. I was the one who never lost control.

I squinted my eyes, expectantly. I shuddered like a teenager, feeling his body against mine as he stroked my back down to my buttocks. I winced at the touch of his lips, when I finally received that kiss that seemed like it would never have come. I opened my mouth, grabbing his head, dipping my fingers into his dark, short hair. Then I pulled away to look him in his eyes.

'I'm with someone, Peter.'

'I know. I'm not jealous.' He shrugged and winked. His teasing expression suddenly appeared. 'Obviously someone like you must be with someone.'

I didn't know what he meant by "someone like you". I preferred not to investigate. In fact, I much preferred to start kissing him again.

'You must be with someone too, right?' I don't know why I turned the question on him.

'Obviously.' Peter let his hands slide down my arms, then leaned them on my hips, pulling me hard against him.

'Obviously.' Obviously this made us two insensitive, assholes, traitors.

But I wanted him and I couldn't resist. No, I didn't want Peter Wiles. I wanted the boy I met on a Sunday morning on the street. I wanted freedom. I wanted someone who wasn't constantly asking me what I meant to do with my life and my days.

'You won't have claims on me, Peter. Will you?' I touched his face and lips with my fingers, looking into his eyes. 'You won't want to know everything, have everything. You'll let me free, Peter. Will you?'

'Do I look like a little egocentric intellectual's jailer?' He lifted my chin, gently kissing my lips and then biting them slightly.

'Good, because we have nothing in common.' I put my hands on his arms. In that moment I realized that his right shoulder was crossed by a tattoo that ran down his arm to the elbow. It looked like a tribal, ancient image. I would have looked at it more carefully if Peter hadn't raised me in the heat of kissing me with a passion that I was unable to hold back or reject. I clung to him as I felt his body quiver with mine.

'Nothing in common. No claims.' He sighed in my ear before kissing me on my neck, taking my jumper off with a quick, sure gesture.

He let me fall on the bed and I took his hand and pulled him on me.

'Nothing in common. No questions, no claims, Peter. Never.'

CHAPTER 15

Waking up and not finding him in bed was nothing new. Although this time things had gone very differently. I bit my lips, remembering his touch, his kisses, his gestures. I had seduced Peter Wiles. What a good girl! Probably now he could throw me out of his house, as he had told me. At this point I'd better mentally prepare myself and start dressing. As soon as I recovered the clothes Peter had very artistically launched around the room.

When he came back, I was wearing my underwear and my t-shirt. I had spotted my jeans, but my jumper was still missing.

'Are you leaving already?'

'Yeah, before you kick me out of your house... that's what you said!' I shrugged, trying to put my jeans on and keep myself balanced.

'It's three in the morning, Amantine.' I noticed Peter was wearing a blue shirt and boxer shorts. I thought he went out and I didn't want him to find me still there when he came back. I had completely lost track of time. I thought it was still evening, not late at night. 'I ordered pizza. I'm hungry.'

'Pizza at three in the morning?' I looked at him as if he was a madman just escaped from the asylum. I had never eaten after hours. 'It would be the first time in my life.'

'What a sad life you must have...' This time it was him who looked at me head to toe like I was a Martian. 'Anyway, if you want to try this new experience after having been in bed with a sex god, the pizza will be here in a few minutes.'

'Do they deliver you pizza at three in the morning?' I crossed my arms and couldn't resist the temptation. 'But Peter... tonight between us... I mean... did something really happen? Because I

honestly don't remember. Haven't we just slept, like last time?'
Take that, sex god!

He crossed his arms, copying my position, and glared at me,
as if he was reflecting on how to properly get even with me. Then
he walked the few steps that separated us and grabbed me by the
wrists. I simulated a weak resistance, but I surrounded him with
my arms. Just then the doorbell rang.

'Saved by the pizza!' Peter let me go to go downstairs.

I got ready to eat pizza at three in the morning. Whatever was
happening I liked it, I enjoyed it, it excited me. I had never felt
like that before. And I only knew that I wanted it to continue.

And so we ate pizza half-naked on the bed at three in the
morning. I looked at him. Every moment as if it was the last time.
Aware that at any moment he could and wanted to send me away
and never see me again. Not that I feared that moment. I feared
more the loss of absolute freedom and excitement that I felt with
him and that invaded my bowels and my blood.

Peter jumped out of the bed. I saw him stopping in front of a
much more modern and evolved stereo than the Parkers' one,
that took a good part of a wall in the room. He probably wanted
to listen to music. Maybe one of his CDs. As the music started,
too loud for my habits, I realized it wasn't the same one I had
bought. The voices also seemed different to me. Of course, in
my CD they were very young. But this voice was single, not
alternating. And it was rough, almost wild, vibrant. Angry and
painful at the same time.

'Is it you... you...' I asked, already sensing the answer. But
he couldn't know I had bought one of their CDs and I would
recognise the voiceprint.

'I never listen to our music, Amantine. I can't stand my
recorded voice.' He smiled, coming back to me. 'Anyway, it's
Nirvana, "Smells Like Teen Spirit". Don't tell me you've never
heard about them, girl!'

'I'm a little egocentric intellectual, as you call me. I don't
listen to this music. I played the viola for two years, during high

school.' I frowned, involuntarily dragged along by the aggressive guitar riff and that scratchy voice.

'The viola? Did you play the viola?' From his expression I didn't understand if Peter was going to feel bad or laugh in my face.

'Yes, the viola. The musical instrument, you know? The one you play...' I vaguely imitated the gesture. 'But I wasn't very good, I wasn't good at all, in fact.'

'I'm familiar with a Viola, yes. And I played her well too.' He burst out laughing in my face, then pulled me towards him.

'You are a jerk! You know that, don't you?' I tried to stay serious, but I laughed too, on his lips. I was on my knees on the edge of the bed with Peter standing in front of me. He took my hands, intertwining his fingers with mine.

'Yup. And now you will dance with this jerk...'

He forced me out of bed. He began moving to the rhythm of music, trying to make me twirl in his arms. Uselessly. I was too stiff, a piece of wood, two left feet. I had never danced to that kind of music before. Peter, however, seemed born to move his body following those notes. It was as if he became part of it, as if they were enlivening him with a lifeblood and an almost supernatural force. I followed his movements, enchanted, bewitched.

'I don't...' I tried to explain my embarrassment as he struggled to guide me. 'I can't dance, Peter. I studied ballet, along with the viola. But I did only one year before my parents realized that I wasn't great at dancing. However, you are...'

'I was a dancer at the beginning. It's not complicated, you just have to move your ass and wiggle, little snob. Like this, try, it's not difficult...' Without any hesitation he patted me on my bottom. 'Follow me.'

I followed him, somehow. Without succeeding. I felt embarrassed and completely out of step. I understood I was a disaster. I felt like a monkey trying in vain to get out of a very claustrophobic cage. And that cage was my body, absolutely unaccustomed and maybe unfit for those free, sensual and wildish movements.

'Come here, Amantine.' Peter drew me to him, tightening his hold on my waist and making me stick to him. He moved to music, making my body follow his movements. 'Here you are, do you feel the rhythm now?'

'Actually, I feel something else...' I burst out laughing, leaning my forehead against his.

'You, vicious little bitch!' He let me go, then he caught me again, holding me even tighter.

Maybe it was the dance, it was the music, it was those songs. But the only certainty at that moment was that with Peter, I was an entirely new Amantine, completely unknown and unrelated to the one with whom I had lived my whole life.

We fell on the bed exhausted and he was sweeter but also more intense, more passionate. He still hadn't thrown me out of his house, and I was less and less willing to leave, in any case. I got up and went rummaging through his CDs. I also looked at the Darkest Storm's ones, but I remembered that Peter didn't like listening to his own voice. So I looked for something else.

'The one you played before... Nirvana, you said? He has a great voice... even if I find it painful, suffering.'

'He's Kurt Cobain, silly girl. Nirvana is the name of the band. Yes, however, you're right.' He frowned, becoming suddenly serious, thoughtful. 'One of the few contemporaries I consider brilliant. I admit I envy him, even if normally I'm not the type to envy anyone, he's a few years younger than me... he'll have a great career, way beyond normal success.'

'Hmm... let's see...' I didn't know any of those singers and bands. I was out of touch with the world. Out of Peter's world, at least.

Then the face and body of a girl in a white dress appeared on the case, her breasts on display. I wondered how a dress like that would look on me. I read her name: Madonna. Of course, I knew Madonna! I had heard about her at least! I took out the Nirvana

CD and inserted the Madonna one. Turning around, I saw Peter looking at me curiously as if I were a little animal he was studying the movements of, for an experiment.

'I know her!' I exclaimed enthusiastically as the notes of the first song, "Material Girl", started.

'Of course, Madonna, obviously. Who doesn't know Madonna...' He nodded, sighing and giving me his usual condescending grimace. He rolled his eyes. 'But really, it almost amazes me you know she is a singer and not the one you pray to in church.'

'Sooner or later I'll make you sit an English literature exam, Peter Wiles.' I began to shake myself in time to the beat. I seemed to gain more fluency in the movements and more energy. 'And you'll look bad. I will humiliate you so much that you will remember it forever! So my revenge will be accomplished!'

'Really threatening...' Lying in bed, leaning on his side, he was staring at me attentively. I no longer felt embarrassed, I liked being looked at by him. And I felt safe in the dance. 'Come here, *Material Girl*.'

I reached him, hopping. 'I've improved, right? I'm becoming really good as a dancer!'

'Let's say you're a little less horrible than before.' He focused his green eyes on mine. His words didn't offend me this time and I didn't want to reply with another joke to his one.

I lay my hands on his bare shoulders, ran over his tattoo with my fingers and stroked it slowly as he rested his head on my chest, holding me. He was different than before. Once again, I found myself surprised, confused by his attitude. In that moment, ours seemed to have turned into a more human, more alive relationship. And I realized that I had to leave immediately if I didn't want to lose myself.

'What time is it, Peter?'

He reached out to check the watch he had left on the bedside table. 'Almost seven.'

'What?' I had asked just to say something. I wasn't expecting it to be already so late. 'Oh, damn it... I have to go! I have to go now!' I stirred around the room trying to put clothes, bag, jacket, shoes together. Then I stopped. What day was it? 'Sunday... Monday...'

'It's Tuesday, sweetheart. But where do you want to escape to?'

'To university, Peter. Work. Study. Research. I'm a university researcher, remember? Not a pop star who can switch the night for the day and...'

I ran my hands through my hair. I also needed a shower and to make myself presentable. It would take me at least half an hour to reach Russell Square and then the university. Or maybe I had better change in Euston... No, I didn't have time, not even to think.

'I'm done! Screwed! I must be there before eight. Frey will kill me. There is also the American, we must take him for breakfast before presenting him at the conference. And then Gregor, the evil licker... he will take advantage once and for all to destroy me, annihilate me... take me out!'

'Can't you call them all and say you've got a fever like you did on Sunday?' Peter remained unperturbed in front of my turmoil. On the contrary, he showed an absolute and total indifference. For him, everything was easily solved with a phone call.

'You don't understand, Peter. It's my life we're talking about! My future...' On Sunday it was just about my boyfriend, that was all. The thought flashed through my mind. This made me think of how horrible I was, as a human being.

'Calm down, little girl. You try to fix yourself, I'll go downstairs and make you breakfast. Or I'll ask Gordon to make it if he's already on duty.' I didn't expect Peter's offer to help me, although making breakfast for me wasn't a big help. I wouldn't even have time for that.

'No, no... I don't have time!' I put on my clothes, one after another with frantic fury. I ran to the adjacent bathroom. I was in a horrible state. It seemed like I had been partying all night long. That was exactly what I had done. Fortunately, we didn't drink alcohol! That was the last thing I needed, being drunk as well.

I ran downstairs after making myself at least vaguely presentable. Peter handed me a cup of coffee and a chocolate muffin. I just sipped my coffee, full-bodied but very bitter, and stopped myself from instinctively spitting it back into the cup.

'Strong. You need it to wake up, Amantine.' Peter almost forced me to bite the muffin. 'And take this. It's called a Walkman, inside there's a tape with rock and pop music. At least it will fire you up a little and you won't fall asleep on the street. You need to put the earphones in your ears.'

I automatically nodded to every word and took a quick look at myself. Yes, I had everything, or at least it seemed that way to me. 'Thank you! Goodbye, Peter Wiles.' I hurried to the door and opened it, ready to go out and rush into my world again.

It just took a moment. A moment in which instinct prevailed over reason. And in that moment, I closed the door, went back to Peter and kissed him on his lips. A passionate but sweet, slow kiss. As if we had all the time in the world. And above all as if I had not the slightest intention of leaving.

'Good luck, little intellectual.' He returned my kiss, stroking my neck with both his thumbs. 'Now go, move your ass. And destroy those strutting brontosaurs.'

CHAPTER 16

Peter had been right. The music kept me awake, preventing me from falling asleep on the street. Awake to such an extent that I had to keep myself from not wiggling on the tube as he had taught me, not to move my ass as he said.

I arrived at the university miraculously early, even before Gregor and Frey. And even there I had to keep myself from dancing in the corridors. I didn't wonder what was happening to me. It was just happening. I could be bright and active. Sooner or later I would collapse for lack of sleep and tiredness, I knew it. But at the moment I held on perfectly. I even held the confrontation with that miserable Gregor. I had no idea where that energy, that vitality, had sprung up in me.

I left the university in the early afternoon without knowing where to go and what to do for the rest of the day. I didn't want to immerse myself in my study and research. I knew I couldn't waste my time, but I needed a bit of rest, a little peace, especially mental.

I took a bus to the centre and found myself in Oxford Street with my Walkman and my headphones. Not mine... Peter's. Humming "You can't hurry love", determined, I walked into a music store. I had read the names on the tape and tried to memorize them.

I bought the Nirvana CD, the same as Peter's. I focused on Phil Collins, Wham!, Culture Club and Queen. They were in the compilation he had lent me. Then I decided to follow my instinct, maybe some female voices. And maybe even something more alternative. I would astonish Peter. I wanted to see his expression when I showed them to him!

I stopped, bewildered, at the till. This meant that I had to see him again... Of course, I had to! I had to return him his Walkman and his tape. Then I could listen to my CDs at the Parkers and... Parkers! In the evening I would have to take care of Jinny probably. Not that I wanted to. And anyway, I could think about it later. Maybe I could make up an excuse.

I found myself in the only place where I wanted to be at that moment. In front of Peter's house. I rang the bell and almost immediately the grim, suspicious face of Mr. Gravedigger appeared. Gordon, the butler. Instead of sending me to hell, this time he greeted me with something that could very vaguely resemble a smile and indicated to me to enter.

'Thank you, Mr. Gordon.' I passed him, saying in a mellifluous and teasing voice, 'Don't tell me, I already know. Mr. Peter Wiles is in his room, upstairs.'

'No, miss. Mr. Wiles has gone out. But he instructed me to tell you that you can wait for him in his room. And in case you're hungry, Mr. Wiles...'

'No, forget it. I'll wait for Peter in his room.' I wasn't hungry. I wanted to dance and jump into Peter's bedroom. And to unleash with him on his arrival.

I took off my jacket and my jeans and sat on his bed, looking around for something belonging to him. I didn't have a clear perception of what I was looking for. But I wanted to find him, even in that almost bare room. Bed, wardrobe, bedside table, stereo, CDs. Nothing else. He had no books. I was used to gauging people's personalities from the books they read and kept. But there was no way to find Peter there, to discover something more. I had seen his CDs, I had known his bed, I could have looked at his clothes. But the truth was that the room appeared to me like a desert of solitude without him in it.

I sighed and jumped off the bed and looked in the bag of CDs I had purchased. I had been busy; I had bought ten. I unwrapped the Blondie one and put it in the stereo, nodding and moving in time. I particularly liked a song and went back to listen to it several times. "Call me". There were also verses in Italian and in French. At the third listening, in addition to dancing, I knew it by heart, so much I was able to sing it out loud.

'Ohoh, he speaks the languages of love.
Ohoh, amore, chiamami... chiamami.
Ohoh, appelle-moi, mon cheri... appelle-moi.
Anytime, anyplace, anywhere, anyway!
Anytime, anyplace, anywhere, any day!
Call me... call me, my love.'

I didn't notice him. I didn't know for how long, leaning against the door frame, he had been watching me. When turning, I noticed him and froze, embarrassed, placing a hand on my mouth.

'So you want to compete with me, little bitch!' He pounced on me, wrapping his arms around me. His kiss almost broke my breath. He paused for a moment, gazing frowningly into my eyes. 'Do you want to sing too? Take my place away?'

'Are you kidding, I'm not a time-waster myself! I do a job of high intellectuality...' I coaxed him to me to kiss him again.

What was I doing? I had tons of tasks to complete. Frey had entrusted me with some of his students' work to be corrected within the week and I was wasting my time with Peter Wiles.

'I see...' Peter nodded, wrinkling his nose. 'And I'm not up to it. So you're here because...' He left the sentence purposely pending.

Because I can't resist. I only thought it. 'To give you back your Walkman, nothing else.' I shrugged. Peter noticed the shopping bag on the bed. 'Oh... I bought some random CDs, I did a little shopping today.'

'Did you buy some random CDs? A few viola, violin and cello concerts?' He peered at me suspiciously, raising an eyebrow.

'No, no... pop, rock and hard-rock music.' I crossed my arms and stared at him proudly. 'Don't think you're so special, pop star. I understand music too!'

'You have an upsetting presumption and arrogance, Amantine! Because the truth is that you're just a know-it-all little chick...' He threw himself on the bed, engaging himself in my new CDs. 'Phil Collins... Blondie... Nirvana, Wham!, Culture Club, Queen... Iron Maiden? You go in heavy girl, you even throw yourself on heavy metal... Alice Cooper...'

'Yes, I wanted some female voices... I already know Madonna, so I got Blondie and Alice Cooper. Just so as not to give too much importance and predominance to you bad boys.' I leaned on my elbow in front of him. I stared at him, slightly narrowing my eyes with a sensual and provocative approach. I learned quickly. Even his music.

Peter looked at me seriously, then bit his lip. He stretched completely, laughing wildly and running his hands over his face and eyes. 'Oh my God, you'll drive me crazy little snob! Alice Cooper is a man...'

'You're kidding me, are you? Her name is Alice...' I jumped over him, furious. The asshole was having fun confusing me and dampening my enthusiasm!

'Listen to the CD if you don't believe me...' He continued laughing, gripping my hips. 'So you'll hear his sweet and soothing soprano voice.'

He stood up and I clung to him.

'However, the fact remains that you are an asshole, Peter Wiles.' I tilted my face to kiss him on the neck. 'I understand... a bit like George Sand, George Eliot and the Brontë sisters... they used male pseudonyms to publish but they were women. But I don't understand the need for a man to give himself a feminine name in our time...'

'But my dear Amantine... "What's in a name? That which we call a rose by any other name would smell as sweet." Don't you think the same?' He smiled and kissed my lips gently. I moved away from him, irritated, rolling on my side.

How could he know Shakespeare to the point of citing him by heart? This wasn't right, it wasn't fair. He was with impunity invading my field.

'I played Romeo in a school play...' He smiled, trying to catch me back and to slip a hand under my shirt.

'That's Juliet's line!' I replied, struggling to push him away.

'I know... but there was this girl who played Juliet and always looked at me with shining eyes, like this...' he blinked a couple of times, imitating a feminine flirt. 'And while she was acting, she wanted to say *take me, take me...* And I took her and memorized the line!'

'Yes, I can imagine. She said something like: "Romeo, doff thy name, and for that name, which is not part of thee, take all myself." But I'm sure she meant Romeo... not Peter!'

'You can't know what she meant, you were not there!' He grabbed my hands, blocking my arms back and laying me on the bed. He had immobilized me. 'Say it...'

'Say what?' I moved my hips, struggling to free myself. Or maybe not, but I wanted to give him that impression.

'That thing that Juliet says... take all myself...' He brought his forehead to mine searching for my lips. 'I like the way you say it...'

'Forget it, Peter Wiles. I won't even think about it!'

'Humm... you know, Amantine, I was wondering... Who knows if you're ticklish here...?' He passed his chin over the hollow between my neck and my shoulder. I tried to resist, but his stubble tickled and made tears well in my eyes. 'Yes, you definitely are.'

'Take whatever you want...' I almost lost my breath. 'But stop it... stop it or I swear I'll choke you in your sleep...' He still didn't give up, he insisted more and more sadistically instead. 'All right, take all myself, bastard! Take all myself, Peter...'

I managed to tighten my legs around his and moving my face I found his lips, engaging him in a passionate kiss. I couldn't take a break due to the passion I felt for him. Nor could I hold it back or deny it. I was willing to stop by, to give him back his Walkman and show him my CDs. Then to get on with my usual life. Now suddenly my life was becoming a hindrance to the expression of my desire for him. I didn't know if Peter Wiles was aware of it. I was starting to be, too much. But I didn't care. My cry of freedom was stronger than everything, than my will, even than the reason and the logic that had always dominated and led my existence. Maybe Peter Wiles had already taken all myself, without waiting for me to ask him or to allow him.

CHAPTER 17

It seemed to me I was leading a double life. In fact, I led a double life. I was still living at the Parkers, trying to juggle the university, without stumbling into Gregor Jackman's constant traps and officially remaining Geoffrey's girlfriend.

I sheltered whenever I could in Peter's home. Besides, I had someone and he had a relationship too, as far as I understood. I don't know where he kept her hidden, but she was somewhere. And anyway, we had agreed from the beginning. No questions, no claims.

His house telephone, meanwhile, knew all my dirty lies. From there I called to justify all my absences and my delays. I used everyone, one against the other, to hide my story with Peter. He was the only one who knew everything. No questions, no claims, but Peter Wiles was the only one not to receive my constant lies, my evasions.

I had lied to my parents and my brother too when they hadn't found me on the Parkers' phone. I was always too busy with my research for the department, helping Frey with his students' thesis, or spending the evening at Geoffrey's. I would go to hell, in the circle of liars and maybe even in the lustful one. But I already burned every time Peter touched me. It would make little difference.

Sooner or later it would be over. I was aware of this. Sooner or later one of us would be over it and we would go our separate ways. He was a pop star and I was a university researcher who had no intention of compromising her career.

Maybe I would go to live with Geoffrey, taking with it all the consequences implied with doing that. Like a good girlfriend should. Cohabitation that heralded marriage, children, family. That was my destiny. Peter Wiles could only be a musical break and a temporary entertainment. Our worlds would return to run on parallel tracks to never meet again. In the meantime, however, it had been going on for almost two months.

When it was possible for both, I spent the night with him, in his house, in his bed. I just wanted to live the moment, let me wrap, charm, cradle in his arms to confuse his breath with mine. I woke up often, I watched him sleeping, I felt close to him. Closer than anyone else, as if there was a bond between us, a sort of familiarity, an intimacy that was precluded to the others. Yet I had known him for much less time than Geoffrey. Geoff had been the first one for me, he should have meant a lot more probably. But with Peter everything was different, almost more alive, truer. As if with him my body and even my thoughts could take a dimension and a consistency.

I approached him, leaned my head into the crook of his shoulder, but being careful not to wake him up. I wanted to stay that way, in a perfect silence. I would have remained like that forever, every day of my life. Yet I didn't know what I felt, I couldn't identify it, or I didn't want to give it a name. I closed my eyes, breathing slowly, and touched his chest with my fingers. I felt he was mine. Totally mine. Yes, Peter was mine. At least at that precise moment.

I felt his sudden touch. A kiss on my temple and his hand that at the same time stroked my hair. An automatic gesture, accomplished maybe while he was still wrapped in his sleep. I didn't want to open my eyes and find out if he was awake. It wasn't important.

'Amantine...' he whispered, still kissing my forehead and then descending to my cheekbone. 'I know you're awake, Amantine. Don't pretend to me. I can hear your little brain processing.'

'Paradoxically, you're the only one I don't pretend to, Peter...' I sighed, following the lines of his tribal tattoo from his shoulder to his forearm. I had discovered that he had five others, more or less hidden. Over time I had learned to know them all, but that one remained my favourite.

'I would expose you in a second, Amantine. I'm too smart for you.' He fixed a lock of my hair behind my ear. I raised myself on one elbow to look him in his eyes.

'It would be too tiring to lie to you as well, Peter. But if I wanted to I would fool you without a problem. You're not that smart and you can't compete with my highly above average intelligence.' I expressed the concept, convinced, without hesitation.

'If you wanted to fool me, I'd feel bad, Amantine. Really...' He bit his lip the way he usually did when something troubled him or bothered him. 'Because... I believed... I was under the illusion that I was something different to you, unlike all the others to whom you habitually lie...'

I didn't expect it. His words confused me so much that I didn't know how to answer. 'Peter, I...'

Peter got out of bed with an absorbed and contrite expression. Eyes down he started towards the bathroom door.

'Peter, I... Would you really feel bad if I...'

'You're incorrigible, little egocentric snob.' He turned to me with his lips shut and tilted his face. His green eyes shone ironically, amused. 'You believed me! I told you I'm smarter than you. Why should I care if you commit yourself to lie to me as well? As we said? No questions, no claims. So, for sure I don't expect that you, a professional liar, always tell me the truth!'

'Asshole! Worm! Ignoble bastard...' He had caught me off guard and I hadn't had enough time to prepare a good supply of effective insults.

'If I make you a nice hot bath and I give you an aphrodisiac massage of mine will you forgive me, queen of deception?' He gave me his helpless puppy dog look. I wasn't able to resist him. I couldn't. And I had to be on guard because if he wasn't smarter than me, he was still a worthy rival.

Peter was my safety valve, in every sense. At the university, the situation was discouraging in its obstinate stability. I no longer understood what I hoped to get from Frey. I had once again asked Geoffrey not to intervene, it wasn't worth it. Or maybe day by day I was less and less interested in the role of servant assistant of the great professor. I was increasingly tempted to leave the field and give up without fighting. If I wasn't worthy enough why did I have to claim something that I wasn't entitled to? No, it was insane for me. If my strengths, my abilities were not enough, I had probably overestimated myself. I hated to admit it, but I had no alternative.

And when I had no alternative to the life I had planned since childhood, there was one and only one shelter for me. Peter Wiles. He listened to me without interfering, offered me his opinion without imposing himself. He held me, comforted me with his body, his kisses. Just him who was part of an environment that had nothing to do with the one I belonged to, helped me living and persisting in my world. And I finally could breathe again.

CHAPTER 18

Peter's house also served as a library. Whether or not he was there I took my books, my research and went to study at his place. Gordon, the impeccable butler, knew it and let me pass. He also made me tea with delicious muffins or slices of cake as a snack. I wondered how many women he had seen going through that house. And how he called me in his own mind, what name he had for me? Probably "Peter Wiles's greedy lover."

At university, I didn't want to stay longer than necessary, I would risk kicking Gregor in the balls and other lickers of his calibre. At the Parkers I would have no peace with little Jinny, who most of the time preferred me to her mother and clung to me like a jellyfish; I didn't know how or why, I had always been grumpy, distant and grim with children, even when I was a child myself. In the library in the centre I often had trouble finding a place and people chatted without excessive respect for others' peace and quiet.

It wasn't an excuse. Peter's house was the most peaceful and comfortable place for me. I had excluded Geoffrey's apartment from my options just because it was Geoffrey's. This implied that he would put pressure on me to act in his own way. So for him I officially remained, as a good girl, studying at the university between the closet that served as a study reserved for the English department's assistants and the English library that had little to do with his Sociology department. If I knew he was dropping in to say hello, I'd make sure he could find me where he expected me to be, then I'd sneak away.

When Peter was home, we worked hard to behave ourselves. Well detached, composed and concentrated, a bit like when I had been at his place the first time and he didn't even touch me, I absorbed in my sheets, he in his notes. I wondered if he would ever let me listen to what he wrote. Most of the time I had to turn my back on him not to give in to temptation. Seeing him so absorbed and concentrated roused in me drives and an attraction almost stronger and more irresistible than normal.

'Amantine...' I felt his eyes on my back.

'Humm...' I had begun to actively investigate John Keats. I intended to ask Peter about Jacob but for one reason or another I hadn't done it yet.

'I was thinking...'

'It would be something new, I understand...' I giggled, twiddling with my pen in my fingers. I knew what to expect from him. He would grab me from behind and we would roll together on the couch or on the floor. I bit my lips almost impatiently.

'Why don't you move to live here with me instead of carrying on having to make up stories for everyone? It would also be more comfortable.'

I waited. When would the part in which he was making fun of me for being caught up have arrived? But Peter remained silent.

I turned to him. 'So? When is the wicked joke coming?'

Peter shrugged and ran a hand through his hair, holding it back. 'There isn't any. The idea of you living here with me already contains in itself its perfidy for the emotional and physical stress that I would subject you to daily basis...'

'I'm with someone, have you forgotten?' It sucked as an answer. I sucked as a person, actually. I craved to roll in Peter's bed day and night but *"I was with someone"*. I knew it. But I kept going anyway.

Geoffrey didn't deserve my betrayals. But at the same time, I deserved my freedom and my fun. I justified myself by repeating that I wasn't a serial traitor. In fact, I had never betrayed him before. Never, not even once. Not even with my thoughts, as far as I could remember. With Peter it was something else. It wasn't betrayal, it was free expression of myself, without inhibitions or emotional or sentimental implications. Peter was Peter.

'Oh right, indeed your being with someone makes a big difference. You're always here anyway...' Peter put the guitar down on the sofa and crossed his arms.

'If I bother you, I can also avoid...' I put my papers down and stared at him, frowning.

'Sure. And because you're bothering me, I suggest you come and stay here with me. I must have a twisted mind.' He had raised his tone of voice a bit. Were we arguing? No. But I didn't like him to behave like that with me. I didn't like it at all. And the fact that for a moment I had been touched and tempted by the idea to move with him I liked even less.

'Sorry... that is the point...' I lowered my face. I would prefer he made fun of me. I preferred the usual Peter who mocked me and then lifted me and dragged me to bed.

'Amantine... it was just an idea to help you with that boring paperwork of yours. Don't take it as a tragedy or a marriage proposal.' Peter reached out for me and messed my hair with his hand.

'You'd be the last man in the world I'd marry, Peter. I'd almost rather marry Gregor Jackman.' I gave him a fleeting kiss and burst out laughing.

'Who would be... the irreducible asshole licker, right? Not the brontosaurus professor?' Peter drew me to him and intensified the kiss.

'No, the brontosaurus professor is Hermann Frey. And don't call him that... Frey is the real man of my life, my great platonic love!' I had always called him that. Frey was one of my greatest literary passions, at least the only one or almost, still alive.

'Poor thing... he loses all the gifts you keep hidden from the waist down...' Peter crossed me with his look, puckering his lips.

'But how vulgar you are!' I hurled myself at him, forcing him to throw himself back with his back on the couch to grab me.

'Here... in fact, what I was saying!' He took me by my waist, making me sit on top of him. 'But are you sure this is not what the nasty old man wants...'

'No, I really don't think so. Frey doesn't even return my platonic affection, for sure.' I clung to him, wrapping my arms around his neck. Peter's idea seemed crazy. Frey wasn't that type.

'Maybe you're not his thing. Maybe he prefers... something else...' Peter suggested, pressing both hands on my buttocks and juggling to unhook my trousers with his teeth. 'Maybe he gets it on down with the licker...'

'No! No! No!' I burst out laughing and shook my head repeatedly. The image suggested by Peter was rather embarrassing and I was visualizing it regardless of my will. 'Don't make me think of such things, Peter!'

'It could be true, sweetheart...'

'I know. But Frey... No, he wouldn't do it with one of his students. And then he has been married for years!' I sighed disdainfully. I wouldn't have believed it even if I had seen it with my own eyes. 'Frey is an upright man, he would never do it! He's not the type...'

'You don't look like the type who cheats on your boyfriend, but you get off with any guy you pick up on the street!'

Peter's tone was playful. But I felt hurt, as if he slammed my immoral conduct in my face. I was a naughty girl. Even worse. And not only did I know it. He knew it too. And he was right. I was a filthy slimy bitch. He hadn't used those exact words, but the meaning was the same.

I moved away from him in silence and raised myself. I went back to sit and, looking down, picked up my things, put away all my notebooks, my books and my notes in my bag. I put on my shoes and got up. I walked to the entrance where I retrieved my jacket that I had placed on a small armchair.

'Amantine...' Peter was right behind me and grabbed me by my arms and I ended up with my back pressed against his chest. 'You didn't take it seriously, did you? Tell me you didn't take it seriously and now you'll turn around and laugh at me for putting one over on me this time...'

His tone was different from the one I'd been used to during the two months of us being together. Peter changed it often as he wanted. He had various nuances between ironic, joking, mocking. Then there was the serious one, the a bit pissed off but never too much one, the bored one. In some moments his tone of voice had also been tending towards sweet, tender. But this painful nuance I had never perceived in him. He understood he had offended me. And he was regretting it. But the real problem was that he was right.

'I'd better go, Peter...' I didn't turn around. I couldn't. Instead, I struggled to tear myself completely away from him. 'Better if we move on with our lives. Let's end it this way. We had a good time, you made me feel good...'

'It's not true. You wouldn't leave.' He sighed behind me, embittered. 'We are both a bit tense, even for work. Why don't we relax... I have a CD I want you to listen to, Amantine. Simple Minds. You never listened to them, did you? You'll like them.'

I had to break up with him. It was time. I didn't want it to become harder. Ours was a squalid, absurd and senseless affair. I had to make the right decision. Seriously commit to Geoff as he would like to, as my parents wished. As friends had long suggested to me. As I also suggested to myself.

I just left. I didn't say *"Goodbye Peter"* as I had done so many times before but without any desire to really leave, to disappear from his life. This time I left in silence and closed the large front door behind me. He didn't do or say anything else to hold me back. Still standing outside his front door, I was reached by the melodic notes of "Don't you (forget about me)" by Simple Minds.

CHAPTER 19

Commit seriously to Geoff. Focus on my future. For two months I had completely lost my mind and with it my perspective. Even my university career had been affected. It had been stuck there, waiting for me to come back and take care of it. Even now I was thinking almost more about music than about literature.

Peter's world had invaded mine and I had been the one to allow it. So I had to get back to myself as soon as possible. I couldn't abandon the environment in which I had grown up and had always lived. The party was over. Real life awaited me. It was the right and wisest choice for me.

I was trying to be calm and peaceful with Geoff. The days flowed, each one like the other. The approach of spring, instead of instilling serenity, filled me with anxiety, frustration and irritability. I had become intractable and it wasn't just Gregor Jackman's fault or the situation with Professor Frey. I avoided Notting Hill like the plague which wasn't easy because the Parkers lived in the area. The temptation to walk casually by Peter's house was irresistible, almost corroding me. But I resisted.

My back down was another. To enter a music store in the centre, to hold in my hands Darkest Storm's CDs, to meet his eyes, his sullen, ironic, seductive look. I didn't want to buy them, just watch them and then move away. But I left the shop with the Simple Minds' CD containing the last song I had heard outside Peter's front door before I left for good. No, I wouldn't forget.

Maybe out of guilt or because of the pressure I felt subjected to each time we were together, my relationship with Geoff was deteriorating day by day. I didn't dare to blame him, I took full responsibility for it. The situation improved when we had friends around, but when we were alone I felt an unbridgeable emptiness. More lonely than when I was alone.

'Geoff, maybe we should give ourselves a break…'

One Sunday at his place I decided to take control of the situation and talk to him. I had been with Geoffrey many years. Then Peter came along. Maybe I should be alone, really alone for a while to be able to understand. To try and get to know myself a little better.

'Do you want to leave me to go back to the one you betrayed me with every day for the last few months?' he interrupted me abruptly.

I felt myself blushing with shame. He knew. He knew it and hadn't told me anything!

It seemed as if Geoff's blue eyes were shooting arrows at me. I didn't know how to reply. I couldn't deny the evidence and a simple "I'm sorry" wouldn't have been enough. It was true, I had betrayed him. Why had I done it? Geoff was handsome, kind, intelligent. My conduct had been deplorable.

'No, Geoff. I'll never go back with…' I didn't dare say his name. Mainly because even imagining him, lightning appeared before me. Peter smiling, Peter teasing me, Peter holding me to himself teaching me to dance. His kisses, his body, his skin. Incredibly, I was able to perceive his scent too. 'But it's still better that we take some time… I don't expect you to forgive me.'

'No, Amy. I'm not going to lose you.' Geoff's answer surprised me and partly shocked me. There was, however, no resentment in his voice. 'I know that my future is with you. I've always known it, from the first moment I saw you. And I know he… he's not for you. He will never give you what you really need. What he does has nothing to do with us. And then he has so many women that…'

What could Geoff know? Had he investigated? About me, about Peter. How? For how long? I didn't want to ask, I didn't want to know the details. He had done it, it was a fact. So why hadn't he told me anything before? How could he resist without talking to me? Without attacking me or insulting me?

'I don't want to talk about it, Geoff. I don't want to hear or know anything.' Geoff's apartment had suddenly become tight, oppressive. Actually, it was oppressive to discuss Peter with him. The problem was between us. Peter was now part of the past. Indeed, the real problem was me, only me. I was the one who wasn't ready for a serious relationship, I was the wrong one.

'All right, all right... I'll give you some time if that's what you need. But promise me you will not go back to him...' Geoff's voice cracked. I was making him suffer. I felt like a monster. And at the same time, I felt trapped. A monster trapped in its own cruelty. A monster without feelings. Geoff had always loved me. And I loved him too, of course I did.

'I won't go back with him... He had never been an option for me. He wasn't anything important.' And whatever Peter had been, it was useless to explain it to Geoff. I would hurt him even more. And he probably wouldn't have understood anyway.

Trapped. Although Geoff had given me time, I still felt trapped. Like I had a noose around my neck that tightened more and more, then even more, strangling me.

With Peter I felt light. Maybe just because there had never been claims between us or promises. I was free, with a sort of enthusiasm for life that I had never experienced before, not even as a young girl.

'Thank you, Geoff.' He hadn't insulted me or condemned me. I didn't deserve such a good man, I was aware of it. 'I just need some time to recover. Then everything will be fine, I promise.'

'We've been together for a long time.' His eyes had become sweet and calm again. He stroked my face and I put my hand on his. Maybe it was true. He was right. I squinted my eyes to receive his kiss on my lips. 'We just need to find each other again Amy, it was just a bit of tiredness. I won't let you go. I love you, I can't lose you.'

CHAPTER 20

It had been right to interrupt the affair with Peter. Right for me, right for Geoff, right for everyone. About that I had no doubts. And now I felt quieter, Geoff knew everything and forgave me. I had no more secrets, apparently, at least.

The sense of boredom and irritability, however, didn't go away. On the contrary, it persisted and dominated me. Besides, I was tired of staying at Doris and Rupert Parker's home, I felt bound to their schedules, to their spaces. But leaving it would automatically mean moving to Geoff's house and I still didn't feel like it.

'I know it sounds absurd… but I don't feel ready.' I decided to open up to Rachel, whom I had met during the lunch break. At least, I wanted to try to explain to her how I felt. She was the friend with whom I was better able to talk to about my personal problems. 'And Geoff also gave me some time when I asked him, so it's all my fault.'

I was afraid she would tell Trevor everything, since besides being her boyfriend, he was also one of Geoff's best friends. And Trevor, of course, wouldn't remain good and silent.

'You can't force yourself if you don't feel like it.' Rachel placed her fork on the edge of the plate and leaned back on the chair, peering at me carefully. 'On the contrary, my opinion is that it would be even more wrong towards Geoff. And you too, Amy. Feelings can't be forced, not even by ourselves. They are either there or they're not. You can't control them.'

'But I have feelings for Geoff! I've always had them…' I tried to divert the subject to the professional sector. I didn't want Rachel to reveal our conversation to Trevor, especially the details about me and Geoff. I decided that she wasn't right as a confidant, she wasn't suitable. She was too connected to both.

'It's a bit the university, as well. I seem to keep working in vain, for the glory…'

'Has the other man nothing to do with it, by chance?' I immediately understood who Rachel meant. But I decided to play dumb. Sometimes I was good at pretending to be clueless.

'Gregor Jackman, yes, he's a big pain…'

'Amy... you understood clearly I didn't mean him…'

'So apparently it's public knowledge that I'm a…' I raised my voice too much and two guys from the table next to ours turned to us. I clenched my fists. Who was I to take it out on? Perhaps only on myself. The fact others knew it didn't change what I was.

'It's not public knowledge. Geoff opened up to Trevor and Trevor told me. That's all. A mistake or a crush can happen to anyone.' Rachel closed her light eyes for a moment and sighed softly. 'Even between me and Trevor... there have been some difficult times, let's say. But then we recovered, and it never happened again. We're fine now. The important thing is that it really was just a crush and nothing else.'

Else? No, it was nothing else. 'Look, Rachel, I don't know how to explain... It was as if... as if in his presence all my worries, all my anxieties magically vanished. It was like living suspended in limbo, in an unreal world. Freedom in its purer form, every moment, every instant became more intense, more alive, more vibrant. From every point of view, I felt free to express myself, spontaneously, without barriers and without limits. As if I could manifest every sensation, even the most hidden, even the most insane and irrational, shamelessly, without embarrassment. Without fear of being continually judged.'

Now Rachel knew. And at this point I didn't care, she could even tell everything to Trevor. I had tried to put into words what my adventure with Peter had been. I needed it. Besides, she was the only friend with whom I could confide in about it. I already knew I did wrong and I had hurt Geoff. I would understand if Rachel judged me bad and unworthy of her company and so preferred having nothing to do with me. But at least I was able to express my feelings to someone, which were authentic, real. I couldn't deny or hide them, pretend they never existed.

'Amantine... Are you really so naïve?' The look Rachel laid upon me wasn't sullen or disdainful, as I expected. It was more tense, worried. 'How couldn't you realize it? What you feel for that guy is definitely else!'

CHAPTER 21

I didn't want to know and didn't intend to keep talking about it. Else? Between me and Peter. No. Just the thought was unacceptable to me. Rachel didn't understand anything of what I had tried to explain. Maybe because she wasn't there in those moments it was impossible for her to understand the relationship that had been established between Peter and me. We had agreed from the beginning: no questions, no claims. Our story was based on this. Certainly not on "else".

I didn't want to answer her. I stood up with the excuse of a university meeting. After all, we had finished lunch a while ago. I realized that I shouldn't have to succumb to the need to tell someone about my personal events. In fact, no one had ever really managed to understand me in all my miserable existence.

I hid in the university library. If possible, for the rest of the day I would prefer to avoid interacting with the rest of humanity. I no longer had Peter's house to shelter in and I could only hope not to be disturbed. Meanwhile, I continued with my research, as much as my emotional instability allowed me.

My beloved poets, perhaps, would have appeased my troubled and afflicted soul. But they too were abandoning me and partly disappointing me. It was as if I always missed something. As if I really was not good enough to recognize mysteries, secrets, more original interpretations. As if I always kept myself within the limits imposed and I was not enterprising enough to dare more.

These were the great geniuses: enterprising, obstinate, active, perceptive, brilliant and with an excellent dose of unconventionality and audacity. Thus, results noteworthy were obtained. Then there were the lickers like Gregor Jackman who obtained the results in a different way: hanging out for years in the department, offering performances and services to every professor within arm's reach to curry favour with them. He had no limits, he didn't even have a sense of decency. But this way he had obtained a substantial number of letters of recommendation that would ensure him his position at the faculty.

I felt like a failure compared to him. Evidently, I couldn't count on my genius as a scholar and I wasn't even good as a licker. A lost cause, in short.

'Oh, you're here...' Here he was, speak of the devil. Gregor came up beside me and stood by my side. I felt his breath on my neck, like that of an evil spirit ready to attack.

'I'm working, Gregor. Do you have anything to tell me?' I tried to stay calm, take control of my nerves. If I had to be honest, the blame wasn't even all his own. It was my general emotional state, very close to collapse. Gregor Jackman could only be the last straw that would break the camel's back.

'Yes, I have something to tell you.' Clearly, he was having fun leaving me hanging. And lately he was acting like he was my direct supervisor, not Frey. He felt the intermediary, the only one who could intercede for me and for other poor subordinates to the absolute divinity, Hermann Frey. I hated him.

'Get a move on, then.' I didn't have to be rude and I knew it from experience. He would take even more pleasure tormenting me. He was a sadist, evil and vengeful.

'You should fix Frey's speeches for the conference cycle next week...' He leaned down, leaning his elbow on the library table so he could notice my reaction even closer. I pondered, instead, that he was in the perfect position to receive a nudge in the balls.

'Excuse me... didn't he entrust them to you?' Yet, Frey entrusting Gregor with his speeches to edit, broke the myth for me. But I could understand... He had a lot of commitments and work to carry out and maybe he could have missed some details.

'Frey only gave some guidelines on the topics he will discuss... They should be actually written. They are educational conferences, open to common people, to the crowd of illiterate plebs, not intended for the academic world. So you could do it...'

Of course, being speeches open to common people, to the crowd of illiterate plebs, I, the poor fool on duty, could deal with them!

The anger blocked my words. A grip oppressed me, tightened me from the pit of my stomach. I waited a few moments before being able to answer. I concentrated on the book and the notes I had in front of me.

'No,' I simply said. Just no. Without adding anything else.

'The order comes directly from Frey. I can't take care of it. He entrusted me with a new research on John Keats, so...'

John Keats? No, this was too much!

'John Keats...' I whispered. Meanwhile, I held the pen tightly in my hands. So strong I could break it and splash blue ink everywhere.

'Yes, I showed him some notes and Frey was enormously interested and enthusiastic...'

Since when did Gregor start working on Keats? I raised my eyes. If I could, I would have killed him instantly with my look. No, he couldn't have done it. And I couldn't have been so stupid!

'Our little secrets should be kept well hidden, Dr. Amantine Delamar. Not mislaid everywhere. We know we live in a world of thieves and opportunists...' Gregor ran his hand over his evil red beard. Bastard! Damn bastard! And it was all my fault. 'Disseminating notes and remarks here and there is never a good thing...'

'John Keats is mine...' I mumbled, more to myself than to him.

'And since when would you establish the exclusive possession?' His idiotic chuckle invited my violent instinct even more. I didn't know how to hold back.

I could only go to Frey and cry my truth. I was the one who started the research on John Keats. And as a silly beginner I had scattered tracks and notes everywhere, allowing the bastard to take advantage of it. He wouldn't believe me. I would be defeated at the outset. And physically attacking him was out of the question.

I tried to breathe regularly, the minimum necessary that allowed me to get up from there and disappear without damage to property or injury to human beings. Actually, to property and the slimy worm that stood beside me.

I managed to get to the bathroom and locked myself in. Bastard! And Frey also encouraged his pettiness and his servility with the benevolence he showed him. He was an old brontosaurus without character who was flattered by the most squalid and manipulative of the lickers. Peter was right. Gregor didn't go down on Frey physically, but surely he did it with his boundless ego!

But John Keats was mine, damn it! And that bastard was taking him away from me! He was mine, John Keats, mine only! I stamped one foot on the ground with fury, then collapsed along the wall of the bathroom, bursting into sobs, without even trying to wipe away my tears. I didn't even remember the last time I had cried.

CHAPTER 22

I couldn't stay locked in the bathroom forever. I would have done it too, maybe let myself be sucked down the drain, that was how I felt. Instead, I was forced to compose myself and leave it, hoping that the jackal was not still perched in the library waiting to hurtle on its prey again.

Fortunately, he wasn't there. I couldn't breathe, I felt suffocated. I just wanted to collect my stuff and disappear, at least for the rest of the day if not my life. Going and suffering somewhere unknown and hidden, alone and in silence.

There was nothing I could do. Only succumb and obey. Or seek consolation in Geoff. But I already imagined how he would react. He wouldn't tolerate seeing me treated unfairly and the idea of getting his father involved would re-emerge. This would make me a despicable being, building a career through acquaintances and influential friendships, not very different from Gregor. Other means but identical purpose. Make a career of no merit.

I took the Underground, getting off at Hyde Park Corner. I needed to be alone and calm as much as possible. Why? Why did nothing in my life go well? It was as if my plans were destined to collapse one after the other. I had planned everything with such care and meticulousness, but evidently, they were castles built on sand, without foundations.

I lay down on the park's lawn and closed my eyes. The representation of a splendid castle on the sand, built on a beautiful bank, was a clear vision in my mind. I saw it collapsing without trace, only a few grains scattered in the wind until they completely vanished. My life wasn't going according to my plans and I felt shocked and desperate at the sense of powerlessness and by the injustice that I wasn't able to fight.

I covered my face with my hands. No, I couldn't cry again. I needed to distract myself somehow. Maybe a Walkman would be the answer, like the one Peter had lent me. A bit of music, a bit of dancing. I could always go and buy one in town. Or I could…

I could not follow the reasoning, but as it happened, I found myself outside his house. I looked at it across the street as if it was a monument or a work of art to be admired but not approached. I didn't dare cross the road and ring the bell and I had no idea how much time had passed. Until unexpectedly, the door opened and Gordon, the superefficient butler, appeared stiff and upright. He looked straight at me, as if he had noticed my presence for a while. He had probably seen me standing there, while gazing out one of the windows.

We stood staring at each other. I across the street and he at the door. I was the first to surrender. I raised my hand to greet him. Gordon nodded impassively, and as I showed no sign of wanting to move, he turned, ready to close the door.

'Peter!' Only then I ran across the street, not even looking for any cars coming. I passed the gate and climbed the few steps. Gordon shifted sideways to let me pass. I reached the living room and looked around. Instinctively, I was already moving towards the staircase that led upstairs.

'Mr. Wiles is not at home, Miss Amantine.' Gordon carefully closed the front door and turned to look at me with his usual composure.

'I understand, I understand. He doesn't want to see me…' I frowned and lowered my face. Inside I felt in turmoil. I needed him. From every point of view, I needed him. 'Besides, he's right… I wouldn't want to see myself, either.'

'No, Miss Amantine. Mr. Wiles is really not at home.' He underlined *really* with his tone of voice. Of course, this didn't mean Peter was not angry at me. 'He's out of town, busy promoting the new single, he'll be away for a few days, I believe.'

'Hmm...'

I felt as if the whole world had collapsed on me. Not just a sand castle. But Gordon wasn't lying, I was sure of that. By now I knew him well enough, and when he was hiding the truth or refraining from expressing an opinion, he stared impassively into the void. Now he was looking at me, in my eyes. I didn't understand why he had opened the door, seeing me standing on the other side of the road.

'You can leave a message if you want. I'll make sure Mr. Wiles gets it as soon as he comes back.' The tone of the perfect butler was more friendly than usual. Should I take advantage of it? Actually, the real problem was that I didn't know what message to leave for Peter after the way I had left. 'Maybe you can leave an address or a contact number...' Gordon suggested. A small notebook and a pen appeared from a pocket in his jacket. Obsessively efficient!

'Yes, an address...' But which address? The Parkers' house or their phone number? No, better not. Geoff's house? Forget it! Rachel's place, maybe... no way! Perfect, I didn't have an address. Not an address where Peter Wiles could contact me. 'Tell him he can find me at the university library every morning from Monday to Friday between nine and noon, English department. As long as I don't murder the bastard who stole John Keats from me. In which case he will find me in jail.'

Gordon was still writing when I finished talking. Was he really noting down everything I said? I left Peter's house more tormented than when I had arrived. I was wrong again, I shouldn't have looked for him. I was risking complicating my situation even more. And then maybe, regardless of his being out of town, he wouldn't want to see me on his return anyway.

CHAPTER 23

Leaving the Parkers' house would mean automatically moving in with Geoff. Again, for a change, I was trapped. Maybe I had never left it. Yet I loved Geoff. But I didn't want to afflict him with all my dramas, he didn't deserve it. Our situation was already complicated and unstable. I couldn't completely loosen up with him, I always had difficulties letting go, to express myself.

My brother Alain's phone call from France gave me hope for a way out.

'So you really intend to move to London? And when exactly?' His idea of taking medical specialization in England seemed fantastic to me. More than anything, for me. Leaving the Parkers' home and going to stay with Alain to help him fix the house or apartment would be a great excuse. 'I think you should get here as soon as possible. In the meantime, I can start looking by myself…'

'Calm down, princess. I understand you miss me, but there is still time.' Alain laughed at my enthusiasm, perhaps excessive. 'My course will start in September. I will move to London not until the summer, before it starts. I'm still busy here in Paris for now.'

Summer. We were only at the beginning of April. Damn it! I decided not to insist further so as not to make him suspicious. If I asked him to hurry the arrival, to be here earlier, he would be intrigued. And maybe it would involve our parents, too, and the disaster would be complete.

I didn't expect or demand anything, just to drag myself forward in some way. I had written all of Frey's speeches for the conference cycle and I hadn't even been invited to take part among the academics. Obviously, the following was composed of the licker and a few others chosen.

In the library I was also tired of working on my research. I was mostly wide-eyed, staring at the same page for endless hours until the words began to sway in front of me and my eyes became blurry. I was advised to wear reading glasses because I was reading and writing so much. Actually, it wasn't a matter of resting my sight, but of limiting the anger and the tension that constantly gripped me. Why should I have to commit myself so much if the fruits of my labour were taken away from me?

I adjusted my glasses better on my nose. They made me feel ridiculous with that blue frame. They gave me the appearance of an intellectual snob. But maybe it was really what I was. He called me that too.

I nervously bit a fingernail, alternating my gaze from the book to what I had just written in my notebook. It didn't have much to do with academic research. I was inventing a fictional story about John Keats's life. Just to release some of my nervousness.

Someone in the meantime had sat in front of me. I only perceived the shadow, but I didn't want to check if it was one of my colleagues or a student. As long as he didn't bother me, there were no problems.

The guy cleared his throat. I raised my eyes and saw a long dark beard, a shapeless blue hat and a book that he held up and whose title I couldn't read. He had to be a student, then. One of those a little rebel and alternative, anti-conformist. I tapped my fingers on the table, then relaxed my hand as I retraced with my eyes the last lines I had written.

I jumped, feeling a finger touching the back of my hand.

'Sweetheart... you're incredibly sexy with those bitchy and hysterical intellectual glasses. I could lose control right here, right now.'

Beyond his long dark beard, the blue hat that covered his forehead, his grimace was his own. And in his hands, he had a copy of *Romeo and Juliet.*

'Peter...' I sighed, recognizing his green, laughing eyes. I turned my hand to grab his. 'You are here...'

'I was afraid I wouldn't find you, actually...' He shrugged, stroking his long beard repeatedly. 'I was afraid I was too late and you had already acted recklessly, knowing you.'

'What...' I stared at him, puzzled. I clung to his hand as if to a lifeline.

'Wait, how was the message... as long as I don't murder the bastard...'

Then Gordon, the super butler, had really marked everything.

I placed my hand on my forehead and bit my lips. 'I'm sorry.'

'Murder is not a good idea at all, Amantine. There are other ways to stop yourself from boiling over.'

We were drawing attention. I nodded at him to keep silence and looked down. I hated to admit it, but I had missed him. Now I had him in front of me it was as if the vitality in me resurfaced and a new stream of energy returned to flow through my veins.

'Is there a place where we can be alone, sweetheart?'

I closed my notebook and the book. I put them in my bag and got up. With a look, I motioned to him to follow me. No, there wasn't a suitable place, actually. The only one was Professor Frey's office, of which I had a copy of the keys. Frey and Gregor were at the conference. Once we reached it, I searched for them in my bag.

Peter was immediately behind me and with one arm from behind he grabbed my waist. Somehow, I managed to open and we entered. Peter turned me against the door, tore off his fake beard and kissed me furiously.

'Peter...' I clung to him with all my strength, searching his lips desperately.

He lifted me by pressing me against the door as I clung to him. I didn't have to do it. It was wrong. But I couldn't stop or think clearly. Passion silenced the small and feeble voice of my conscience.

'As far as I can see, you missed me a bit…' Peter reached down into my blouse and began kissing my neck.

'Oh my God, Peter…' I trembled with impatience, just like him. But... 'Peter, we're in Frey's office... we can't…'

'Lock us in!' he suggested, fumbling to lift my long skirt, one of those I usually wore at university as an alternative to dark trousers. 'But what's this stuff, Amantine, you look like a nun...'

'Don't make obscene thoughts, Peter! I can't…' Meanwhile, I locked the door. I had to calm down. It wasn't for this that I had called him. 'And then you were away, you did whatever suited you…'

'I was away for work. Don't you keep up with when we are on tour, Amantine?' He pulled away from me, crossing his arms, frowning.

'Honestly, I don't. Why should I care about a pop star's band tours?' I sighed trying to control myself. I couldn't let myself be dragged with him into that vortex that I could never resist. 'And then you call it work, that, really?'

'Yes, of course... for your work is only the intellectual one, I guess.' That's it, he was getting angry. I didn't want to, but I couldn't allow us to return to how we were before. I had looked for him, but... 'But do you know what the real work is, Amantine? A work that is exhausting and without big gains... To deal with a bitch like you!'

'Why are you here, then? I stopped by your place, it's true.' I bit my lips slightly and stared determinedly into his eyes. 'But you... you dressed like this, in order not to be recognized, I suppose, you came to the university, you looked for my department, then the library…'

'At the risk of being found out, exactly. Because maybe you don't know it, but it often happens that someone recognizes me. Not the snobbish intellectuals living on a different planet, but ordinary people, yes, they recognize me.' He nodded seriously. 'Then there is also the fact that I woke up early in the morning to be here as soon as possible and I returned at four in the morning when I received Gordon's message. Actually, I barely slept.'

'Thanks...' I wasn't quite sure it was the truth. Knowing him I could have also found out that he was making fun of me. He was smart and was good at telling lies, he could get away the biggest whoppers.

'So, what do I deserve?' In a moment his mischievous smile reappeared. He gripped my waist and lifted me. I let him do it and wrapped his shoulders with my arms. Meanwhile, holding me tight, he moved quickly backwards.

'No, no Peter!' I exclaimed as soon as his intentions were clear to me. 'No, not on Frey's desk...'

Peter moved the books and the papers placed on the heavy, solid wooden furniture, with his arm. Part of the volumes slipped to the floor. 'I've never done it on a university professor's desk... Would you deny me that too? I don't know when or if I'll ever have the chance again...'

'But it's not... not...' I tried to restrain myself, but my body didn't listen to any reason. I followed his movements and, completely bewitched, I clung to him. 'It's... unethical...'

He burst out laughing on my lips, spreading me completely and pulling me onto him. Meanwhile, my white blouse had flown over Frey's black chair. I laughed too, grabbing the belt of his jeans. Uncontrollably, bound by an excitement and a yearning that I didn't know how to and didn't want to fight anymore. Then I met his eyes and I felt completely lost. Lost and ready to start all over again.

CHAPTER 24

This time I was aware of it. I had to act honestly and free Geoff from the bond of our relationship. I wasn't the right woman for him. I was wretched, ungrateful and treacherous. Unworthy of his love. The truth, whether I liked it or not, was that I couldn't refrain with Peter Wiles, despite my attempts. I was a human being with its weaknesses, and I was forced to admit it. I wasn't proud of it, but Peter was my weakness.

'I have to leave Geoff...' Turning to one side, I waited for Peter's reply. I knew he wasn't sleeping even though his eyes were closed.

The story with him had started again, for three days at full speed. Since his return the contriving and deceit had begun again for me. But it was time to put an end to it, forever!

'This means you won't be with that famous "someone" anymore. I think I'll miss him, it was like having a threesome sometimes...' Peter opened his eyes for a moment, gave me a gloomy look, then closed them again. At the same time his lips folded in an amused grimace.

'Don't be an insensitive asshole, Peter. It's not funny! On the contrary, it's a very sad and painful situation...' Sad for me and painful for Geoff. How could I leave him this way? How could I hurt him so much, again?

'I got it. You don't want to feel guilty alone, so you look for some company and get me involved too.' He opened his eyes again and turned to one side, imitating my position.

'I can't betray him anymore. He's not like...' I pointed at him with a wave of my hand. 'In our normal world, mine and Geoff, we don't usually do these things. We don't go to bed with just anyone and normally we don't betray who we're going steady with...'

'It also happens in your normal world, don't worry. As it doesn't necessarily always happen in my world... that for you is abnormal, I gather. I wasn't born a pop star, Amantine. I was born too in the world that you call "normal". My job doesn't define me. Only maybe I have more chances than all the other mere mortals, but then again, I might even decide not to take them.'

He was strangely serious. Maybe his speech made sense. I was the tangible proof of it. I had betrayed Geoff repeatedly and for months I had carried on a double life. It was not necessary to be a pop star or be part of the show business to be a naughty girl.

I sighed and lay on my back, staring at the ceiling. 'I am a huge disappointment to everyone. Even for myself.'

'Will you remain being so pathetic for much longer? Because if so, I'll throw you out of my house immediately, so you won't have to worry about dumping your "someone" because you will miss the raw material with which you make him cuckold...' He turned around, adjusting himself once again to copy my pose.

'Do you know how much of an asshole you are, Peter? I'm just a game to you, an entertainment...' It was one thing to know something and another to feel it clearly slammed in your face. Peter never made the effort to be subtle when he had to say something.

'I am too, for you. Wasn't this the point? No questions, no claims. So why should I keep you here and put up with you if you're not as much fun for me anymore?' His comments didn't stray from the truth, on the contrary. He was right.

But I remained silent. I didn't know what to say. That was because I couldn't talk to him about Geoff and my guilty conscience towards him. I would have tried hard to amuse him, a reason the words were not coming. In that moment I didn't even know if I wanted to stay there or not. I wasn't in the mood to have fun. My relationship with Geoff had come to an end because of me, at university they shamelessly exploited me and then took all the credit. No, there was nothing fun in my life right now. I closed my eyes. I wanted to sleep. Maybe for a few months or even a few years. One hundred years as Sleeping Beauty, and then wake up in a different and fairer world.

I opened my eyes again, feeling a touch on my forehead. Peter still held his lips, and when he pulled away, he watched me from a short distance away. I stroked his nape gently. We remained silent. His silences had a more disruptive effect on me than words.

'I'll try to be funny...' I sighed and ran my fingers over his chest.

'You're not in the mood to be funny, Amantine.' Peter pulled away from me and sat up. 'It is not fitting well in your mind, the idea of hooking up with me, am I right? Because even if you don't have it anymore, I continue to have that famous "someone". Even though I don't break balls like you continuing to talk about it...'

'I have no intention of hooking up with you, idiot!' I raised myself too and crossed my arms, irritated. 'Only that my "someone" expected something from me and now I can't...'

'Nor could you ever be, you would still want to roll in my sheets for eternity. So your poor "someone", whoever he is or will be, would remain eternally cuckold,' Peter reiterated, chuckling.

'Are you by any chance pointing out that I will remain eternally a slut?' I crawled, trying to hit his chest with my knee. 'I'd like to remind you that I've never, ever, ever been like that before meeting you!'

'Never, ever, ever...' he laughed loudly, imitating my voice. 'You make me feel like the evil tempter of a chaste and innocent soul, Amantine. When you first arrived here, you knew exactly what you wanted from me. And how you knew it!'

'It's all your fault! I was destined to be a good girl with upstanding behaviour!' I snorted, annoyed. 'I was determined to follow certain patterns, for myself, my family... I had planned everything right, and differently...'

'Tell me a bit about your family. I would like to know a little more about the environment that generated this little snob with delusions of grandeur and upstanding behaviour, since apparently I was the one to bribe you.' I thought he was joking, but his expression was serious.

I lifted my shoulders indifferently. 'My father is a diplomat, my mother an astrophysicist. I can't even define my nationality, because I am a mix of cultures. I speak five languages, even if not all of them fluently. I spent my childhood and early adolescence in Paris, the summers in Italy and Switzerland. I travelled a lot, visited many countries. I know art, international literature...'

'All right, all right... You're really intimidating me now, Amantine...' He drew me into his arms. 'How much I adore the sound of your name, it's incredibly sensual...'

I frowned. Just what troubled Geoff. 'He, I mean "someone" in short, calls me Amy... just because he considers it... not that he ever told me, but I understood it. I understand...' I was talking about him already in the past, even if it was not over yet, I hadn't left him yet. I decided to change the subject. 'My mother wanted to call me Amantine because she was passionate about George Sand as a young girl. Have I ever told you about George Sand? After all, my brother was called Alain in honour of Alain-Fournier. But if I ever have children, I'll give them names just because they sound cute to me.'

Peter kissed my shoulder and held me closer to him. 'And this George Sand was getting off with an Amantine?'

'No, Peter, George Sand was Amantine. Her real name was Amantine Aurore Lucile Dupin. George Sand was her pseudonym, a male name to fight prejudices against a woman author. They didn't believe a woman could be just as good as a male writer. But she was nonconformist and independent, fighting against the prejudices of her time and... hmm... she had a lot of romantic relationships...' Here, I had it coming. I was expecting the sarcastic and somewhat vulgar joke from Peter, who would inevitably try to make fun of me.

'You have only me instead, don't you?' He kissed my shoulder again, holding his lips. 'Beside the "someone" you will get rid of soon…'

'Who knows... maybe I'll make a habit of it with pop stars in general…' I turned my face and kissed his temple. 'Now you tell me something about yourself, I don't follow your scandalous life in the magazines…'

'Hmm... South east suburb of London, my mother was a housewife, my father a teacher… I have an older brother, Harry, a good guy, unlike me. My father died when I was seventeen. I think that's all. I'm a musical virtuoso, that you already know... I'm the coolest and the most talented in the band and I create self-esteem issues for all the others.'

I stroked his arm gently. 'Peter, I'm sorry... I didn't know about your father…' I rolled over, holding him and stroking him softly.

'You couldn't know. But now don't become emotional, sweetheart…'

He leaned his forehead against mine. I was fine. I was fine in his arms. And it wasn't just about passion and sex, I didn't understand what was happening to me. I only knew I was finally well and feeling free, even more than before. Although now we were not having fun, but just talking about ourselves. But maybe it was just tiredness, just the need for some peace, some tranquillity.

'Can we take a nap? And stay this way, just for a while…' I didn't dare to confess that I wanted to stay hugged even while I slept. I didn't dare to confess it, not even to myself. But when I opened my eyes, I found that Peter was still holding me in his arms, he hadn't let me go.

CHAPTER 25

'So, will you talk to him?' Peter was watching me while I was busy cooking chocolate biscuits in the kitchen. I was scrupulously following Gordon's recipe in time to Cyndi Lauper's song "Girls just want to have fun".

'I'm trying to have fun, Peter.' I fixed the embroidered apron on my hips. 'Why do you want to interrupt my fun? To reproach me then for not being funny and kick me out? I'm sorry for you, but it's not going to work!'

The topic of discussion was Geoff. And the lies I had started to tell again from Peter's home phone. But I still needed a few days to make it more acceptable to him. I had to recover from stress and collect my thoughts.

'No, on the contrary. I wanted to ask you to move here with me. If you learn to cook it would be even better, so I can give Gordon a little vacation from time to time.' He came closer and pulled me to him, pinching my bottom.

'Hmm…' It was hard to resist him. The truth was that once I left Geoff, I didn't know what would become of me, of us. Peter would continue to have his official girlfriend. I didn't care who and where she was. But she existed and Peter had pointed it out to me just a few days before. As long as I was with Geoff we could be on the same level.

'Hmm yes?' Peter kissed my lips, first slowly then more intensely.

'Weren't you afraid I wanted to hook up with you?' I stroked his hips and put my hands under his shirt. I was strongly tempted to accept but I didn't want to give him the impression of surrendering so easily.

'I absolutely need a little maid to cook biscuits for me, Amantine. And since you're already here...' He took my face in his hands and stroked my cheeks with both his thumbs. 'Then you're sexy with that little apron... you awaken my perverse fantasies even more than when you're wearing the nun's long skirt...'

'Look, I could even accept, Peter Wiles. Just out of spite, to get even!' I smiled and brought my lips to his, biting him tenderly. 'And I would ruin your existence, every day and every night. I'm an ultimate pain in the ass when I really put my mind to it.'

So, right or wrong, I went to live with Peter. This implied abandoning the Parkers' house, gradually. First some clothes, then my books, then my accessories and all the rest.

And finally, I got to the hardest thing, talking to Geoffrey. Take full responsibility for the situation and accept the insults that he could fire at me. He had every reason. I insulted myself too from time to time, reflecting on my last months' conduct.

But this didn't change the situation. I was selfish, bad and insensitive. Maybe I felt good with Peter because he was selfish as well, bad and insensitive like me. Better this way, after all. If Geoff considered me a shabby and vulgar whore, he would forget me faster and with no regrets. He could start a new life with a more honest and more worthy girl than me.

From his engrossed and miserable look, I understood that he already knew. Again. As he had understood last time. I had met him one evening at his place. This time it would really be the end for us. Then I probably would stay at the Parkers for the last night. It didn't seem right and proper to me to immediately rush to take refuge in Peter's arms after having hurt Geoff again.

'Of course, as I thought.' Geoff's reaction was calmer and quieter than I had expected. His blue eyes stared at me, inscrutable. I feared it might be the calm before the storm. Geoff had never been a violent man, he had never raised his voice in all the time I knew him. And he had never even been sarcastic or angry. But this calmness destabilized me, it seemed unnatural even for a guy like him. I didn't know what to expect and I felt intimidated.

'I'm really sorry, Geoff. But try to understand...' No, what was there to understand? That I liked to stay glued to Peter always, and I wanted him constantly? They were not the most appropriate words to use during a breakup. It was useless beating around the bush, the cause was Peter. Another man. And my irrepressible desire to feel freedom and passion with another man.

'I can't understand!' Geoff sprang up from the living room sofa where we both sat. He with his head in his hands and I on the edge, as if I felt a bit on the brink and a bit in danger.

He headed to his room and I thought he wanted to be alone. Instead he came back immediately and threw something on the sofa, not far from me, so that I could see. An open magazine from which Peter Wiles and a very young and very blonde girl were winking out, smiling and clinging.

'And don't bother checking the date on the cover... it's this week's!'

'Geoff, I...' I reached out to take another look at the photograph and the article. It didn't seem to me the time and place to read it shamelessly, but I discovered that the girl was a model and her name was Lolita. Lolita? Peter was dating a Lolita? I looked back at Geoff. I felt horribly deceitful. The wicked witch of fairy tales. 'I knew it...'

'You knew it? And you're still...' Geoff's expression towards me turned from astonished to horrified. 'But... How is it possible that you can accept such a situation, Amy? He is with you, he is with her... He deceives you and you know it. And you're fine with it. Don't you have dignity? Don't you have self-respect? Are you so in love with him that you've completely lost your mind?'

In love with him? With Peter? What was he talking about? 'I'm sorry...' I wasn't looking for dignity when I went to Peter. And not even love. And it was neither dignity nor love I received from him. But I couldn't reveal the truth to Geoff. It was already hard enough like that. I was already hurting him enough without getting into details. 'I'd better go.'

I got up and instinctively picked up the magazine. Geoff didn't speak, didn't look at me. I left his apartment in absolute silence. I had hurt him, and I had hurt myself too. My feelings for him still existed, they had always existed. It wasn't his fault if I wasn't happy. It wasn't his fault that only with Peter Wiles could I feel alive.

CHAPTER 26

My prickly throw of the magazine at Peter reminded me of Geoff's same gesture to me. But it was done now. Peter ignored the magazine but looked up at me.

'Didn't you say you would go to your friend tonight to give the final farewell?' He laid the guitar aside and rested his back on the sofa, stretching and putting his hands behind his head. 'With "someone" how did it go? Don't tell me he made you change your mind and now you're getting ready to repeat the same pathetic scene for me...'

'Are you with someone named Lolita?' I ignored his questions and hinted at the magazine with a glance. I had totally forgotten my decision to spend the night at the Parkers, and instead of continuing to their home I had stopped by Peter.

Peter stretched again and with a yawn he took the magazine in his hands, just long enough to see the photograph. 'Oh, yes... this picture. It doesn't completely do me justice but it's not bad...'

'Lolita...' I sighed, standing, still in the same position.

'Yes, it's her. My "someone".' Peter nodded, picking up the guitar. 'Have you decided what you're going to do tonight besides standing there?'

'So I'd be the other woman of a guy who is with a Lolita!' I didn't decide to sit down or leave. Perhaps the breakup with Geoff and all the accumulated stress was affecting my nerves.

Peter raised his hand as if to ask permission to speak. 'One of the other women...' he specified without particular interest in what I had to say. 'And then Lolita is not really her name... it's a stage name.'

'And what's her name then?' I decided to sit on a corner of the sofa, as if I unconsciously refused to get comfortable and relax.

'I don't know. I call her Lolita. The whole world calls her Lolita.' He answered me absently. Besides the guitar he had also taken up his notebook.

'But you're with her... It's not normal for you not to know your girlfriend's name!' I crossed my arms. Why did it matter to me after all? His business! I was tense. Maybe it would have been better for me to go to the Parkers.

'Often we don't talk much. We do something else... She can do certain things with her mouth...' He glanced at me amusedly.

'Peter!' I didn't want to hear anymore. But I had been the one to ask. 'And anyway, she's too tall for you...'

'She must be tall to do her job, she's an international top model. She's over six feet tall but she's not taller than me.' Peter laid the guitar and the notebook back again, turned to me and tilted his face, frowning. 'Let me understand, Amantine. Are you getting jealous on me?'

I sprang to my feet, irritated. 'What? You're dreaming, really... I'm just asking, just to know...'

'Because I've had some jealous scenes in my life and I remember they were vaguely similar. But if you say it's not, I believe you...' He shrugged.

'No... it's that...' I sat down again, closer to him and the magazine. 'I just wanted to say that she doesn't seem right for you. She doesn't seem your type, that's it. She's too tall. Too skinny, I mean...'

'I will give you a detailed list with photos and sizes, so you can choose the next one for me. All right? You'll have to accept Lolita for now.' He smiled and pinched my nose. 'How did it go with "someone"?'

'Not well... I was almost afraid...' I rubbed my forehead with my fingers. I didn't want to think again about the conversation with Geoff, I didn't want to relive it, not even to tell Peter.

'He didn't hurt you, did he?' Peter's look became dark, almost worried.

'No... I mean, not hurt...' I closed my eyes. Not physical hurt, of course. But I still felt rotten, emotionally. 'He already imagined it, after all he knew it before. I got the magazine from him. He can't understand how I can accept this situation... he can't understand why I... In short, he thinks I am a poor little woman without dignity who yearns for a celebrity's attentions. Well, he didn't use these exact words but this is his idea. He believes you are using and manipulating me... and that I don't even realize it...'

'If he knew it's you using and manipulating me instead, poor man...' He sighed, rolling his eyes. 'You even want to choose my next Lolita!'

'Hmm... not so tall, maybe...' I forced a smile. I tried to get Geoff's words out of my mind. He couldn't understand what attracted me to Peter. I didn't understand it either. I only understood how I felt. And I felt good. Even if there was that very tall model named Lolita. Even if there were other women.

With Peter I lived, and I didn't have to pretend. He had destroyed the universe that I had meticulously built, but I couldn't and didn't want to be without him. In return I had conquered myself, my freedom.

'And possibly not a pain in the ass like you, Amantine. I assure you that you can be more annoying than three six foot two models combined...' He drew me to him and I didn't resist. I ended up on his lap, my head resting on his shoulder. He searched for my lips and kissed me tenderly, stroking my back. 'I only need one like you, sweetheart...'

CHAPTER 27

The good thing was that I no longer had to hide and make up lies. The downside was that my world would soon be aware of my story with Peter and I would be targeted. After Geoff it would be the Parkers' turn. Then some common friends. And soon my parents too. It was unavoidable. Probably Geoff would try to talk some sense into me and bring me back on the right path through my parents' intrusion, perhaps my brother's, Rachel's... And I would be alone against all giving explanations that didn't have a rational logic.

The day after the breakup with Geoff I decided to go to the Parkers to pick up the last of my things.

'I'll still be available if you need me for Jinny...' I had to try, at least, to sweeten the pill. After all, it couldn't matter so much to them where I was, not being directly involved. But I had to tell the truth to Doris. Thankfully, she was alone at home when I arrived—with Rupert it would have been even more embarrassing.

'So, from a chance meeting it became a real relationship...' Doris seemed fascinated by the idea, but doubtful at the same time. 'But are you sure about it? Do you think you have a future with him?'

A future? My future with Peter didn't go any further than living day by day. But it was absurd to try to explain it to others, including her. 'You can never be sure of anything or anyone really...' Here, a vague and diplomatic answer.

'But I was wondering if you were aware of his problems...' Doris sipped her tea and put the cup back on the table.

I remained silent. I swallowed a sip of tea too, not to be obliged to answer immediately. 'Yes, sometimes he has some problems with the band, I know. But they are normal things, I guess...' I tried to remember what Peter had mentioned to me about it. Very little. And I hadn't asked further.

'No, Amantine. Not really...' Doris frowned, narrowed her light eyes and seemed to think about how to measure her words. 'What I meant... you know about his past drug and alcohol problems, right?'

I didn't know anything, of course. I forced myself to maintain my composure. But it was as if something inside me screamed. Why? How could she say that? Was the crusade against Peter, probably called by Geoff and my parents, already started?

'He never showed any sign of having these problems with me... they might be rumours, gossip...' I didn't know how to go on and I didn't even want to.

'It was in every newspaper, how can you not know? About a year ago they wanted him to leave the band because of his unreliable attitude. They feared he would ruin them, compromise them, they almost kicked him out... He was abusing alcohol and drugs since he was a kid, even before he joined the band...' Doris was far too convinced. But I didn't want to listen to her. I was even more convinced than her.

'I understand you all don't agree with this situation... but none of this is Peter's fault, it was my decision. It's not right to smear him...'

I didn't want to listen anymore. I moved in my chair as if I was getting up. Peter didn't even drink alcohol. I tried to recall all the episodes I had lived with him. I hadn't paid particular attention because I didn't drink either. Fizzy drinks, water... No, I had never seen him drinking, least of all taking drugs.

'Amantine, I absolutely don't want to smear Peter Wiles or ruin your relationship with him, but just warn you...' Doris laid her hand on mine in an attempt to reassure me. 'Of course, it's also possible that his problems are in the past and now he's completely changed. But do try to be careful.'

I nodded without enthusiasm. I still didn't believe it, but it was useless to argue anyway. 'Okay, thanks.'

I just wanted to leave. Walk alone, maybe in the park. Clear my head, cancel this bad feeling and then go back to Peter to feel free and happy again. With him, with the music. With the sadness that always turned into a smile.

'Are you in love with him, Amantine? I see it from the face you've made, from how you defend him…' As soon as I got up, Doris copied me. She knew that I would soon move towards the door.

Of all the answers I could have given her, I opted for the simplest. What was happening between me and Peter wasn't easy to explain even to myself. I certainly wouldn't have done it with Doris. I needed a little serenity. I needed to respond as she expected in order to make her and all leave me alone. 'Yes, I'm in love with him.'

CHAPTER 28

I was in love with my freedom. This I had discovered with Peter Wiles. I couldn't give up on this. In all my life I had never felt the sort of euphoria that I only felt with him. Even the problems at the university were much less of a burden. They certainly hadn't vanished, but at least I no longer lived in the constant temptation to kill Gregor Jackman, cut him into pieces, hide him in a suitcase and send him to some unknown destination.

After a few days, rather than trying to find a way to confirm Doris's allusions, I removed them from my mind. I didn't ask Peter and I didn't want to find out something through the newspapers. There could be a kernel of truth, but I didn't care. Doris said that Peter had started as a kid, even before joining the band. I had no right to investigate his private life and his past.

Fortunately, no one intervened anymore in mine and so everything proceeded with relative calm. At least until the afternoon when returning I found a shady individual wandering around the living room. Short and grizzled hair, dark and piercing eyes, he looked me over from head to toe as if I were an insect to trample on. Like Gordon initially had looked at me suspiciously, but not with the intrinsic cruelty in that man's gaze. He was tall and heavy-set, wearing a blue suit with a white shirt open at the neck. I fleetingly glanced around looking for Peter, or Gordon at least. I didn't find them. The stranger instilled in me a sense of insecurity and danger, I suddenly felt fragile.

'So it's you...' He didn't move from where he was, next to the CD shelf that Peter kept in the living room.

'It depends on who you're looking for and who you are...' I answered, trying to keep an impression of tranquillity. Whoever he was I didn't like him, especially I didn't like the hostile expression with which he stared stubbornly at me. But I wasn't a child. I could face him. I had faced even worse.

'Simon Jennings, Darkest Storm's and Peter Wiles's manager.' He approached me, keeping a few steps away. 'While you, as far as I know, are the one who will permanently ruin his career. As if he hadn't done enough damage alone!'

'Oh no, you've really got the wrong person!' I raised my hands defensively and stepped back. 'I really don't know anything about Peter's career, and I don't even care. We are just...' Here, how could I define us? 'Friends... more or less... For the rest of it, he has his own life and I have mine.' He had Lolita! Why the hell was this guy complaining to me and not going off to break her balls? Better to reiterate the view. 'I'm sure you've got the wrong person, anyway.'

'Then why are you here?' The guy's tone became even harsher, annoyed at my words. 'Do you want everyone to know you're his girlfriend? Do you want to try to bribe him? Do you want his money or take advantage of his fame? Or are you in love with him? It could be though... you look smart, you want to screw him over properly in my opinion!'

'I already told you I don't care that he's a celebrity... It's Peter, in short!'

Why did I have the distinct feeling the guy didn't believe me? He didn't care about my explanations, he accused me regardless. He had already decided that I was guilty and that was it. And then what was it? The "People who believed that I was in love with Peter Wiles" day?

'Peter Wiles is causing inconvenience to us all... and it's your fault! He refuses out of town promotions, he doesn't get involved in the new CD's launch and he leaves rehearsals early... All this to run back home, to you!' As Peter's manager advanced towards me, I instinctively pulled back again. The more he raised his voice, the more I felt small and helpless. 'He has threatened to leave the band and start a solo career. You convinced him! What have you done to him to make him lose his mind completely?'

'So, I see you don't really want to understand!' At this point I raised my voice too. 'There's nothing between me and Peter... nothing...' I nervously bit my lips. I didn't want to tell the truth to that man and especially not the details of my private life, but I didn't have an alternative if I wanted to be left alone. 'I'm not Peter's girl at all! I only sleep with him! I picked him up on the street... and what we do has nothing to do with love, feelings and all that nonsense. And I'm not bothered about his career that I don't really care about!' I didn't know how he would interpret my revelation, but at least I had said it. 'And now if you don't mind...' I dodged him and set off towards the stairs to reach the upper floor. 'It's been a long day and I'm tired! There are also people working in this world, not everyone goes around getting involved in other people's business!'

I said it, this too! And maybe Peter would go mad at me for offending his manager and throw me out once and for all. Maybe this time I would deserve it...

I went into Peter's room and lay down on the bed. I didn't want to go down and deal with that Simon... what's his name... I did wrong, I shouldn't have talked to him like that. But I had to shut him up, I had to defend myself and defend Peter too.

I closed my eyes. I wouldn't move from there until his return, not wanting to risk saying something that I shouldn't. I didn't want him to get angry with me and send me away. Now that I seemed to have settled in my situation, these absurd stories began with his manager and his career. Peter was not a singer or a celebrity to me. It was Peter. I didn't ask for more from him.

CHAPTER 29

I woke up in the morning and didn't find Peter at my side. Maybe he had gone to sleep in another room. Or he had remained on the sofa. I dressed quickly and went downstairs and found Gordon, who had prepared breakfast as usual. I didn't dare ask for either Peter or the manager. Returning the day before I had found the door open, but I had no idea how that guy broke into the house. Peter had given me a copy of the keys. Maybe he would want them back as soon as possible.

As if the surprises had not been enough at the university, I met my brother Alain, leaning against the entrance door of the department.

'Didn't you say you wouldn't come to London until the summer?' I hastily greeted him. I was glad to see him, but I feared the real reasons for his sudden arrival. Lead me back to the path of reason and common sense, I imagined.

'What's the story with you living with a singer?' Alain's tone was more intrigued than irritated. He seemed to wonder how it had happened and why. Why to me, above all. He ran his hands through his brown hair and looked at me as if an alien had taken his sister's place. 'I didn't believe you were the singer type, and famous no less... Are you living the life at least?'

'So the word has been spread and they sent you to talk some sense into me? I can't say I wasn't expecting it...'

I kept walking again, I had to stop by Professor Frey's office to hand him some text revisions. After what had happened with Peter, I hadn't been able to look at my mentor's desk in the same light, I looked away every time.

'Yes, I knew it too. Your beloved boyfriend has made a big mess... ex-boyfriend...'

Alain followed me, giggling and trying to keep up. Most likely if he had moved to London earlier all the big mess he was talking about would never have happened because I would have avoided moving in with Peter.

'I had to leave Geoff... I had been thinking about it for a while. He was starting to expect too much from me, and I wasn't ready. So it couldn't work.'

I didn't want to go further with the explanations. What I cared to point out was that between me and Geoff it was over. Not with whom I had decided to live afterwards.

'And what role does Peter Wiles have in all this?' Alain didn't seem willing to give up. Whatever he would say or do, I wouldn't change my mind anyway.

'Peter is just a friend...' I wondered how many times and with how many people I still had to justify my connection with Peter. I already had enough and probably the worst had not yet arrived. 'And anyway, Alain... I'm twenty-seven, I'm older than you. You're not the one to tell me with who I can or I can't... live with.'

'I'm here because I promised our parents I would talk to you... And since I was here I kind of like the idea of a tour of London. Anyway, your dear Geoffrey, as far as I know, went to whine to his father who reported the news to Dad...' Alain gestured to make me understand that the news had spread like wildfire. From Geoffrey to his father, to our parents, to mutual friends...

'Damn it, I was hoping it would stay between us! Not that it became a state matter with whom I'm having...'

I stopped in time and sighed resentfully. Whatever, Peter would send me away anyway. I just wanted a bit of peace and fun in my miserable existence. Why did they have to ruin everything? I bit my lips hard. I didn't want to burst into tears of rage in front of my brother.

'He would take you back, this is the real drama!' Alain raised his eyes and then shook his head in disbelief. 'He must be crazy to want to go back with you, poor cuckold...'

'Alain!' He wasn't saying anything that wasn't true but calling Geoff crazy for wanting me back was implicitly making me out to be a slut.

'Between a madman and a tattooed pop singer I don't know what's worse. Our parents still relentlessly vote for the madman and support your return to him, but I'm currently in the process of suspension of judgment...' Alain continued undaunted with his unsolicited opinions.

'I've my part to play in this story too, if you don't mind. And no, I have no intention of being taken back by Geoff, whatever your judgment about it may be.' Instead of finding peace and freedom, my cohabitation with Peter was turning into a nightmare. 'Anyway... where are you staying in London?'

'In an apartment with some friends... but I'll only stay for a few days this time.' Alain shrugged indifferently but it annoyed and irritated me that he had spoiled his plans just to come and talk to me about a matter that only concerned me in the end.

'I'm glad to see you, Alain, but you shouldn't have come here for this purpose. It's absurd that I can't live with whomever I want.' I had now arrived at Frey's door. 'So you can report to who sent you that I'm old enough to make my decisions.'

Since morning I couldn't wait for the afternoon to come, then the evening. I just wished for the day to end so I could go back home. I felt tired and in a state of desolation and dejection I couldn't escape, not even concentrating on work. I had never before reflected on the fact that what I called "home" was actually Peter's home. Perhaps because I had never worried about losing it.

When I returned, I found Peter on the couch with his legs crossed and the guitar across them, it was a habit of his. He didn't look up at me, he seemed so absorbed in his world that he completely ignored me. A grip tightened my stomach and I stood still a few steps from the entrance. Then I summoned my courage and sat down beside him, striving to behave as naturally as possible.

'Simon told me he met you...' He sighed as he kept staring at the guitar.

'So I guess he already told you what we said...'

I didn't even know what to hope for. Whether he already knew it or to be forced to tell him the truth myself. Although the truth certainly didn't help my case.

'That you're here just to sleep with me and you picked me up on the street. Yes, he told me. He told me everything.'

He still didn't look at me, he didn't smile at me. He didn't even give his ironic, amused glances. He was angry. I had intruded into his private life, his career, his relationship with his manager and his band. I even went into the details. He had every reason to despise me and want me to leave.

'Okay, Peter... I'm sorry. Just give me time to pack...' I bit my lips hard. I didn't want it to end this way. I didn't want it to end at all. Where could I go? To Alain's, I mean, that is, to Alain's friends. Maybe they would have a little space for me too.

'Are you going on holiday?' Peter gave me a puzzled look. 'You didn't mention it to me.' He frowned in that way that I found every day more sensual, provocative.

'No, I... I thought...' I closed my eyes for a moment, striving to find some peace. 'I thought you were angry at me because I wasn't very kind to your manager, and you wanted to send me away for what I told him... about us...'

Peter put the guitar down, his gaze turning dark as his green eyes shot sparkles at me.

'Now you must explain to me what happened to the little intellectual snob and egocentric I met a few months ago! Where did you hide her, Amantine? Because you worrying about that dickhead Simon Jennings and convincing yourself that I want to send you away just for telling him the truth is really a nonsense!'

'But I...' I looked down. I wanted to cry, again. And I didn't want to cry, I had never cried before. Only in the last few months I had weakened. Not just for what happened with Peter's manager and for the fear he would kick me out, but for the situation as a whole.

'Come here, sweetheart...' Peter reached out for me, looking for my hand. I didn't play hard to get and let myself be drawn to sit on his lap. Then I pressed my body into his as he wrapped me tightly in his arms. 'You've held too much tension, baby. Tonight, you and I need to relax and have a good time.'

I nodded, placing my forehead on his shoulder. I stroked his chest and his arms as he gently kissed my face down to my neck. 'You didn't come back last night...'

'Humm... you really want to know everything I do, Amantine? I didn't think you were interested and that I had to tell you everything.' Peter pulled away from me for a moment to look in my eyes. Looking for an answer that I didn't even know myself or maybe I didn't want to reveal.

'No, of course you don't have to. I just worried a little...'

'Let me remind you that you're only here to sleep with me, your own words.' He burst out laughing, pretending to bite my neck. 'I understand your insatiable desire, but you can't expect me to be available every night!'

'Oh but... you're an idiot, Peter! I'm not like that at all!' I tried to move and get away from him, but Peter held me back by grabbing my hips and surrounding my waist to keep me from moving.

'Forget it, you can't escape from me! You're my prisoner, sweetheart...'

I had no intention of escaping. I hugged him with all the strength I had, I hugged him feeling happy, peaceful, relaxed. And finally alive, once again. 'Peter...'

'The only movement you're allowed is from here to the bed upstairs.' Peter managed to get up and hold me in his arms. 'And I'll take you there now. You'll stay there and you'll be mine for the whole night. So suck it up!'

That night, something changed between us, in me. Irrevocably. Peter looked me in the eyes like he had never done before. He was joking, laughing, making fun of me as usual, but at the same time it was as if everything in him was new, different, more passionate, deeper, more intimate. He seemed to know every part of me, every fragment of my skin. But not just my body and my human desires. Even my soul, my thoughts. And I wanted him, I wanted him with every part of me.

There was still in Peter a fragment of that teenager who maybe had suffered too much, who maybe had let himself be corrupted by something that had hurt him, that had destroyed him and that he still couldn't express. I didn't dare ask, I could only be there. I could only feel his warmth, wait for his caresses, his kisses, his words whispered softly as he held me, his unique way of touching me, moving and then surrounding me with his arms, holding me on his chest.

Yes, something had irrevocably changed between me and Peter that night. And I didn't have either the strength or the will to stop it, to repress it. I could only surrender. I could only hope to have him every night, like that night.

CHAPTER 30

The last days and nights with Peter had been wonderful. Sweet, funny, passionate. We listened to almost all of Peter's CD collection. I learned the complete discography of The Doors, Queen, and Led Zeppelin, what would be the soundtrack of my life and that would bring me back to him, forever. Despite owning them he always avoided listening to his own CDs, the Darkest Storm ones, regardless of my continuous and incessant requests that often wandered between pleas and threats. He was ashamed. There was in him that childlike and tenacious part that made him adorably stubborn.

At the same time, however, my professional life was falling apart. The guerrilla warfare with Gregor was increasingly turning into a fight to the death and more and more I had the distinct feeling that I was going to be the one to succumb.

He had taken John Keats away from me out of spite, but apparently once he got him, he didn't know what to do with him. He expected me to carry on the project with him, or rather, for him.

I hadn't spoken to him or anyone else about the fictional life of the poet I had started writing for my own pleasure. I rarely reminded myself, either. It was like a vague dream, a little crazy idea not worthy of sharing. The academic world in which I grew up would reject my silly extravagance, taking away my enthusiasm. The academic world most of the time also rejected true poetry, beauty in its purest form, the melodious sound of spontaneous words, of a less refined and perhaps meaningless language. Jacob's beauty, in short. The sound of my name, which Peter liked without getting lost in absurd meditations and search for meanings.

I began to wonder if the poets of the past really wanted to be studied like that, analysed, plumbed, inspected, almost vivisected, like lab rats.

I was interested in that moment, for the first time, in beauty for beauty, an end in itself. The beauty in pain, a bit like the jointed roughness and strength of Kurt Cobain's voice, the intense and passionate love of Romeo, the dedication and abandon of Juliet.

I shivered, often, at the very thought. Where was I throwing my life? On which basis did I build my world? On something distorted, not true... or that survived only on the surface, but didn't belong to me, my nature, my deep soul. I denied what made me alive and happy to cling to an environment that rejected me, that didn't accept me. I unfairly suffered for something that probably would have never satisfied me, even if I reached it.

Professor Frey didn't defend me. Professor Frey always took Gregor's side. By now it was clear who would be his successor. I rejoiced within myself, my rebellious spirit exulted every time I was called to report to his office, knowing I had violated his sacred wooden desk making passionate love with Peter Wiles on it.

I didn't care anymore. What I thought I wanted with all my heart, I still partly wanted, but it wasn't so inalienable. It was no longer a matter of life or death. However, I no longer knew how to give up pure beauty, joy, and freedom.

I took a walk in the centre as soon as I got out of the university and completed what I had been thinking about for some time. I stepped inside my favourite music store and bought all the Darkest Storm CDs they had available. The new single included.

The cashier, with a thrilled expression, told me that the new CD would be available from the first of June and that the entire band would attend to sign CDs and meet the fans. I replied with as much enthusiasm as I could not to disappoint her. Maybe she believed that I bought all the band's CDs having been taken by an irrepressible passion and had considered giving me all the details about it. In fact, she was partly right. The irrepressible passion really existed.

I left the shop elated with my purchase, just like a little girl, a little raving fan. A bit as if I had fooled Peter nicely. I wanted to take him over completely and his work, which I mocked at the beginning of our story, was part of him.

Was it worth it? Breaking up with Geoff for him, and flying in the face of Gregor Jackman, Frey, my world? Annihilating the environment in which I had grown up and had always considered mine. Dispersing forever my past as a little snob and egocentric intellectual, as Peter called me.

Maybe it would be a good idea to leave London, at least for a while. Maybe go and stay a while in Paris or Milan. A change of scenery to understand what I really wanted, to be able to detach myself and think without pressure. A sudden grip tightened my chest, and my heart quickened. No. I couldn't. I didn't want to. Maybe I could postpone it for another time.

Then there was that thought that didn't leave me. The one I didn't dare to talk about with Peter. Alcohol and drugs. Surely Doris had exaggerated the scale of the problem. The gossip newspapers generally feel a petty pleasure in destroying people's reputations, and I knew it, even if I was completely outside that environment.

I was tempted to continue to the Parkers' house to ask Doris for further information about it, but I abruptly changed my mind. I would make more trouble for myself. Doris and Rupert Parker, my parents, Geoff... I hadn't heard from them for a while.

Alain had blissfully set off for Paris once his mission was completed. His conclusion was that if I liked the adventure with the famous singer, he certainly wouldn't prevent me. He also asked me to have Peter sign a number of autographs and then pass them on to him, maybe he would need them to pretend he was friends with the singer, pull and bed some pretty girl, once he moved to London. My brother was an immoral jerk almost as much as me. But apparently our parents and Geoff were not aware of it and trusted him, hoping that he would convince me to make the right choice by backtracking on the path I had taken.

Anyway, the situation was getting unnecessarily complicated. And to think that I had decided to go and live with Peter because with him everything seemed simpler!

A part of me, the reflexive and rational one, was desperately trying to stop everything and go back, before sinking deeper into the abyss. But now it would be like throwing myself into the void from a running train because the other part, at this point the most influential and the most intense, the one that caused me shivers, thrills and irregular heartbeats, no longer listened to the reason and only wished to let go, surrender body and soul to what I felt for the man I felt every day more and more was mine.

CHAPTER 31

I entered the house already looking forward to the now familiar and comforting scene of Peter sitting on the sofa with his guitar. I was disappointed at not finding him. I wanted to talk to him. Maybe leave here, or at least try to.

At times my rational part clung on details related to the career, the situation, the future. What kind of future could I have with Peter? The words echoed in my mind like an annoying drum, a deafening and pitiless lullaby. They mercilessly hit me and sank me, in fact. What kind of future could I have with Peter? And turning the tables... What future could Peter have with me? Peter, after all, had his Lolita and if the relationship ended with her, he would have another one, then another one and another one. Until, sooner or later, he found the right one, the one for whom I should disappear because she would impose her presence at Peter's side at all times.

I looked around in the huge, almost empty living room. I had never paid much attention to it before. It was a bit as if the furniture was an annoying and cumbersome element in there.

Peter loved the space. Creative, mental and even physical. He didn't like feeling oppressed. In addition to the CD shelf there was very little. A shelf with some books. I wondered how they had ended there. Maybe they were just part of the bare furniture purchased by Peter and he had never really read them. Maybe they were not even his.

I was looking for objects that would tell me something about him. But beyond the guitar, the CDs and those books I couldn't find anything. The notes that he sometimes wrote disappeared with him every time he left the house. Or he hid them in a place out of my reach.

I ran my finger along the books on the shelf. History of music, biographies of ancient and modern musicians, an art history book about Kandinsky, a Shakespeare poetry and sonnets book. I took it in my hands and leafed through it, there were some pencil notes written here and there. Before I could read them, the front door opened.

'You're judging me by my books, aren't you?' Peter smiled and joined me, gripping my waist with one arm. He seemed in an excellent mood, he was calm and relaxed. 'I understand, little intellectual snob, I'm finished...'

'It's a bit like if you judged me by the music I listen to... or I buy.' I glanced distractedly at the sofa where I had put the shopping bag with the CDs.

'Oh my God, I'm expecting anything now... Let's see what you've bought this time.' As soon as he had the CDs in his hands, his smile faded and his face darkened. 'Worse than I thought, Amantine. Did you really spend money on this junk?'

'Of course... and the enthusiastic cashier told me that the entire Darkest Storm band will attend on the first of June to sign autographs for the fans. I think I'll stay there from dawn to get to the front row!' I joined him and tilted my face, trying a seductive expression. 'Above all, because I would like the autograph of one of them... maybe written here...' I unlaced the first buttons of my blouse, showing him my chest.

'You're a silly girl, Amantine. I could have given them to you if you wanted them, you didn't have to buy them...' Peter threw the CDs on the sofa and grabbed me by the hips, bending his head to kiss my breasts. 'As for the autograph, however... I must first inspect the area...'

'Hmm... I wanted to... contribute to your success...' I sighed, dipping my hands in his hair.

'Oh, thank you so much then, sweetheart...' Peter lifted his face to kiss my lips. 'You have my CDs, you know my books... In a little while you'll know everything about me!'

'I was just wondering if the books have any meaning for you or have been put there by chance, without real interest. Those related to music seem quite obvious to me, the book about Kandinsky... Maybe if you transferred to figurative art, you might be similar to him, there's a sort of spiritual dimension you have in common... Shakespeare however... it's the second time we come across Shakespeare after the quote from *Romeo and Juliet* that you only know through a school play in which you played Romeo... But basically, I would say that the poems and sonnets book is there just for show, a literary note among everything else. Maybe you've even flipped through it, absent-mindedly though... There are some pencilled notes, which are probably not yours. It seems quite worn out. You might have found it in a flea market and told yourself "Why not!" But no, I don't think you've read Shakespeare's sonnets, it's not stuff for you, pop star...' I took a break even though Peter was silent, he looked so involved and fascinated by my analysis. 'You are not a romantic, Peter... In the sense that I don't think you are well disposed towards the romantics as Jacob is. That's funny... For a long time, I wanted to ask you is there any news of him and for one reason or another I never did. Now he came up like that. I was wondering where Jacob is... If he still spends Sunday mornings in the same place, I didn't go through there on Sunday at that time since... His must be a hard life, alone, abandoned, on the road...'

'Not really... Jacob is not exactly what it seems, what you believe.' Peter smiled, running across my face with a finger. 'Jacob is a poet, a free spirit... Sometimes to feel completely free he runs away from home. Everyone has his own means, Amantine.'

'I like it. At the end it's a bit what I did too...' My freedom, however, where did it go now? I felt like a little fish trapped in the net, struggling to get free but without success. Indeed, remaining even more trapped. And my net was the man in front of me. I had to leave. To reflect. To regain my freedom. Not to give up. For fear that if I waited longer it would be too late. 'Peter, I think maybe I should...'

'Then hate me when thou wilt, if ever, now,
Now while the world is bent my deeds to cross;
Join with the spite of fortune, make me bow,
And do not drop in for an after-loss:
Ah, do not, when my heart hath 'scaped this sorrow,
Come in the rearward of a conquered woe.
Give not a windy night a rainy morrow,
To linger out a purposed overthrow.
If thou wilt leave me, do not leave me last,
When other petty griefs have done their spite
But in the onset come; so shall I taste
At first the very worst of fortune's might;
And other strains of woe, which now seem woe,
Compared with loss of thee will not seem so.'

Peter recited Shakespeare with perfect and vibrant intonation, without interrupting, without lingering, staring into my eyes. Did he understand it then? Was it the only poetry he knew? There were shorter, simpler ones. Why had he chosen just that one? Had he perceived my intentions?

My fingers trembled, stroking his face. No, I didn't want to leave, and even more I didn't want to leave him.

'Peter...' I searched for his lips and kissed him with tenderness mixed with an unknown ardour. Every kiss, every gesture between us always seemed to acquire a new value, irrepressible, overwhelming but of a sensitivity never experienced before in my life.

'Are you leaving?' He took my hands, intertwining his fingers with mine. 'Again, Amantine? I feel it by now... I can sense it when you're troubled.'

'No. No, Peter. I thought about it but no, however...' I lowered my face. I wasn't ready to convince myself to leave, to live with the idea of me far from him. It seemed unacceptable to me, at that time. Even worse than giving up my freedom. 'What do we have here, Peter? Music, yours and others. Some books. What you know and I don't know. The poetry that I know and that you perhaps ignore. Shakespeare that you know better than I believed. Your bed upstairs.'

'Yes, it seems to me that's all more or less... maybe something is still missing...' Peter looked around with amused expression, then he became serious again, concentrating on me, holding my face in his hands. His green eyes had turned bright, lit with a renewed passion. 'Don't leave, Amantine.'

'We don't have a future, Peter. We are so different... We can only have a present. Here, now.' I placed my hands on his, stroking them gently. 'Do you think it will be fine for us?'

'The present is perfect, I would say.' He wrapped me in his embrace and I was lost once again, along with my fragile intentions. My reason was forced to succumb and our fiery and impetuous kisses prevailed.

The words of Shakespeare recited by Peter had dug a new groove inside of me, reaching in my heart's recondite areas, the existence of which I had always ignored. There would be no way for me to leave him. To hurt him and myself. The freedom that I so longed for didn't exist in me, without him. Because he was my freedom.

CHAPTER 32

I watched him sleeping. He seemed so peaceful... I carefully inspected his features, the line his eyebrows painted on his face, his slightly parted lips. And I wondered how it was so simple for me to leave Geoff after so many years together and impossible to leave Peter after only a few months. I wasn't looking for an explanation, but a truth that I would be forced to accept now.

I cuddle up in his arms, hoping not to wake him. Or maybe just enough to notice me, hold me close to him and then go back to sleep. Peter Wiles was much more than what he looked at first sight. And much more than what I had thought I could find in him.

He stroked my back, kissing my forehead. 'Sometimes I fear I won't find you...'

'I'm still here, however.' I raised my face to kiss his lips. 'I'm sorry I woke you up.'

'Actually, I was already awake. And I felt a little like I was being watched.' So had he noticed it? It didn't matter. He closed his cycs, thcn hc opcncd only one with a grimace. 'You bought it, hmm... You really thought I was sleeping like a sweet little angel!'

'You were ready to trick me, however, like an evil tempter. But I have to admit you're cute when you sleep... and when you pretend, too.' I crossed the tattoo on his shoulder with my finger. 'I like it very much.'

'Hmm... sounds almost like a compliment. Maybe I should mark it on the calendar.' He took my hand and brought it to his lips.

I would have never left. In all my life I had never had such an intense relationship with another human being and between me and Peter Wiles the connection now went far beyond physical attraction. He had also managed to bury my platonic love for Professor Frey.

I winced from a sudden and unexpected thump, then repeated knocks. I took a moment to realize that they were knocking on Peter's bedroom door. It had never happened before. Since I had been seeing him it was the first time someone had disturbed us in the bedroom. Instinctively, I retreated in a corner, tempted to hide my head under the blanket. I glanced at Peter in terror, waiting for him to tell me what to do. Maybe it was Lolita, coming to his house without warning...

'Calm down, sweetheart...' Peter smiled, stroking my hair. 'Whoever it is I will immediately get rid of him.' He got up, picked up his shirt from the floor, put it on, reached the door and left the room.

I perceived Gordon's serious but slightly excited voice. 'I'm terribly sorry to bother you, Mr. Wiles. But Mr. Jennings is in the living room and he insists on talking to you. I tried to calm him down but he's really very upset...'

'Don't worry, Gordon. You can tell Mr. Jennings that I don't want to be disturbed and that he can wait forever. And if this is not clear to him you can tell him that he can go fuck himself.' Peter's voice, unlike Gordon's, was calm and quiet, even saying those not very polite words.

The idea of hearing Gordon repeat those same words made me smile. But the awareness that Jennings was in the living room and had something to confront Peter with was increasing my concern.

I got out of bed and hurriedly searched for my clothes. I didn't have time to put my shirt and jeans on when I heard a great commotion outside the door. I recognized Simon Jennings's voice. His screams, indeed.

'And so you made arrangements without consulting me!' The man's anger was clearly expressed in his higher and higher tone. 'If you carry out your intent I will ruin you, Peter Wiles! There is no man who has cheated me and has remained unscathed! It's a promise!'

'Get out of my house, Simon! Go away if you don't want me to lay my hands on you and...' I hardly recognized the anger and the emotional tension in Peter's voice. It was completely new to me. I had never heard him like that.

Before I could think or understand what was right to do, I rushed to the bedroom door that Peter had closed behind him when he went out, and opened it.

'Here she is, the one responsible for all this! The one that has swollen your head with ideas above your possibilities!' Jennings's accusations slipped past me without me understanding what he was talking about. Perhaps this was why I couldn't reply promptly. On the contrary, I was so stunned that it even stopped my instinct to intervene in Peter's defence.

'Don't you dare!' Peter hurled at him, grabbing him by his jacket. 'And now out, walk out now, while you still can, before I kick your sorry arse out of my door!'

Simon Jennings wriggled away from him. 'Yes, out... you're out, Peter! You have until tomorrow to go back to being yourself, and concerning your wonderful projects without the band... you know that I have enough connections and power to ruin your career and reputation forever! We know well how unreliable you are with all your vices... Vices that I myself have been forced to indulge and cover for seven long years! The one you're sleeping with now is just another vice, only more destructive than the others... I hold an exclusive contract, Peter, I'll rip you to pieces! You'll lose everything, I promise you!'

Simon Jennings continued to rage even going downstairs. I heard him slamming the front door. Peter waved to dismiss Gordon, who was incredulous and helpless in front of the manager's aggression, at least as much as me.

I remained silent, motionless, waiting. Even Peter stood still where he was, his head lowered.

'Peter...'

I walked the few steps that separated me from him and hugged him even though he didn't return it, keeping his arms down at his sides. I didn't ask him any questions, so as not to oppress him further. It was enough for me he could feel my presence. He would give me explanations only if and when he wanted.

We went back to the room and sat down on the edge of the bed. Peter's state of dejection and prostration was intolerable to me.

'Peter...' I said his name hoping he would understand that I was there for him. I didn't expect that he would confide in me.

'Leave it, Amantine. You know what I think... That you really should go...' He ran a hand through his hair, nervously, without looking at me.

'Peter... do you really think I'm ruining you? I don't understand how, though...' Simon Jennings's words echoed in my mind. It was what he had said at our first meeting too.

'It's not your fault, Amantine. It's me. Let's say you happened at the wrong time... But it's me asking more from myself. It's me who no longer agrees to continue with a stupid way of doing music that is functional only to attract horny young girls. They are the ones buying our music, our appearance... I would like to leave something more than this to the world, do you understand Amantine? Yes... you understand... you can understand.'

Yes, I understood. 'But what your manager said... can he really hurt you with that contract?'

Peter nodded briefly. 'I'm trapped, Amantine. I've tried to suggest something new, different. To make Darkest Storm evolve, but they don't accept what I write. I'm trapped and I have no way out. I can't even offer my pieces to other artists!'

'But if you feel so bad, you will damage them as well in the end.' I couldn't resist offering my opinion, even if not required. I wanted to understand, try to help him. 'Why don't they let you go? You could find an agreement, it would be better for everyone...'

'Simon fears it would be the end of Darkest Storm without me. Especially right now. The band's end would mark his failure as a manager and a substantial economic loss.'

Peter stroked my back with his hand. I laid my head on his shoulder. I was a fool, I had never considered that there were all these interests behind a band's success.

'They can't bind you forever, Peter.' I raised my head and stroked his face. I was looking for a useful solution for him and considered and discarded options one after the other. 'The contracts expire sooner or later. You could look for a lawyer to help you...' I considered someone who could help him in my father's circle of acquaintances. I hadn't taken advantage of Geoff's father's connection with Professor Frey for myself, but for Peter I would do it, I would bend. I would try to find the best. 'My father could know someone... I will ask him to help you, here!'

'Little intellectual snob...' Peter kissed my lips, then leaned his forehead against mine. 'It wouldn't help, unfortunately. But knowing that you would do it means a lot to me. I didn't want to involve you in all this.'

'But I'm involved, Peter! You host me here...' It wasn't the only reason. And I knew it. Maybe now he knew it too.

'Three years. I'll be tied to them for three more years.' Peter sighed and put his head in his hands, pulling away from me. 'Three years without being able to accomplish anything of what I believe in. Three years perpetually replicating the same style, the same gestures, the same movements, the same rhythm, the same words, the same singing voice... All the same as when we were eighteen and we were at the beginning. Only now I'm twenty-seven. In three years I will be thirty, too late to innovate, to return with something new... I will never be remembered as a true artist, Amantine, but only as one of those momentary and easily replaceable phenomenon destined to disappear without leaving a mark. So much money accumulated in a few years, then the defeat as soon as other younger and cuter guys than us take our place. Simon doesn't care about this. He wants to squeeze, squeeze us until he can get nothing more from us. This is my destiny. To be forgotten by everyone.'

'No! No, Peter...' I took his face in my hands and forced him to look at me. 'No, Peter. Listen to me now. I won't let this happen to you. Three years? All right. If there is no other way, we will wait three years.' Without realizing I had unconsciously fit myself into Peter's future life scenario. 'But it will be three years in which you will work unceasingly, every day. Three years in which you will write and produce the best you can create, so as to be ready when you'll be finally free to start your true artistic career. I don't understand anything about music, you know... But I understand what it means not to be considered for what you are worth because I've lived it every day, for years. To expect more, to know that we have something good to offer to the world but to be bound, not to be free to express ourselves because others prevent us.' I said everything in the spur of the moment, without thinking. Perhaps Peter found my words foolish and childish, overflowing with an absurd, reckless, utopian, and even a little insane hope. But I myself was fool. I myself nurtured my secret dream, the one I had not yet revealed to anyone because there was nobody I trusted completely.

'Amantine... How beautiful your name is. So much I could write a song about it, sooner or later.' Peter held me in his arms so hard he risked breaking me. When he let me go, I saw the hint of a smile on his face. 'Three years... In three years you could be my manager, you would tear up someone like Simon in the blink of an eye!'

'Of course, I certainly could. Then remember that I will be the one choosing your next Lolita, so...' I felt calmer now that I saw him feeling better. Three years. Would I still be with him? For a moment the thought touched me, but I struggled to get rid of it, to get it out of my mind. To succeed, I clung to my dream. 'Peter, I...'

'Are you hungry? Gordon might have prepared our breakfast if he didn't have a heart attack after that deranged Jennings's visit.' Peter pinched my nose, then got up and grabbed my hands.

'No... I mean yes, I'm hungry too. Peter, I haven't told anyone yet, but... I have a dream. Not as big as yours, I'm not an artist. But...' I stood up, holding my hands in his, I sighed deeply before expressing my request directly. 'You... would you read my dream?'

CHAPTER 33

Peter had agreed to my request with enthusiasm. He wouldn't be able to offer me a professional judgment, not being a scholar, but I didn't care. I trusted him, the sensitivity I had rediscovered in him, our intimacy, not only physical but also emotional, mental. I had found a kindred spirit even if belonging to a completely different world from mine.

So, once I fixed my notes and rewrote the story to the point I got to already, I entrusted Peter with my fictional biography of John Keats. I had continued to work only at home, away from the prying eyes that circulated in the university.

I never expected to find Geoff there, a few weeks later, right in front of the main entrance. I couldn't ignore him and besides it seemed obvious that he was waiting for me.

'Hi, Geoff...' I didn't know what to say except a polite greeting. I couldn't pretend that I was glad to see him, not after he spread the news of our breakup by telling his father and my parents all about me.

'Amy... Amy, we have to talk.' He raised his hand towards me as if to lightly touch me, then lowered it. His blue eyes were deeply sad and wrapped in that dark jacket he looked a bit slouched.

'As far as I know you've already talked enough. Now excuse me, I really have to go.' Maybe I shouldn't have reproached him. I had made him suffer, repeatedly. And he, for suffering or for revenge, had reacted as he could. The only solution was to leave things as they were and not go any further, hurting each other.

'I'm sorry, Amy. I know I shouldn't have told anyone everything. But I... I can't be without you.' He was making the situation even more painful with his insistence. He was making me feel guilty just for the simple fact of me being well and feeling happy overall.

'We already talked about it, Geoff. I'm sorry, you can't imagine how much…'

'What does he give you? Sex, a life on the edge? Perhaps parties with famous people...' Geoff shook his head bitterly. The look he was giving me had changed, from suffering, it became disgust. 'That man is not right for you, he will never be. You'll regret it, Amy. One day you'll regret it.'

'Anyway, it's my choice and I'm ready to suffer the consequences.' I tried to stay calm so as not to become hostile and unkind, speaking out of turn. But who was he to make claims and to establish what there was between me and Peter, what was right for me? 'Please, Geoff, for what there was nice between us over many years, stop interfering. Let me live my life, even if you don't agree with my decisions.'

'Yours is just a wild fling, Amy. It's for all the years we've spent together that I can't let you throw it all away!'

I couldn't listen anymore. I left him without replying, I rushed into the university and then straight into the bathroom, hoping he didn't think of following me. So many years with Geoff and he still didn't understand me.

I struggled throughout the day to ignore the episode and conceal everything in a remote corner of my mind. I concentrated on the evening, on the job that awaited me. The real one, the secret one. Peter urged me to continue firmly and enthusiastically. I did the same with him. Others might never have understood how our universes, so distant to be almost counterpoised, could blend perfectly.

'Maybe I have reached an agreement with Simon and the others,' Peter told me that evening with his green eyes shining with enthusiasm. 'They will look to introduce someone new to the band in my place, however I will stay low until the new member is integrated. Hoping that the fans will welcome him and soon become attached to him, too. Then little by little I will leave and be free. If all goes well, even before the end of the three years I can start collaborating with other artists.'

'It seems like a good solution!' I was happy for him. And I was happy to stand by him. So much that I would like to be still there when he finally achieved appreciation and success through his real artistic merits. 'You will make it, Peter. And soon we will listen and dance all night long to your music too, and not just that of others. You won't hide from me anymore.'

CHAPTER 34

'If you refuse and tell me to go to hell you will have my full understanding, Amantine.' Peter was watching out for me coming home that evening. I couldn't understand the reason for such an agitation. The new Darkest Storm album would be released in a few days, but it had never seemed to me that Peter worried much about it.

'I should first know the details of the indecent proposal you intend to make me...' Chuckling I clung to his neck to kiss him on his lips. 'Ice... ice cream, strawberries... you and I locked in somewhere for nine and a half weeks...'

'And you undressing for me in silhouette? Maybe!' He frowned and snorted, a bit annoyed. 'Unfortunately, not. We have been invited to Rebekah and Joseph Stevenson's anniversary party in their Gloucester huge mansion. More than just a party, it will be a social event that will cost a fortune with a waste of food and money that could feed the third world...'

'And you are forced to take part in it? I guess you need it for the launch of the CD and everything.'

I felt alienated and excluded from certain aspects of Peter's world. Show biz, celebrities, money thrown away into stupid parties and expensive clothes. But he, whether he wanted it or not, had to deal with it almost every day. And I was willing to support him, to advise him as I could if he needed me.

'Amantine, I...' He bit his lips nervously, looked away from me for a moment and then stared back at me. 'I would like you to go with me.'

I was dumbfounded for an unquantifiable period of time. Go with him? Me? To the Stevensons' party? Regardless of how totally unrelated to their environment I was, they were so famous that I knew them too. He as an international tennis champion, she as one of the highest paid actresses at the time. Even if I wanted to, I couldn't ignore them. They had been everywhere for years.

'I... Peter...' I would consent all his requests without discussion. But that one? 'No, Peter. I'm sorry but I really can't...' I couldn't. What would I do at such an event? What would I talk about? My extraneousness to Peter's world would seem even more evident. It would mark our distance even more.

'Yes, I understand, I'm sorry, sweetheart. It was an absurd request.' Peter nodded, stroking my hair. I quivered. Above all, I felt guilty and cruel. I knew it wasn't easy for him to deal with that environment. He loved music, art, he loved to create emotions through his talent, but he barely handled the pressure of being forced to live with most public figures. We had talked about it.

'All right, Peter. I'll go with you if this is what you want. But don't rely too much on my irreproachable behaviour, because I can't guarantee how it will be.' We had achieved a sort of partnership and we lived together in the spirit of mutual support. I wouldn't leave him if he wanted me by his side.

'Actually, I want you with me because I'm worried about my behaviour, not yours.' He touched my cheek and stroked it lightly with his thumb. A familiar gesture now. 'With you, I know I can resist, Amantine. In fact, if I haven't killed Simon Jennings yet and instead we have found an agreement, it's only thanks to you.'

'I don't think I've been very helpful in this, Peter. Your manager has no particular sympathy for my cause, it's no secret.' What I was beginning to think about were the details. Maybe futile and irrelevant to us, but not unimportant in that environment. How would Peter introduce me? As the other woman? As a friend? As his confidant or his secretary? 'What will you say, Peter? About me, I mean. If they ask who I am...'

'Whatever I say the newspapers will write what they want anyway so it doesn't really matter much.'

He didn't comfort me at all. I would prefer to avoid all this media circus. If someone had told me a few months before I would have called them crazy.

'I hope they won't photograph me, at least. I hate being photographed, a bit like some ancient civilizations. I'm convinced that by photographing me my soul ends up locked in the lens and stolen, subtracted forever. I would be destined to remain a poor creature that wanders about this world without a soul... In fact, at every photo I lose a piece of it...'

Peter followed my speech seriously, then burst out laughing. 'You're having a laugh, aren't you Amantine?'

'Did you really believe that?' I pinched his arm, then pulled back, still trying to lure him to me. 'But it's true, I can't stand being photographed. Anyway, I always look awful, other than with an expression halfway between hysterical and furious. Then seeing you, now I fear the worst!'

Peter grabbed me from behind, lifting me up. I struggled for a while pretending to want to break free, before giving up and clinging to him. I was losing my world, more every day. Or rather, my world was flowing into his. Like our bodies and our souls, day by day.

I still didn't intend to give a name to what I felt for him, even if a part of me was desperate to express it, even to scream it. But I restrained it, I held it back, forcing it to keep quiet and good so as not to risk losing moments that I considered precious, unique. What I was aware of, however, was that although I didn't give it a name and a voice, I didn't decrease the level, the essence of my feeling. On the contrary, I greatly amplified it.

CHAPTER 35

The release date of the new Darkest Storm CD was approaching. It also meant that my time was running out because two weeks later I would have to go with Peter to the Stevensons' event. I waited that day with unspoken horror. I had also asked Peter if it wasn't more sensible for him to go with Lolita, his official girlfriend.

I was just one of the other women, after all. Not that I found myself very much one of those lately, because in the end I was the one living with him and spending almost every night with him, unless he was out of town for work. It didn't happen often anyway, and I didn't complain.

Lolita was an international top model, always around the world for fashion shows and fashion shoots. About the other women Peter didn't talk, so that I began to doubt their existence. In any case, the agreement "no questions, no claims" remained valid between us, even if, as far as I was concerned, it was starting to wobble a bit. If I couldn't stake claims, many questions would arise. Perhaps too many.

As summer approached, I was involved in minor university commitments and that gave me a few more hours to work on my project. I hadn't revealed to anyone other than Peter, who couldn't help me with the material but supported me with firmness and continuous encouragement. I tried to reciprocate in the same way.

The spark that flew between us from the first moment had not extinguished yet, nourished by the fire of a passion that was growing, more intense, more alive. But as we often repeated, we only had the present. Better not to think about the future.

Above all for me it was better not to think about that damn VIP party to which I had consented to go. Only for Peter. I wouldn't have done it for anyone else in the world. The mere thought took my breath away, my head was spinning and I felt weak. Yet I didn't believe I was the type to be intimidated by that sort of thing. From time to time lately I also had annoying stomach cramps, unbearable sometimes. All because of the tension accumulated over the last few months!

'I'm not obliged to take part in the presentation of the CD and the signing of the autographs, right?' I bit a chocolate muffin while Peter was still half asleep, wandering in the kitchen.

'Didn't you say some time ago that you would line up from dawn to get an autograph here?' He patted his chest and stared at me with an offended expression.

'Why should I wake up at dawn and stand in line when I can get one of the band members here, and do whatever I want with him? What can I do with a miserable autograph drawn with a pen if I can have much more?' I bit my lips, blinking several times, intentionally, in order to provoke him.

Peter frowned and scratched his temple. 'As long as that member of the band comes home tonight... With unleashed fans ready to tear their underwear for him, you never know...'

I crossed my arms and stood motionless, looking at him. Still and silent.

'I know that you're swallowing the scenes of jealousy, the ones that I'd really like to receive... Since the time of me and Lolita in the gossip magazine you've become very cunning, sweetheart. I had fun that time, it's a pity!' Peter snorted and bit half the muffin at the same time.

'Rather than be crowded out and jostled by your fans, I'd prefer to go for a walk in the park or along the river. You never know, I could even meet a nice boy... You know, after the first one I picked up on the street I could make a habit of it...' I smiled and amiably sipped my coffee. 'So tonight, in case you come back, you might not even find me here. Just to warn you... I could be the one not coming back.'

Peter didn't reply. He approached me, tore the coffee cup from my hand and pushed the whole breakfast in a corner. He lifted me onto the table, sitting me there, resting his hands on the sides of it. His eyes on me were serious, almost resentful. He almost angrily grasped me and kissed my lips vigorously, stroking my back and pressing his body against mine. I returned it, clinging to him with my legs and arms, I moaned and dipped my hands in his hair.

'Just decided to leave you with a souvenir, sweetheart... In case you decide not to come back tonight...' Peter shrugged and pulled away from me. His mischievous look made me smile. I would come back that night. I would come back every night.

'I could very well come back, but I would get bored if I didn't have anyone to entertain me...' I tilted my face and sighed before jumping off the table.

'Amantine, Amantine... The day I launch something totally mine, I'll want you with me and you won't be able to say no.' Peter had unexpectedly changed the subject. From playful his expression had become very thoughtful. 'It could take many years, maybe you would forget me... but I'll want you with me anyway.'

'Peter...' I would be there. Even after many years. Whatever happened to us and between us. 'If I forget you, I wouldn't be me anymore.' I stroked his chest, kissing him on his lips. 'I'll be your other woman forever, face it!'

He nodded, returning the kiss, stroked my face tenderly. 'You're my favourite other woman, do you know that? Tonight, I'll try not to be late, sweetheart. You can do what you want with me.'

CHAPTER 36

I didn't understand the importance and the extent of that event until the day I had to face its preparation. For Peter it had been simpler. For men it was always simpler and if there were rare occasions when I envied them there were just these.

Choice of clothes, accessories, makeup, in short, everything that generally excited girls was for me an exhausting ordeal. When shopping with friends I had always ended up defeated and in a bad mood. On that occasion I completely lost my cool.

Hair, that a hairdresser had come, specially to style me, or rather, tame me. After all, I was Peter Wiles of Darkest Storm's chaperone. I never realized I had hair until that moment. After two hours of torment it came out a thirties hairstyle that I was sure would inexorably collapse by the beginning of the evening if I didn't keep my head still. I pretended to appreciate enthusiastically, so as not to disappoint the hairdresser and his artwork.

But the real massacre was the make-up. I cried bitter tears because of the eye shadow, eyeliner and mascara. My mother's friend who insisted that I made the green specks of my eyes stand out was an amateur in comparison. I didn't believe someone could put all that make-up on just one pair of eyes. The make-up artist looked like Leonardo struggling with *La Gioconda*. Instead, it was just me. And in the end, when he allowed me to look at myself in the mirror, I had to learn to become familiar with the diva version of myself.

First thing, however, there was the selection of the dress. They had brought me a selection of clothes. When Peter said I didn't have to worry because he would send me someone to help me prepare for the big event, I didn't think he meant that they would dress me from head to toe.

After a dress fitting, that seemed endless to me, I refused the proposals of skimpy dresses with which I would have felt more naked than dressed and ended up choosing a dusty pink dress, in lace but high-necked and long, down to my calves. It marked my waist but not excessively my shape and had a long row of little buttons on its back. The matching shoes were the same colour as the dress. They had heels a bit too high for my taste, but with some goodwill I could accept them.

I was not a doll to dress and model. I knew what I liked and what I didn't. I listened to the experts' opinion but not very well, and still not enough to allow them to obscure or make my judgment waver. I intended to accompany Peter, to make my entrance into that world that was totally unknown to me, but without forgetting who I was.

When it was almost time to go and my dressing was complete, I went downstairs. To get me ready, they had locked me in a guest room so as not to be disturbed. By Peter, mainly.

Coming downstairs I met Gordon first and he looked at me so incredulously that for a moment I feared he didn't recognize me. Peter came up behind him, he appeared from the kitchen, crossed the living room and reached the bottom of the stairs. He passed Gordon, looking at me.

I feared he was unhappy with my choice. He didn't speak. He was serious. Worryingly serious. Maybe the dress was too chaste, that was the problem. I was convinced there was nothing wrong with makeup and hair. I still had time to change and take advice from the experts for something more suitable. But when he gave me the freedom to choose, I thought he meant that I could choose what I considered was most appropriate.

I reached the last steps with one hand on the banisters and sighed. 'I understand, I'll go upstairs and change. I'll follow orders and I won't do it my own way anymore, I'll stop being a whimsical bitch!'

'Amantine... you're the most beautiful whimsical bitch I've ever seen...' Peter took a breath and stretched out his hand to me.

150

Strangely, it seemed that he didn't dare touch me. He ran his eyes over my dress, and then returned to stare at my face.

'Hmm... You're kidding me as usual...' He looked well in his elegant blue suit with a lighter shade shirt and bright tie. I had never seen him like this before. He looked good even though it was much easier for men. 'And it's just a wickedness from you because if I answer you as you deserve, I risk ruining something of what they put on me... or breaking a heel.'

Peter didn't reply. I was now in front of him. He put his hands on my waist, drawing me towards him. 'I've changed my mind.'

'Would you make me know what you are on about, Peter Wiles?' I put my hands on his shoulders. I felt him quiver, maybe he was tense, worried.

'We're not going to that stupid party anymore. We stay here, just the two of us... You and me.' He searched for my lips and involved me in a slow, deep kiss. As soon as he pulled away, he shook his head. 'I don't want them to see you or ruin you.'

'Peter...' Was he serious? Did he really like how I dressed and all the rest? Or... 'You're ashamed of me...' I tilted my head and wiggled my nose.

'I don't want them to see you because I want you only for me, Amantine. So we stay here...' He rubbed a hand on my back, brushing his fingers over all the little buttons of my dress. 'I want to unbutton them all, one by one... take off your dress, then let your hair down...' He kissed my lips again and then let the kisses run down my neck.

'And then the hairdresser and the make-up artist you called just for me will kill you.' I took his face in my hands and smiled. 'Peter... you're terrible! You're ruining my make-up, wrinkling my dress...'

'I don't care. I'm not joking. Amantine, we're not going to that party! We order pizza if you want... we dance all night, but don't mix with that rabble.' Yes, he was serious. He wasn't joking at all.

I hugged him. I didn't know if he wanted me to avoid the embarrassment of an environment that wasn't mine or avoid the embarrassment for himself. But I knew I couldn't let him, even if I wished with all of my heart to stay home, alone with him. 'You must go, Peter. You have to do it for your work. There will be many important people. If you don't want me to come, I can stay home, I don't care at all. I know I can't compete with all those actresses and models. But it's good for you to go and if you don't show up you risk compromising your career.'

'Okay, then.' Peter nodded resignedly to my words, took my hand and interlaced his fingers with mine. 'But you come with me and don't abandon me for the whole night. Without you I don't even leave home, sweetheart.'

CHAPTER 37

I imagined my fate that evening. Clung to Peter. Or at least I wanted to be. Even in the car I couldn't tear myself away from him. The road to Gloucester seemed endless to me. Hours and hours. It seemed much more than it should have been. I was terrified of ruining my makeup, hairstyle and dress.

Peter was quiet and a bit absorbed beside me as the driver drove safely to our destination. I had always been a detached person, definitely not very emotional. I didn't understand why I became so anxious. Or maybe I did. But I was still reluctant to admit it.

The driver stopped at the entrance to show our invitations. Beyond the great gate of the mansion, which seemed more a castle than a mansion from the distance, my already fleeting serenity wavered even more. I looked away from the window and turned to Peter.

'Don't be impressed.' Peter shrugged impatiently, then smiled. 'We will manage to survive such shameless ostentation.'

I nodded, holding his hand. I wasn't a Cinderella visiting the Prince's palace. I had been moderately used to luxury and comfort, I was hardly amazed. But what I was facing far exceeded my expectations.

From the gate to the mansion we travelled a long stretch of road. They probably had spent a fortune on the lighting alone. The sun was setting and from the car I was already lost in the twinkle of the avenues leading to the castle.

I could no longer watch without feeling uncomfortable and I turned to Peter. I realized that his idea of staying home and ordering pizza was not bad at all.

'Do you think there will be many people?' Rhetorical question.

'Some members of the aristocracy, some famous actors, producers, directors... So you can see in person all those you usually find in gossip magazines or tabloids.' Peter glanced out the window and sighed.

'But you know I don't read gossip magazines!' I winced, vaguely disgusted. 'Peter... maybe next time we order pizza, okay?'

'If you dress up like that for the occasion, we can do it, sweetheart.' He looked back at me and smiled.

Meanwhile, the car suddenly stopped. Without needing to look I realized that we had come to the Stevensons "modest little house". Peter nodded to the driver, got out of the car and came to get me. He opened my door and held out his hand.

'Don't leave me for any reason, Amantine.'

'Yes, don't worry...' I sighed, looking straight at the mansion. I felt small and useless in front of that immense brick thing with a colonnade and giant windows. On the whole, it could almost compete with Buckingham Palace. 'I'll follow you even into the bathroom!'

'Don't let me get any ideas...' Peter grabbed my hand and held it in his. 'Take a deep breath when the show starts. We'll have to do the parade to go and greet the gentry, we can then eat some expensive crap. Maybe first we pretend to greet some of the guests. Then we scram towards the outdoor swimming pool, which is huge, of course, I take off your little dress and...'

'Peter... how many times have you been here?' Concerning Peter's plan, I was mainly interested in the finale.

'Three or four times...' He sighed as we walked inside.

Peter feigned smiles to some people passing through. I noticed beautiful women and a couple of men that appeared familiar. Were they actors? I was very bad recognizing celebs because I had never been passionate about cinema and television. Surely I would make a show of myself.

The women's clothes were so eccentric that they made me look like a convent school girl, and they bothered me. They annoyed me the way they looked at Peter and winked in his direction, as if I wasn't there. That I officially was nothing to him didn't change things, indeed probably increased my uneasy feelings.

Beyond the grand entrance there was a refreshment table. In fact, I should say tables. The amount of food was unimaginable, I had never seen so much laid on. More than a refreshment, it seemed destined to feed the nation for a month.

In the distance, at the entrance to the hall, I saw them and recognized them. Rebekah and Joseph Stevenson welcomed the newly arrived guests. The hall vaguely resembled the Hall of Mirrors in the palace of Versailles. They probably had taken inspiration from it. Obviously, being as beautiful as those two were, they didn't have self-esteem problems.

'Peter, my dearest...' We hadn't yet arrived before them, and Rebekah had already called Peter with a wave of her hand. 'I saw the other boys around, I was afraid you wouldn't come.'

Her voice was sweet, soft and smooth. She was wearing a turquoise dress that didn't hide anything, indeed it wrapped her, revealing every detail of her shape. It wasn't skimpy, but in its own way it made the beauty of Rebekah's body even more evident. She wore heavy make-up with strong definition that accentuated her features: cheekbones, beautiful black eyes and full lips. Her dark hair was wavy on her shoulders.

'Here I am, anyway!' As soon as we were right in front of them, Peter and Rebekah hugged, even if very innocently. Then the woman's gaze slipped on me.

Meanwhile, Joseph Stevenson also joined his wife and consequently stood before us. He and Peter greeted each other with a pat on the back. Joseph was a man of disarming beauty, emanating an uncommon charm and physicality. A lock of light hair covered his blue eyes, making his virile look even more sensual. The black jacket showed off his broad shoulders. I looked away so as not to seem too intrusive.

'Who did you bring us here, Peter? Who's this beautiful girl?' Joseph looked at me, composed but intrigued.

'The beautiful girl is Amantine Delamar... and she's my girlfriend,' Peter answered without hesitation.

I did my best to smile and remain unperturbed and I shook hands with our hosts. But... his girlfriend? Rebekah and Joseph didn't have anything to say about it at the time.

'What a good girl! You got the only Darkest Storm with a shred of talent. What do you do, dear? Are you an actress or a singer? A new up and coming star?' Rebekah kept smiling amiably. Too much for my taste.

'No, I'm...' I glanced at Peter, searching for help. He stood in silence and looked at them with that somewhat sarcastic expression, one of those I had seen him do before. I wasn't that good at lying anymore, especially if caught off guard, so I only had the truth. 'I'm a university researcher in English literature.'

Peter grabbed my waist, drawing me to himself. 'I've been lucky. Beautiful and smart.'

I could have killed him. Once away from the magnificent couple I would beat him to death, I decided.

'I could kill you but there are too many people around!' I dodged him as soon as we stepped away. 'And stay away from me, so that you don't spoil me, I'm already struggling to keep myself composed with this stuff on.'

'I couldn't ask for anything more than you take everything off, Amantine. You'd just be doing me a favour.' Peter burst out laughing, wrapping my waist.

'Why the hell did you tell those two that I'm your girlfriend?' I crossed my arms and snorted. 'And why didn't you come up with some idea when she asked me what I do? The university researcher of English literature...' I raised my voice without realizing it. 'Did you want to let me pass for the evening extravaganza? And then Lolita... What will Lolita say?'

'Do you really care what Lolita will say?' Peter narrowed his eyes and fixed a lock of my hair that stuck out from my hairstyle. 'Wasn't she too tall for me?'

No, I really didn't care about Lolita. I felt uncomfortable. 'I do not know... I feel like you wanted to do something eccentric by bringing me here. Of course, I was the one to say what I do with my life. I could make up a story... And then Lolita is your girlfriend anyway! I...'

'Lolita is in Hollywood, Amantine. She cheated on me with an actor... Don't you read the newspapers?' Peter sighed and shook his head with a desolate expression, then stroked my arms, drawing me to him so that I ended up close to him. 'Everyone will be laughing at me now, they consider me a poor cuckold. So I thought that if I too...'

'So... now I've switched from being one of the other women to a standby girlfriend?' I frowned, biting my lips. Was he kidding me? Yes, definitely.

'Of course, sweetheart. Always without questions and without claims, as you wish.'

Did I really want it? Was he so convinced? Because I was not anymore.

'All right, Peter. I'll be your spare girl for tonight. Just to save your ass!'

Peter stroked my face gently. His green eyes had become intense, almost eager. 'How long will we go on like this, Amantine?' He put his arm around my waist and kissed me impetuously, indifferent to the people around us. 'And if I catch you again looking at Joseph Stevenson with that dreamy expression...'

'Are you getting jealous, Peter?' I giggled, stepping and turning away from him and then I turned around to look at him. Peter shrugged, pouted, shaking his head. I came closer and smiled, stroking his face. 'Because it vaguely sounds like...'

'Here you are, you have finally arrived!' A tall guy with slanty blue eyes approached us.

'Tyler... it's been a long time!' Peter threw a sidelong glance at him and added nothing more.

'Knowing you, I thought we couldn't count on your presence.' The guy let his gaze slide over me, then he took my hand and brought it to his lips. 'Anyway... Tyler Grey, I can't hope that my colleague here will have the dignity to introduce us.'

'Oh... I'm Amantine Delamar.' I didn't know if I had to make a bow, a curtsey or a twirl considering the guy's chivalrous ways. I recognized him as one of Darkest Storm, a bit from his words and also from the memory of the band's image on the CDs I had purchased.

Three other guys came up and introduced themselves to me: George Tennison, Steve Woodhouse and Rick Adams. Outwardly very nice, very clean, very polite. The classic good guys, rebels enough, but without exaggerating. Totally different from Peter's "punchable face'. Surely, given time, I could associate their names with their faces.

Since I knew a bit more about music, I was realizing that the band's name, Darkest Storm, was perhaps not that suitable for a predominantly pop band. It suggested something obscure, maybe it was more appropriate to a heavy metal or hard rock band. I had never questioned Peter about the origin of their name. Perhaps they had chosen it to achieve contrast, to draw attention.

'Okay, guys. It was good talking to you. See you in the near future...' Peter took my hand, holding it tightly, and motioned to move away. 'We're going to get stuck into the buffet, then we'll walk around.'

He dragged me away giving me barely time to say goodbye. In the meantime, I recognized other familiar faces among the guests, but I didn't have enough time to frame them to find out who they were. I was too far out from the environment and Peter was too anxious to drag me away.

'Peter... your friends...'

'They're not friends... they're little poisonous snakes.' He turned his gaze to me and frowned. 'This is not an easy environment to handle, Amantine. They all seem very friendly, very polite, very lovely. Hugs and kisses, but most of the time it's just a façade. True friendships are very few, almost non-existent.'

'That also happens in normal life, Peter. Even in my environment...' I identified myself in his words. It was the same for me. All pretences, schemes and exploitation of the others' work. All sweet talk, but people ready to fool you at the slightest sign of weakness or excessive integrity. I had experienced it the hard way.

'Now, we'll eat something at the buffet. Then we'll walk around just to show we attended the event of the year. We're going to hide in the huge Stevensons' swimming pool, maybe. Then we go back home, because I want you all for myself tonight.'

Peter's program seemed reasonable to me. But I wasn't particularly interested in either the buffet or the swimming pool. I wanted to be in the car that would take us home.

The buffet was varied and delicious, but all too rich and elaborate. I hardly swallowed anything. I felt watched. I wasn't used to being considered Peter Wiles's girlfriend and I preferred to know in advance the part I had to play. The idea of not knowing how much truth there was in my portrayal made me nervous. I had been Geoff's girlfriend before. Awful, I know. I had behaved badly towards him and made him suffer. With Peter I wouldn't be able, as I hadn't been able to go away and leave him when I should have. But it wasn't true, I wasn't really his girlfriend. Between me and Peter it was only an appearance, a pretence, an act that I was increasingly struggling to cope with.

We walked along the avenues in the mansion garden, silently. Detached, as if each of us was immersed in our own thoughts. My relationship with him had grown lately. Maybe it was just me, maybe I was the only one to feel that way.

'Thank you, Amantine.' I had never heard Peter's voice so warm and deep.

'It has been nice. In short, it's not a place and they're not people I would hang out with every day, but...' I smiled and shrugged.

I kept walking, not realizing that he had stopped a few steps behind me. We had reached a small bridge that crossed a pond on which some water lilies floated and that led to another part of the tidy garden and towards the outdoor pool.

'No, Amantine. I meant... thank you for staying. For not leaving me.'

'I wanted to stay, Peter. I really wanted it. I still want to.'

I turned to him, slowly. His green eyes on me were brighter than ever. Or maybe it was the lights, or maybe the moon, or that moment that felt like infinity, eternity. He looked at me without saying another word. He simply looked at me and I held my eyes on his. He looked at me making me feel, with just one glance, the most beautiful woman in the world. And I realized in an instant that no other man could make me feel like Peter Wiles at that moment. Because I would never want to be looked at like this by any other man.

CHAPTER 38

'Amantine...' Peter held out his hand to me. 'Listen to me, Amantine...' His voice trembled. Touching his hand, my heart quickened. I nodded and smiled.

My smile died as soon as I saw the man behind Peter, heading towards us. Simon, Darkest Storm's manager. I hoped he hadn't sought us out just to make us another scene. He looked hostile, as if he was preparing for a fight, confident of winning it. Up to now, I was relieved we hadn't met him, but apparently, we had no way out. The desolate expression on my face forced Peter to turn around.

'What do you want?' Peter's tone was dry and annoyed. He was hoping to avoid him too.

'I promised the guests that you would play some songs from the new album...' Simon focused on Peter, ignoring me. What did it mean? That they, *had to* perform?

'You're kidding, aren't you?' Peter knew nothing about it. He couldn't force him. Especially because Rebekah and Joseph hadn't talked about it, so it probably had to be Simon's idea, that they didn't even know about. Selfishly, I didn't want to be alone in that place, without Peter beside me. Although I understood that maybe it was a good opportunity for him.

'Not at all. The others are ready, except you.' That man was disturbing. I didn't like Peter having to deal with him, but he had no choice.

'I'm not ready. They could do it without me.' Peter turned to me and took my hand. 'In fact, we were just leaving. You can say you didn't find me.'

'Do you want to be known like that, Peter? Do you know what most of these people think about you? That you are unreliable, difficult to manage, and that it is advisable not to work with you. Do you want to confirm their opinions? There are important journalists here tonight.' He was blackmailing him. And if this was not blackmail it looked a lot like it.

I felt Peter's hand quiver in mine. 'My answer is still no. As I told you, I'm not ready, I don't care about the consequences.'

Peter was proving to be even more obstinate than him. But he couldn't refuse, he would get in trouble. And I didn't want it to happen.

'Peter...' I clung to his arm to attract his attention. 'Peter, I think you should perform with the others... I'll be all right in a corner listening to you.'

I didn't want to leave him. And I didn't want him to leave me alone among those people. But it was right. It was his job and the performance this evening could affect his future.

'Just a couple of tracks,' Peter said. 'Then we'll leave!'

Simon didn't reply but preceded us by walking towards the mansion.

I realized that it would be the first time I'd see Peter with his band, except for that quick TV appearance in which I recognized him at Doris's house. I didn't think about it. I would see the pop star, the celebrity. In the months we had spent together, I had only known the man.

Maybe I felt intimidated by what he represented for the rest of the world, maybe I rejected it and that's why Peter had never imposed on me, rather he preferred to hide himself. It destabilized me to discover another aspect of him. But I had no alternative.

I made eye contact with him as we were about to reach the mansion. I smiled, striving to look calm. The truth was that I wanted him only for me. Mine was selfishness, I had to hold back. I had to share him with others. No questions, no claims. After all, I knew it, from the beginning I knew about the other women. No questions, no claims. We got along exactly on those bases we had established from the beginning.

I was forced to let him go. We had reached the back of the mansion where they had set up an improvised stage. Peter stroked my face, gently moving his thumb on my cheek. His habitual gesture completely relaxed me.

'I'll do this, then we'll go home. Who cares about the park, the swimming pool and all the rest. If you don't want to stay here you can go to the buffet, or...'

'Are you trying to prevent me from watching the show, Peter?' I leaned towards him kissing his lips. 'It's not going to work. I have to behave like a good spare girlfriend. If we want to keep up appearances it must look real.'

In the meantime, however, I had to let him go. Just a few minutes and he would come back to me. Peter sighed deeply, nodded and walked to reach his colleagues. But unexpectedly, halfway, he turned to look at me, in my eyes. I remained enchanted, perceiving his words among the instruments' chords, the chatters and laughter of everyone else who waited to attend their performance.

'Amantine... do you want to make it real?'

CHAPTER 39

I stayed at the back. The event was for a small audience, but there were still many people, more than I thought. I didn't follow the Darkest Storm's performance. I saw and heard him only. His way of moving on that improvised stage, his voice. He stood out from all the others so much that they almost disappeared compared to him. Perhaps it was my impression influenced by the bond I had with him.

Peter's personality annihilated the others even when they alternated the singing. I listened to the first piece, "Here for you", then the second "Take me back". Pretty and catchy songs but not exciting, common love words repeating themselves. Peter was right, he deserved better. Even from the little I had learned to understand about music, I knew he was right.

Two pieces. I wished the show was over. Peter had said just a couple of tracks. Instead they went on with a third, a fourth. The more they went on the more it seemed to me it was better to escape that world, not to be part of it. The enthusiasm of those present probably pushed them to continue.

Peter had forgotten me, maybe. I couldn't do anything but wait. I decided to get away for a few minutes. I had to think, understand. Above all, try to deal with the evolution of my relationship with Peter. With that part of him that I didn't know yet, but I couldn't deny even though it was so distant from me. Our two worlds had somehow met and coexisted, intersecting each other. I couldn't pull back now. I didn't want to. But he was also the one who continued singing, to perform on stage increasingly encouraged by the approval and applause of the audience.

I found myself in front of the buffet table, but my stomach was completely closed. All that elaborate food, instead of whetting my appetite, made me sick, so I had to look away. I refused a glass of champagne that one of the waiters offered me. I wanted to go home. I wanted pizza. I wanted to lie in bed with Peter, in his arms. I was becoming fragile and scared as I had never been in my life and I didn't understand why. I had never been so emotional. It was like I was no longer myself.

'Weren't you enjoying the show?'

No, not him. Not now. While Simon Jennings came up beside me, I had to stay strong and recompose myself before showing signs of weakness.

'Not particularly.' I glanced at him sideways. 'In fact, I hope it ends soon.'

'Does Peter know you're not a fan of his?' An evil grin painted on his face as he grabbed a sandwich.

'Of course he knows. He himself is not... Not a fan of Darkest Storm he's forced to stay in.' Maybe I shouldn't have taken up that position with Simon. I stopped before pushing myself too far, in terms of insulting him.

'Yours is an impossible relationship. You will drag him where you want and then ruin him...' Simon took a step toward me. I almost felt overwhelmed by the enormity of his bearing. 'And there are aspects of Peter that you don't even know. You don't know his problems, you don't know what he could become. He tries to live up to you, he is striving, but he will never succeed. He is weak, prey to his vices and continuous depressive crises.'

What was he saying? Was he crazy? Peter wasn't at all like he described him. And why should he ever try to live up to me? It didn't make sense!

'Didn't you know?' He jumped in before I could say anything. 'You are too strong for him, beyond his reach. And you're too wrong. When you realize it, you will leave him and destroy him even more than he has already destroyed himself in these last few years.'

'Review your plans, asshole, because I have no intention of leaving him! You're just a sleazy climber. And you're taking advantage of Peter's talent, you're holding him against his will because you're inept, without him you're worthless, you're nobody. But I won't let you. Don't you dare hurt him because I swear that you'll be the one who's destroyed, I will use all the means at my disposal!'

I walked away. I was about to feel sick and I didn't want it to happen in front of that slimy, mean man. I wished I had a place to escape, but I didn't know where to go, I felt trapped. That immense property was too big and too impersonal for me. I no longer heard the music. Perhaps they had finished.

All I had to do was find Peter and get out of there. We had to talk. We had to understand. And even if it cost me to expose myself, I had to express what I was feeling, all of it. Then maybe disappear forever, as Simon Jennings suggested. One thing was certain. I wasn't strong, I wasn't at all.

Returning to the back, I saw two of the guys still on the stage. They were handling the instruments. Among the guests I couldn't locate Peter, but he couldn't be far. I waited in a corner for a few minutes. Maybe not seeing me as soon as they had finished, he had gone looking for me. As people got back inside or flowed to the sides to reach the main park, I felt flooded with an annoying and unpleasant feeling. I felt lost, abandoned.

I had nothing else to do but go back inside. Maybe I should ask someone if he had seen him. But who? Maybe one of his colleagues. I didn't even remember their names. The first one who introduced himself, maybe... Tyler Grey, yes, Tyler.

'Tyler...' I approached him while he was talking to a busty girl with short red hair. 'Excuse me... I'm looking for Peter, have you seen him by any chance?'

While Tyler shrugged with a desolated expression, it was the girl who answered. 'I've seen him around with Delly... I think they were planning to take one of the guest rooms...' She nodded to one wing of the house.

I felt my pressure dropping suddenly. I had never experienced such a sensation in my life. As if I lay on the ground but I was still standing at the same time. I nodded without replying, but still I couldn't move from there. I had to force myself to move, turn around and start walking. I didn't know exactly where I was heading. I only knew that I had to find Peter. In any case. After all, we were not... A couple, absolutely not. It was just acting, there was nothing true. We were not really together, so...

'Hey...' I felt my arm grabbed. For a moment I deluded myself that it was him. 'Amantine... listen...' It was Tyler. I looked at him without seeing him but clung to his jacket.

'You ... would you help me find Peter, please?' I didn't even recognize my voice, so cracked, so feeble.

'Better not, Amantine. Listen... if you want, I'll take you home, then...'

I shook my head. The guest rooms, the girl said. Where could the guest rooms be? She had pointed at this side. I reached a wide corridor and started to walk along it. I stopped in front of the first door. I was an intruder in someone else's house. I was an intruder in a world that wasn't mine. Even in Peter's life I was an intruder. I forced myself and opened the door, just enough to look inside. I saw a man lying in bed with two girls. I closed it immediately, taking two steps back. It wasn't him.

I crashed into Tyler who followed me to the next door. 'Stop... if you don't want to see...' He held me by my wrist. But I had to see. Otherwise I risked not believing it. And no, I didn't want to believe it. Or maybe I wanted to believe anything else.

Second door. Now I didn't care anymore, not even to keep up appearances. It seemed to me that I was living in a lucid dream, or rather one of those from which one wakes up with the sensation of falling and struggles to find a foothold, something to hold on to. With the difference that I had nothing, I had no one. Only a world that wasn't mine and clothing that I wasn't used to.

This time I didn't just peek. I opened the door. I closed my eyes, then opened them wide. I felt my throat tighten, as if someone was holding me tight, too tight, to strangle me. Instead there was no hand around my throat. It was just me. The knot in my throat that didn't go down. The sob that didn't find a way to explode, to free itself. Then it stayed there, still. Absurd, all absurd and senseless. As if I was doing an identification. Yes, it's him. The tattoo on his shoulder so familiar now. His arms that were not holding me. His way of moving. His lips on a body that wasn't mine. Yes, it was him.

I turned and started walking. Incredibly, I managed to keep my balance on those heels as my world sank. No, it wasn't my world. And not even his. It was the world we had built together, the one formed by mine, his, the two of us. It was our world that collapsed, crumbled. Yet, I knew it. No questions, no claims. We had been clear from the start, why was I surprised? I had no right to be hurt or even slightly affected. Yes, I knew it.

'Can I take you home?' Tyler was right behind me. I nodded without replying.

Home? But where was home? Peter's home? Yes, I believed that. I followed him like a robot and found myself sitting in a car, with Tyler driving. When we had already left, just a few minutes later, I realized that I hadn't said goodbye to anyone. But maybe it wasn't the kind of party in which people at the end say goodbye and thanks. Maybe it worked like this. Arriving with someone and leaving with someone else.

The landscape was passing by, in front of me. I saw everything and couldn't see anything. Past images, excerpts of life and poetry, passed through my mind. I didn't know yet what to love meant, as Jacob had said. And maybe it was better to never know. Not even approaching to suspect it. I gripped my chest with my hands, as if to hold my nausea.

'Maybe you should have stayed.' If Tyler was trying to make conversation that wasn't certainly the right phrase.

'Maybe I should never have...' Attended the party. Enter a world that wasn't mine. People who betrayed. But at the end I deserved it. I received what I had given. I had betrayed Geoff, I had been cruel, insensitive. The difference was that Peter and I were not really a couple. So, we couldn't even talk about betrayal. I shouldn't have expected something that didn't exist.

I realized I had arrived when Tyler's car stopped in front of Peter's house. Maybe I should have asked him to drive me elsewhere. But where? Anyway, I had to take my things. And then...

Tyler got out quickly and came to open the door. 'I'll take you inside.'

The keys. I didn't have the keys. I had gone out with Peter, I had a tiny handbag that I had forgotten in the other car when we got out. 'I don't have...'

While I was thinking, Tyler had already rung and Gordon had already opened. He stared at us in silence. If he was surprised to see me with Tyler, he didn't show it. He laid his eyes on me, as if waiting for a word from me, but faced with my silence he withdrew at a nod from Tyler, without saying anything.

I seemed to have completely lost the ability to respond, to pronounce words correctly. But I was calm. So calm. To the point of being close to giving in to sleep. Maybe then I would wake up and find out that none of it was true. Or that it was way too much.

'Are you all right?' Tyler's presence was the only thing that brought me to reality and prevented me from sinking into the catatonic state I almost yearned for. He stroked my arm and I nodded, shivering. I felt cold. It was June and I felt so cold. 'You know how these things work... don't take it the wrong way.'

I stared at him and met his thin blue eyes. At that moment they seemed more magnetic than I remembered. No, I didn't know how these things worked. I knew I had been punished. I had paid. I was paying. I deserved it. But still I was silent. Even me who lived by words, who had read so many, written, interpreted, and studied. I kept silent. I kept silent not to collapse, not to fall apart. I kept silent in the effort, almost inhuman, to control myself.

'We can get even, the two of us if you want... I'll comfort you...' Tyler put his hands on my shoulders and let them slide down my arms.

'Stay away from me!' The voice finally came out from me, but almost like a strangled cry. I pushed him away with all the strength I had, even though it wasn't much at that moment.

'I already told you, don't take it wrong. You'll see that tomorrow Peter will be back at home as a good boy, but for tonight... After all, he's like that. It's not the first time he's come to a party with a girl and then gets off with another one... even more than one.'

He made me sick. He made me throw up. Tyler approached me again, grabbing me by my side, pushing me against the wall. I shook my head trying to get rid of him. 'No! Don't touch me...'

'Don't you like me? Don't tell me Peter is cuter than me because I don't believe you.'

Peter wasn't cuter than him. But it was Peter. And I felt like I had forever lost a part of me that had become essential. My freedom, my joy of life. The closeness, not only physical.

Tyler probably didn't understand or maybe he misunderstood because he interpreted my silence as an invitation and drew me to him by my wrists, trying to meet my lips with his.

'Let me go...' I didn't want to. I didn't want anything from him. Only that he let me go. It was as if the world had started to turn again but in slow motion, at a different pace than mine. Or it was my pace that had undergone a change compared to the rest.

I ended up, in spite of myself, in Tyler's arms. He kissed my face, my neck, ignoring my weak physical resistance. Peter... why had he left me alone? Why had he abandoned me?

I remembered his words, the ones I had heard as he walked away to reach the others, when he turned to me and looked me in my eyes. "Amantine... do you want to make it real?"

'Peter...' I sighed heavily.

Scenes of us appeared before my eyes. Our first meeting, the note he had left me, our first time in his house. The music. The books. William Shakespeare. The poetry. Waking up in the morning in his arms. And yet his words. "Amantine... do you want to make it real?"

'Peter...' My heart dropped without anyone there to pick it up. I collapsed on myself like a puppet, a broken doll. And again, his eyes in mine. "Amantine... do you want to make it real?"

Tyler let me go and I slid to the ground. I had lost a shoe, my beautiful dress was creased, had lost all its charm. I realized my hands were shaking. And I was getting colder.

'But then you...' Tyler bent over at my side. 'Amantine...'

'Don't hurt me, please...' I could only rely on his mercy because I had no more strength in me to rebel and fight. My weakness had locked me in a wrapped prison from which I couldn't get out, free myself.

'Amantine...' Tyler lifted my chin, forcing me to look at him. He stared at me almost in disbelief. 'You truly love him, you're not attracted to him just because he's a celebrity.'

A celebrity? No, it was Peter. Only Peter. I remembered when I was asked if I was in love with him some time before. I had answered yes to avoid discussing. I had not considered the issue. For too long I had not considered the issue. Also, because I had never loved before.

'Yes, poor girl. You love him.' Tyler resolved, pulling away from me, standing up and composing himself.

'Yes...' I whispered to myself. The revelation caught me suddenly, overwhelming. I loved him. I loved him and I was desperate. 'Yes, yes, yes!' My breath came back, unexpected. Yes, I loved him. In spite of my world and his. Against my will. With all my heart I loved Peter Wiles and there was nothing left for me. I punched the floor in pain, in anger. I knew what it meant to love. My moment had arrived. But the moment when I finally understood it also coincided with the moment when I realized that I would rather never know.

CHAPTER 40

I called a taxi as soon as Tyler left, getting rid of his presence. I was able to stand up and reach the phone. Then somehow, I managed to collect my things. My passport, what I thought was essential. Not everything, it would have been impossible. I didn't care. I just wanted to run away, as soon as possible. Pieces of me would remain scattered in that house, anyway. I took myself to a random hotel in the suburbs.

After spending a day locked in the room in total darkness, I called Rachel begging her to come to me. Somehow, I told her everything, even though it meant reliving what had happened. Aloud, not just in my mind. I had no choice, and I had no one else to talk to.

'I'm going to stay in Paris.' I ended my story, determined. I had reached that conclusion inside myself, during my first night away from him, in a strange bed. I was leaving to get back to myself, I was leaving to keep living, and maybe to force my heart to forget.

'Are you really sure? Amantine, you know that I've been friends with Geoff for years. But are you really sure you want to leave Peter?' Rachel looked at me compassionately. She was right, even I felt compassion for myself. I had been stupid! 'From what you told me maybe there was a misunderstanding... Maybe you should talk to him, explain to him how you feel. Maybe he didn't understand he was so important to you...'

'No, I'm not sure. But I have no alternative and there is nothing to explain. I have broken the rules that we imposed from the beginning. In fact, I was the first to establish those rules, so... my mistake!'

I bit my lips, shaking my head. Love in our rules was not an option. After all, there had been Lolita and I had known it from the start. Lolita or another one, what difference did it make? Just none. The mistake was mine.

'What are you going to do? Leave the university, everything else...' Rachel sighed and stroked my hair tenderly. 'Don't hurt yourself like that, Amantine. It seems you want to punish yourself. You fell in love, there's nothing wrong with that.'

'You know what I think, Rachel? The evil I've done, I'm receiving it in return. I hurt Geoff. Now it is my turn to suffer. And regarding the university... With the academic career I have no hope here, it's nothing new. Frey has already chosen for some time.' I was tough, ruthless. With only one person: myself.

'You really should talk to him, Amantine!' Rachel rubbed my shoulders. The slight pressure hurt me. I was a nervous wreck, I realized.

'It's useless, Rachel. Gregor is the chosen one.' Suddenly I didn't care. My university career now seemed to me like a distant past. All that I had left were my sheets, notes for a book that I might never continue.

'I mean to Peter. Ask him for an explanation, at least.'

Asking him for an explanation when everything was so clear and obvious? No. Never.

'I can't. Obviously, it had to end like this.' The images of him tormented me. Those of the last evening together, as he held me in his arms, just before leaving. While he was trying to convince me not to go to that party, to stay home. The two of us, alone. I could no longer torment myself, I had to remove those scenes, those words. Remove them forever. 'I was wrong. I have been punished. I'll pay for my mistake, all the way.'

CHAPTER 41

I had thrown my life away. Or so I thought. In Paris, in a small rental apartment. Mine only. The absence growing inside me every night annihilated me. I felt myself precipitating like in the dream in which we always fear falling. It had become a constant for me now. But I was awake. Always awake. With the last words he had spoken to me, his voice, his eyes wearing me out continuously.

"Amantine... do you want to make it real?"

Maybe I would never sleep again. I would never find peace again. Then I realized that I wasn't alone anymore, and it wasn't only the absence growing inside me, but a presence.

I thought about writing. A letter to him, everything. I stopped at the first word. My heart knew things that words were not able to express. Was this love? Losing control, voice, courage. Getting lost in a labyrinth without being able to get out.

I wouldn't love again. No one anymore. For any reason. I just wanted to be me again. But with that presence inside me, I couldn't succeed in my intent.

I went to see my parents. I hadn't revealed anything, committing myself to be the usual Amantine, the one they knew or thought they knew. They didn't understand. How could they, anyway? The disappointment for the university, yes, had been the one that pushed me to move away from London. The other thing better not to talk about, it was finished as it was born. In nothing.

A few days later I managed to put together a few sentences in the letter I intended to write. Reading it, it didn't even seem written by the old me. Even the handwriting wasn't mine anymore. Trembling, uncertain, as if it had been conditioned by my own despair.

I didn't recognize myself. Broken phrases, unrelated to each other. *"I left"*, I told him. *"It's better for both."* Who was I trying to convince, myself or him? *"We had good moments."* Yes, of course. No denying it! *"You always have your world, I have mine. We knew it would end sooner or later. That evening I realized it."* No, actually, I didn't realize anything. *"Our lives will keep flowing. Everything will be fine. Our separate ways."* I couldn't resist, instead. *"Peter... I'm in Paris, Peter."* Written at the end, the phone number I'd had installed. The address of my apartment at the bottom of the letter and on the back of the envelope. I couldn't do more, I couldn't say more. I wasn't able to. I was a miserable beginner. I loved for the first time, for too short a time.

Two weeks and no reply. Then half of the third. And I had to make a decision quickly, otherwise it would be too late. The presence would impose itself, every day a little bit more. I could only give up.

'Are you sure, miss?' The nurse sighed, tilting her head. She pitied me. She was right, I was a miserable creature.

'Yes, I'm sure. I have no other choice.'

September 1998

CHAPTER 42

The start of a new academic year was always hectic, at least for me. Notes, programs, nervous colleagues. New confused students that reminded me of Peter Pan's lost boys. Maybe I let myself get too involved. Maybe I was investing too much of my life in them. I was trying to give my best. After all, I had always done it. But if on one side they deprived me of everything, from another they gave me confidence and I wouldn't fail in my commitment. So the new Sorbonne students, like those who had preceded them, would have the best of me.

Geoff reproached me for neglecting my family. But I was good at dividing my time properly. I had been doing it for more than five years now. He had nothing to complain about. I gave him and our children, William and Madeline, all that was left. There was the tranquillity of a daily life, devoid of great expectations, but also of emotional turbulence. Everything proceeded on a straight track, without acceleration and without stops. One day after another. Seconds, minutes, hours that kept turning while life flowed and I let it slip by me.

A husband. Two children. An academic career. All socially acceptable. I had done my duty, as a good girl. Now I could hope to be left alone.

The dream, the only survivor, was also the only one I had not abandoned after my departure from London. I was able to

177

publish it over the last year. And it had been successful. With the public, with the critics and even with the academics. In that order.

Some critics and some academics had turned their noses up at it. But thanks to a good band of admirers I had almost become a celebrity in that field. There was even speculation on who would be the next poet or author I would deal with. A life like a novel. Looking more at feelings than for a chronology of events. We are born, we live or we exist, we die. Common destiny. But I was looking for tangible signs of a passage, I was looking for emotions. Words that mark silences, beating hearts. Many lives in just one. Lives that lightly touch upon each other, changing destinies.

Was it really what I wanted? Surely what I had thought I wanted. Because what I wanted, I had to suppress, to kill inside me. Not talk about it anymore. As it was born it died, murdered by reality and perhaps even by rules that I had contributed to, and imposed by myself.

A clean break with the past. But it wasn't possible because the past was everywhere. So I had learned to live with it. The past was a public figure who was evolving by making people talk more and more about him. After leaving the band, he started his solo career. Great difficulties at the beginning, nobody willing to trust him. Except me who from afar still believed in him. Except my heart that didn't want to give up, despite what I had seen with my very own eyes.

They didn't believe in him, they mocked his madness. However, it was his absence from the band that annihilated the others. They were nothing without him. They had lasted about a year before collapsing inevitably, forgotten and replaced by younger, fresher, nicer boys. And it hadn't even taken that long.

In the end I had made peace with myself and established that it was useless to try to escape. If I had to continue to run into him, then I might as well follow him attentively.

I hid his CDs in a secret drawer of my desk. I also kept some photos and some articles, especially the positive reviews. He was good and I understood that. He had nothing to envy of the artists he made me listen to. I also followed them, as a reflex, with the unconfessed purpose of keeping that indissoluble bond alive.

The early death of Kurt Cobain of the band Nirvana had devastated me, as if I had lost a dear friend. That day I walked around the city completely stunned, almost without remembering my duties, or where I was and why. His voice stood between me and my past. And the past had a name and a mischievous smile. Green eyes.

I had been right in believing that no one in the world would ever look at me like him that night. In fact, it no longer happened. As much as he always loved me, not even my husband looked at me like that. Just as well for Geoff, because I couldn't have returned it to him.

I knew he had a son with a German model, the same year I had Madeline. After some time he got married, but to another woman, an American singer. They had gone on their honeymoon on a tropical island. Their marriage had lasted three months. I had also started to read gossip magazines. And I learned that you must never deny something regardless.

The pain I felt every time I read about him with another woman was still standing where it was born that night. Like a nail into my heart. I left it there intentionally, almost fearing that in a forced attempt to remove it, it would be completely broken or crumpled up on itself. So I lived with it, nourished it, cuddled it sometimes, but with light caresses so as not to overburden it too much. It kept me company and after the Sorbonne's students, my husband and my children, it took the third part of me.

CHAPTER 43

Although it still seemed impossible to me, my brother got engaged. Seriously this time, he specifically pointed it out on the phone. After all, I got married too, and I would have never thought it possible. But he didn't do it for lack of an alternative. Even more incredible, his girlfriend was a theatre actress who had some parts in a soap opera. Her name was Marianne. So we were waiting for Alain and Marianne for lunch.

Our house overlooked the Champs-Élysées. In a short time I had become a splendid Parisian. Perhaps the fact of not having roots helped me to adapt more easily to changes, a bit like the chameleons that change skin according to situations, good at camouflaging in the environment.

Geoff had had more difficulty living in France but had agreed to move. I wouldn't return to either London or elsewhere in England. And I had refused any other option. After all, my parents have lived in Paris for years. It was my birthplace, so in a way it was a bit like coming home.

I had an excellent lunch prepared. Forgetting to ask Alain what his girlfriend liked, I relied a bit on my own and my brother's taste. With Italian cooking I was hoping not to make mistakes, usually everybody liked it.

Me starting to cook was always out of the question. The best I could have been asked for was a half-burnt omelette. I had once tried to make cookies. I was determined to learn. But it had been in my previous life. It belonged to the past. I couldn't move the nail from my chest. It wasn't the most appropriate time. Alain and Marianne were about to arrive.

Welcoming them, I tried to behave like a good hostess. Even if it was just me, in the end. I adapted the mask to the occasion, every time. With my brother a little less than with the others, but I didn't know Marianne yet so a certain solemnity was a must. I found her pretty, simple, rather thin. Far enough from the flashy girls who Alain had always dated. Being an actress, I was probably expecting her to be different, or I probably expected Alain's usual standard.

As I, Geoff and Marianne sat down in the dining room, Alain had lost himself chasing my children in the house. He was crazy about them, especially William. Maybe because he was his first nephew, maybe because he was a boy and he felt closer to him.

Meanwhile, Marianne watched me, intimidated, almost fearing my judgment.

'Alain told me that you're an actress...' I left the sentence hanging, just to break the ice.

'Yes, I act in the theatre, mostly. I work with the National Theatre. We stage Shakespeare and the classics often...' Marianne was shy, refined and she spoke Queen's English. Almost embarrassing. I could express myself in different languages but in none did I ever achieve such magnificence.

'Fantastic! I love theatre.' Not that much, actually. I attended it from time to time. As a young girl it had been part of the baggage of general education imposed by my parents. Then I had gradually abandoned it.

'Marianne is extraordinary, you should come and see her in London one of these days!' Alain had finally decided to join us at the table, diligently followed by William and Madeline.

I nodded as I was losing myself in their conversations and, little by little, I abandoned them. London. I had returned only once, in passing on the occasion of Alain's graduation. Accompanied by Geoff and my parents. I had followed the ceremony, my body was there while my thoughts wandered elsewhere, they had reached Notting Hill and then...

'Mommy, when are we going to London?' William drew my attention, his green eyes on me.

181

'Sooner or later, William...' I turned around a little bewildered, the lunch was going to be served and it could be a good excuse. 'Excuse me, I'm going to the kitchen to check if we're ready.'

London. William was not the only one who wanted to go. I was also shivering, just like a child. I trembled every time I heard the word, unable to control the mental image, the nail in my chest still hurting me.

The silences between me and Geoff, the banality of our conversations in the last years, did nothing but amplify my desire. The past was calling me back, almost sucking me into a vortex, summoning my name. And I wasn't expecting anything else but an opportunity to answer it.

CHAPTER 44

After September, the rest of the year slipped away in a flash, almost without me noticing it. I found myself at the end of December hoping that Christmas holidays would end quickly, so that I could resume my daily university routine.

Staying home psychologically destroyed me. I was a very bad wife and a very bad mother, but I tried not to show it too explicitly. I simulated cheerfulness and a sort of prepackaged happiness. Besides, I was not the only one. Maybe I pretended less well than others, and from time to time I got lost in myself. But I was allowed to. Those thoughts were only mine, I didn't invite others to be part of them nor did I torment them with my dissatisfaction that I never made clearly visible. I stroked my heart to heal the wound. Then I came back to the present and I was still Amy for Geoff or Mommy for William and Madeline.

My study was my refuge. I was ready for a new work. I was pondering on dealing with George Sand or George Eliot. One of those two George's, anyway. Did I maybe risk being too directly involved with the one who carried the same name as me?

The telephone interrupted my profound reflection. I stared at it, bored, tempted not to answer. Then I picked it up trying not to show too much annoyance.

'Hello…?'

'Amantine Delamar? It's Gregor Jackman…'

Gregor Jackman? That Gregor Jackman? Of course, unless he was cloned or there was one with the same name that coincidentally knew mine, it couldn't be anybody else but him. How did he find my home phone number?

'Oh... of course. Gregor Jackman, what a pleasant surprise...'
Fuck you, Gregor Jackman. What the hell did he want from me?
Wish me Merry Christmas, belated, six years later?

A few years after my departure from London, the asshole held
the office of Professor Frey who had left his position.

'Dearest Amantine, I call you to express you my best
wishes...'

Could I spit him in the eye through the phone? No.

'What do you want, Gregor?' Here, better to get straight to
the point and avoid wasting time on pleasantries. If Gregor
Jackman was bothered calling me, it was because he wanted
something substantial, not wish me a Merry post-Christmas.

'I've seen your book around. You have had success beyond
all measure in these last months. They also recommend it as a
Christmas present in the bookstores!' His voice was becoming
shrill.

'And you're the Grinch and you hate Christmas? What's your
problem?' I snorted, moving away from the phone for a moment.
'Nobody forced you to buy it.'

'No, of course. But the department has instructed me to invite
you for a seminar on your book. Intended for students of
literature and creative writing. I've been good at finding you
through our dear Professor Frey, I couldn't wait for the
resumption of the classes.' Gregor paused, probably waiting for
my reply. It must have pained him to be forced to contact me. Or
maybe he had just waited for the Christmas holidays, hoping he
wouldn't be able to track me down. 'So, what are you doing?'

The temptation to tell him to go to hell was irresistible.
'Gregor, you can go...' But... London. I would have the
opportunity to return to London. Even for just a day. 'When
would it be? I should get organized with my classes here,
anyway...'

I used an indifferent, almost annoyed tone. A part of me,
intimate, invisible to the human eye and ear, was gloating. But

at the same time, I was tightened by a painful grip. Desire and fear at the same time.

'The last week of January. It would be a great opportunity for you too, Amantine, because then I thought we could...'

'All right.' I didn't care about the rest. I didn't want to listen to him. 'I'll contact you on the department phone for details as soon as classes resume. Now I really have to go, Gregor. I have an important appointment. It was a pleasure to hear from you. Happy New Year!'

Bullshit! I no longer held the emotional tension and I wasn't sure I could control the detached tone of my voice. So I hung up quickly, just giving him time to reply. But now I had to move on to the second phase of the "project": tell Geoff. Find the way to mention Gregor's call and offer, then... Then let him know that I had already accepted it, without the need to consult him.

I decided to wait for the evening. Then I thought about waiting again, for the children to be in bed. It was just a business trip to London, not a guilt to atone. London didn't imply... Yes indeed, it implied moving the nail from my heart, hurting me. But it was a lure I couldn't resist.

I adopted a neutral tone in communicating my decision to Geoff. 'It's a very good opportunity,' I concluded after reporting Gregor's offer all in one breath.

'I really don't think so. Amy... didn't you think about the children?'

'It's only for a couple of days... and I won't be on the other side of the world!' I suspected it would have been easier for him. Although he didn't appreciate Paris, he didn't hold good memories of London. And indeed, he was right. 'However, we can ask the babysitter to stay longer. She already does it when I work more than usual. Or the children can stay with my parents for a few days.'

'We mutually had agreed to stay here, Amy. I remind you of that offer I received last month for that job in America... it's still valid.' Geoff's tone became cold, stiff.

'But it's not the same thing! For me it's just a lesson, just one day, two at most...'

Geoff had received the offer to move to America. He could collaborate with one of the greatest sociologists in the contemporary international scene. But this meant forcing me to give up the assignment at the Sorbonne. For me it was inadmissible as a hypothesis.

'In fact, it's not the same thing. Especially because you have a reason to stay here, just as you have a reason to run to London now!' I didn't understand what he was talking about. Nor the need to become upset and raise his voice. 'Just when "someone" claimed he will never leave England and London because it is where he has lived the most important story of his life!'

I was still struggling to put the pieces together. Geoff's gaze on me was hostile, almost furious. I turned away and left the living room to go and take refuge in my study. It was "the room of my own", like the one wished for by Virginia Woolf. In this case it would protect me from my husband's incomprehensible anger.

'Just the right time to go to London! Perfect timing!' Geoff's altered voice reached me there too. His words didn't make sense.

London. The most important story of his life. I didn't want to believe it. I didn't even want to know when and where he had made such a statement. It was all wrong. I sat down at my desk, covering my ears.

London. No, it wasn't him. It wasn't me. Not for him. For me, yes. For me always, despite everything, despite everybody. Every day, every night. Before my eyes forever, for six years now. His last look, his words.

"Amantine... do you want to make it real?"

I would be back in London. Just for one day, just to savour the moment, the closeness. Just to try, at least for one day, to live a little.

CHAPTER 45

My heart had started beating differently since landing at Heathrow Airport. Since the plane had begun to glide softly, I had to fight against the tears that flooded my face against my will. I had turned and leaned completely against the window so as not to make a show of myself.

What could I do? Where would I hide? Maybe it was a mistake. Where would I hide all those feelings that invaded my soul, my blood. Where would I go and vent my cry of freedom, of life?

When the plane touched the ground, I felt the sense of home taking over me, overbearing. England. No, that wasn't the reason and I knew it. As I had always known I never had roots until I had been the one to create them for myself.

I had left my children to relive that sense of freedom and life. I was a bad mother, I was aware of it. But I couldn't turn it down. Gregor's offer had only met a need that I could no longer ignore. There was the call, the hook that had begun to attract me so insistently.

I arrived in the morning. The meeting with Gregor would be in the afternoon, to define the topics that I would address in the lesson the next day. Time to take a shower, wear something comfortable and leave my luggage at the hotel in Piccadilly, to take a walk in the city centre.

Nothing had changed too much compared to my memories. I didn't expect it. I didn't want to go shopping. And I wasn't even hungry. The music shop where I stocked up still existed, of course, but had expanded. I entered for a quick walk around, but immediately left as if I didn't even know why I had entered.

Because I knew exactly what I was looking for and where I wanted to be. And it wasn't there. I walked all the way, implacable, at a rapid pace. Maybe a part of me deluded itself that tiredness would force me to desist. But no. I was collapsing and I was scared. But I progressed, maybe with inertia but progressed.

I stopped only in front of the Notting Hill underground staircase. Exactly at that point. The scene still flowed before my eyes. I bit my lips hard. Everything had to end there, where it started. I knew I would not have to go any further. I had the moral duty to stop, to calm my heart down, my heart that had begun to beat too impetuously, as if to forcefully reject the nail that for six years had held it in a steady throb.

But my will no longer counted. I had turned into pure instinct, I moved with a single and constant rhythm towards my goal. I didn't even know if he was still there or what I would find. When I reached my goal, I stood still, staring at it, that white house with blue shutters, on the other side of the road. It was a scene I already lived, which had already crossed me. I relived it a second time as if in a stream of consciousness, reabsorbing it inside me.

I tried to look inside. Another element that remained constant was my stupidity. This time the level exceeded the previous one and considering the fact that I was a few years older and I had a more compromising personal situation, this carelessness didn't serve me well.

Yes, I was determined. I had to leave, to get away quickly. But something inside me, a small part still too sensitive, wriggled and rebelled. It was like a little girl, fragile, innocent, delicate, asking me to stay. Only a brief instant would be enough. Just seeing him for a moment. Even from afar, even in backlight.

He had never answered my short letter, he had never looked for me. Maybe he considered our affair forever closed and I should have done so too. I had to leave immediately. I would just make myself even more ridiculous. A deep breath before forcing my steps in the opposite direction.

If it were not for that fragile, innocent, delicate little girl, she refused to give up on evidence. On the contrary, she suggested to me to write a note with the address of the hotel in which I was staying, the number of my cell phone and put it into the mailbox.

Shamelessly, boldly. I found a piece of paper and a pen in my bag and obeyed her before giving time for the opposed rationality to intervene. I crossed the street to finish my work. But this would also mean the end of my hope, of my fantasy. He wouldn't look for me, wouldn't reply to me, as he hadn't replied to my letter.

I held the sheet tightly in my hands, crumpling it. I had to leave. I had nothing left to do. Say goodbye, more calmly this time, and go away. Forever, above all. I grabbed the railing while a last rebel instinct still held me back. I looked down and closed my eyes. It made no sense. To physically say goodbye to that place, when inside I had never gone away, I was still living in that house.

'Miss...' I raised my head at the sound of that voice. I saw him, it was really him. So... he still lived there.

'Good afternoon, Gordon.' I sighed trying to stop the trembling of my voice and my body. 'You look well, I'm glad. I... I was leaving...'

Seeing the butler would be the only concession I would receive. He was always the same. I bowed my head slightly, raising a little smile. Finally, I managed to turn to get away. In fact, I almost ran.

'Miss... Miss Amantine...' Gordon hastened to take a few steps to reach me. 'I'm sure Mr. Wiles would like to see you if he knew you were here. He wouldn't forgive me for not stopping you, this time.'

I didn't understand the meaning of his words, but it didn't matter. 'I'm... I'll stay here only for a day or two.' I couldn't say anything more, but I handed him the crumpled note I held tightly in my hand. 'I have to go now, Gordon. I really have to go.'

CHAPTER 46

I had to make an effort not to continually think about the episode with Gordon. And about what would follow. I needed total mental clarity to deal with that asshole Gregor.

I don't know why I expected changes. Only six years had passed, not sixty. The university was still there, imposing and majestic. Actually, the real changes had taken place inside me, not in the environment I had left, from which I had escaped from one day to another.

Returning to my old department aroused mixed emotions in me. It was like re-emerging in my old life, as if I had never left, and on the contrary I had come back just to pick up where I left off. Regrets? Yes, I had. Too many.

Even Gregor Jackman remained the same. Cynical, sinister, petty, opportunist, manipulator. The usual old Gregor. He had cut the red beard, emphasizing more the sharp chin.

We agreed about the lesson I was going to hold tomorrow. He wanted to introduce me as his old and esteemed colleague. Maybe he deluded himself that sooner or later I would return the favour, but he was wrong. I would not ask for his participation at Sorbonne, I wouldn't impose his nefarious presence on those poor students. Although I didn't appreciate the manipulations that Gregor had always used, if I considered him an innovative and brilliant scholar and researcher, I would have admitted it. But he wasn't at all. And I wasn't either, I'd just been lucky with my book on John Keats.

'I was reflecting that you could come back for more lessons after tomorrow. I had the task of reorganizing the semester, unfortunately Professor Jones has had a stroke and in short is no longer the same as before...' Gregor spread his arms, desolate.

So he had invited me with an ulterior motive. It wasn't just an isolated seminar lesson. And he hadn't done it to be invited in turn. That man was even more infamous than I thought he was.

'Jones of creative writing? Of course... And here I take over to help you get rid of him completely.' I frowned at him. Not only did he want to use me as a stopgap. But as a stopgap for a subject that wasn't mine! 'I remind you that I teach at Sorbonne, Gregor. I'm not at home knitting.' Though I often wouldn't have minded, I thought. Indeed, I could consider it as an alternative. It would certainly be more productive and rewarding.

'We can find a way to make it work, Amantine. I've already contacted the Head of your Department at Sorbonne...'

If I could, I would have crossed the desk with a jump to strangle him. How dare he! I wasn't a pawn to move on his personal chessboard.

I looked down. The desk. The desk that had been Frey's. Frey's office. I found myself in a confused state, between anger and past memories that were re-emerging in an impetuous way. As if I relived the scene on my body, the sensations on my skin, like a fire that took my breath away, preventing me from breathing regularly. I remained so suspended, between anger and desire.

'I... I'll see you tomorrow for the lesson.' I felt myself blushing to the roots of my hair and didn't want Gregor to realize it.

I had to go back to the hotel, immediately. I took a bus and then walked with my head down until I got to my room. I felt guilty. And I did feel it, even more than I did a few years ago.

I was a traitor, a no good. I returned indifferent to the crime scene. My resistance was becoming increasingly inconsistent. And yes, I was also reflecting on the proposal of that worm Gregor, someone I despised, just to satisfy my craving. Until the point I would fall down.

My head was bursting. I couldn't find any justification for my conduct. Because it wasn't work at all and I knew it. It was about wanting to relive the past at all costs. Gordon's words had not left me since he had said them: 'I'm sure Mr. Wiles would like to see you if he knew you were here.'

I pondered the idea of going to see Rachel or Doris to spend the rest of the day. I discarded both options, I hadn't even warned them that I would arrive. And I didn't want to talk, to discuss, to explain, to tell. I didn't want, above all, that my new life intersected with the old one. I tried to distract myself by recapitulating the points I would deal with during the lesson. All for nothing, I knew them by heart and anyway I wasn't focused.

Maybe a good sleep would be right for me. Instead, I looked for my Walkman in the inside pocket of my hand luggage, lay down on the bed and closed my eyes. A compilation I had created a few years before. Starting from "Smells like teen spirit", the soundtrack of my past life was even more present in me than ever.

CHAPTER 47

The lesson, despite everything, was a success. I didn't think it would excite me so much to delineate aloud the creative processes that had pushed me toward John Keats's fictional biography. And I never would have imagined finding such an attentive and participant audience. In the end, I was forced to stay to answer the questions of some students interested in my work. So, even from the professional point of view, I hung in the balance between research and creativity, as in the private sphere I was between real life and dreamed life. It was probably my destiny.

After a compulsory lunch with colleagues, congratulations, greetings and pleasantries, I was finally free. I had called Geoff when I arrived the day before. Then I also called my mother to greet the children. It seemed useless to call again, I would be going home the following day.

I didn't want to wander around London's streets alone, it was cold and raining, so I went back to the hotel immediately. I was a coward. I invented excuses when I knew perfectly well the reason for my return. I wanted to wait. Simply wait, aware that maybe what I waited for would never come to me.

I lay down in bed. I didn't want to fall asleep, I only wanted to free my mind a little from the sense of oppression that I fell victim to so often lately. I ended up falling asleep, however, then waking up with the feeling of an unfinished dream. I saw myself in front of that house. Enter, look for parts of me that remained there. Then look at the door like an enemy. The door wanted to exclude me, send me away. However, I wanted to hold back. I wanted to stay.

I had dreamed of him a few times. Four, to be exact. I clung to those dreams for the next few weeks and then resigned myself to letting him go. And I continued to recall the last words he addressed to me, like a mantra.

Now there was nothing left for me but go home to my family and resume my life. Refuse Gregor Jackman's tempting offer. Behave like a mature and responsible person.

It was also perfectly useless to keep waiting in the hotel. I checked out the window, it had stopped raining. Better to go out for a walk before it was too late. I could buy some gifts for William and Madeline instead of waiting for the last moment at the airport.

The journey to London and my lecture at the university had been an episode. And so I should consider them as an episode, not an attempt to recapture what I couldn't definitively store as past.

I reached the entrance of the hotel and waited a few moments. I realized how difficult it was to stay still there, poised between two lives. Maybe I would be forever.

I remembered what Rachel advised me to do a few years before. Maybe I should have talked. But I had talked, in fact, I had written. And I never received an answer. Only silence which in its way is a strong and clear answer.

But... if I had talked to him directly? If I had the courage to ask him for an explanation? No, everything was useless. I had never been a brave person, far from it.

I stepped away from the entrance to let two people go by. I didn't even know where to go. I hadn't changed since the morning, nor fixed my makeup and my hair. Maybe it would be better to go back to my room and compose myself a bit.

Just as I was turning to get back inside, I felt myself being yanked. My bag, damn it! I resisted, holding it back with all the strength I had. A bag-snatcher had jumped me, right in the city centre!

I took a few seconds to be able to react, I was paralyzed by fear.

'Let me go, bastard! I'll call the police...' I could hardly breathe, but I was trying to regain my voice to attract attention. I hadn't even been able to identify the man dressed in black. 'Help...'

'Always the same impulsiveness! Do you really want to get me into trouble, sweetheart?' I found his face a short distance from mine. 'What I intend to steal is not your bag, for sure.'

I ceased to wriggle and remained motionless. I had the distinct feeling of low blood pressure but somehow I held myself up. I scanned him with my eyes. I met his green eyes first. Black hat and scarf covered the rest of his face.

'It's you...'

'Yes, Amantine. It's me.' He put a hand on my hair and touched it lightly. 'Let's get out of here, before they really mistake me for a pickpocket.'

He took my hand. I followed him without asking questions and without resisting. I was biting my lips hard. I didn't want to cry. But I had never felt so sad and so happy at the same time. I didn't care about anything, not even about the silence that had been between us. Not even about the answer I had never received. Not even about his "betrayal" that night.

I followed him for several minutes, my hand grasped in his, until we walked more and more away from the centre. I had lost track of time and space. Suddenly he stopped and drew me to himself. He opened the door of a car and let me get in. I obeyed him immediately. A few moments later he was sitting beside me on the driver's side.

He turned to me and looked at my face as if he wanted to catch every detail, every little change. I felt insecure, shabby. 'I still can't believe it... You're right here, sweetheart. And you're even better than I remembered.'

'I can't say the same.' His gaze on me. I felt crazy for how much I missed him. 'I mean... I see you in the newspapers every now and then, so I already knew... I'm happy for you, Peter. You managed to achieve what you wanted. And what you deserved.'

He turned and took the steering wheel in his hands. 'Let's go home...' He left the sentence holding between request and question.

I couldn't reply, my wishes didn't coincide with my duties.

'Peter, I... Maybe it's better not to. Maybe I shouldn't have...'

'Look for me? Why did you do it then, Amantine? If you didn't want to see me again...'

He let the steering wheel go and turned back to me. A few more years hadn't altered his appearance, but I found in him a despair, a torment that he didn't possess before.

'I wanted to see you again. I really wanted it. And apparently I've been lucky to find you in town...' I forced a smile, shrugging.

'I wasn't. I came back as soon as I received Gordon's message. And it's not the first time...' Peter sighed and started the car.

I didn't stop him. I would have let him take me wherever he wanted. We remained silent. Yet I had so many things to say, emotions to express after all this time. But more than anything else I wanted an explanation.

'Why... why did you leave, Amantine?' Peter's question floored me. I wouldn't have expected him to be so direct. I wouldn't have been either.

'You should know what happened that night...'

I felt choked. I didn't want to show him so clearly my emotional state, my feelings. I turned to the window. It had started to rain again. I remembered all too well what our agreement had been. We were not a couple, I had nothing to expect from him.

'Did you care? About me... did you care?' His voice came in a sigh, faint, hoarse.

'Hmm...' I put my hand on the window, almost to catch the first drops of rain that flowed outside. 'I thought... there was something between us... I believed... I was silly.'

'You were not the only silly one, Amantine. Because I thought the same too…'

I leaned my forehead against the window and closed my eyes. I didn't have the strength to articulate other words. When I opened them, the car stood in front of Peter's house. I let myself be guided and I entered. I was too weak to refuse, too distraught. And the truth was that I really wanted it. See the interior of that house again, even for once, just one last time.

I looked around with a vague smile. 'Peter... nothing has changed here.' Everything remained in the same place. But maybe we had changed. Indeed, certainly. I struggled to appease the memories, the mind that created continuous images of how it could have been between us. Images of my dreamed life, with him.

He threw his hat and scarf in a corner and took off his coat. 'Would you like something to drink? Or to eat? I can call Gordon...'

'No, thank you.' I shook my head and approached him. Seeing him like that still had the same effect on me, like the old days, despite everything.

'Amantine...' he sighed, lowering his head as we faced each other. Then he looked back at me and frowned. 'It was water. Just water. I... I had been drinking years ago. I had been an alcoholic up until I was twenty-five. I used drugs, not hard but for sure they were not good for me. I started at seventeen, just before joining the band. They were complicated moments... I wasn't a good boy, in short. And it wasn't anyone's fault, just mine.'

'You don't owe me an explanation, Peter...' I didn't want to know. I didn't want to hear. 'Really, there's no need.'

'No, you must let me explain. I... I stopped for a few years. With everything, drinking and drugs. For my job, because it was the most important thing in my life. I wanted to be taken seriously. I knew so many others...' He ran a hand through his hair, closed his eyes. 'But I wanted to be considered as an artist, one that could be trusted. I thought about compensating my non-exceptional talent with reliability, I wanted to be trustworthy.' He blocked with a wave of his hand my attempt to intervene. 'That evening... before performing... to clear my voice, I had taken a few sips from one of the water bottles that they distributed to me and the other guys... and we started playing. Then between one piece and another I drank again, from that same bottle.'

'What are you trying to tell me, Peter?' I was lost in his story. What his words were suggesting to me seemed too crazy to be true.

'I thought it was just water. I wouldn't have...' He shook his head slightly, went to sit on the couch.

It hurt. Continuing that conversation was hurting me too much.

'It's all in the past. It had to go that way, Peter.'

No, it didn't have to. Why? What happened? What was inside that little bottle of water? I didn't want to know. Nothing could change what had happened, anyway.

Peter nodded, looked up at me as I stood. 'How are you? What have you done with your life in these six years?'

'I live in Paris. I am a researcher at Sorbonne. And I teach, too.' I smiled and sat next to him but remaining distant.

'What you wanted. I hope they give you the consideration you deserve...' Peter raised a smile, raised a hand to rest it on mine that I kept intertwined on my knees. Then at the last moment he gave up. 'Are you married... have you…?'

'Yes. And I have two kids.' My voice cracked. I said no more in an attempt to control the lump in my throat, ready to burst into tears.

'I have a son, Matthew. Actually, I wasn't sure he was mine, me and his mother...' Peter shrugged. 'We didn't have a stable relationship, that's it. We had to run some tests. I didn't want to accept it. Now I'm glad he's mine, he's a good boy. Then I had been married but it didn't work... well, it worked just for a few months...'

'Three months. I read about it.' I nodded and looked at him, tilting my face. 'I'm following you, Peter Wiles, I'm a little stalker.'

'You? Have you devoted yourself to the gossip magazines, little intellectual snob?' Peter smiled, running his hands through his hair. 'I'm a very common subject for them.'

'You're one of the favourite subjects of French gossip magazines, too.' I chuckled to ease the tension. With poor results as far as I was concerned.

'Your kids... what are their names? If you want to tell me...'

'Of course, I want to tell you... William and Madeline.'

'William... like William Shakespeare.' He rose from the couch and moved to the shelf where he kept his books. 'I remember you said you would choose the names for your children just because they were cute, with no connections...'

'In fact.' I stayed sitting on the couch after giving him a quick glance. I tried to regain control of myself before getting up and reaching him. 'I found them cute.'

'Shakespeare, however, is still here, along with the others. Only one is added...' Peter took a book from the shelf to show it to me.

I recognized it immediately. 'Oh no, Peter!' My book on John Keats. 'You really didn't have to...'

'Why not? This, however, is just one copy... I have bought many more in these months. It was my Christmas present for friends and relatives. Even if only because I actively took part in the initial project, if you remember...' Of course, I remembered. And my heart grabbed, thinking about it. 'Then I wanted to contribute to your success in some way. Just like you bought my CDs.'

'I... still buy them, for that matter... I have all of your four solo albums. The singles as well.'

I smiled and clasped my hands tightly. I had to leave. I had to leave quickly because I wouldn't be able to resist anymore.

'Amantine... Do you remember that poem... that Shakespeare's sonnet?'

A step towards me. Then another one. His fingers placed a lock of my hair behind my ear, then brushed my cheekbone. His green eyes peered attentively at my every emotion. No. He couldn't do it. He couldn't do this to me.

'Peter, please...' I broke away, firmly. I was trembling, inside and out. The nail that gripped my heart was tormenting me painfully. 'I have to go. I can't, I really can't... it can't happen.'

I looked for my bag. I didn't even remember if I had brought it home or not. Maybe I left it in the car. I saw it at the entrance and rushed to leave.

'You don't see. It's already happening!' His voice reached me and pierced me like a dagger, freaking me completely out. 'You went away, that night... and all you left... it's still here... I'm still here...'

I felt him behind me. He grabbed my arm and held it for a moment before letting me go. Every contact with him caused me waves of terror and desire that I wasn't able to resist.

He was right. As far as I was concerned, it had never stopped happening. In that house I hadn't only left some of my material objects. I had left my heart, even though I was living in another city, in another country.

I turned. I wanted to look at him in his eyes, touch his face one last time. I passed my fingers on his temple, sliding them along his cheekbone and cheek. I had to do it. I had no choice this time.

'Goodbye, Peter.'

'No...' He closed his eyes as my hand moved away from his skin, forever. He didn't hold me back. He didn't say anything else.

I turned my back again to get to the door. The nail that oppressed me seemed to stick even more tenaciously into my chest, piercing my heart more deeply. I was saying goodbye to my freedom, to my life. Another time. That door... that door I had dreamed of and had to pass. That house where everything had remained the same, exactly as I left it one night, more than six years before.

'Peter...'

I had no choice. I could only beg forgiveness. From a God I wasn't even sure I believed, from heaven. From who I was about to betray. And also from him, from love that called me without resigning. Without hearing neither the voice of reason nor that of decency.

I could only hear the voice of my passion at that moment, which like a melodious song brought me back home, to him. The desire of his arms ready to welcome me, his lips on mine, on my face, everywhere.

'You're here... you're here, sweetheart...'

He held me so tight that he almost hurt me. I clung on to him with fury, afraid of being forced to break away again. I let myself go to a radiant smile, almost mad, as if the desire for life and freedom had returned to breathe in me.

I found myself in tears as my lips met his, while his mouth explored mine. I grabbed him by the head to force him not to stop, not to let me go. I just wanted to taste that kiss that I thought I would never receive again.

I followed him on that familiar way, up the stairs to his bedroom. I didn't know how many other women had passed that way and I didn't even care. It was ours and everything had remained the same. Even us in that moment. Even me in all the six years of distance.

My hands couldn't get away from his skin as he undressed me slowly, pondering every gesture as if he were to memorize it forever. Our caresses became more and more painful until we let ourselves fall into each other, unable to resist any longer. I had the absolute certainty of never having left. Everything was back as before. Everything was wrong. Or maybe everything was so right.

CHAPTER 48

Six years hadn't really passed. Maybe it was all a dream, our separation had never happened. I had simply slept, close to him, in our bed. I found the warmth of his kiss on my forehead again, his arms wrapped around me. No, six years couldn't have passed. We could still have everything, as happened every morning after our awakenings. Breakfast, music, our great projects. And that bantering that every time pushed me more and more hopelessly into his arms.

'Peter...' I tried to move, stroking his chest gently. With my finger, I retraced the tattoo on his shoulder, always my favourite. I kissed his face, then his neck. I knew he was awake but that he was pretending he was sleeping. It was at that moment that I noticed a new tattoo at the base of the neck. He didn't have it before. It was an elegantly designed letter "A". I retraced it with my finger, several times.

Peter turned and jokingly bit my hand.

'Spiteful, like you always were.'

'You were not sleeping anyway...' I giggled, kissing his lips. 'You were tricking me, like you usually do... you did...' With my words, we were serious again, both of us. I eagerly searched for another topic of conversation. 'This... is it new?' I stroked again the tattoo on his neck.

'Yes... I did it for *All of me*... my first solo album.' He frowned, sighed and pulled himself up with his back. 'I wanted to remember it forever. A symbol of my conquered freedom.'

'I'm happy for you. I've listened to it so many times, it's great. All your new albums are.' The moment was approaching, inescapable. That I rejected it with all my might, didn't change the situation. 'Peter...'

'I know. I know you, Amantine. You're about to tell me it was a mistake. But you also know that it's not true. It hasn't been one this time and it has never been ever before...'

He got out of bed, turning his back, almost ignoring me, looking for his clothes.

'Peter... it's the situation that's wrong. Before I...' I left the subject hanging. I got up too. I located my clothes, grabbed them, and began to dress almost in anger. 'I have to leave...'

'Sure.' He answered mechanically, as if he didn't care. He was hurting me. I walked to the bedroom door, but I found him in front of me blocking the exit, his eyes on mine. 'Are you happy, Amantine? I mean with...'

'Do you think I am not? Maybe you think that if I was happy, I wouldn't have slept with you...'

It was as if Peter had guessed who I had married and why. Even though I didn't reveal my husband's name. I wondered if he had looked for me, in his own way.

'It was you who said that, not me.' Peter's face tightened, he looked away from me and moved away from the door, leaving the exit free.

'We have ups and downs, like everyone.' Suddenly I realized I had no other words to define my marriage.

Happy? No, we had never been. Serene? Yes, maybe at the beginning. If I hadn't had that pain constantly corroding my soul. The daily life with Geoff was completely different from the daily life that Peter and I had during the period in which we had lived together. Geoff belonged to my world of academics and intellectuals. I couldn't even compare the two situations.

'You can always divorce, Amantine. I did it. I mean... it can happen...'

'Peter... what are you talking about? I...' Sure, it could happen. Indeed, it happened to many others, more and more frequently. But I...

'The little intellectual snob Amantine Delamar is too perfect to divorce like mere mortals, I know.' His tone was not joking, but dry, detached.

'I'd better go.'

He was hurting me. Perhaps he didn't even realize it. I would collapse soon, but not in front of him, I couldn't allow it. Because collapsing in front of him would mean not being able to leave him anymore.

'Amantine... I'm sorry, I didn't mean to...' He stroked my shoulders and arms from behind. He put his lips to my nape, causing me a shiver. 'I'd like to see you again before you...'

'I have to leave in the afternoon, Peter.' My heart was desperate for a solution. Maybe an excuse to postpone a few days, only one or two. To give me peace once and for all, to put an end to the story with him and not to return home too shocked and weakened. But no, I couldn't. 'I feel guilty enough already.'

'You'll leave me again. This seems to be becoming a habit, but...'

'There's no alternative this time.' I wasn't leaving him, alone. I was also leaving myself. My happiness remained inextricably in his hands. 'You have... you have your music, Peter. Your world...' I couldn't resist and turned around. Just one last time, one last time his eyes on me, one last time the shape of his lips, his face. 'Who knows, maybe you'll meet the right Lolita one of these days and then...'

'It's not the same thing! Amantine... I would have never been with another woman that night if I was conscious, if they hadn't drugged me... I'm not trying to justify myself, but I didn't even want to go to that damn party, and you knew it! I wanted to be with you! I looked for you... I looked for you as soon as I recovered, but... I couldn't find you. Then I thought you...'

He took a step back, then another. He ran his hands through his hair, turning his shoulders angrily. I stood still and watched him. The nail in my heart seemed for a moment to be annihilated, to vanish. But it was only a momentary sensation, an illusion. It was breaking it right now, mercilessly. Peter turned back to me. The tears in his green eyes took my breath away.

'Didn't you understand, Amantine? As long as we kept joking, didn't you really understand that night? When I asked you if you wanted to make it real... I would have never betrayed you like that, because I wanted only you... I loved you!'

A tear ran down his face, quick at first. Then it stopped as soon as it reached his lips. I reached to him to dry it but held back. I felt myself collapsing on the ground. Exactly like that night. When Tyler forced me to admit the truth.

Just one thing I could do. The one I could do for the better. Run away. Away from that room, from that house. Away from him. Forever. Once outside, I kept running. Without even knowing where I was going. I ran for simple need, the need to tire my heart to the point of forcing it not to suffer, not to break. Or to break with fatigue, maybe, but not for that unbearable pain.

I was forced to stop, however, because I fell to the ground. I didn't even know where I was. I could no longer distinguish the residential neighbourhood to which I had come. There was no one on the street, but I wouldn't have cared anyway.

I wanted to cry, really cry. Cry for the life I had lost, for the happiness that would never touch my life again. I wanted to say it, aloud. To the wind, to the sun that appeared shy in that pale English sky, to that false and hypocritical world that had welcomed me back, but to which I hadn't belonged anymore for some time. Because I belonged to him.

'I loved you too, Peter. Against everything and everyone, even against myself. I loved you too. And I still love you.'

CHAPTER 49

Getting back to my life was a miserable illusion for me. I imagined it. Nothing would ever be the same because I knew the truth. He loved me. He wouldn't betray me. Although we were not a real couple. Despite our games, despite our constant joke about ourselves and our relationship. As much as I had stubbornly insisted that I wouldn't have tolerated any question or claim, my heart belonged to him, rebelling against my own will.

In the following days I did nothing more than fantasise about what my life with him would have been like. If we hadn't gone to that party. If I had talked to him, demanding an explanation.

I realized that the result of my behaviour would be to further wear my relationship with Geoff out. I wished I was stronger, able to control myself. I couldn't. I was thinking about Peter constantly, day and night. I worked in my study until late with the excuse of having found the inspiration for the new book. It was just an excuse not to share the bed with my husband.

As long as I thought that I was nothing to Peter, I had been able to live with that thought, and be able to move on. But how could I stop dreaming, building a parallel and imaginary life in which he and I were still together, happy, in love?

Even my children were adapting to my absent mother figure. They were so small... and I wanted to be different, at least for them. Get over myself. Sometimes I could, others I couldn't. They were more connected to my mother, to the babysitter, even to Geoff. I often noticed from their gaze that they looked at me fearfully, almost intimidated. I never had a very developed maternal instinct, not even with little Jinny, the Parkers' daughter.

Meanwhile, the date of my brother's wedding with Marianne was approaching. I was helping them with the preparations. Actually, my mother was helping them, I was just trying to make myself appear at least vaguely participating, offering slivers of my time between my many commitments. The university and my new book. For two weeks I had been using them as a shield to protect myself from the pretensions of the world. I could be credible, at least with others. My heart, on the other hand, always took other directions. One in particular, London.

'So, the invitations have all been sent, right Amantine?' It was my mother's voice. I had met her for lunch, and it awakened me from the state of stupor in which I fell more and more often. 'Amantine... you're not well...' My mother put her hands on the table that separated us, stretching towards me. 'Your face is tired and you're so pale.'

'Too much work, Mom. The university, the new book.' I reassembled myself immediately, ready to declare my usual excuses. I had become good.

'Honey, you need to slow down a bit or you'll collapse one of these days.'

My mother tilted her head slightly. I would have given anything to have her emotional and physical serenity, her consistent well-groomed appearance. Everything in her life had gone according to her plan. And if something escaped her control, she had been able to adapt and put the pieces back together.

Marianne, for example... She had confessed to me that she didn't think she was suitable for Alain, regarding culture and temperament. Then she got to know her better and now she had a better relationship with her than she had with me. My parents were profoundly similar from that point of view, they marvellously adapted to every situation as well as adapting to each other. Maybe it was one of the reasons they got along so well.

But I wasn't like that. I couldn't even adapt to a man with whom I had all interests in common. 'I know, Mom. I'll take some time...' Here, standard answer.

'How are things going with Geoffrey and the children?' My mother's dark eyes scanned me inquisitively.

'As usual.' I shrugged. What did we still have to discuss in that Parisian taverne adjacent to the university? Everything was ready for Alain's marriage, best not to analyse the details of mine too much. I took a significant look at the watch I kept on my wrist. I had no lessons in the afternoon and I wasn't late, but it didn't matter.

'Amantine... you know how I feel about it.' No, a lecture from my mother, I couldn't stand it. 'Geoffrey told me he was deeply opposed to the idea, when you wanted to go to London.'

'Oh, of course! He has been always excellent in this! Telling all about our business, whining to his father about this, and to both of you...'

The memories of the past resurfaced, fuelling my anger even more, my intolerance. I noticed my hands were shaking. By now I had exploded, I could no longer take back what I had said. Tears began to sting my eyes. It wasn't good. It didn't work like that. Amantine Delamar wasn't supposed to cry in a public place in front of her mother. Amantine Delamar accepted and moved on, firmly grounded in her world, in symbiosis with all those who belonged to it.

'Marriage is important, Amantine. In our environment above all... I've always thought this way.' No, I didn't want to listen to her. It was a lesson I already knew by heart. 'But now I'm getting old. I've been lucky and I'm not complaining about my life. I started to consider other people's lives. Our friends. Alain and Marianne at first seemed to me the most absurd and messed up couple I had ever met. And then... there are. You and Geoffrey, so similar, so perfectly born for each other. But instead...'

'I'd better go, Mom.' Her detailed analysis of my married life was making me uneasy.

'Have you thought of separating, Amantine?' She took me completely by surprise as I was about to get up from the table. What the hell was she talking about?

'No. I... no...' How did she come up with an idea like that? 'Mom, you know that's not how it goes. I mean…'

'Sometimes there is no other choice. Why did you marry Geoffrey?'

Her question forced me to stay seated. As far as my parents knew, my daring adventure with the singer was over and I, as a good girl, went back to my loving boyfriend's arms again.

'I had to.' I gripped my hands tightly, intertwining my fingers. 'I just had to. And I won't backtrack on what I have done.'

CHAPTER 50

A few days later I received an e-mail from Gregor Jackman with an ultimatum. Take it or leave it. My feelings were not enough, the conversation with my mother was not enough. With the pressure I was under, that's all I needed, Gregor Jackman… A man I despised both personally and professionally, but who offered me a unique possibility, an escape. He offered me London on a silver platter. And for the umpteenth time in my life on one side there was the heart, on the other the reason. On one side the desire to see Peter again, on the other the responsibility towards my husband and my children.

I opened and closed the e-mail a number of times. I started writing my reply and then erased everything. If I talked to Geoff it would result in a discussion in which he ordered me to refuse. I was absolutely sure. And indeed, how could I blame him?

But my heart rebelled against everything and everyone. It invoked only a name, a body. His hands caressing me, his lips. I wouldn't have peace. I had to see him again, at least one last time. To say goodbye definitely. Calmly this time, with serenity. Without desperation, without running away.

I replied to Gregor Jackman, swallowing my pride. I accepted his offer to teach creative writing. I would split between London and Paris. I would suffer the consequences, I knew it. But after all, what could Geoff do besides raging? Leave me? No, he wouldn't. He would get over it. And I... I had betrayed him, and I was getting ready to betray him again. I was guilty now. I had made too many mistakes and I probably deserved unhappiness in my life.

I couldn't face the truth. I lied to Geoff and told him it would be some occasional lessons. Then I lied again, saying that my assignment had been prolonged. I read the hate in his eyes. As if he already knew.

I left the children at my parents' home and made arrangements with the babysitter. My mother understood but didn't ask me any questions. I felt treacherous, cruel. I tried to blame life and destiny, then I had nothing left to do but assume my responsibilities. I was a weak woman, I had always been. I couldn't resist the desire to be reciprocated by the one I loved, to have him for me.

From the airport I rushed straight to Notting Hill, even before going to the hotel. My fear was that he would despise me as I had run away, and that he wouldn't want to know me anymore.

Gordon told me that Peter was out of town. I left him the address of my hotel again and my cell phone number, begging him to warn Peter as soon as he could.

'Stay here, Mrs. Amantine.' Gordon gave me an almost affectionate smile, perhaps even a little compassionate. 'I'll make you a cup of tea or something to eat. Don't go to the hotel, I'm sure you would feel better here.'

I nodded, trying to show myself composed, detached. Instinctively, I would have hugged him, but I knew I would embarrass him. He was right, anyway. I would feel better there. I bit my lips so as not to cry, but was forced to wipe my face with my hands. 'Thanks, Gordon. I... I would just like a cup of tea and one of your muffins, as I used to. I'll wait for Peter before I cancel the hotel.'

I was a monster. I would move for three days a week to the house of the one who was, in effect, my lover. My name said it all. But why did being a monster make me so happy? Because waiting for him filled my heart with joy, enthusiasm, hope. I was a monster, an immoral woman, an adulteress... with the complicity of an austere English butler.

I waited for him until evening, arranging my notes for the lesson I was going to hold the next morning. All as it used to be. Then, hour after hour, the feeling of completeness began to leave room for fear, emotional tension. I couldn't be sure he still wanted me. I had deduced it from Gordon's invitation to stay, but...

I closed my eyes and crouched on the sofa, drawing my knees to my chest. I just wanted to try and relax a bit. A few minutes, no more. Instead, I fell asleep.

'Baby...'

I opened my eyes and found his face a short distance from mine. 'Peter...' I hugged him. 'Gordon told me I could stay, I...'

He didn't answer. I found myself on his lap with his lips on mine, on my face, on my neck. My hands clung to him desperately. I was his. Body and soul. I was his beyond all reasonableness, beyond any sense of guilt. Maybe the flames of hell would envelop me one day, but for the moment I wasn't thinking of anything else other than living that paradise made only of the two of us, together.

CHAPTER 51

Thus, my double life began. Again. Peter and I were fighting week after week against our respective commitments to be together for a few hours. A whole day if we were lucky. In those cases, I considered myself the luckiest woman in the world. He never told me again he loved me. And I didn't say it to him. Maybe by tacit agreement. If we had declared ourselves looking into each other eyes, we wouldn't have had the strength to say goodbye every time. It would have broken my heart to leave him to return to my other life.

He had not asked me anymore to separate from Geoff. He knew that my marriage was now only a formality. After all, it had been from the beginning. I had to marry Geoff, he had waited for me for so long and forgave me so much. For a few years I had deluded myself that I could achieve serenity with him if not real happiness. After all, I had been fond of him for a long time. I couldn't leave him and expose him to the comments of our little hypocritical world. At least I owed this to him. Then there were the children. It was no longer just the two of us, I had to protect them too. If I chose to follow my heart, I would mess up too many people's lives.

I couldn't be with Peter at important moments. I had never been, not even before. Before that damned night that had separated us. Just thinking about it, I felt bad, like a cruel grip that was wearing me out internally. So much so that we removed it from our conversations, as if it never existed. It had happened. It was useless to revive the past. I wished the guilty one would pay for the harm he had done to us. But this wouldn't give us back the life we had lost. However, Darkest Storm had broken up after Peter left. And Simon Jennings had ever since been looking for someone who could replace the gain he had with them. Peter had signed a contract with one of the biggest record labels explicitly refusing that Simon be involved in the deal.

I supported Peter as much as I could. Indirectly, as a spectator, witnessing his success. I was the lover he had to keep hidden. The gossip magazines continued to attribute to him flirts that he neither confirmed nor denied. It hurt me, but maybe this way they would avoid further investigation into his associations. I remained the mysterious woman nobody talked about. I was always afraid that sooner or later the gossips would keep me from staying at his house. I feared that our worlds would collide once again, destroying us.

Then there were those moments... those wonderful moments that I defined in my mind as "our daily life". Sitting on the sofa at home, I read, wrote and arranged my notes for the book or for the lessons. He tried new chords, new melodies on the guitar and he marked everything in his precious little notebook.

'Hmm... hmm...' Suddenly I put down my sheets and, closing my eyes, leaned against the back of the sofa. Some notes, played by Peter, were as if they took possession of me, of my mind, of my soul, as stanzas of a very sweet poem. So much I wanted to taste, feel, live them. I perceived them as the fulcrum of our story, the melody of our life, of our love.

'Amantine...' Peter put the guitar down and stood next to me, his green eyes anxious, worried. 'Is everything all right, my love?' With his thumb he wiped a tear that was running down my face.

He had called me my love, maybe inadvertently. And I had lost control of the beats of my heart. I took his hand and placed it on my chest.

'Peter... don't let it go... that melody. It's ours...' I kissed his lips tenderly and then ardently. 'Don't lose it...'

'All right, baby. But you have to help me find it again...' Peter hesitated again on my lips, then almost forcibly moved to grab the guitar. 'Help me write our song, Amantine...'

He resumed playing, remembering the melody. I didn't know how to help him, I could only take advantage of my poor and remote knowledge of music and notes to recall what in my mind would become our song.

So it happened. From that moment on, our worlds began to flow even more into each other without being able to stop, as our soul, our heart that couldn't help but surrender and follow its call.

I realized that Peter Wiles was the man in my life. He would be the only one for me, always. I would love no one else but him in the course of my existence. Regardless of who he was and what he was doing. I would have loved him even if he was an ordinary boy I met on the street. Indeed, maybe it was precisely for that reason that I loved him. Because for me he was an ordinary boy I met on the street on a cold November morning.

CHAPTER 52

One evening Peter came home with a more mischievous expression than usual. I immediately understood that he had a surprise for me.

'Did you win a special prize, Peter?' I reached him, wrapping my arms around his neck. 'Or maybe they offered you some very important collaboration? Not with a beautiful girl, right? Do I have to act jealous? I know how much you enjoy that.'

He put his hands on my hips and gently rubbed me. Strangely, he remained silent. I sighed nervously and stared expectantly. Finally, he decided to speak.

'Not me, sweetheart... you. And I hope the jealous scene from me won't be necessary.'

I didn't understand the meaning of his words. I stared at him, puzzled, urging him to continue. 'I invited someone for dinner, Amantine. He will be here soon.'

'What do you mean someone for dinner? Are you crazy?' I ran a hand over my forehead, reflecting on where I could go and hide. Locked in the bedroom seemed the only option to me. 'Oh God, Peter... if someone sees me here...'

'It's to see you that I invited him to dinner, sweetheart...' Peter held me by my forearms and smiled. 'Are you going to stop fidgeting? Try to be a good hostess and behave yourself.'

'But Peter... you know, I mean... I don't want to ruin you...'

He took my face in his hands, gently stroking my cheeks. 'Did you listen to me, Amantine? I invited him for you, not for me.'

'But I'm so...' In jeans and a t-shirt. And I had no idea of who or what I should expect. 'Peter Wiles, if you don't tell me immediately who's coming and what I have to do with it...' I searched for something threatening enough to shake him, but I was running out of ideas.

'Can't you think of anything wicked? I don't believe it!' He burst out laughing, hugging me. 'You're losing your touch, sweetheart.'

I was about to answer him, but we were interrupted by the ringing of the bell. Suddenly I realized that there was no dinner ready on the table. Gordon hadn't prepared it and I hadn't seen any chef going around the kitchen.

Turning towards the entrance I could hardly recognize the man standing in front of us. No, it couldn't be him. Dressed in jeans, a shirt and a sports jacket, he could have been between sixty or seventy. He smiled at me, bending his head slightly in a warm greeting.

'Nice to see you again, my dear.' Then he glanced at Peter. 'Have you already ordered pizza, my boy? For me, onion rings as well.'

'Jacob?' Jacob. I couldn't believe my own eyes. The one who had been in part the architect of my relationship with Peter Wiles was now in front of me, after years. Cleaned up and refurbished.

'Jacob, yes...' Peter confirmed. 'Or J.D. Sanders, if you prefer.'

J.D. Sanders, one of the greatest and celebrated contemporary poets and author of critical essays and novels as well, was right there in front of me. Inaccessible and rather wild-eyed, they said. He lived in solitude, surly and grumpy, he kept the human race away, he mistreated academics and critics, he refused interviews. He had also turned down an invitation from Professor Frey many years before. I had seen only one of his photos on the back of a book, perhaps the only one that existed. Obviously, I didn't connect him to Jacob. How could I have imagined it? But actually... Yes, it was him. Aged, but definitely him.

'Exactly.' Jacob nodded absently, his eyes focused on me. Disconcerted, I glanced at Peter, then looked back at Jacob, J.D. Sanders, still disbelieving. 'I've heard a lot about you, my dear.

Apparently, you took my suggestion about John Keats. I've read the book, you have been kind. I wondered if you could reserve the same treatment for me as well. If I have to give myself away to a biography, I expect it to be well written but with a bit of animation, and a bit of light-heartedness. Maybe by a nice pretty girl who loves poetry, music, true beauty. I don't want stiff brontosaurs with delusions of grandeur around.'

CHAPTER 53

J.D Sanders, unrepentant recluse, entrusted to me and me only the rights to write his biography. The news went around, if not the world, certainly the country. And our environment, above all.

The official story was that the great poet, impressed by my work on Keats, had decided to contact me. That sometimes it popped into his head to play homeless and hang out on the streets of London to discover the real life and that there was an antecedent bond between me, him and Peter would always remain a secret among us.

Peter had known him through ancient bonds between their families, before they both became famous. His paternal grandfather had been a teacher of young Sanders. We started working together and everything proceeded wonderfully. So, both in London and in Paris, I had become a sort of celebrity too in the academic world.

I spent most of my time with Peter and Jacob. When we met at Peter's house, we were careful not to get noticed. I couldn't do anything else but regret the life I could have with him. And blame myself, most of the time. Or destiny. Destiny that had conditioned my stupidity, my fear of expressing the feelings I had begun to experience.

What remained, constantly, was my sense of guilt. I continued undaunted to hide a truth that would upset so many lives. Often I tried to hide it from myself too, as if it didn't exist, but then it re-emerged disruptive, relentless.

I took refuge in the present. It was all that Peter and I were allowed to have. The truth and the future could wait a little longer. Better times, maybe.

'My grandfather and my father were teachers, little intellectual egocentric.' Peter had teased me when I started working with Jacob. 'If I had become one myself, maybe I would have tried the academic career, so we could fight to steal each other's place.'

'No, Peter. I don't think so. We would probably have allied against Gregor Jackman and we would have torn him apart! Besides making love on his desk... Oops, we already did that!' The idea of having Peter as a collaborator was still tempting. In fact, I wouldn't have minded.

'Don't unleash those memories in me, sweetheart, or I'll want to do it again! We destroyed him, anyway. I guess he didn't take well Jacob's choice to make you his official biographer.'

I didn't answer him but held him closer to me. I didn't know if the idea had started with Jacob or Peter. I only knew that Peter had made it possible. And I knew that, although unfortunately it was impossible for us to spend our life together in the limelight, there would be nothing in the world that I wouldn't do for him. How could I keep hiding something so important?

'How I wish that...' Peter sighed then shook his head, lowering his eyes.

'Peter, there are some things I should tell you...' Courage? No, I didn't have it at all. But I couldn't keep silent anymore. The right time would never arrive.

'Me too, Amantine. But I don't want to hurt you...' He raised his green eyes, staring into mine, he suddenly seemed very serious. A wave of frost took over me and crossed my body, reaching my bones. Did he want to leave me?

'Do you want to...' I pulled away from him, curling up into a corner of the couch. I felt the cold of not having his arms around me anymore.

Peter reached out his hand to mine. 'Amantine... I don't know how to tell you... It's about my son, Matthew. As much as I didn't want him, now he's here... So, it's a complication that I have to try to solve...'

A complication. What was he trying to tell me? That he was going to go back with his mother to give the child a family? Something like that? After all, it was what I was doing too. I couldn't blame him.

'You want to go back with your child's mother, I understand...'

'What? No, Amantine! Absolutely not.' He squeezed my hand hard and brought it to his lips. 'I've already been wrong once... more than once, in fact. I'm not going to make mistakes again. What I was about to say... Matthew will stay here with me for about a week. I have to spend some time with him. And I would like you to know him, he's a cute boy, but... When I got married he was small, he didn't understand. But now he talks and he could say something about you. I don't know if it's a good idea for him to see you.'

'You're right, it's not...' No, it wasn't at all. For anybody. Maybe another time, maybe when there was less confusion among us. In our relationship, in our lives, in our careers. Maybe when the kids grew up a little bit. 'I won't come here... we won't see each other for as long as necessary...'

'I'm so sorry, baby...' Peter drew me to him. I asked nothing more than to take refuge in his arms. 'You won't leave me for this, will you?'

'No, no Peter. I won't... I will never leave you...'

Never. After all, I hadn't really left him even in those years of separation, of detachment. I hadn't left him when I left his house the first time with the intention of behaving myself and returning to my official boyfriend. I had never left him. Not even that night when I discovered him with another woman and realized I loved him so much that I felt like dying. When I had escaped alone, desperate... And although I had tried, I couldn't get rid of what I considered a burden. Not out of goodness, out of maternal instinct... but because it was his. At the cost of sacrificing myself and one of the things I most cherished in the world, my freedom.

'Good. Then we'll find the way.' Peter smiled, kissing my lips. 'It will only be a little more complicated than I would like it to be.'

'Peter... that night...' I hated to remember it. But there was that sentence, those words that hadn't given me peace, for years. And sometimes they came back to me, I still felt them with the same intensity, as if they had just been pronounced. 'When you were about to go to the others to perform... and you told me...'

'Amantine... do you want to make it real?' Peter nodded, stroking my face, holding his hand on my cheek. I put my hand on his and our fingers intertwined.

'Hmm...' I kissed his lips. A slow, sweet kiss. A kiss that contained my answer in itself.

'Why do you think I said you were my girlfriend?' Peter sighed, holding his forehead against mine.

'Because Lolita had betrayed you with a Hollywood actor and you needed to save appearances so as not to be taken for...'

His hands stroked my back, holding me tighter. 'I hadn't cared for Lolita for months. I hadn't cared about anyone, besides you.'

I slid my arms around his neck, wrapping them closely. 'So, I wore myself out unnecessarily for all those months...'

'You were my little egocentric and snob intellectual... How could I admit that I was crazy about you so much that I gave all the others up? You would have laughed in my face... or run away from me, as you can do well. You would have accused me of not respecting the rules... "No questions, no claims". You repeated it so often...'

Peter loved me. And I loved him. How could we be so foolish? And how could I have been so superficial and stupid that I didn't realize it?'

'When you left, Amantine... All of you remained here. Everything you left. Your books, your CDs... your clothes... even the dress you wore on the night of the party. When we were walking in the park and we reached that little bridge... you turned to me. You were the most beautiful woman I had ever seen in my life. And I promised that I would talk to you... I couldn't hold back anymore, even risking losing you. Once we got home, I would have asked you...'

Peter hesitated and stopped, as if frightened by his own words. I put my hand on his chest and felt his heart beat hard. I realized something I had always missed. Years ago, during that period of being together, and even recently. Peter was terrified, maybe not as much as me, but almost. Peter was afraid to express his feelings, he was afraid of love, he was afraid of a relationship with another person. He was afraid of losing, of suffering.

This had condemned us to unhappiness. The constant denial of a feeling that we both strove to suffocate, in our own way, but which we could no longer repress. The external circumstances were to blame, but not on their own. It was ours, above all. It was mine. I realized how much it had cost him to confess he loved me when we met again after six years.

'Peter... do you want to make it real?' I took his face in my hands and looked into his eyes, serious, determined. 'Because I want it. I want it now as I wanted it years ago. As I wanted it that evening, on that little bridge... when I turned and you... I want it with my body and soul, Peter. Even if it's complicated now, even if...'

'Yes, Amantine. I want to make it real... I want to be with you. I want you to be my girl. Even if now you are another man's wife...' I saw an intense, vivid light in his eyes. The light of hope, the same that was born in my heart when we composed our song together. 'I want to find the way... because for me it has always been real with you. From the first moment.'

CHAPTER 54

Thus, another year passed. I obviously didn't achieve Peter's popularity, partly because I was working in a completely different setting, but I was becoming a well-known person. If, on one side my skills were finally recognized, on the other, it complicated our situation.

I could never be there at Peter's public presentations; I couldn't attend to share in his successes. And he couldn't publicly attend mine. Geoff was always at my side, even though we had almost become strangers. He accepted everything, as always. But he wouldn't let me go, now less than ever. Even the initial outbursts had diminished and then ceased altogether.

I was now almost certain that he too had another life outside our domestic walls. But he was better than me at enduring the situation. In any case, day after day, my emotional tension increased and I realized more than ever that I could never live the life I wanted. Then there was that truth to corrode my soul, that truth that I still couldn't confess. Not even to the man I loved with all my heart.

The children were growing up and already judging my absences, my lack of participation in their everyday life. William, above all. He was only seven years old and I read in his eyes my deplorable behaviour and the esteem and the affection he had for Geoff, instead.

Then, to complicate even more our already precarious situation, blackmail came. A picture of us taken at the entrance of Peter's house. The money request not to sell it to the newspapers. Peter subdued himself to that wretched extortion and paid. For me more than for himself, not to ruin me publicly.

It was at that moment that I realized that for us the end was coming, or the need to find a way to solve our dramas. We would receive other blackmail attempts, other threats. The temptation to unveil everything, to leave Geoff, to tell everybody to go to hell, was great, immense.

But then there were William's eyes, those green eyes so sweet but so severe at the same time. Every day I saw him growing and every day I realized that he would never forgive me. I cursed myself for not having acted before, at once, immediately. I cursed myself for accepting Geoff's marriage proposal and for not having the courage to stay alone. I also cursed Peter, I cursed Simon, I cursed Darkest Storm, that damn party.

Why... why didn't I accept Peter's idea to stay home? Eat pizza, listen to music all night, watch old movies lying in our bed... Why didn't I tell him that I loved him? Why didn't I wait for him that night to scream my pain at him, in his face, to tell him the truth?

That truth that I still hid in the depths of my soul, among my wounds. That made me weary and tore away from me even the moments of serenity, of life in his arms, of love. I was scared, once again. He wouldn't forgive me either. I would lose him more than I had lost him in all these years. More than I was prepared to lose him when I realized that I had no choice, I had to let him go once again.

He never asked me again to leave my husband, to give up my life. Yet at some point I might have done it. Sowing pain and anger, in a purely selfish act, I would have left everything and everybody for him.

Peter, in the meantime, was starting to get success in America too, but they required his constant presence. I could have taken the children and followed him. He had been right when we discussed it sometime before. It happened so frequently to many people, not just to the showbiz celebrities. Why not to me? Why couldn't I be free?

I only knew I could not hinder his career. It wouldn't have been right, he had worked so hard, he had suffered too much to get his artistic value recognized.

'You have to go, Peter.' How many times would I have to leave him again, giving up happiness? How many times would my heart be broken by emerging memories?

'I'm fine like that. What I have here is enough for me, Amantine. Really, it's enough for me.' He kissed my lips gently, then held me close to him. 'I've always said that I would never leave London. I haven't changed my mind.'

'Peter... you can't give up your career.' He looked away from me. Besides, the gossip about us was spreading. They had recognized me, his girlfriend of that night and were starting to put the pieces together. 'You must keep fighting. Your talent must be recognized by everyone, in America as well.'

'Do you know how much I want you with me, sweetheart?' He bit his lips almost angrily. My mind was struggling to find a solution that it couldn't find. When would I see him again? And how? Where?

'I'm always with you, Peter. I've been with you from the first moment. I want to make it real, remember?'

I hid my face on his chest. A part of me kept rebelling, desperately wanting him. A solution could be found. We were not the only ones who had to face a complicated relationship.

But what would it mean? To lose the children... Geoff would tear them from me if I left him. Would it come to that?

For Peter's career that was taking off right then, it would be a disaster. A relationship with a woman who left two young children because of him. Or that impudently dragged them to another country. Americans knew how to be damn puritans sometimes. Already the rumours in England were spreading. They would be more interested in the details of his private life than in his music. I couldn't allow it.

'Peter, I want you to... dedicate yourself to your music. Completely. I want you to go to America and stand up for yourself. I want you to work with the best in the world.' I looked up firmly, stared into his eyes. Without hesitation, without a tear. 'If you really want to do something for me, Peter... Do you remember the artists you introduced me to since we met, who you taught me to admire? Now, I want you to commit yourself to reach their greatness. I don't want you to settle for a good level, you have to be excellent. You have to promise me. If you do this for me, Peter... I will always be with you, my darling. Together we will find the way...'

October 2009

CHAPTER 55

Other years passed by us. More and more often I wondered what had become of my perfectly planned life. Nothing had gone as I had planned. And I missed it a little. Not so much that life itself, as the very idea of my accurate planning.

But what I missed most were those days, those months of freedom and light heartedness, of pure joy. I would have given anything to get them back. To be able to go back and change the course of destiny, of our story. I missed being happy with little and the memory oppressed my soul without granting me break. Those months when I instinctively chose him, feeling completely happy, without realizing it. And I continued to choose him still, even after so many years.

I followed his public life day by day and shared his most resounding successes as well as the bitterest criticism. I suffered in silence at each new flirt that they attributed to him, aware that I couldn't make any claim on him. Just as I had asked years before, "no questions, no claims". I never imagined that those silly words would turn against me.

In over eight years we saw each other several times but only on seven occasions had we managed to spend a few days together, although at the beginning we did everything to keep in touch. E-mail, phone... reading his words, hearing his voice was enough for me. Seeing each other once a week or at least every two weeks had become physically impossible.

We had sworn to ourselves that the distance wouldn't separate us, that we would resist despite the difficulties. But there wasn't only the physical distance between us, there wasn't only the ocean. An infinite series of complications, impediments, setbacks. Both our jobs, family, especially mine, children who were growing, as was their growing need for my constant presence, their questions about my prolonged absences.

The temptation to take them with me to the other side of the world always existed. But once again I had to put my selfishness aside, as I had done with Peter, allowing him to pursue success in his career. I had to learn to sacrifice myself. Not to mention that Geoff would never allow me to go so far with the children.

I felt more and more like a burden that Peter was forced to drag along. Even if I didn't live with him. I feared that the very idea of me, the feeling that united us and kept us bound began to weigh on him, to wear him out, almost like a condemnation from which sooner or later he would want to free himself.

A few months after his move I couldn't resist and went to see him in New York. A whole week together. He wasn't famous in the United States yet, so we managed to remain incognito in the apartment he had rented. While Peter, during the last days of my stay, planned our other probable meetings, I was getting ready to say goodbye and let him free. It wasn't right to keep him tied to me, it wasn't fair to him in that regard. I had to find a way to end my selfishness. I had always been selfish with everyone in my life, but I couldn't be with him anymore.

I hadn't left him in words, I wouldn't have succeeded. I allowed a gradual separation between us, while Peter was more and more busy with his music, building his career.

During the first two years we managed to see each other every time he returned to London, or other parts of England. But incognito, always in a hurry. In an East End hotel, in another one in Richmond. Once in Liverpool, once in a Yorkshire village.

For me it was no longer possible to go to the United States to stay with him. Each time it was like renewing the wound, the pain of separation.

In the end, dominated by the tension, by the anxiety of being discovered, we could hardly speak, laugh, or be happy together. We were condemned to an impossible relationship. The difference from before was that we were becoming more and more aware of it. And we resigned ourselves to accepting it as if neither of us had the strength or the courage to fight anymore.

Then there was the truth, but at least it was a burden that I alone was forced to wear. That truth that became increasingly difficult to confess and with the passing of time took on enormous and inhuman proportions from my point of view.

Would he hate me? Would he stop loving me completely? Or... maybe he wouldn't believe me. Day after day doubts crowded my mind. I should have told him right away, as soon as we found each other again. Without reflecting on his reaction, assuming my responsibilities. Instead, as always, as a constant misfortune in my life, I had lived waiting for the right moment that never arrived. By now my biography could be summed up in five words: woman condemned to make mistakes.

I tried not to think about what our life would be like if I'd waited for him that night instead of running away. But sometimes... sometimes I couldn't help myself. I visualized the scene, like a lucid dream. The scene of our explanation, the scene in which I would reveal my secret to him. His reaction. In the parallel story that I deluded myself to live, he would be happy. And I would be too. We would have supported and loved each other for the rest of our lives. A sort of happy ending fairy tale that I had always been inclined to mock. But the truth was that for us I desired it with all my heart. The truth was that a tiny part of me was still deluding myself of being able to obtain it, despite the years, despite the pain... despite the secret that I still kept hidden in my heart.

Why had he kept choosing me among so many beautiful women for so long? I felt more and more tired, aged, sad. What was left of what he had once loved in me? Almost nothing now. What had happened to my great aspirations, my enthusiasm, my smiles, my strength, the brazenness with which I had gone to look for him so many times? Nothing, really.

So, gradually, I started to let him go. I avoided seeing him for a year, making up one excuse after another. Peter deserved a better life than I could offer him. He deserved a better woman than me.

I found him again in the spring of 2006, in the private hall of a Paris bookshop. Sitting in the fourth row on the occasion of the presentation of my new book, this time on George Sand. I had decided to start a research on women who used male pseudonyms to publish their novels. It was a job I had thought about a lot, it was important to me. I decided to start, beginning with the one from which my mother had taken inspiration for my name.

He had hidden his face with a beard, wore a hat and thick glasses. But I recognized him immediately, at first glance. My husband and my children were with me. There was not even a brief greeting alone together, surrounded by journalists, critics and press officers. But he was there, and his presence tightened my heart, torn between pain and desire. I felt the memories press and pinch my eyes, to the point they watered. I remembered the morning he appeared at the university disguising himself in much the same way so as not to be recognized. And then in Frey's office, on the desk. We were crazy. But it was us and I already loved him, even without knowing it yet.

At the end of the presentation he approached me to shake my hand and ask for an autograph, like many other participants in the event.

'Congratulations, Mrs. Delamar. I really enjoyed your book.' His tone was detached, like his phrases of courtesy, his own gaze. His green eyes partly concealed behind the glasses expressed no feelings towards me. I felt a chill in my heart, so much that I wished I had not seen or recognized him. I would have preferred if he had not approached me. Until he pronounced those words. 'I don't know how much fiction there is in your biography of George Sand. But I confess that reading it I did nothing but think, Amantine... I wish it was real.'

I struggled to hold back my tears as I wrote the dedication and autographed the book. *"It will always be real, Peter. Amantine, little snob and egocentric intellectual."* I looked up at him, closing the book to give it back to him.

'I've done my best to make it real, I'm sorry I didn't always succeed.'

'I will always look for something real in your books, in your words, Mrs. Delamar. I like your way of writing and storytelling. Since your first book on John Keats.'

He had shaken my hand again. And this time I felt the heat emanating from the contact with his skin. Then he disappeared into the crowd. Without me being able to follow him to cry out that I still loved him, with all my heart, as I had never been able to tell him. That I always loved him, even if each of us was going our own way, getting on with our own life.

I should have avoided keeping him bound to me by writing those words on the front page of my book, but I couldn't resist. All I wanted in life was to be loved by him.

Then I saw him, last time, on a cold December day in 2008. On the occasion of Jacob's death. Or more accurate, J.D. Sanders. In the background "The Show must go on" by Queen, which he had requested himself, as he was a big fan of Freddie Mercury. And those same words were also so much ours, once again. So much ours they frightened me.

"Inside my heart is breaking
My make-up may be flaking
But my smile still stays on…"

We were saying goodbye to the one who had contributed to our union. To the one who had predicted to me that one day I would know what it meant to love. I had learned much more, actually. I also knew what it meant to suffer for love and for its loss.

Peter and I had grown up. During the funeral ceremony we now looked into each other eyes, no longer expressing any feeling or emotion in public. Or maybe we were just more trained to hide them.

For my part they were still there, even more intense than before, almost more desperate. I had become good at managing them, controlling them. I kept buying his CDs, one after the other. Even his videos, recordings of his concerts. I also bought the works of the artists with whom he collaborated. I read the serious reviews written about him. But for a while I completely avoided the tabloids. He had had relationships that I preferred not to know about. I had no right to be jealous, but I was, incessantly. And unfortunately in this now, there was nothing fun anymore, just for me an immense pain.

After the ceremony I had let everyone go, including him, remaining alone at Jacob's grave.

'Goodbye, Jacob.' I knelt down, stroking the tombstone gently. 'You're... one of the most beautiful people I've met in my life. Maybe the most beautiful ever. I'm sorry I wasn't there for you enough during your last moments... I'm sorry...'

I ran my hands over my face, sighing deeply. 'What can I do? Sometimes I think about what my life would have been like if that Sunday morning...' I found my face flooded with tears. 'But I have no regrets... No, I will never have regrets. Maybe I would never have known what it means...'

Being tight in his arms, once again. 'I have no regrets, too, you little snob and egocentric intellectual.'

'Peter...' Kneeling beside me, he wrapped me in his embrace. 'Peter, why did you come back? If they saw you here...'

I hugged him tightly, after almost two years in which I had to do without his warmth, his breath, his eyes on mine. I cried desperately on his shoulder and felt his tears mixed with mine.

How different we were from our first meeting. Of the two kids who just wanted to have fun, eat pizza and dance all night, there was nothing left. We had become two pale and blurry figures in dark coats, in which despair won, over will, over courage.

Pulling away from me, he took my face in his hands. 'Just for a minute. Let me look at you, sweetheart. Let me bring your eyes, your lips with me…'

'There's not much to look at, Peter. I got old, I'm tired…'

He was too. A few wrinkles furrowed his forehead and his eye contour, more than anything. And some white hair had started to appear at his temples. But nothing had changed for me, my feelings for him remained intact, indeed they had grown with time.

'On the contrary, you're so beautiful. Even more than before, Amantine…'

His green eyes so shiny, his lips. I couldn't resist and I kissed him, first clinging to him desperately, then stroking his face, drying his tears. I kissed him with all the passion I was capable of. In a cemetery, kneeling before Jacob's grave, running the risk of someone surprising us.

'Peter… Peter, there's one thing I have to tell you.' Was it the right time? Maybe not. But I had to take advantage of the strength that I felt reborn in my heart. We were together. In the presence of Jacob, if not physical at least spiritual. Yes, it had to be the right moment. 'Peter, my children…'

'I know, I know, baby. You did well choosing them, I understand you...' Peter kissed my forehead, then my lips again. He nodded, raising a smile.

'No, no. Peter, it's about…'

William. It was about William. There was a reason why I gave him that name. Not because I found it cute. A deeper reason. William Shakespeare. Shakespeare's sonnets. The one you had recited to me, asking me not to leave you.

'Mom…' Madeline's sweet, slightly suffering voice, behind me, hit me like a stab.

I got up suddenly, completely detaching myself from Peter. He stood up too, and embarrassed he waved to my daughter who was approaching us.

'We were... saying goodbye to Jacob for the last time.'

Any justification from me would have been useless, superfluous. I had no idea what Madeline had seen or heard. She was only thirteen. What judgment could this tender and beautiful teenager have made of me, whose eyes were so similar to mine?

'I know, Mom. But... I saw a guy who was taking pictures of you and...' Her anxious look passed from me to Peter, then came back to me.

'It doesn't matter, honey. Let's go home now.' I surrounded her shoulders with my arm, holding her to me.

'William and Dad have already gone. I didn't want to leave you alone here and I came back...' Madeline nodded, raising a smile. Her eyes continued to scan Peter, who had remained standing in front of us. Then unexpectedly she held out her hand. 'I... I'm Madeline.'

'I'm Peter...' He smiled, shaking her hand and gently stroking her hair. 'Take care of your mother, dear. She... was very close to Jacob. It's a great loss for us.'

Peter patted my shoulder fleetingly, to definitively say goodbye. I stood staring at him as he walked away, carrying my heart with him. He turned once more, however, hearing his name being called. But it wasn't my voice calling him back.

'Peter!' Madeline smiled at him, waving her hand. 'I'll take care of my mom. I promise.'

CHAPTER 56

The incompatible strangeness between me and Geoff had only increased. After the decision to let Peter go permanently, I tried to give my marriage another chance. The last one. I was looking for civil conversation with Geoff. After all he knew, it was completely useless to try to deny, or hide it. In the end I always gave myself the same justification, as I had done years before. I had never betrayed him with other men. Just with Peter Wiles, just with the only one that mattered to me.

The attempt had not worked. On the contrary, it made us even more alien and hostile than before. To the point that Geoff started drinking and more and more often reproached me for ruining his life. It was true, he was right. But as much as I was sorry, I couldn't change things. Or maybe I could. We could break up, really break up, as happened to many others. Our children were teenagers now, if we managed the situation peacefully, they might understand.

One morning when we found ourselves alone at home, I galvanized myself and decided to speak to him openly.

'Geoff, I was thinking... We've been through a lot, but...' His hostile gaze, his blue eyes expressing anger, were focused on me like sharp blades. I tried to express everything I wanted to say without interruption. 'You often reproach me for ruining your life. And it's true, you're right. So maybe we should just separate. You could still have the chance to start a new life with a better woman than me. The kids are grown up a bit now, they would understand if...'

'Are you willing to tell William and Madeline the reasons for our separation?' Geoff interrupted me, but he answered quietly, unperturbed. 'Because in that case you know they could choose between us. And you've never been their favourite, especially William's. Then, while you're at it, you could confess all the rest. It will be interesting to see their reaction.'

They would blame me, and they would hate me. I had never been a good mother, I had never been present and understanding enough, attentive of their needs. And Geoff, among other things, did nothing but remind me.

I didn't know if his close and deep connection with William had been calculated or born spontaneously. He couldn't have been so perfidious, so sadistic. But as far as my conduct was concerned, he was right, I could only admit it. I had been a disaster from all points of view.

The only aspect that was saved in me was my career. In the end it was precisely what mattered most to me about twenty years ago. I couldn't imagine that I would later consider it almost irrelevant, superfluous. Certainly, I was no longer the Amantine who Peter had loved, the little snob intellectual who he loved to make fun of. Nothing was left of her in me. Or maybe it was he who made me like that, and without his presence by my side I was fading, day after day.

'If you think you can get rid of me, you're wrong.' Geoff resumed talking before I had the alertness to reply. 'You'll be the one caught in the middle. You and your lover. They even took a picture of you hugging at a grave, you should be ashamed of yourselves!'

'You knew about him... you always knew. Why did you still want me, Geoff? After I left you, after...'

I didn't understand his fury. From the beginning, after my betrayals, I had never understood it. Why had he taken me back all those times?

'After you continued to betray me all these years?' Geoff crossed his arms and challenged me with a provocative smile. 'Because I knew you'd always come back to me. As I know it now, too. You will always come back to me because you are afraid. You are afraid to be really with someone, but you are even more afraid to be alone. Maybe you don't love me, but you don't love the other one either. You are afraid of your career now too, that's why a part of you rejects it. You wanted it until you actually achieved it, until you became someone in the academic field. Now it's almost a burden to you. You are afraid of your children, to tell the truth. So rather than risk losing them you prefer to persist in this situation. Do you see how well I know you, Amy? Better than him. And maybe even better than you know yourself.'

'No...' I shook my head, annihilated by his words. 'No... I'm not like that.'

I felt tears stinging my eyes. If this really was what he thought about me, why did he keep me bound to him? Why didn't he let me go? For anger, for revenge?

'And you are afraid to leave this world. After all, you are a superficial and conservative little woman, incapable of great passions and great gestures.'

Geoff sank the knife into my chest even more deeply. I understood only at that moment that the man didn't love me at all. Maybe he had never really loved me. Maybe he had wanted me, he had stayed with me and had only taken me back out of habit or for the sake of having a hold over me after my betrayal.

I didn't reply. I reached my studio, the room of my own, and locked myself in. Geoff had hurt me deeply. And he had succeeded so well because I recognized a kernel of truth in his words.

He was right, I was afraid, terribly afraid. I had been afraid to confess my love to Peter. Even Peter had never been that unbalanced, but I was the one to impose certain rules on our relationship. The one insisting on them constantly. The one who ran away from him instead of facing him. Always me, the one denying him the truth by hiding the secret that involved him too. And yet I had not changed, I was the same fragile and frightened creature. I realized that probably that truth was only one and I had reached the maturity to deal with it. I had learned what it meant to love, but I was still unable to love myself and to trust the people I loved. That was why I continued undaunted to condemn myself to unhappiness.

CHAPTER 57

The days, the months piled up on me, without mercy. Geoff's words had hurt me, but they led me to reflect on myself, on my behaviour. I had always looked for the best solution, I was convinced of this at least. I was beginning to understand that maybe it wasn't the best, but the easiest, especially for me. The one that wouldn't have forced me to face dramas and separations. I accepted my grief so as not to have others suffer the pain that would inevitably have poured over me, because it was me who would have been the cause of it. Combined with the disdain towards me. Geoff's, my children's, the rest of my family, friends, colleagues. And maybe even Peter's.

My everyday life remained suspended, studded with a series of shameful "ifs". If I had confronted Peter that night, if I had told him I was pregnant, if I had left Geoff when the children were still small. But now it was completely useless to complain, I was the main one responsible for the unhappiness of many.

Everywhere in the world couples separated. Often couples with small children. So too were some of our acquaintances. But not me, I remained anchored in a marriage without love, fearful of my husband's threats, worried about the judgment of the world. Geoff was not entirely wrong, calling me a superficial and conservative little woman.

But the truth, my truth, what was it? In addition to the son I was still denying Peter the other truth was hidden in Peter himself, in my relationship with him.

If he... Here it is, the truth behind which I concealed my biggest "if", probably the dominant one. If he hadn't loved me enough? Maybe it was precisely the fact that our relationship had been constantly facing opposition that it kept the flame alive. If he hadn't accepted me and our son? If he hadn't loved me with the same passion, the same intensity?

I didn't run that danger with Geoff, I didn't risk it. I had never risked anything with him. Our marriage had been a failure from the beginning. I had failed as a wife. Lately also as a mother, despite my efforts.

I hadn't feared failure, not even in the academic field. But Peter was still my happy island, my safe harbour. If I failed with him, I would have had nothing more, no one. Nothing to take refuge in, no dreams to feed on, no fire to keep alive, intact, incorruptible. No love to give all my heart to.

Here, Geoff was right, again! I was afraid. Madly, unreasonably, irrationally afraid. I risked, in my own way, but at the same time I demanded certainties. Not that this would protect me from pain, because in the last few years I had done nothing but suffer.

Having arrived at these little edifying conclusions about myself, I realized that I could no longer spend my time regretting the past. I could only live the present. Face it, above all. Talk to the kids. At sixteen and fourteen they would be able to understand. At this point I also had to risk they would choose Geoff by denying me, I was aware of that.

Then... then Peter's turn would come. Seek him and reach him, wherever he was. Tell him everything. Beg him to forgive my silence, ask him to allow me to stay with him if he still believed there was a chance for us.

I hadn't seen him since Jacob's funeral. I hadn't even tried to contact him during the following months. But his voice kept me company every day. I heard it penetrate my soul and stay there to warm my heart from the cold of his absence. As if every word he spoke was dedicated to me. Words of love, words of anger, indignation, accusation, revolt. I rediscovered them, every day different, strong and delicate, passionate and tender.

I realized that something in him was changing, once again. His output after Darkest Storm's times had greatly improved from every point of view. Although I wasn't a musician, it was clear enough to me that with his latest album, released in June, he was taking a different direction. More intimate, more suffered pieces. Less sung, in a way. His voice, in some passages hoarser, deeper, producing in my heart an uncontrolled, devastating vibration. He spoke of suffering, of loss... and also of a truth that he believed he knew but escaped him constantly.

I found our story in "The Lover's Song". Our song, the one we had composed together. I immediately recognized its sweet and slow melody. I never thought Peter intended to include it in one of his albums after so many years. I was convinced that he had archived or lost it during his various tours between Europe and the United States.

But I never imagined that I could listen to it one day, in the form of a real song. Maybe because it was totally different from the others and unsuitable for the albums that had preceded his latest work. It almost seemed like... Yes, it seemed like a part of Jacob had survived in Peter. His poetic, sweet, passionate components. Those components of pure beauty so important in J.D. Sanders's work that had led him, from time to time, to detach himself from the world, from the cynicism of those who thought themselves important, renewed, to become a mere human being among other human beings of any gender, of any social background.

Here was what was new in Peter Wiles. A man who was no longer just the light-hearted and irreverent boy I had met at the intersection of two streets on a Sunday morning in November. He was not even the singer who was struggling to express himself, to free his talent from the mediocrity that had been imposed on him by the musical genre of a band that had long been too narrow for him.

Peter had conquered himself. Probably his latest work would get less public success than the previous ones, perhaps even by the critics. But it was really him. My boyfriend. The man I had fallen in love with.

Those words, some of those words extrapolated from his lyrics... So true, so ours. They seemed like a message that I could no longer ignore.

"I don't even know why I chose you... You have never been like the rest of them... Not even close..."

"You know what you want but I'm not sure you still want me... I'm just a guy you met a Sunday morning... maybe forgotten..."

"So hate me whenever it pleases you, but if you are going to, do it now..." In a more modern key...Shakespeare's poem.

"It's not just a song for you... you're everywhere, everything. My friend, my lover, my deepest love..."

"Tell me your secret... hidden behind your eyes, your heart... your books, your promises... The lover's song is ours... My lover's song it's only yours... And I keep on waiting, waiting... waiting for you to say forever or goodbye..."

Maybe they were just words scattered in songs. Words that could be found anywhere. As many others. Maybe Peter had only taken a past story as an inspiration. But that story was ours.

Reach him and tell him everything. The truth. My secret that would become ours. Stay with him. Live with him and face the world in his arms. I was ready, finally. And if he still wanted me, mine would never be a so long, a farewell or a goodbye forever, but a together forever.

CHAPTER 58

Timing was not my ally. It had never been in my life. A few months, I told myself... I'll wait for the Christmas holidays to pass. I couldn't let the bomb blow up during the family yuletide celebration.

In the meantime, I still tried to contact Peter through his e-mail address, the one he had always used to communicate with me since his departure. Then I also tried to call him in America and on his private number. Nothing, no reply. Maybe he was moving around promoting his album; from his website he didn't seem to be on tour or visiting other countries.

Instead the bomb had blown up on me. Devastating, disruptive, cruel. While trying in every way to avoid them, I was used to seeing Peter on the covers of gossip magazines with beautiful women. Actresses, singers, models especially with whom they attributed flirts and relationships.

Every damned time my heart was in a grip that for a while prevented me from breathing. It was inevitable. What I once felt, those first little pangs of jealousy, were nothing compared to the feeling of dejection in which I felt myself collapsing. I felt betrayed. And yet the married one who had not wanted to give up marriage for years had been me.

I didn't think I had to endure worse. And the worst came when I read, in one of those magazines, Peter Wiles's wedding announcement with an actress, the young new Hollywood promise, Kendra Scott.

I didn't follow cinema attentively, but I had heard about her. Twenty-seven years old, beautiful and talented. She was the same age as me when I started my relationship with Peter. It would be a stylish wedding between two celebrities.

And I felt more than ever forgotten, put aside. I had never before felt so excluded from his life. And it was all my fault. I had definitely lost him now. Forever. Even if it was a completely different forever from the one I had imagined. It was a forever that broke all my illusion, that caused me a physical illness, the sensation of swallowing sand until I suffocated.

I was even more hurt by reading Peter's statements about his fiancé. He spoke of great love, of total emotional and physical harmony. I analysed how they looked into each other's eyes, as he was holding her side while she showed the engagement ring.

Kendra Scott had light brown hair in delicate waves that brushed her shoulders, clear and bright blue eyes, a perfectly oval and delicate face, full lips. In comparison I felt myself falling apart. Peter would no longer come to collect me, he would not be there for me anymore. He would not even see me in any comparison to her.

I had lost him irremediably. He had fallen in love with someone else, a beautiful young woman, who wasn't me. She had his heart, his body, his voice. I would be alone. And what had seemed to me written for the two of us, for our story, was just a song. Maybe just for that reason he had written it. To break our bond once and for all.

While he continued to wait forever, it was he who had been the one who said goodbye to me. He had left me alone with my secret, with my lies, with my fears, with the misery of my existence. I had lost his heart. And of mine there was nothing left but a cold shell destined to melt or burst. With another "if" that was to be added and to increase mercilessly the multitude of my remorse, of my regrets.

CHAPTER 59

More time. Days, weeks, months. Nothing left for me to do, but to remain silent. My pain, my defeat. Continue to play the part of the devoted wife. With William and Madeline however, I was making my best efforts, even if with poor results.

Most of the time I had the impression that William ignored me rather than answering me badly. Madeline, on the other hand, had a tender attitude with me, almost protective even if I couldn't understand her silences, the lack of intimacy towards me, as if she didn't trust me.

I remembered that day at the cemetery, at Jacob's grave. My daughter's promise, a girl only thirteen, to Peter. What had she seen? What had she heard?

The picture had appeared in a weekly magazine although we were portrayed from afar and I had my back to the camera. Despite everything, it was undoubtedly us. It was a single photograph, a frame, because none of the major magazines had wanted to create a scandal involving J.D. Sanders's name. Also, Peter and I were old hat. Our past relationship was well known now and two former lovers fondling each other at a mutual friend's grave was not a sensational scoop.

But Geoff had had time to see it and to point the finger at my immoral behaviour. Madeline hadn't talked about it anymore even though I often caught her staring at me confused, as if she was meditating on my intentions. And William... William was probably not aware of it or he was so indifferent towards me that he didn't mind it. He went in and out of the house like a guest, he didn't talk to me. I wasn't sure, but I had the feeling that he was gradually drifting away from Geoff too. And sometimes he assumed that tormented, restless and a little absorbed expression that inevitably reminded me of his father.

The wedding date was set in spring. I had done everything to forget that date, that day at the end of March. I asked for nothing more than to pass it, to overcome it. That day flew by me like any other day. I didn't want to know or see. Never.

So it had passed. Even that day, like many others that had preceded it. I thought something essential changed from the moment we were both married. It didn't. My feelings for him persisted unchanged. The world kept turning. The sky hadn't exploded, or the sun fallen. I had nothing else to do but to congratulate him who maybe had finally found the right woman, the one who would make him happy. I preferred not to know anything, not to read magazines, not to watch videos, not to receive any information. I had also stopped listening to him, closing everything that concerned him in a casket that I would not open anymore. It had been a painful but necessary rift.

Summer came. More and more often I found myself in tears without a real reason. Or rather, I accumulated motives for a while and then collapsed in the most unexpected and inappropriate moments and places.

I felt like a hurt child with a broken heart. And it was probably like that. My heart, still childish and maybe not entirely capable of loving, had been destroyed. I had nothing left to do than try to reassemble it and move on. I wouldn't replace Peter with another love. And I would never learn to love my husband, by now I was sure of it. But I was also certain that my children deserved a better mother. Above all, an adult, aware, responsible, rational mother. For this reason, I had to commit myself to become wise, to finally grow up, to mature. Gain their trust. And maybe one day I would be able to deal with the truth as well. I would find the way.

However, I still needed a few days off to recover my strength after the disappointment. Peter Wiles had managed to upset my plans in addition to my mental balance. But the truth was only postponed. I just had to understand how to act to reveal everything in the most painless way possible.

This pushed me to accept Rachel's invitation to follow her on a trip to Italy. She had promised her contribution in an art history manual on the main European museums. The meeting with the other authors was set up in Florence and she needed an interpreter because many of them were Italian and French. I knew hers was just an excuse to get me out of my state of prostration and dejection. But it was only for three days and I had a great need to change the environment and think about something that wasn't family, university or... him.

The meeting had been concluded in less than half a day, Rachel and the other authors had agreed on the parts to be divided. I was pleased to have been of help and take my mind off my everyday problems and anxieties. We had two free days left to visit the city, the museums and have fun in the shops. I had never loved shopping but now anything was fine to distract me.

'Maybe I shouldn't ask you, Amantine...'

After wandering through the city, Rachel and I found ourselves in a café in front of the Uffizi. I looked away, pretending to admire the happy flow of people around us. I wanted to disappear in some remote corner, maybe lose my memory and never come back. Rachel tilted her face, ran her hands over her light hair and didn't go on.

'Ask me, I already imagine...' I looked back at her. As much as I tried to escape I couldn't go very far, my thoughts always brought me back.

'Between you and Geoff... I mean, do you think there's a chance? I know it's none of my business, but... there are things I think you should know.' Rachel looked embarrassed. In fact, quite a bit, as if she expected me to anticipate what she didn't dare to talk to me about.

'I suggested to him to separate some time ago. Things between us haven't worked for years, many years... If only he had granted...' I sighed looking into her eyes, shrugged and shook my head. I was tired, morally and physically. 'From the beginning it didn't work, to tell the truth. We shouldn't have... I shouldn't have...'

'I don't know how to tell you, Amantine. So I'll just tell you even if it's not up to me. First because you're my friend... then because you have to know it to make your decision.' Rachel bit her lip. Her whole speech seemed to be a prelude to something that she hoped I could guess by myself. She remained silent for a few moments before continuing. 'In short... Geoff has another woman. I found out from Trevor, actually I found out by myself and he was forced to confirm it. I heard them talking in Trevor's study when Geoff came to London a few weeks ago. They believed I had already left, but I had forgotten a book. Of course, then I had a fight with Trevor who was encouraging him to betray you...'

'I hope you have made peace, I would be sorry...' I was more concerned about my friend's romantic situation than mine.

'Have you heard what I just told you, Amantine?' Rachel's eyes widened on me. She probably knew that there were problems between me and Geoff, but maybe she didn't suspect that we had come to the end of the line, quite a while back. He had a lover. And I didn't care.

'I cheated on him too, Rachel. And you know it. Before our marriage and even after. With the same man, no one else. Because I loved him. It's not a secret. Apparently now his turn has come, even if I had suspicions for a while.'

There wasn't much to say. In fact, I deserved it. And the truth was that Geoff could have all the women he wanted. I had been out of the picture for a long time. I had been deeply fond of him, but love was something else. Love, I had lost it forever and it would never come back to me again.

'Why did you marry him, Amantine?' I seemed to relive the same conversation I had with my mother some time before. 'You loved someone else, I know... Peter Wiles.'

'I shouldn't have.' I shouldn't have married Geoff. I shouldn't have loved Peter. Both things. 'The truth is that I don't even know if I love myself, since I've been so good at making myself unhappy for so many years. I tried... to do the right thing for me, for my children and also for Geoff, instead...'

'Why don't you try again, Amantine?' Try again? Try again to make my marriage work? No, it was impossible.

'Rachel, you just told me that my husband is cheating on me... not that I don't deserve it, but...'

I called the waiter with a wave. I needed another coffee to take a break and continue the conversation. Rachel didn't seem inclined to change the subject.

'A cappuccino for me, it's delicious here.'

I ordered for both. I had to make a change in my life, but I didn't know how, where, when.

'Anyway, I didn't mean that...' Rachel slightly narrowed her blue eyes, then she looked back at me. 'Why don't you get back Peter Wiles, Amantine? If you still love him, after all these years...'

'Because he just got married, Rachel. Don't you read the newspapers?' I blushed, it hurt me even to think about it. Instead of helping me, my friend was carelessly twisting the knife in my wound. 'And then... have you seen her? A young and beautiful actress. And, by now, I am...' I closed my eyes, biting my lips hard. 'I'm a poor, shattered, old, hopeless woman...'

Rachel sighed, raising her eyes to the sky. 'As soon as you go back to Paris, you sign up for a good self-esteem course, my dear. Do we want to try to lure some nice Italian guy in the meantime? In my opinion, you wouldn't have any difficulty. You have nothing less than that actress, you're just very sad and unhappy, that's it... and it shows.' Rachel's words were not comforting me in any way. They were dictated by friendship, not by reality. 'And anyway, are you convinced that that marriage is real? You know how the stars work... Maybe it's a charade, they only did it for the publicity.'

'No, Rachel. I really don't think so. Peter wouldn't do that, he's not the type, I...' I knew him well. He wouldn't do that. He wasn't like that. Even his first wife... I never thought he'd married her just for publicity and convenience. I was sure that at that moment he really wanted it.

'If you are so sure. Anyway, I read that he wants to put Shakespeare's poems and sonnets to music. I didn't think he was interested in literature.'

Rachel knew more than me. But since when did she start following Peter's career?

'Yes, he... he has always been interested.'

I wanted to change the subject. But I didn't know which one to bring up. I didn't want to think about Peter, Shakespeare, the two of us. About that sonnet that he had recited to me and that I had found in the song. I didn't want to think about him asking me not to leave him. About our second chance. I had been so stupid to miss that one too. I took comfort by thinking that probably between me and Peter it wouldn't work anyway, and he would eventually leave me for a younger, more beautiful, more successful woman, one from his own environment. No, Peter definitely wasn't thinking about me anymore. Maybe he still felt affection towards me, yes. But nothing more.

'So, do you think it's a coincidence?' Rachel smiled enthusiastically and thanked the waiter as he served us coffee and cappuccino. Then she became serious again, addressing me. 'Are you sure that testing the literature water is not a way to get closer, to stay linked to you?'

CHAPTER 60

By now I had reached the age and the life experience in which nothing could surprise me anymore. Not even the fact that my husband, one morning like many others, reached me in my private room and announced that he was leaving me to go and live with his "new partner". Yes, that's right, it's how he called her. She, the new partner, was twenty years younger than him, had been his student and was expecting a baby. And he wanted to do things right.

I looked at him almost without feeling any emotion, clinging to the book I was reading as a lifeline. I only wondered how he, who had never wanted to let me go and had used all the means in his power to prevent me, announced to me the separation so frankly, from one day to the next, expecting me to accept without replying.

A part of me wanted to create problems for him and dramas out of rage, for revenge. But it was only a small part of me. In fact, I couldn't behave like a deceived and betrayed wife. Because even though I actually was, I couldn't feel like that. The truth was that I didn't even feel I was his wife.

'I would have preferred to have known it before,' I simply said. 'I mean... I would have preferred it to have happened before.'

Now all was useless, even to burden him with his behaviour. But I couldn't help but think about it. Yes, definitely, I would have preferred to have a chance too.

'You'd go back to him, wouldn't you?'

I sensed a vibration of anger in Geoff's voice, but I didn't lose my cool. Maybe he forgot that it was he who left me, it was he who was expecting a baby from another woman. I wondered what his upright father would have said. But perhaps, after the stroke that struck him on a late summer night, there was very little he could say now. Of course, at the end of October Geoff hadn't waited a long time.

'I wouldn't go back to him. I would stay with him. I was already back.'

I couldn't resist that kind of cruelty, more or less unnecessary. It was my fault, but Geoff had forced me to stay by his side. He could start a new life, I had lost everything.

I looked at his blue eyes that seemed so terribly tired now, rimmed, the marked wrinkles on his forehead. He had aged badly. Maybe it was my fault, I hadn't made his life easy. Or more likely, dealing with the passing years is not the same for everyone. I wondered if he made this new beginning, to get the happiness he had never had with me. Maybe the new partner would give him everything he had always missed.

At least I had been happy, even if only for a while, even if I had never realised it. I hadn't even managed to savour that happiness. I had loved and had been loved, always without realizing it. However, I still had the memories that I could recall in my time of need.

'Now it's too late, I guess.'

Of course it was too late. It even seemed that Geoff had done it on purpose, calculated according to the scheme of a cruel revenge. Let me free, knowing that between me and Peter it would no longer be possible. Or maybe it was just a treacherous joke of fate that unfortunately had never been my ally.

'Yeah...' I didn't know what else to add. In fact, the truth was that I didn't want to show him my suffering, my regret. I got up from my desk and turned around, towards the bookcase behind me.

'Do you believe me if I tell you I'm sorry, Amy?'

He flanked me, reached for me and touched my shoulder. I moved and took a step back to keep him from touching me.

'No, I don't believe you. I know I've made my mistakes but you...' I hid my face in my hands. I retraced our history in a few moments. So many years. So many years lost, thrown away. 'You should have left me when I betrayed you. Insult me, throw me out of the house. I have not been able to do it, I...'

I no longer wanted to deal with him. But being already in my study, in my shelter, I had no other place where I could hide. By now everything had been said, I just wanted to interrupt the conversation.

I left the room and went to the living room. Maybe I just needed to leave the house for a while. To go for a walk in the centre, along the Seine. Or take refuge in a cafe, in some bookshop, in some flea market. In short, to find any way not to think about what could have been and had not been, instead.

'You are trying to lay your blame on me! But I won't let you!' Geoff unexpectedly followed me and grabbed me by the wrist, tugging at me. I stared at him, almost in disbelief. 'If you... if you were not so infatuated with that damned singer...'

I pushed him back to get free. 'You never wanted to understand this, Geoff. I wasn't infatuated... and he's not...' Did he really believe that it was that, that attracted me to Peter? The fact he was a singer? A celebrity? 'I never cared about who he was! It was him that I wanted... it's him that I... Or maybe that's what disturbs you, that has always bothered you. That I saw him as an ordinary boy for whom I had genuine feelings. The fact that you could treat me like a stupid little girl who had lost her mind for a singer from a successful band consoled you!'

'I should have let you go and get fucked by that wretch! Now I understand it, finally. Instead of getting to...'

Geoff's fury towards me would never end, I understood. His false understanding was only an act. I wondered if it was also the claim to start a new life with a much younger woman. Show the world that he had done better than me, in the end. Whatever his intent was, I didn't care anymore.

'Instead of raising his son?' I barely breathed, narrowing my eyes.

'I took pity on you, don't you understand?' Geoff grabbed me hard by my shoulders. 'And I thought... I deluded myself that you could love me if I did this for you! What future could you have with an alcoholic who takes you to a party and then takes drugs until risking an overdose? With someone who...'

I stood petrified, looking at him, without the strength to wriggle away from him, to free myself from his hands that were clenching my shoulders like a vice. How... how could Geoff know?

'You were not there... How could you know what happened that night?'

I saw him blushing. 'I... You told me when we were...'

'No! I've never talked about it! Never, with anyone!' I regained consciousness of my actions and freed myself with a tug. I had raised my voice. Worse, I was screaming. I strove to remember. 'I certainly never told you! I'm sure!'

I had only talked about it with Peter. With Rachel... but I told her about Peter's betrayal, that I caught him with another woman. Not that he took drugs, because at the time even I wasn't aware of it.

'I might have read it in the newspapers... That bloke has had those problems all his life, I mean...'

Geoff backed off looking away from me. He was lying to me, it was obvious. And I... I still felt too upset to deal with the situation lucidly.

Geoff took the opportunity to turn his back, cross the living room and walk the few steps that separated him from the main door.

'Tell me the truth, damn it! Geoff, how the hell did you know?'

I wouldn't allow him to leave like this. I demanded answers.

If Geoff knew that Peter had been drugged... he probably knew about it even before he married me. Even before I knew it myself! He didn't even listen to me... When he reached the door, he opened it ready to leave, to escape to seek shelter in the future that awaited him, without bothering about me and my despair.

'Tell me or I swear I'll make your life a living hell! I will never grant you the divorce. I'll force you to stay with me, like you...'

I put my hand on my chest, trying to catch my breath. I didn't feel very threatening, I couldn't even scream anymore, even my voice had stuck, scratching my throat. I felt devastated, more than anything else. My heart was about to explode, I was sure. I would probably die, without hope of salvation, of redemption, of truth.

'Amy...' Geoff came back to me and put his arm around me, supporting me. I had the sensation of fainting, of slipping to the ground as if my feet had lost contact with the floor, I no longer felt its consistency. 'I... Amy, I swear I only heard about it later.'

'Tell me... the truth, please...' I clung to his shirt, banging my fists on his chest, but almost without force, without energy. 'Please... I need to know...'

His blue eyes so shiny, so distraught would have moved me to pity in another moment. But now I no longer felt anything, no feelings. He knew...

'I loved you... I would have done anything...' Geoff took my face in his hands, looking me in my eyes. 'But not that... I wouldn't have risked killing for you. I knew it only later, you must believe me.' He breathed deeply while I was losing track of time, of space and especially of his words. 'It was an agreement between the band's manager and... my father. That man, Simon Jennings, wanted to stop Peter Wiles from leaving the band at any cost. My father wanted you to leave Peter. So...'

'So they made sure I left him, drugged him and...' I closed my eyes. And then my life had been destroyed. And also Peter's. 'When did you find out, exactly?'

'Amy...'

'When did you find out, Geoff?' I thought I was going crazy. Peter. I knew they had hurt us. That they had separated us. I also knew that it was my fault, I should have stayed...

'A few months after you left London. When you had already settled in Paris...' Geoff's voice was calm again, even though he still looked at me fearfully. He seemed torn, exhausted by a truth that had escaped him in an extreme moment of anger towards me but that he didn't believe he had to face. He was probably willing to hide it forever, instead of being forced to confess everything. 'That man was dangerous, Amy. He didn't want Peter Wiles to leave the band, it would be his source of income for years... But Peter was constantly threatening to drop everything since he was with you. My father had contacted him to convince him to put himself between you and Peter and create problems, he had given him some money. He didn't mean that way, but ... The situation got out of hand. They agreed to give Peter a small dose during a performance, a tablet dissolved in water, I'm not sure. Then they had to make sure that you saw him with another woman who was willing to take him to a room... If you cared about him, you would have left him. That party was the perfect opportunity, but... the truth is that Jennings didn't just want to drug Peter, he wanted him dead. He knew he would leave them anyway, as soon as possible. He must have thought that the sudden death of a band member could increase interest in everyone else... You know how it happens. As soon as a celebrity dies, sales of all that he has produced skyrocket… And so the band, in his memory, would continue to be successful, allowing him to make a lot of money. If he had left them on his own initiative, however... So they increased the dose, making my father participate in the plan, after having implemented it. The blame would have fallen on Peter Wiles, he already had alcoholism and drug addiction problems...'

I had no words. Maybe I didn't even need them. Peter. They could have killed him. And all because of me. I felt an inexpressible pain that spread from the centre of my chest all over my body, numbing my limbs. They had taken advantage of my feelings to weave a cruel and perverse plan. And I had done nothing but follow the script that had been written for me.

'I loved him... I was expecting his baby...' I found myself repeating something I had been aware of for almost twenty years now.

'I know, Amy. I... I was afraid something would happen to you. You would have gone back to him immediately if I had told you. You'd be back in his world, abandoning yours, ours.' Geoff sighed, shaking his head. 'I don't want to justify my actions... The truth was that I wanted you for me, as well. I would have done anything to keep you if I have to be honest... Anyway, he was a drug addict, an alcoholic, he would have just met his fate if it happened...'

'I... I hate you!'

I felt fragile, lost. Peter... How could they think of hurting him? That evening was immediately before my eyes, for the umpteenth time. His smile, his words, his way of looking at me, of holding me. And the man standing in front of me, the man I had married... knew and had kept silent, deceiving me for almost twenty years.

I couldn't hold myself back anymore. I no longer wanted to hold back. I could only vent my anger, my despair. I hit Geoff with a slap that was so strong that he was baffled. Then again and again...

He didn't react at first, then he managed to free himself away from me. He grabbed me by the wrists, clutching them violently, so much so that I feared he meant to break them.

'My God, calm down Amy... calm down or you'll hurt yourself...'

'You hurt me... you...'

In tears, I was struggling to wriggle free, to hit him again.

'You're crazy... raving mad...' I was forced to stop. The voice and the look of my son, a few steps away from us, expressed pure disdain and resentment. For me. Exclusively towards me.

'William... William, listen to me...'

What could I tell him? The truth, there was nothing left. It was time. My turn had come. He had to know what they had done to us. He had to meet his father at last. Maybe it was too late, maybe he would never forgive me. But he couldn't continue to believe in a lifetime of lies, of deception. A life that I had helped to create but in which I'd fallen into without the ability to free myself.

'Go to hell! I won't stay here with you...' In his eyes I saw Peter's eyes. Peter's eyes looking at me with hatred. What had I done? Growing up, William's voice was beginning to sound like Peter's voice, however, now his tone was such, that never before had I ever felt him so hostile towards me. 'You're just a shabby slut! It was all your fault, you ruined everything! I don't want to see you ever again!'

Did I deserve these words from him? Probably I did. I stood petrified as I watched him going out, leaving our home. Where would he go? What would he do? I should have found something to stop him, to get him back. But I had the sensation of living the scene from the outside, as if I were more aware of it than being part of it. As in my whole life I had been a helpless spectator. I was losing him, just as I had lost his father.

'Amy... he'll get over it, he didn't mean it...'

Geoff's voice called me back to reality. I nodded without even listening to him, without looking at him. He had taken everything from me. Or at least he had contributed more actively than I thought. The love of my life had risked dying and I was involved. My husband knew it. And now I had lost my son too.

Without another word, Geoff moved towards the entrance. I looked up to see the door closing after he had left the scene. From our home and from my life.

CHAPTER 61

As much as I felt lost and disoriented, it was up to me to take decisions. Maybe it had been good to lose everything, after all. Especially for someone like me, always too attached to her certainties. My world, the one that oppressed me but in which I had persisted exclusively, was crumbling and I had nothing left to stay anchored to beyond myself.

My husband had decided to leave me. Finally, maybe, it had been the most sensible thing he had done in his life. Even my son had left our home. He had gone to a friend's house and then took shelter with my parents. He had inherited from my mother an almost crazy scientific passion for the universe, satellites, planets, space. Something for which I had never shown the slightest interest. This led them to deepen their bond, especially in recent years. A fortune in this devastating situation, William was only seventeen years old and I couldn't allow myself think he was alone in danger.

William was a good boy. He despised me but he would never get into trouble. I... I had to admit it, at least to myself. My fear was that he would get into trouble, as Peter had begun to do at his age. It didn't have to happen, I couldn't allow it.

Madeline had chosen to stay with me, instead. Maybe because the situation with Geoff would be too embarrassing. Or she didn't feel like abandoning me as well. She watched me, as always, in silence. She was aware of the separation and of the reasons as well, rather of the triggering reason. She knew about the baby Geoff was having with another woman. But she had received the news calmly, without losing her composure.

'Dad told me. About the baby.' It was her comment about it. Then she had scanned me in her somewhat absorbed, almost inscrutable way. 'He asked me where I would like to stay... I'll stay here if you want me. I'd like to stay with you.'

I had a daughter more mature than her age. Maybe she was my lifeline. The only one I had left.

'Of course I want you here with me, honey.' I forced myself to smile, kissing her cheek. 'We're left alone, but... without men around we can do pyjamas parties day and night.'

'And watch so many comedies eating chocolate and popcorn!'

Madeline gave me a radiant smile, her eyes full of tears. I wished a happy life for her, and I realized that from then on, I would do anything for her to have it, to make all her dreams come true.

I decided to talk to my parents. I hadn't explicitly announced my separation from Geoff yet and there were issues that couldn't be dealt with fleetingly or during a coffee catch-up.

I joined them one morning, taking advantage of the fact that the kids were both at school. Sitting on the living room sofa, in a few words I told my mother and my father about my conversation with Geoff, including what they had tried to do to Peter Wiles during that party about eighteen years earlier.

From the contrite expression of my father I understood that the news didn't catch him completely unprepared. And not just the one concerning my separation.

'I suspected it.' He added no more, sighed deeply and adjusted his glasses on his nose. 'Some of Raymond Carter's conversations, Geoffrey's father, had led me to believe he was involved in some plot against that singer. But I was convinced that between you and him it was a flash in the pan, a crush, it wouldn't have lasted anyway...'

Perfect. My father, Frederick Delamar, a great diplomat, involved in a shady drug deal and attempted murder. There was no salvation for me. And I didn't have the strength nor the desire to argue, to fight, to cry out against my world that in the end had been the cause of my failure, of my defeat.

'We have nothing left to say…'

I looked from him to my mother. I shook my head and got up, ready to withdraw.

'Amantine, you can't leave this way!' My mother's dark eyes stared at me, almost hostile. 'You must take on your responsibilities too. Years ago I told you, if you can remember, that maybe it was time to think about a separation with Geoff. Why didn't you do anything about it? Explain to me why…'

'Leave her alone, Antonia... After what Geoffrey has just done to her…'

My father's conciliatory tone intervened to stop the questions and unfinished businesses with my mother. She was right. And I knew it.

'No, Dad. Mom is right. It was mostly my fault.' I bit my lips to hold back my tears. 'I... I was scared. I am still, actually. I'm desperately looking for someone to share the responsibility of my mistakes. Someone to unload this pain of mine because I can't stand it alone, it's unbearable. I tried to avoid the worst in all these years, until I was overwhelmed.' I went back to sit down and prepared to continue, twisting my hands. 'If you believed that between Peter and I was just a crush, you were wrong. But I don't blame you for this, I believed it too. However... it has been going on for almost twenty years. For this reason Geoff left me. I would have preferred that he did it first, to be honest. Between me and Peter it never really started, but it has never finished. I believe... that we would have been happy if we were allowed to be. If I had allowed myself to be.'

A deep sigh. My parents stared at me in silence. Both. Almost as if they didn't dare to speak.

'And I realize that the biggest impediment to my happiness was just me. Mom... you're right when you say I should have thought about separating from Geoff years ago, instead of waiting for him to get rid of me. I should have faced the situation, tell the truth to Peter, to everyone, to myself. Being with Peter, with the children... Fighting against Geoff who would surely

have prevented me from taking them with me. Tell Peter that...'
I paused. I had to say it. For the first time I had to say it. I had
never expressed it aloud, never so clearly, not even with Geoff.
'Tell Peter that William is his son.'

I closed my eyes so as not to be forced to deal directly with
their reaction. But then I opened them wide. I had nothing to be
ashamed of. On the contrary, there were many things I had to be
ashamed of, I was spoiled for choice. But not that one. I loved
Peter. And there hadn't been a moment in my life when I
regretted keeping William.

'We already imagined it, Amantine.' My mother's tone was
calm, peaceful. 'The break up with Peter, and then you were
going back and seeing Geoff again... Getting married so hastily,
when it was obvious that you never loved him...'

'I... I was able to hurt everyone, including myself.' I
shrugged. What else was there to add? 'But at least I'm relieved
that Peter is fine and happy now. After all... Geoff's father was
paralyzed and probably will not recover now, Simon Jennings
had no luck after the band's breakup, no one wanted him
anymore. I just have to put together the pieces of my life once
and for all. First of all... tell everything to Peter as soon as
possible, even if it's too late for us now. He must know that
William is his son.'

CHAPTER 62

Divorce documents. Geoff hadn't wasted time. He had acted decisively and resolutely, I had to give him credit. He had pointed out, in a telephone conversation, that with the baby on the way he would prefer to speed up the process. Obviously, I consented to everything. He would leave me the house and custody of the kids he would see according to the terms of the consensual separation.

With Madeline, the situation remained stable. She was always my sweet little girl. I just prayed that time and life would never change her. William, however... he tolerated me; from the way he attacked me while witnessing the quarrel between me and Geoff, I had feared the worst. But he preferred to stay with my parents or at a friend's house. I watched over him without bothering him, without annoying him further, aware that sooner or later it would be time to reveal the truth to him as well.

My intention, however, was to face Peter first. Telling everything to William with the knowledge that his father would accept him would be easier for me and for him too. No, easy wasn't the right word. Less shocking, perhaps. Less traumatizing. That my parents knew it already was a relief.

The problem that I faced was how to contact Peter. I hadn't succeeded when I tried the last time. Maybe he hadn't wanted to answer me on purpose because of his marriage. If that was the reason, he probably would continue not to answer me.

I also felt obliged to let Peter know what they tried to do to him during that party. It was his right to know everything. He no longer had any relationship with Simon Jennings as far as I knew, but by warning him he could take precautions for the future. That environment was dangerous... No, any environment could become so, surrounded by the wrong people.

Time, especially in these last years, seemed to have no mercy on me. Another year had almost flown by and I had made up my mind to talk to Peter before William turned eighteen. Between November 2010 and February 2011 there was not much time left. It was ironic that Peter and our son were born in the same month, almost the same day.

Not receiving an answer and discarding all the other unattainable options, I had only one option left. Try searching for Peter at his London home. I was pretty sure I wouldn't find him, but maybe... Maybe I would find Gordon. Maybe I could beg him to get in touch with Peter for me, to report my message to him.

This time I really needed to see him, to talk to him urgently. More urgently than all the other times. And I also had a great desire. Selfishly, I dreamed of finding him in front of me, looking into his eyes, studying his features, stroking his face. To feel, for the last time in my life, the sensation of his gaze on me.

I reached Notting Hill with my heart in turmoil. I felt even more tense than the first time. Indeed, of all the times I had come back to look for him after many years. And I was certainly more desperate than ever because of the feeling that Peter had no intention of either seeing me or talking to me. That he had built a happy life with another woman. Not that he didn't deserve it. He had every right.

I stopped in front of his house. I joined my hands and intertwined my fingers tightly, almost to the point of hurting myself.

'Please... Please, Gordon...' I sighed to myself.

I didn't even dare ring the bell. I was hoping in my heart that Gordon would anticipate my call as it had happened other times when, seeing me standing in front of the house, he had opened the door.

No, I couldn't wait for hours and make my fate depend on destiny, on chance, on the luck that Peter's English butler looked out of one of the windows, saw me and decided to come and open it for me.

I rang and waited. No reply. I tried again. Two, three times. I had to be patient, give him enough time to get to the door. Unless... Peter had permanently left the house, abandoned it or sold it to others. Of course, now his life was elsewhere.

I looked down, disappointed. Everything was lost now. Even the house where my love for him was born. I retraced its interior in my mind. The living room, the sofa, the shelf with his books, the kitchen. The stairs leading to the upper floor, our room. Even the one where I got ready that evening, the dress I had worn. Where they had dressed me, styled me, put make up on. Then I had come down to him and...

'Madam...' I heard someone clear his throat. A man. 'Madam, are you looking for someone?'

Looking up I saw a young blond boy at the top of the steps in front of the door. Pale, gangly, he looked about thirty years old.

'I... I'm looking for Peter Wiles...' I sighed, frowning.

'I'm sorry, Madam. No Peter Wiles lives here.' Perfect accent, nothing to say. Gordon's rejuvenated photocopy.

There was still the chance that he would tell the truth. That the house no longer belonged to Peter. But I had to try again.

'Can I talk to Gordon? He knows me.' I sighed more deeply, struggling to hold back the emotional tension.

'Gordon is...' The young blond man narrowed his eyes and shook his head with a slightly desolate expression.

'Oh no, my God... Gordon...' So I lost Gordon too? Of course, he was old. And it had been years since the last time.

'No, Madam. I mean... Gordon is on holiday with his wife until mid-January. I replace him when he is not here and when... well, when we wait for Mr. Wiles in London.' Gordon's substitute opened up, with somewhat vague smile, losing some of his stiffness and composure. 'You're... a friend of Mr. Wiles, aren't you? I recognize you now.'

A friend. A refined way of saying that he recognized his master's lover. Or maybe one of his lovers. Maybe he had seen me in some newspaper years ago. Or... It wasn't the time to get lost into inconclusive reflections.

'I'm Amantine Delamar. I need to talk to Peter. It is necessary for him to contact me, urgently. Maybe he won't want to do it, maybe... But I beg you, it's important... really...'

I couldn't even put together a meaningful phrase, my voice trembled. A shame thinking that I was a literature university teacher. How could I be convincing to that young man with a clean and virtuous expression, he who was not Gordon, he who didn't know me as well as Gordon?

'Don't worry, Madam. I'll deliver your message to Mr. Wiles. I'll make sure he contacts you as soon as possible.'

The young man whose name I didn't know nodded with a conciliatory smile. He seemed almost pitied at my state. I had to have looked desperate. In fact, I was.

'Thank you. Thank you so much.'

I gave him a note, he took it from me up at the gate. I wanted to ask permission to enter the house for only a few minutes, but realized that it would be too much to ask.

When he went back inside, I was still there. It wasn't the place. It was not even that particular home. It was him, Peter. My heart was with him, it belonged to him. Peter was my home and he would be forever. Wherever he was.

CHAPTER 63

I lived waiting for a message from him, a call from him. I stayed a few days at Alain and Marianne's house in London before returning to Paris. I didn't want to leave the kids too long. William and Madeline needed me. Or maybe it was me who needed them.

'Amantine...' I immediately recognized his voice, as soon as I picked up the phone to a private number.

'Hello, Peter...'

Just hearing him say my name caused me a deep turmoil, a kind of heat that rose from my chest to block my breath. And the tears involuntarily filled my eyes, clouding my sight. Fortunately, I was alone in my study.

'I know you looked for me.'

His tone remained detached, however. It wasn't him. I mean, it wasn't the usual Peter and it wasn't his usual way of talking to me.

'Yes, Peter. I've been looking for you for a while and so... I went to London, to your house...' Needless to underline the obvious. He already knew that I had gone looking for him. 'Here, I... I need to see you.'

'Why?'

No, it definitely wasn't the usual Peter. My Peter. But it was also normal, I think. He was no longer my Peter, for a while now.

'I can't tell you on the phone... Peter, please...'

Since I knew him it had never happened. I never had to beg to see him. I was talking to the man who came back just to meet me, who ran to me even if he was out of town. Out of the country, as well.

'Amantine, I'm sorry, but I'm busy.' Sure, I knew it. My eyes narrowed and I nodded sadly, even though he couldn't see me. I heard him sigh at the other end. Wherever he was he had never been so far from me. 'I mean... I have a lot of work on at this time.'

'I understand, but I...' How could I make him understand that mine wasn't a whim? I really needed to see him. 'Peter, as soon as you have a moment. It will take only a few minutes. Tell me where, I'm willing to reach you.'

Actually, I wasn't sure that it would only take a few minutes. To confess to him the truth yes, certainly they would be sufficient. To tell him that his manager and my ex-husband's father had agreed to separate us, to drug him with the intention of killing him. To tell him that when I escaped in despair, I was pregnant with his son...

Yes, a few minutes would surely be enough. But to accept and assimilate everything, I had no idea how long it would take him. Days, weeks, months, years... Maybe all his life.

'Okay, listen to me...' I sensed a sort of inclination in his voice, as if he was yielding to a compromise while keeping himself cold and detached. 'I'll let you know, Amantine. As soon as I can.'

'Peter...' The temptation to tell him at least the part about my separation from Geoff was irresistible. But I held back to prevent him from thinking that this was the main reason for my call and that I was expecting something from him. And it wasn't like that, although I couldn't deny the hope that the news would provoke some reaction in him. 'Thank you, Peter... I'll look forward hearing from you, then.'

The message was clear. I still loved him. He didn't love me anymore, though. He had never been so cold with me. He had never treated me with so much detachment. But it was obvious. There was another woman by his side. A young, beautiful, successful woman.

I put my hand on my forehead. I feared that my head would explode, struck by an intense and sudden pain. It hurt. It hurt too much, the awareness of having lost him. My most remote illusion had been destroyed by his voice. His voice that once asked me "Amantine... do you want to make it real?"

I shivered and stroked my arms. Sitting on the armchair in front of my desk, I raised my legs, drawing them to my chest. It would never be real for him again. Never again. In any case, it wasn't for myself that I looked for him. It was for him. For our son. My suffering, this time, took second place.

CHAPTER 64

I had nothing left to do but to divide myself between work and children. Waiting for Peter to find, among his various commitments, a few minutes for me.

With Madeline, the situation was stable. She was quiet and tended to give a lot fewer problems than a common teenager, even if I suspected that she wasn't expressing herself clearly with me.

William remained a world apart. He had come back home and seemed to have calmed down, but soon he would turn eighteen and I was afraid his was just a sort of quiet before the storm. For his part, towards me, he had created a curious competition in which he tried to show me that he was able to achieve better results than I did in the school environment. The danger of him falling into harmful addictions didn't seem to exist. But he never revealed his dreams, his aspirations, to me. I didn't even know what course of study he wanted to undertake.

Both my children, as by tacit agreement, didn't express themselves about Geoff's decision to leave us to start a new life. William no longer blamed me for the ruin of our family, but at the same time I doubted that he had forgiven me.

My mother had been more successful than me in gathering his confidences. I heard from her that Geoff didn't want him with him, in the house he shared with his new partner.

'Obviously...' I couldn't deny being upset by Geoff's choice to remove us from his existence. As far as I was concerned it was understandable, but he also involved the kids, William above all.

'I don't think it's for the reason you believe...' My mother was more condescending than I was towards my ex-husband. 'Geoff is just trying to build a new life and for now his situation has not yet stabilized. He loves the kids... both. I've talked to him.'

'Apparently you have a better channel of communication than me with anyone...' I sighed, sipping the tea in front of me. 'I inspire coldness and detachment in everyone, lately. William can't stand me.'

'It's not like that, but...' My mother, as usual, was working to keep control of the situation. I wasn't able to act lucidly, maybe I had never been. 'It's not an easy time. And when you tell him... Well, it will be even less. But sooner or later you will have to do it. Did you manage to talk to Peter?'

'No. He called me and told me he would contact me as soon as he was available for a meeting...' I bit my lips and refrained from going on. Three weeks had passed, and he hadn't called me back yet. By now the second week of December had passed. Maybe he would come back to England for the Christmas holidays, but I couldn't be sure. 'He may have forgotten it or not have the slightest intention. And I don't know what to do. I've always had very bad timing, unfortunately. Or it's destiny that enjoys playing with me. And then I don't even know how... how can I give him such news? After all these years? Apart from my divorce... Tell him they would have killed him... But above all, talk to him about William... Anyway, if he doesn't contact me, I'll have to decide to go and look for him myself.'

I was in Peter's hands. Literally. I had to submit to his decision. Peter, Geoff, my children. I no longer had control of my life, of my future. But maybe, by taking an account of my past and my present, I had never really had it.

'Amantine...' My mother leaned towards me, barely touching my hand with hers. 'You know that I have a rational mind. I have never been in such a situation myself, so I don't know how to advise you. But based on the facts, on what I know about this story... You know that man, his character, his strength, his weakness... so much so that you would have left everything for him. You will find the way. About the rest, I give you less rational and perhaps much more trivial advice. But it's the one they recommend in most love stories. Don't think too much. Follow your heart.'

CHAPTER 65

Almost another month had passed. The Christmas holidays were over, a new year started. No news from Peter, apart from those I was constantly looking for on the internet and on his website. I was hoping to find out where he was or maybe get some news about his public and private life.

I had repurchased his CDs. The new ones and also the first ones, those with Darkest Storm. From time to time I lost myself looking at his face portrayed on those covers. He was about William's age. Fortunately, he didn't look embarrassingly like him, but he had the same gaze, the same colour and shape of eyes. When he squinted them and stared at me with scorn or contempt, he became even more like him. I was able to find some photos of Peter's other son, Matthew. That kid, yes, looked like a photocopy of Peter as a teenager. Although he probably had got his mother's blue eyes.

I ran my finger over Peter's image, the picture that portrayed him so young, rebellious and bold. Then I hid everything in the drawer of my desk, as relics of a secret past even though I no longer had a husband from whom to hide my passion for another man.

In mid-January I lost hope. I decided that I would not return to look for him to beg him again. Or maybe, considering the importance of what I had to reveal to him, I should.

While I was torn between trying to remove his thought forever and the necessity for him to know the truth, I finally received his communication. A message to my e-mail address. Formal, impersonal, almost telegraphic. He was in London for a few days. If I wanted to reach him at his house, he was willing to spend a few minutes of his time with me.

I immediately booked the flight and announced to the university that I would be absent for two days for personal problems. I prepared a bag with the strictly necessary. I called my mother and asked her to take care of the kids. I wouldn't spend more than two days to complete my mission. Arrive in London, talk to Peter and return to Paris. But it was the upheaval that I would bring into his life, in everyone's life, that terrified me.

I lived the departure and the journey as if dragged by events, almost without my active participation. When I arrived in London, I went to Alain's house to leave my baggage and to prepare for the meeting. I tried to dress in the simplest way possible; cream-colored shirt, dark jacket and trousers. I untied my hair and wore just a bit of makeup. I wasn't going to impress him or attract him, but I didn't want to show myself too destroyed by the signs of time and circumstances.

And in a moment, I found myself there again. Notting Hill, outside his home. And what scared me the most was the feeling that I was getting ready to face an enemy, a hostile person. Not Peter.

The very idea hurt me, wounded me. I forced myself several times to review the speech that I had ready for him, as if I was repeating the notes for a lesson, finally arriving at a conclusion and withdrawing as painlessly as possible.

My plan was well outlined. I would talk to him about my divorce and then reveal to him what Geoff had discovered about that party. Finally... William.

But unfortunately, it wasn't a matter of notes for a lesson, so I could structure a line by creating links between one topic and another. It was life. Ours. And Peter wouldn't remain silent to listen to me as armless as my students. Peter would demand answers, Peter would react. Although cold and distant towards me he wouldn't remain indifferent to such news.

It was Gordon who came to open the door for me. I just had time to greet him and inquire about his health. He replied with a vague smile and helped me to slip off my coat before retreating looking a little lost, leaving an atmosphere of silence and palpable tension reigning in the house. Probably among all the moments I had expected over the years to talk with Peter I had chosen the worst.

I saw him sitting on the couch, at his usual place. He kept his eyes on me. Not a smile, not a word. He didn't even give a sign of wanting to get up to welcome me, to greet me. He looked fit, in his sportswear. Jeans and a green military shirt that made his eyes stand out. I found him more charming than ever, but with a look of weariness that had nothing to do with his physical appearance. An emotional weariness.

'Peter...'

I almost didn't dare to approach him, without his explicit encouragement. I had to force myself to move a few steps towards him.

'Amantine...' He sighed deeply, narrowing his eyes, then opening them up again and scanning me almost in anger. 'You have no idea... how much I wanted to avoid meeting you again. How I would have preferred not having to see you ever again.'

'Yes, I do. I understand.'

I stopped and gripped my hands so hard that I hurt myself. I bit my lips, lowering my face. I didn't want to lose control and burst into tears in front of him. I added nothing more, realizing that I wouldn't be able to hold back sobs.

'Why, then?' His tone still seemed firm, unyielding.

'Because... I had no other choice.'

I remained motionless between the entrance and the living room. Without the courage to get close to that frost that surrounded him, to the rejection towards me that I had read in his eyes, in his voice.

'Why are you doing this to me, Amantine?'

Suddenly I felt his pain. Still distant, like a far away echo. It was as if another person had taken possession of his body, but a fragment of Peter was still there, hidden in an obscure space of his soul. And if on one side he begged me not to bring him back to the surface, on the other he implored me to make him re-emerge, together with the feelings that still inevitably bound us.

'The last thing I want in the world, Peter, is to hurt you.'

And the first thing I wanted at that moment was to hold him in my arms, kiss him, confess to him all my love.

'I'm a man without will, apparently. I couldn't resist.' Peter stood up, approaching me with a few steps. 'Yet I tried. Every day when I avoided replying to you, calling you... for me it was like a victory, a conquest. I was very happy in recent times, before you arrived... again...'

'Forgive me, then. I never wanted to upset your happiness, Peter.'

In this situation, maybe we had to talk to each other like that. Standing, motionless as statues, a few feet away. We scanned each other almost like two caged animals, unsure of who would give up first, abandon the armour. Probably me. As much as I struggled to keep control, I felt my heart explode in my chest.

Peter shook his head and shrugged. 'What do you have to tell me that's so important, Amantine?'

I realized even more that I couldn't implement my great plan. I couldn't recite the little lesson that I had prepared as if he was a student ready to absorb my teachings. Divorce, party, son. No, not even creating the most appropriate connections. Not with him. It wouldn't work.

In that body, in that indifferent and hostile look towards me there was still Peter. My boyfriend. The love of my life. The only one with whom it had been real to me.

CHAPTER 66

'I've followed you... your career, I mean...'

I wasn't sure there was a God or some saint who could inspire the right words in me but if this existed it was time to manifest itself.

Peter slightly narrowed his eyes, he didn't seem to understand what I intended to tell him. He wasn't entirely wrong, I didn't even know where to start. His wary way of watching me reminded me of William and disturbed me even more deeply, so much so it forced me to look away.

It was at that moment that I remembered my mother's words during our conversation a few weeks ago, words to which I had paid little attention. "Follow your heart." "Don't think too much." "Follow your heart."

I firmly raised my eyes on him and sighed, opening up to a sweet, warm smile. I could only try to express my feelings.

'I've missed you, Peter. I've missed you every day, every moment.' I moved towards him fearfully, then more firmly.

Peter backed away a few steps without replying, but I wasn't intimidated by his silence or his retreat. I realized that it wouldn't be easy to break down his reservations. He was just defending himself, he was protecting himself by building a wall between us. But I needed him, his collaboration, to be able to tell him the whole truth.

'A harmless little snob and egocentric intellectual has never made you so afraid, Peter...'

'You... you're not so little, Amantine. And above all, you're not harmless.' I saw him shudder, clench his fists as the light in his eyes, that flame that I knew so well, came back to life, to burn, setting my heart, my senses on fire. 'You are my damnation. You want to destroy me once again... To disappear then and return to your world, from which you have always excluded me, turned me away...'

'That's not true, Peter. I have never excluded you from my world, because you...' A few more steps and I found myself right in front of him. 'You've become part of it since I met you. No, actually... My world has exploded, it has crumpled on itself after your arrival in my life. My world no longer exists, maybe it never existed.'

'It might even be true what you say... but it didn't seem to me, since you've been basking in that world for years.'

Peter quickly ran both hands over his face. I took the opportunity to get even closer, cancelling the distance between us. I stroked his arms.

'I'm sorry. I'm sorry if I hurt you. I've hurt myself too, a lot.' As soon as he pulled his hands away from his face, I found myself with my eyes on his, his lips so close to mine. 'And I'm sorry because, with what I've come to tell you, I'll hurt you even more. But it's important. In fact, it's essential that you know.'

'There's nothing that can hurt me now, Amantine...' He barely touched my shoulder, held his hand for a moment then moved away from me. 'It pains me to treat you like that, you have no idea how hard it is for me. But the last time we met, at Jacob's funeral... I would have asked you to leave everything, to come away with me. Not to leave me again, because I desperately needed you and only you could understand me. Jacob was... like a second father to me. You started talking to me about your children, I told you that I understood your choice, but actually... I would have asked you to follow me anyway, promised you that we would find a solution together. Then your daughter arrived, and everything changed. I couldn't destroy the family and the life of a girl so sweet, so beautiful... I couldn't be so selfish! So I decided that I had to commit myself to let you go, to step aside to start a new life, to try to build something... to be able to stay away from you once and for all.'

'Maybe you should have asked me to leave everything to follow you... Peter, my marriage is over. I'm divorcing Geoff.'

I didn't expect him to be exultant, but not even an absolute silence on his part. He seemed almost resigned.

'I'm surprised that you left your husband.'

Contrary to what he had just stated, he didn't seem particularly impressed.

'He left me. For another woman. He will have a baby with her, so...' I sighed, shrugging. One of my great news items was gone. But it wasn't the most devastating, especially when compared to the others.

'What an incredible man. He held onto you, a tight grip, for twenty years, maybe more...'

He looked at me halfway between ironic and compassionate. He shook his head, pursed his lips, without adding anything else.

'You probably reached a strange agreement, a coincidence that both of you took the solemn decision to let me go for a younger, more attractive woman.' I could have spared him that one. I realized it as soon as I pronounced the last words. Comparing Peter to Geoff was a very bad idea of mine. 'Sorry, I shouldn't have said that...'

'As for me, you shouldn't have even thought about it, considering the fact that I've never been your husband. I could have all the women I wanted, I'm married to another woman... but I'm still here to take orders from you!'

He had raised his voice. It was my fault. I hadn't been able to resist the jealousy I felt towards him. Even knowing I didn't have any right.

'I didn't stay with Geoff for the bond I had with him, you should know it. And I know that many others in my place would have acted differently, but apparently I have never had much courage. It's my biggest fault. No, actually there's another one, maybe worse.' Unlike him, I was just whispering. 'Peter, you know that I...'

'You what, Amantine?' He snorted, addressing me, his expression sarcastic. 'That's the reason why you wanted to see me? To tell me that after years you finally separated from your husband? To announce to me that you are now free and available? A great pity, my dear, because now I am not free! And if I have to be honest, I'm perfectly fine, in fact I've never been better.'

That sounded almost like spite on his part. But I knew it wasn't.

'I know, Peter. And even if I wish we had an opportunity finally, I... All I want is for you to be happy, you have to believe me. Not necessarily with me.' As much as it pained me to admit it, it was true. I would never ask him to give up a life that made him happy, serene, fulfilled. 'Anyway... that's not why I asked you to meet me.'

With a nod, Peter pointed to the sofa, inviting me to sit down and at the same time to continue. He too sat down, crossing his arms.

'Here, it's about that night... about that party, again.'

The impatient look he gave me was far too eloquent.

'Amantine... it's past, we should leave that night behind once and for all.'

'I can't. Not so much for what they did to me, but...' The image of him with another woman came back clear in my mind, as if it had just happened, although the face of that unknown woman was overlapped in my imagination with that of Kendra Scott, Peter's new young wife. 'It's about you, Peter. About what they wanted to do to you.'

'Destroy me? Ruin me? Separate me from you?' Peter leaned back on the sofa, raising his face to fix his gaze on the ceiling. 'We already know. As we know they have succeeded.'

'Peter... Geoff's father had an agreement with Simon Jennings...' I moved to get close to him. 'And the purpose, at least for Jennings, wasn't just to separate us or hurt you. He wanted more... He wanted... to keep you from leaving the band, that's it. At any cost.' I had to say it, even if I abhorred at the very thought. 'Even at the risk of killing you... On the contrary, he thought it would serve to give more prominence to the band, to awaken the interest, if you...'

Peter's expression seemed almost unbelieving at first. Then he became imperturbable, as if he was disinterested and didn't care less about what I had just revealed to him.

'Of course, sales would have skyrocketed with a dead man involved. It doesn't surprise me. And your dear father-in-law would have shared the spoils with Simon? Good job.'

'No, from what Geoff said he was only interested in me... in me leaving you, in short.' I couldn't hold back anymore the indignation I felt towards Raymond Carter, Geoff, Simon. Even towards myself that I had played my part so well in the plot against us. 'Which I did, like an idiot. I was just a puppet in the hands of those bastards! They used my insecurities, they played with what I felt...'

'It wasn't your fault, Amantine. Don't blame yourself...'

Unexpectedly, Peter reached out to me and touched my cheek with his fingers. At his touch I was no longer able to resist, to hold back. I grabbed his hand.

'I shouldn't have left you, Peter. I should have figured out... looked for an explanation from you instead of running away!' I wiped away the tears that ran down my face. 'How many, how many times I have repeated it to myself. I have always been a lucid and rational person, but at that moment I wasn't able to control myself, to think. And yet I didn't know that I left you alone, in danger, that I had risked... losing you forever... that they would hurt you... that you...'

'Don't cry, Amantine. You know I can't bear to see you like this...'

He drew me into his arms. And, recognizing his scent, his warmth, I felt lost and found at the same time.

'How could they...'

I was crying on his chest. For him, for me, for the risk he had run. Even if it had happened almost twenty years before. My pain remained recent and burned me in the depths of my soul, almost to annihilate me.

'Calm down, baby...'

His reaction was too peaceful. A sort of resigned indifference, as if it didn't surprise him what Simon had tried to do to him.

'Peter, you...' I touched his face gently.

'I knew it, Amantine. Anyway, I suspected it.' He held me, stroking my arms as I shivered from the cold, as if frost ran through my veins instead of blood. 'That night... at one point I woke up in that room, not understanding what had happened. I had images in my head, but discontinuous. The two of us in the park, me walking away to play with the boys. And then with... that girl. Initially, I assumed it was you. I couldn't believe that... Anyway, as soon as I could move and get out of the room, I asked about you. I wasn't myself, but somehow I tried to find you in that house, in the park, I managed to get to that little bridge... But Simon Jennings drugged me again, a massive dose with the intention of provoking a drastic relapse, let's say.'

'Peter, if I hadn't left you that night...' I trembled, holding his hands in mine, intertwining my fingers with his. I felt annihilated by remorse, though I probably couldn't have done anything. 'We didn't have a relationship, I shouldn't have reacted like that, even if...'

'Did it hurt you to see me with another woman? I know what it means, Amantine. I've known it for years. However, Joseph Stevenson saved me. For no reason would he accept such a scandal in his house, it would have ruined his reputation as a great upright tennis player. If it had been known publicly that during his parties they were dabbling hard drugs, his career would have been compromised. Of course, if I had died elsewhere, maybe it wouldn't have had so much importance...' The cynicism with which Peter spoke about himself and about the people he hung out with upset me, hurt me. 'So, Stevenson made sure I went home still alive. Then a hard period started for me, I felt very bad...'

I listened to him silently, stroking his face and chest gently. I wasn't there. I was gone. I had left him alone.

'Peter...' I didn't know what to say. I didn't know how to make up for a misjudgement that had forever compromised my happiness but that could have cost him his life. 'Why didn't you ever tell me when we met again? Didn't you have the chance... to report Jennings?'

'No. What evidence could I bring in my favour? I already had drug abuse problems in the past...' He sighed, passing his thumbs under my eyes to wipe away the remaining tears still visible. 'Nothing could be easier than making everyone believe in my relapse. I would have crossed to the wrong side, compromising even the little that remained to me. The only thing I could do was fight to recover, instead... and wait to get rid of them once and for all.'

'The others were in agreement, I think. Tyler Grey made sure...' That I acted like a fool, like a stupid idiot. Worse, like a wounded little girl. 'He took me away from the party. I came here with him...'

'I know. When I recovered, I heard it from Gordon... That poor man still has the remorse that he obeyed Tyler and withdrew. But you seemed to be fine...' he sighed, taking my face in his hands. 'Amantine, what did Tyler do to you? I should have protected you... I said I don't want to talk about it anymore, but it's something I will never forgive myself.'

'It wasn't your fault, Peter.' I hugged him. Aware that I shouldn't have done so, I searched for his lips, even though I knew he would reject me. 'The truth is that I wanted only you... I... I still want...'

I felt the warmth of his lips on mine, his hands gripping my hips as he dragged me over him. I let my jacket slip from my shoulders and in a moment his mouth was on my neck, on my breast.

Then he suddenly broke away, turned me away from him to look seriously in my eyes.

'I should stop, resist... it shouldn't happen. But I'm afraid I won't have your cooperation this time.'

'It's already happening, Peter. I'm sorry...'

I stroked his face, leaned my forehead against his. I kissed him on his lips with the passion held back for years, while with my hands I stroked his chest trying to unbutton his shirt.

'Little intellectual snob...' He turned me over and spread himself over me. He took my hands and intertwined my fingers with his, pushing back my arms. 'How I wish it wasn't too late... How I wish I wouldn't lose my mind every time I see you... I hear you... Amantine, I knew it. I shouldn't have surrendered... met you...'

I hugged him with my arms, with my legs. Unreasonably, irrationally, nothing else mattered to me than holding on to him, to feel him quiver at my kisses, at my touch. As always. Being his, only his, once again.

He could have all the women he wanted, younger, more beautiful. I could find myself other men, less complicated, belonging to my world maybe, more suitable for me. But no one else would ignite in me that spark of life, of joy, of love. That spark that was suddenly triggered, on an ordinary day, without me desiring or looking for it. And that on my part had never been turned off, despite the pain, the time, the distance.

I met his eyes, realizing that the cold, the indifference, the tension between us was only a vague memory. I understood that it was the same for him, that the flame was still alive, intense, palpable. He had returned to be Peter. My boyfriend. The only one it had ever been real with.

I wanted to believe it wasn't too late. I wanted to delude myself that there was still hope for us. I cancelled every thought, every contradiction. Even the restlessness that triggered me what I hadn't yet revealed to him. The fear that he wouldn't accept my words, my truth. I just wanted to live the moment, to have him for myself, even if for the last time. To feel that he still loved me, as I loved him.

CHAPTER 67

The intention had been to meet only for a few minutes. I spent the afternoon with him and then all night. The last thing I expected, even though I wanted it with all my heart, was to wake up the next morning in his bed, in his arms.

It seemed like a return to the past. But I incessantly continued to have hopes, or maybe the most appropriate term was illusions, about the future.

I didn't want to open my eyes. I didn't want to move from where I was. Above all, I didn't want to face the reality that was looming over me. Peter was married to a beautiful young woman. And I had to confess having lied to him for years. I omitted the truth. But it wouldn't make much difference.

'You're awake, aren't you?' His lips touched my forehead.

I moved my head slowly to avoid having to move from where I lay, clutching him. 'If I refuse to admit it, does anything change?'

'No, but you can always try to convince me. You're pretty good at making me do what you want.' He lifted my chin to kiss my lips. 'Sweetheart...'

'Don't say anything, Peter. I know.'

I knew I was forced to give up. It had happened too many times even though now the roles were reversed.

I opened my eyes and found him leaning on his side, with the intent of looking at me. I sighed, passing my finger over his chest, eventually reaching his tattoo.

'Peter...' My mind was painfully looking for a solution. Above all, it was questioning, in the desperate search for an answer. Or maybe even more than one. For what dark destiny between us, must there always be problems, setbacks, separations? It almost seemed as if a perverse curse had fallen on us, raging to make us suffer. I needed to be distracted even just for a moment, I didn't want to face the conversation that would unite us or divide us even more forever. 'What are you working on, Peter? Some time ago I heard about your intention to put Shakespeare's poems and sonnets to music...'

'Yes, it's true...' He gave me a smile, even though a little gloomy, sad. 'But I fear that the great Shakespearean academics and enthusiasts will slaughter me. For that reason, maybe it's not a good idea. I think I'll leave it...'

'Since when are you worried about those strutting brontosaurs?' I kissed his lips and sighed as he stroked my side.

'Amantine, I...'

'Don't say anything, Peter. I know that...'

I bit my lips, moving away from him and turning my back to him. My attempt to hold on to another subject had failed miserably.

'If only we could go back...' He touched my shoulder, playing with a lock of my hair. 'But I can't.'

'You've married a fantastic woman, I realize that. I saw her with you in some photos, I know I can't compete. You did well.' I swallowed hard, the lump that stuck in my throat didn't allow me to breathe normally.

'Of all the women I met, she was the one that reminded me the most of you, in some way. That's why I married her.'

'Are you trying to sugarcoat it, Peter? Thank you, but it's not working...'

I turned, raising a smile, trying to show myself serene, gracious. Instead I felt nervous, possessive, jealous like never before. I was working hard to keep control of myself and keep a detached, almost amused tone. There was nothing funny about our situation. On the contrary. We continued to betray those we were supposed to be with and nothing could justify our actions. Not even love. Or the fate that with impunity continued to separate us.

'She was a little like you at the beginning. She challenged me, she amused me. And of course... always so lively, beautiful, ambitious...' He sighed, closing his eyes for a moment. 'I tried to bring out something that happened to me in the past, just once, with you. Only with her I never managed to be what I was with you. It's as if my cheerfulness, my source of joy has been sucked, drained forever. And in spite of all the time that has passed, you remain you. With her I tried to revive our history, in vain. So I realized that I could no longer remain attached to you, but I had to learn to appreciate her for what she is... Kendra is part of my world, she understands me, appreciates me and maybe she loves me. She tells me often. And I try, too. But now I've proved I've failed again, even with her.'

'I'm sorry. It was all my fault.' I sat up and leaned my forehead on my knees. 'I pushed you to do something you didn't want, you were not willing to do... Evidently being so used to doing it myself, to betray, I didn't worry about you.'

'I didn't intend, it's true. But I wanted it, you didn't force me.' He gently stroked my hair. 'I don't think there will ever come a time when I won't want you, Amantine. I can try, of course...'

'For me it's the same.' I took his hand and brought it to my lips, closing my eyes. Immediately he raised my face to kiss me. 'Peter... Whatever happens, to me it will always be real between us. If I don't tell you... Try to understand, it doesn't mean that it's not real or that I don't feel it. It means that... If I told you looking in your eyes, like now, I would never be able to get away from you, I wouldn't be willing to let you go. It means that I would turn my world and yours upside-down, indifferent to the pain that I could cause to others... betrayals, wounds, scandal... to anyone... to my children, your wife, us... I would crawl over everything and everyone without any scruples to be with you, I really would. You can believe me.'

'Amantine, I know. I believe you. We are the same in this, remember? And do you remember how stubbornly we kept repeating "no questions, no claims"? While I... I meant something completely different... Little intellectual snob, I still mean something different...'

I nodded, wrapping my arms around his neck. 'Peter, I have to tell you something important.'

I wasn't ready. I wasn't absolutely ready to tell him everything, to break his heart and mine. To confess to him what I had taken from him for almost eighteen years. No, I wasn't ready. But I had no choice.

He leaned back against the bed, hugging me, pressing his lips to my forehead. I searched for his hand to entwine my fingers with his. I could have stayed like that forever, for the rest of my life. But prepared or not, it was time. His silence was an encouragement to continue, to express my secret in words.

'When I left... Shortly after I left London, I wrote you a letter. From Paris.'

His lips left my forehead and he tilted his head to meet my gaze.

'I never received it, Amantine.'

'Yes, I understand that. I realized that after we met again. But in those days, I believed you didn't want to answer me. Inside the letter and on the envelope I had written to you where I was, my phone number, the address of my Paris apartment... And there I waited, hoping to receive your answer.' I held his hand tighter. 'I dreamed you came looking for me...'

'I would have come to you, Amantine. Immediately, as soon as possible I would have come to get you. Baby...' His green eyes darkened, showing an immense sadness.

I felt suffocated by regret and by the awareness of having to cause him an even greater pain, immeasurable in comparison to that caused by what I had just told him.

'I thought you didn't care about me. Also, because I was in a condition... I didn't think clearly. In short, I renounced everything. My university career, my life here, you. I didn't want to go and cry to my parents, I wanted to be able to face everything alone...'

'Probably Simon found the letter. Or anybody else wandering around my house in those days. I wasn't very conscious, unfortunately.' He frowned, passing a finger on my profile, on my cheekbones. 'I kept dreaming you... I perceived your voice, I heard you calling me... But I thought it was just the effect of what they had given me. Then to recover I went to my mother's house; it was a very hard time. It was Gordon who called her, against my will, because he had begun to fear for me. He didn't trust those around me and alone he couldn't be in control, in order that they didn't hurt me. I thought I couldn't snap out of it. I thought I was falling into the abyss without being able to get back. I found a picture of you taken by someone that evening and it appeared in a magazine, I always kept it with me, I deluded myself that you were still my girlfriend... And I smiled remembering the story you told me... That taking a picture of you would be like capturing your soul, something like that... like those ancient civilizations... Then I remembered that you went away, you had left me...'

'I dreamed of you too. And there was also something...' Just a few words. Just a few words were enough. The most difficult to pronounce, for me, in all my life. 'The reason why I married Geoff is that alone I couldn't...'

'I don't want to know, darling.' Peter moved away from me, running his hands through his hair. 'If I think... if I think about our life, it seems the result of a perverse set-up. If only... if I hadn't convinced you to accompany me to that damn party. I keep repeating that I don't want to talk about it anymore, but in the end, everything is attributable to that night. What I should have told you before, to convince you that I would never have betrayed you... To the Darkest Storm performance, to Simon Jennings...'

He clenched his fists in anger, refraining from continuing. Needless to continue to repeat the painful stages of a story that we knew too well by now.

'I should have confronted you directly, Peter. Instead of writing you a stupid letter. But my problem was that I didn't feel strong enough to accept your rejection if you hadn't wanted me. This is because I felt as fragile as I had never been...' Now, I had to say it. I couldn't wait any longer. 'That's why I accepted Geoff's proposal. I was afraid. I shouldn't blame him, despite everything, because the responsibility was mine only. He tried to help me... and he convinced me that alone I wouldn't be able to face everything. The alternative would have been to give up, but I didn't want to... I couldn't...'

'You needed someone by your side.' Peter nodded even if he had little conviction. 'He took advantage of the wrong I did to you, for this reason you were fragile... Then there was also the story with the university, I remember. Your professor didn't recognize your merits. You were disappointed. But he shouldn't have forced you, trying to convince you to marry him.'

'No. In spite of the pain I felt, I wouldn't have married him. I would have been alone... It didn't scare me to be alone, if I couldn't be with you. Another reason, with Geoff I have only ever felt affection, nothing more than that.' I covered my face with my hands. Strength. I needed strength and all the love I felt for him. Hoping his would be enough to forgive me. 'Peter... there was another reason. The reason, actually. The only one I married him for.'

For a moment I thought I was reading a change in his eyes. Uncertainty was turning into understanding, almost empathizing with me. Had he guessed what I was desperately trying to tell him?

'I couldn't give it up... it was yours...'

I felt my heart shatter into tiny pieces, as I took his hands and held them in mine. They felt warm to me, while mine had become icy. But it was a cold that pervaded my entire body, starting from my heart. As if I had been wrapped in a spiral of ice that wouldn't have mercy on me, freezing my blood in its veins. As if my only source of warmth and relief was now him.

I looked down at our joined hands imagining what the same revelation would have been like, eighteen years ago.

'Amantine, you're not saying...' He held my hands tightly, then let them go. I realized that he was lowering his face in search of my gaze, while I still didn't have the courage to look him in his eyes.

Should it be like this? Had it to happen just this way? In all the years when I had waited for the right moment, never, not even once, had I imagined or visualized the scene. How it would have been to confess my secret to him, the only other one who was directly involved. I had dreamed this, me of eighteen years ago, who made him part of the recent discovery. But never my late confession.

'I was pregnant, Peter. I don't know if for that reason my pain had been amplified. Or because I realized, right then, that I was feeling something for you that I had never felt for anyone...' I summoned the little courage I had to force myself to lift my face and look into his eyes. 'My heart was broken. I couldn't control my emotion. I didn't want to tell anyone. I realized it only when I arrived in Paris. I wrote you that letter. I didn't get an answer and... I decided that the only thing I could do...'

Peter still held his hands in mine, but without force, without life. With inertia. It almost seemed that the frost that flowed in my veins had infected him too. And he hadn't said a word to me yet. I felt myself condemned by his silence. I felt I'd been annihilated.

'Peter...'

'You have... you have... you lost it...' he whispered. And I realized that he didn't dare to use other terms to define what I had tried to do.

'No. I haven't lost it. And I didn't even... even though I intended...' We stayed still. Both. As if we had no voice, no more breath. As if we had to learn to breathe again. 'I kept it. Our baby. And I called him William. Not just because it's a name I found cute. I called him William because William Shakespeare brought me back to you. I called him William because he is your son and I couldn't have called him anything else. Above all, I wouldn't have called another man's son that name.'

I held his hands with more strength, going up to his wrists and arms. To hold him to me, not let him go. Because I felt that a part of him was escaping me, irremediably.

'Why you...' He began to say something, but he stopped. He didn't even have the strength to speak. And he kept on not looking at me.

'Peter, I... I didn't know what to do. I only knew that I wanted to keep it. That I had to save him, even if at first I thought otherwise.' I stroked his face, then hugged him tightly to me. 'Darling...'

'He... doesn't know?' He grabbed me by the shoulders, pushing me aside, though gently. 'I can't believe it...'

'That's what I feared, Peter. But I had to tell you... He doesn't know, not yet.'

'No. You didn't understand.' I met his eyes. There was no more light. There was no more life. There was nothing left anymore. 'I can't believe you didn't tell me. You disappeared with our baby... you wanted to get rid of him...'

'No, I didn't want to! I... Please, Peter. I was scared, I was alone, desperate...'

'You were not a little girl, Amantine! You should have looked for me!' He turned around quickly, turning his back to me. He remained sitting on the bed, gripping the sheet tightly. I could see his fists quivering, for pain, for an anger he hadn't been able to express yet.

'I thought you didn't want me...' I moved to hug him from behind, but I gave up. I barely touched his back and he withdrew away from me.

'You should have told me anyway!' He turned to me and our eyes clashed. In a moment I realized that nothing and nobody in the world could hurt me more. His green eyes, often so sweet towards me, sometimes restless, sometimes ironic, expressed not only disbelief, but also contempt, anger and above all an uncontrollable pain, a pain for which I felt the physical sensation of a heart that was breaking. It was his. And mine as well, consequently.

'Forgive me... I lived waiting for the right time and I could never...'

'William. I saw him without knowing... At the presentation of your new book, at Jacob's funeral...' He stood up, turned to me and remained standing, looking at me. He seemed to age suddenly. I saw him shiver again, almost stumble. 'How many right times did you have, Amantine, during these years? When we met again after a few years, when you came looking for me... when I asked you to stay with me ... when we were together even if you were married and you were here with me during your stays in London... when I begged you not to leave me... when I told you that I didn't intend to go to America... when you came to me there... when I did everything, transforming my life, my commitments, just to see you even for an hour... The truth is that you've always used me, I've always been an entertainment for you, a diversion from your boredom. A pastime. But I've never been worthy enough! I shouldn't be surprised, you've always said it, from the beginning...'

I had never seen him cry. Not like that. Never, not even at Jacob's funeral. I remained motionless, as if bound to that pain, too big for me to be able to contain it, to express myself, look for a justification for my behaviour. I had been a monster. A monster of cruelty, of selfishness. I had been inhuman. And now I felt myself torn apart by his words, in an atrocious way. As I deserved.

'Peter, please...'

'How many times have I held you in my arms... how many times have I kissed you... All that we have said to each other... And it has never been the right time for you?' He was still keeping his eyes on me, but they were becoming more and more empty, inexpressive. Like without a soul, without emotion. 'I told you I loved you and it was the first time... and it wasn't easy for me. You never did it. Now I understand why. It wasn't real. It was never real for you. That's why you gave my son to another man! Because it made no difference to you. Only now that he has left you... the right time has suddenly come. Suddenly I became worthy of being your son's father... just because you don't want to be alone!'

'No, Peter. No. I destroyed my life, I married a man for whom I felt nothing...' I tried to move, to stand up from the bed to reach him, but my limbs felt like they were paralyzed. I managed to drag myself to him, clinging to his shoulders. 'The only good thing was the children... but I've been awful with them too... And the more I went on the more I didn't know how to do it. I wished to tell you right away, as soon as we met again... But you told me about your other son, you were not sure he was yours, you didn't want him... We didn't have a stable relationship, I thought you might have doubts about me as well, about William... Then things went on and I... Please, forgive me. You're the only man I've ever...'

'But what there was between us was all different, I wouldn't have doubts about you! You have been... the most important person in my life, Amantine. As well as the one who hurt me most.' Peter interrupted me, pulling me away with disdain, and I unbalanced, falling backward, onto the bed. 'I can forgive the first years you were away. I can also forgive that you married another man and... that he was the father of my son. But then? More years have passed, more than ten! And you remained silent... You didn't care, you let me go away, you let our son grow up without knowing...'

Suddenly he stopped. He opened his wardrobe and wore random clothes. A pair of jeans over the boxers, a shirt... As if I wasn't there. He opened another door in the same closet, the last one, the one next to the wall. Then he moved so I could see. There were some clothes I had left there, many years before. And during our long relationship. On the small shelf some of my CDs, some books. And even the dress I wore that night hung there. I recognized it instantly. I hadn't seen it for almost twenty years. I didn't believe Peter had kept everything... including that dress.

I burst into sobs. I felt I was exploding internally and my head was spinning. But I forced myself to take a few steps and seek comfort in his arms. He hugged me tenderly, then almost with fury and kissed me with a passion that left me breathless.

'Peter, my love... I... we'll find the way, now. I promise you. I'll talk to William...'

'No, Amantine. No. Don't speak to me words you don't feel, I don't want them anymore now. I will leave this house now. I'll stay out all day to give you enough time. When I come back, I don't want to find you here anymore. I don't want to see you anymore. I don't want to hear from you anymore. I don't want to know anything about you for the rest of my life. Take what is of yours that is still here. Ask Gordon for a suitcase. Take everything away. If you leave something, I will order that it will be thrown out. I held you in my arms for the last time, I kissed you for the last time. Now I just want to forget that you exist. I want to forget how much I loved you. One day...' He stopped suddenly. His eyes had become even colder, arid. There was not even any more resentment or contempt towards me. There was no more light. There was nothing. 'One day I'll try to talk to William, I'll try to get close to him. If he won't accept me, I will understand. Because he was a victim, just like me. Like your daughter... and who knows how many others. You can keep your ambition, Amantine. Your perfect life, as false as you are. Your world. The world of which I have never been worthy... I would have given up mine for you. I would have given up everything for you. I told you that I loved you. I would have turned my world upside-down for you. I would have given up my career for a bit of happiness with you. I loved you so much tonight, again... I even thought about leaving my young and beautiful wife for you. Because no woman has ever really had me, as much as you had me. You were my little snob and egocentric intellectual, my joy, my sweetheart... my life... my most beautiful song. That song that I thought was ours... but it was just mine.'

CHAPTER 68

There were no words I could say. Or tears that I could shed. I didn't exist anymore. He simply removed me from his life, like a harmful, devastating virus. He had left the house without looking at me again. While I was still trying to hug him, to hold him to me, he pushed me away so as not to allow me to touch him. Trying not to hurt me physically, gracefully, but without speaking, without his eyes meeting mine.

I had lost him. His love, his sweetness, his voice, his smiles. I had lost everything about him. And I had lost myself too. Because it was he who made me alive, sweet, beautiful... it was he who made me feel in love.

Without Peter I had truly become the person he described. Arid, indifferent, selfish, hypocritical, perched in a world that did nothing but tighten a noose around my own neck, immobilized me by crushing me from within. I returned to what I had been before meeting him. The young university researcher with a well-defined path in front of her, severe, incorruptible but without enthusiasm for life. Free but a prisoner of herself and of a world in which she had barricaded herself.

I didn't take anything of mine from his house. I motionlessly waited for his return. Sitting on the bed staring into space. Then I realized that he would not be back until I was gone.

At the door, before leaving, I waited again. Gordon greeted me with a respectful nod after offering me a cup of tea, which I refused.

'I'm afraid this is the last time we will meet, Gordon.' I held out my hand, trembling a little.

'Mrs. Amantine.' He returned an unexpectedly vigorous handshake. 'Don't give up, Mrs. Amantine. It was a pleasure to see you again and I hope it's not the last time.'

I nodded, holding back my tears. 'Tell Peter I left everything here... what was mine... And tell him as well that I...' I sighed, shaking my head. 'No, don't tell him anything. Goodbye, Gordon. Thanks for everything.'

All I had to do was go back to Alain's house and then, trying to disguise my desperation, return to Paris. Get back to my children, my family, my students. While my heart remained in London, in that house in Notting Hill. And with him, wherever he was.

I had been terrible in showing him how much I loved him, years ago. A beginner without excessive luck. And I still was. Indeed, I was even worse. I had destroyed him. And in the meantime I had destroyed myself. But I loved him, despite all my mistakes perpetrated for years. I had never stopped loving him. Maybe in the most wrong way, maybe without being capable of it, but I loved him with all my heart. If only he could understand how much...

My attempts to re-establish contact with him were in vain. All of them. He had removed me from his life. Permanently, this time.

Meanwhile, he no longer appeared in any magazine, not even when I was looking for news on the internet. He also cancelled the dates of public appearances. He hadn't retired from the scene, but it seemed he wanted to hide. His wife often appeared alone at parties, events, awards or in the company of other people. Mostly her sister, her mother, friends or colleagues. I didn't believe their marriage was in crisis, but Peter seemed intent on living secluded from the showbiz he'd belonged to for so long.

In the meantime, I felt increasingly lost, astray. He wasn't mine anymore. I missed everything about him, even memories. Because unlike other times, I had the certainty that he had stopped loving me. I was no longer his little snob and egocentric intellectual. I was no longer his sweetheart. And for this missing part of my life, it was as if my heart corroded day after day, giving me the physical sensation that it would become increasingly small, fragile, useless. One day, maybe, it would vanish completely, ceasing to beat. And I would stop breathing.

William was his son. I had denied him for so many years. Of course he hated me. No love could have resisted and survived such betrayal. Not even the one Peter felt for me. I had heard that there is no worse hatred than the one that was once love. As long as he hated me. As long as the wound I inflicted on him hadn't turned his love into indifference.

I found myself in spring, then in summer without even realizing it. I lost track of my days, months, years. And I, unlike the spring, was fading. I no longer cared about my makeup, my clothing, anything. As if my existence no longer made sense.

There was one thing I had to do, still. Talk to William, who I found more and more spiteful and intolerant towards me. He had turned eighteen. At any moment I expected him to let me know that he was leaving our house forever.

The news was announced on Peter's website on the first day of autumn. In November his new album would be released, of which only the title was known at the moment, *Then hate me when thou wilt.*

Had he done it then? Had he put Shakespeare's poems and sonnets to music? Or was that title just a coincidence? No, it couldn't be. That was our sonnet, in its original form.

Why had he done it? Was he still thinking about me? I had to wait for more information. Day after day I checked his website looking for further news wherever possible. As a daily appointment. Even more than once a day. In the meantime, Peter was still not appearing publicly.

In early October the song titles appeared. Yes, they really were William Shakespeare's poems and sonnets. Those he had underlined in the book I had found at his home. He really had them put to music, then. The penultimate title was a poem by

John Keats, "La belle dame sans merci". I wondered why this choice... And then in conclusion, the last one on the list... I had to reread it several times, I almost didn't want to convince myself. No, he couldn't have done it... He couldn't have exposed it like that, to everyone to see. It was true, however. As if there was nothing more to hide, to protect now. "Amantine's Song".

September 2012

CHAPTER 69

In almost a year, many things had changed. Maybe too many. It had been as if the release of Peter's latest work marked a watershed between the new me and the old life I had dragged along for almost twenty years.

His idea of putting Shakespeare to music and singing his sonnets in a modern way hadn't been particularly well appreciated by academics. He had suspected it. I had told him not to give a damn about it.

But not even his fans appreciated the idea. Too far from who he was. Word had spread that he had been ill-advised by a woman with whom he had had an affair. I suppose they meant me. After a few weeks of discussion, not even too lively, it had all quietened down and ended up in oblivion. Nobody cared about me or bothered me about it. Probably a story of old lovers wasn't so interesting for gossip magazines anymore. Our time had passed. For better or for worse.

"Amantine's Song" was our song, it had already appeared on one of Peter's previous albums. But with its "real" title, that Peter had not bothered to conceal anymore, and while maintaining the same music, it had a sweeter, slower pace. So his latest work was dedicated to me... or at least inspired by me. A goodbye, a memory of the past... or a faint hope for us? I had no idea.

Peter kept from appearing. He didn't reply to criticism. He merely thanked from his website all those who still supported him and understood his choice, his need for a change, to try something new. Growing up everyone feels the need to change, to experiment. I understood him. I would have supported any of his artistic choices, even if against the current flow. I loved him. I would always love him and I always regretted him.

A key part of my change had been the move to Yorkshire. I still held some courses at the University of Leeds, but I had decided to abandon my academic career permanently. My lessons were more focused on creative writing and on the structure of the novel.

I no longer wanted to compete. I no longer wanted to fight to establish myself in a world I had never believed in. I realized that my academic ambitions had always been something for my ego, to show others how intellectual I was, not a job for which I felt joy, love and even inclination. Now I was starting to love what I was doing.

For too long, I had pushed back with all my strength what made me feel alive and happy, my love for Peter and for my creative side that was finally emerging. And curiously this change of direction had happened for both, simultaneously. This made me feel even more a kindred spirit with him. As if Peter and I had been created to be together, to meet again, to link up and fight the same battles. In our worlds, so different, we were similar. Even though I had refused to understand it and I hurt us both.

In Leeds I went out a few times with Ned Douglas, a colleague who taught English literature, passionate about postmodernism. An intelligent, cultured, refined, charming man. I enjoyed spending time with him during breaks between courses, discussing literature and art. So I found it natural to accept his invitations. But I didn't want him, as I no longer wanted to analyse literature scientifically. I had given the study too many years of my existence. I wanted life, joy, beauty. I wanted love, poetry, to read novels to feel the taste of words, to savour them without the need to examine their language and meaning. I wanted my boyfriend. I wanted Peter.

So when Ned suggested to me to intensify our relationship, I politely refused. He accepted my decision without arguing and we were back to being simple colleagues who appreciated each other but nothing more.

Madeline had moved to live with me. William, however, started university in London. His dreams as an astrophysicist had waned and, although he was not convinced of his choice, he had decided to study English literature, following the path of the person in the family he appreciated least, that is, his mother. Maybe it was his way of challenging me and, knowing him, he would surely try to surpass me.

I continued undaunted to look for information about Peter. Every day, I never missed my appointment. I welcomed with perplexity his decision to go back to the scene with a collection of old successes. He also set dates for some concerts, in the moment when they were talking about a betrayal of his towards Kendra Scott. But it seemed that she, too, had betrayed him and that they were close to a separation caused above all by Peter's clear refusal to have more children.

Other gossip, like Peter's alcohol abuse and short temper, I couldn't and didn't want to believe. Peter wasn't like that. He had never been since I knew him. I knew he had had problems as a boy, but he had never been drunk with me. And he had never attacked me physically, not even when he had every reason to detest me.

In any case, I kept track of the news about him every day. Now with the internet it was much easier and faster to find it, there was no more need for me to go looking in magazines. According to the latest news, Kendra was living with an actor with whom she had recently made a movie and Peter was seeing a model. Lolita type but blonder and thinner. And he seemed to be serious about her. The stories even said she was pregnant, while he had refused to have children with Kendra. This, among others, had been the trigger for divorce.

Every day I suffered for him and with him. Every time they accused him, every time they criticized his work... Every time they insinuated wickedness and injustice. I went so far as to no longer be able to stand the fury against him. There were those who claimed that his career was at a standstill and now declining and that it would deteriorate lower and lower. They even accused him of having gone on stage drunk while attending a show.

I tried again to write him an e-mail on the private address that we used to communicate. I knew that almost certainly he would trash it without opening it... or maybe he even closed his account so as not to receive my messages.

I wrote to him anyway. I was feeling it for him, I would always be there for him. I believed in him and in his work and I wanted to convey my support. I loved him more than before. No, I couldn't write this. Not in a cold e-mail message, though it could be my last and only chance.

I prayed that he would answer me. But he didn't answer me. Every day, every night my thoughts were with him. During a journey to London I had even been tempted to stop by his house, even though I knew I couldn't find him. A few weeks later I received the confirmation that my e-mail had been received and read. I hoped that it was he who had received it and that he hadn't entrusted the reading of his messages to some collaborators.

I cried for hours in front of my computer screen. I cried on that confirmation of a message received and read, perhaps not even by him. I cried to the point where I wanted to hold it, caress it. There were millions of words that I still wanted to write to him, words with which I would express all my love for him. Even though it was too late now, even though I had lost him now. Even though maybe someone else would read them, not him. I decided to summarise them in those that would have more meaning for us, for me, even if maybe for him for some time they no longer had any value: "Peter, it will always be real for me."

CHAPTER 70

I was pleased that my relationship with Madeline was growing, intensifying. On the contrary, the one with William was more and more the result of frustration and dejection. The tension and the intolerance towards me grew. Almost as if he suspected the great wrong that I had done to him before he was born. His obvious hostility prevented me from being sincere towards him. I feared his reaction, I feared he wouldn't be able to tolerate the truth. And I kept silent, perpetrating my mistake and my guilt.

He wouldn't forgive me. And because of the bond she had with her brother, Madeline as well would side with him against me. Meanwhile, she was the link between us. She also formed the link between me and Geoff. Our fragile family balance was based on her. Maybe a little too much for a seventeen-year-old girl.

The situation had degenerated when Geoff accepted the academic assignment in America that had been offered to him years before. He left with his new partner and his new son towards the new stage of his life. He was firmly orientated on the new, in short. Leaving our children after leaving me. William had been tempted to join him to attend an American university, but Geoff had made it clear that he wasn't welcome into the new life he intended to build.

All my fault. This as well. Geoff was rejecting the son of Peter and I, the son he had always loved and raised as his own. The one who had always been on his side, even more than Madeline, who was really his daughter. I wanted to tell William the whole truth, more than anything else. But how could I add to Geoff's rejection, the rejection of Peter as well?

'Do you think Dad really doesn't care about us anymore?'

Madeline, unlike William, clearly expressed her perplexities. William's anger was lately silent, unexpressed to such an extent that it took on a proud and mocking solemnity. I don't know where he got it from, between me and Peter. He often seemed like a mix of both in the worst moments.

'No, darling... it's just that... for a long time he wanted to accept that position in America, it's a big step forward for his career. I'm sure that he won't stay for long, only the pre-established time. And anyway, he still has to settle... and in short, all the rest, you know...'

I would rather not have to strive so hard to find excuses for my ex-husband's behaviour. But the failure of our marriage and our family was attributed to me more than to him, I was aware of it. Even though it was he who left me for a younger woman and got her pregnant, it was my responsibility.

Years of betrayals. Years of unrequited love. I could understand it even if it was difficult for me to accept it. Above all, I was paying the price of not taking the decision myself to end our relationship when it would have been difficult, but not so devastating for everyone. I thought it was better to wait for the children to grow up. Instead it had been worse and Geoff had beaten me to it.

'Mom, you... don't you go out with Ned anymore?'

Madeline crouched next to me, pausing the DVD thriller we were watching together on a Sunday afternoon. Now came the time of questions that demanded an immediate and honest answer. Surely Madeline didn't see it like William did. My son would have never asked me details about my love life.

'Ned is a nice man and a good person, but...' I sighed, shaking my head.

Madeline had met him only once during a series of lectures open to the public in which he had spoken about the work of James Joyce.

'But you don't like him enough. Not as you like Peter Wiles.'

It was the first time Madeline had spoken to me openly about Peter after the meeting at the cemetery. Madeline, in the last few years, had begun to express her ideas clearly, that had been the only topic on which she kept a certain reserve.

'Madeline, Peter and I have known each other for so many years...' I was hoping to be able to close and archive the conversation in some way. But I still didn't know how. 'I'm a teacher. He lives like a star, he is part of showbiz. We have nothing in common. Why don't we resume our DVD?'

I smiled, glancing at the movie left on pause on the contrite look of a woman who seemed to have held her breath just because of that forced stop. She could actually be me. My emotional state was very similar. Not just at that particular moment. Always.

'I think you should try with Peter.' My words didn't seem to have had any effect on my daughter. As if I hadn't even pronounced them. 'He's alone and he doesn't seem to be getting by very well lately. And he's still very handsome... much more than Ned, in my opinion.'

I stared even more intently at the woman stuck in the movie in an attempt not to violently blush at Madeline's words. Apparently, we had the same taste.

'Peter and I are friends...' False. He hated me. 'But there has never been…'

I was a liar. An unscrupulous liar. And also, an awful liar in this case. I hoped that my daughter would decide to give life back to the poor woman in the movie and let her catch her breath. And that gave me a respite from my feelings for Peter Wiles, too strong, too intense and overbearing to be dominated and held.

'I've known for a long time that there was a story between you and Peter, Mom. I read it too. And then with that song in his CD he couldn't be clearer. I'm young, I'm not stupid.' She hit me hard and fast. In fact, the stupid one continued to be me.

'Peter is dating a model...' I shrugged and began to play with my sweater's sleeve, pulling it up to cover my hand. I also had the attitude of a restless teenager. Nothing of a university teacher. 'He doesn't care about me.'

'No way! That possessed blonde isn't his type. And then she's too tall! In my opinion it is all faked. He doesn't care at all about that one... but he cares about you, instead.'

Madeline grabbed the pillow she held on her legs and threw it to the side of the sofa.

Funny. They were more or less the same words I had used about Lolita about twenty years ago. *"Too tall for you. She's not your type, Peter!"*

I looked down, biting my lips and remained silent, utterly embarrassed. If he cared about me why wasn't he answering me?

'I'm going to make popcorn, do you want some?' Madeline stood up quickly. 'However, back to the topic of showbiz... I spoke to Aunt Marianne. I would like to study drama in London and enter the National Theatre if I can.'

All right, then. Between Peter and the popcorn this was my daughter's news. Not really news because she had admired Marianne since childhood, but I never believed that she took the theatre idea so seriously. Maybe she had mentioned Peter just to raise the topic and the popcorn was the excuse to run away from me if I didn't agree.

'There's still some time, darling. Another high school year...'

She would have time to change her mind. Or I would have time to turn my life upside down again. Even if London couldn't be an option for me. I had suffered too much in London. I would live every day of my life waiting for him, in London.

February 2014

CHAPTER 71

About a year after our conversation in front of the TV Madeline moved to London. She had been staying at Alain and Marianne's home in South Kensington area for a few months. She liked being with her uncle, her aunt and her cousins for the time being, she didn't feel ready to live alone, unlike William who had from the beginning decided to share a flat with two classmates.

I was still holed up in the Yorkshire village that I had chosen as my residence, continuing to hold courses at the University of Leeds, a place that I loved and that fascinated me but to which I still didn't feel I belonged, although there were all the conditions for it to become the place where I would live the rest of my solitary life. Haworth, the Brontë sisters' village.

I went to London occasionally to see my children. Madeline, more so. William never really wanted to meet me. And every time I tried to bring up a particular subject with him, he withdrew with the excuse of not having time to listen to me. As if he feared what I had to tell him. So much so that I began to believe that William suspected the truth. It probably wasn't that difficult to imagine. But it seemed that he wanted to avoid having absolute certainty by means of my confession.

I continued to regret not having dealt with the situation when I saw Peter and cleared it up with him. And I regretted him. After an unspecified number of relationships and flirts that had been attributed to him, news of his definitive return to England had come.

About six months had passed since his return, which had happened more or less at the time of Madeline's move to London. If I believed in coincidences maybe I might have believed it was a sign of destiny... But maybe it had nothing to do with me, with us. I stubbornly remained in Yorkshire to lead my life as a mature woman now secluded from the world.

However, during my stays in London I never managed to avoid a walk in the Notting Hill area. A couple of times I had also reached his house, one of the two I even rang the bell but without success.

Evidently, Peter was keeping faith with the decision not to see me and not to hear from me again. There was nothing I could do. A bit like with William. I kept being rejected by the two most important men in my life.

Meanwhile, the descending phase in Peter Wiles's career seemed unstoppable. He was now considered a star on his way out. He had released a single in collaboration with a jazz musician, but it had gone almost unnoticed. He had increasingly involved himself in fundraising and supporting charities. I had been tempted again to write to him, but resisted. I couldn't help but continue to love him in silence and atone for my guilt.

I wondered if he would show up with William sooner or later. Or if he had tried to see him. I stubbornly held back in Yorkshire for fear of having to confront both of them and come out morally torn. More torn than I already was.

I dreamed that Peter would forgive me and come back to love me. But by now we had reached an age where it couldn't be helped if hearts had hardened. I had wounded him beyond any possibility of forgiveness, but I wouldn't surrender now that he had returned to England. I also dreamed of my son's understanding. In the meantime, however, time passed, Peter continued to avoid me, and William moved further away from me.

I had nothing else to do but to continue living and to give my best to Madeline who was starting to emerge as a talented young actress. And to my work, on which I was constantly struggling for hours and hours, until late at night. Almost with an angry passion. I was researching, reading, writing. I tried to produce as much as possible so as not to have the feeling that my life was empty, useless. Wasted. At least from that point of view I was having success. I had become almost a celebrity in my field, especially after Jacob's biography, and I had not stopped yet.

But... but there was that moment. That instant at night, before closing my eyes and giving in to sleep. That instant when I thought about him, even more intensely, and I felt him next to me, in my bed. And I promised myself to look for him, to make sure to meet him. At least once again.

I would die sooner or later. I had never thought of it so much before. Not in the same way. I was young and I had always been strong, healthy. I was still well, the years did not weigh heavily on me yet. But they would pass, gone so quickly... And I couldn't allow myself to get to the end without... without a final explanation with him. Even though it was now a certainty that I had lost him, that he no longer loved me. It would have been like leaving unfinished business.

So... I had nothing left to do but to stop being the woman I had always been. Change, even at the age of fifty almost. It was quite horrible to think about it. To think that I had remained so anchored to myself, to the self of my first meeting with Peter.

Yes, I was horrified by myself. An empty woman, without courage. So cultured, so enterprising in some aspects of her life... but so fragile, so scared in others. I had not changed, while the rest of the world was growing and transforming around me. Even Geoff, who seemed to cling to me so much as to love me beyond all my guilt, had left me. And he had done well. My kids had grown up and left me. My parents were getting old but had their own world, where they still combined perfectly. My brother and his wife had found each other and they were still fine together despite the differences.

And then there was him, Peter. What about him? He had certainly changed, grown... Even though maybe he hadn't achieved happiness. But he had returned home, perhaps he understood who he was and recognized the place to which he belonged. Even if he was losing everything, success, fame, and perhaps a bit of himself.

Only I didn't know who I was and what would become of me. I kicked the blankets aside, like an angry little girl who, although locked in her room, didn't give up on the idea of escape. I found myself in the bathroom in front of the mirror. I met my pale, tired face, marked by dark circles. The skin so fragile in some places, the small wrinkles that had formed around my eyes and at the corners of my mouth. My eyes in which those green specks that my mother's friend had advised me to make stand out no longer shone, were now without light. My hair, to which I had recently devoted little care, was scattered over my head, without form, substance, body.

Yet it was always me, Amantine Delamar. Despite everything and everyone. The world changed and grew, and I remained the same confused girl who didn't know what it meant to love. Or maybe she had learned it, but she became so dazed that she couldn't express it in the right way.

I loved Peter Wiles. With all my heart. With all my strength and my weakness. But I had never managed to make him feel it. When we met again, when for years we saw each other in secret. And finally, when I told him the truth about William. I had been good at getting, receiving love from him. I had felt it and I wanted it again. But he had missed all this. Despite my promises, despite my messages, my attempts to recover the situation. Despite that it was real.

I took a deep breath and glanced defiantly at my merciless reflection in the mirror.

'I'll get fit. I'll be back home, Peter. Whether you want it or not, I'll stand by you, this time. You will really feel me, I will love you as I have never been able to do before. Whether you want me, or not. We still have a lot of life ahead of us.'

CHAPTER 72

I was getting ready to return more or less permanently to London, without including detours and without being further slowed down on my path. I felt a little like an aged Scarlett O'Hara, aged and of a bit a loser, who was leaving to win back her Rhett Butler. Prepared to receive all the "Frankly, my dear, I don't give a damn" that Peter would be able to produce and hurl against me.

It was the beginning of the month of Peter's birthday and also William's. And I was invited to the premiere of a play in which Madeline would act. The theatrical and musical work of a young author, entitled *La vie en rose.*

With such a title, the notes of the song and the voice of Edith Piaf kept coming to my mind, but I was curious to see the staging of the play. Madeline was passionate about classical theatre but had expanded her perspectives towards a new type of contemporary theatre with musical influences. She believed that the way to the new talents of the dramaturgy should be opened and insisted that I express my opinion about the theatrical writing of some of her friends.

Even William had been invited to the play. He gave me a formal greeting, showing himself decidedly warmer with his uncle, his aunt, his cousins and especially with his sister. I was his mother. His rival, his enemy. The cause of the ruin of his life. And looking at him, observing his gestures, his movements, trying to catch his green eyes, so similar to his father's, I had further confirmation that he knew. Obviously, he couldn't have absolute certainty. Also, for this reason, he refused me. He feared to receive that certainty from me. He was afraid of it.

It became even more necessary for me to speak to Peter. Now that he had permanently returned to England and I had decided to stay in London and return to Leeds once a week until the end of the course, I had no more excuses to postpone.

I couldn't leave unfinished, unresolved business. Not anymore. Even though mine wasn't the story told in a movie or in a novel. It was life. With an infinity of voids, dark moments, time spent without achieving anything important, concrete, with my days that accumulated, one after the other with no news or expectations.

Because life is often like this. Nothing happens for years, sometimes for decades. Then everything is revolutionized in an instant. Here I am, after years dragged into oblivion, lacking nothing and missing everything, I needed a revolution. Little, maybe. Intimate, recondite, mine only. But a revolution was what it required.

Maybe a bit similar to the one of Virginia Woolf's dear Mrs. Dalloway. Organizing a party and buying flowers could sometimes conceal intrinsic passions, secrets, anguishes, memories, desires that awaited nothing but to be expressed, manifested. Crystallization, the infinite extension of an instant of life, of love. The essential need to exist, a spark of life that returned to shine.

This also happened in me, for me. Expressing myself and revealing myself had become an absolute and vital requirement. Yes, I was a middle-aged woman by now decidedly ready for a little, big revolution.

CHAPTER 73

I had chosen a day in mid-February. A sunny day, despite the cold that was still felt in the icy air from the last month of winter.

I had made myself pretty, I had put more effort than usual in dressing, combing, wearing make-up. Somehow, I found in myself the young woman I was years ago, in my brown hair, in my well-defined eyes, in the delicate lipstick and in the dress with blue shades and soft lines.

This time with more decision. Despite everything, he had never got rid of that white house with blue shutters. Everything there persisted unchanged over time, as crystallized. Including Gordon. I hoped to find him. I needed him. I needed his silent encouragement. Gordon was usually present when he knew Peter was nearby. Always, when he lived in England. So by logical consequence my hope was justified.

I had never deepened my knowledge of Gordon's private life. I knew that he lived in the smaller house adjacent to Peter's, with his wife who I had seen only a few times, fleetingly. And that they had three adult children. I knew that he felt for Peter an affection that went beyond what one has for his employer. So if he told me not to give up he really believed it. Knowing him, he wouldn't have gone that far otherwise.

I didn't hesitate, I rang the bell with a decision and a self-confidence I had never possessed before. I couldn't wait any longer. I had waited too long!

I waited. After a few minutes my self-confidence began gradually to resemble a snowman melting in the sun. I visualized the discomforting image of myself, instead of the snowman. No! I couldn't give up! I rang again by pressing my finger on the bell longer, more fiercely. More minutes of waiting. And finally, the door opened.

I found myself facing the young butler, the substitute one in short.

'Good morning. I need to talk to Peter Wiles.'

I used the forceful tone that tolerated no arguments. The one Peter could have defined as one of a snob and egocentric intellectual. Or maybe better of a woman determined to get what she wanted.

'Mr. Wiles is not at home, madam.' Of course. How could it be otherwise? I was already prepared to start the counterattack, but the young man preceded me. 'But... if you want to leave a message...'

'Sure!' I rummaged in my bag as the junior butler came down the steps to join me at the gate.

Considering that Peter didn't bother to answer my e-mails I had already prepared a letter in which I firmly expressed the absolute need to talk to him, including all my contact details. And in case he wasn't nearby a card with my cell phone number, which he already had, but which over the years that had passed, went without a call, so he could have lost, deleted or destroyed it.

'Tell him it's important...' I left the sentence hanging. I didn't know the junior butler's name.

'Jack...' he suggested to me, in an obsequious tone.

'Tell him it's important, Jack. I absolutely need to see him. It's about...' About our son, above all. Then about us, as well. '...about something we have to solve, a common business, let's say.'

I was aware of not having any hope of finding him at home. Or that he wouldn't allow me to see him anyway. I was hoping to convince him, if not through Jack's words, at least with the letter in which I begged him to meet me to talk about William. He was very likely to refuse both of us, but we had to try. I remembered the last words Peter had addressed to me. He had said he would try to get close to our son. Maybe it was time.

I received a call from him three days later, while I was in Leeds. Outside the university I was contacted by a private telephone number and I instantly understood it was him.

'I'll be in London in the next few days,' he told me coldly, with no emphasis. I didn't recognize his tone in the way he spoke to me, I almost didn't even recognize his voice. 'We can meet in a coffee shop.'

Oh, great. He didn't want to see me at his home. In a coffee shop? Didn't he care about being recognized?

A few hours later he told me through a phone message the day, the time and the exact place. I had four days to psychologically prepare myself, go back to London and meet him in a Notting Hill café. The one where, one Sunday many years ago, I had gone to get the coffee I had offered to Jacob.

I arrived about half an hour early and walked around, lingering in a small used book shop to kill some time. Checking the time every minute, it wouldn't have passed faster.

I couldn't even concentrate on the books I grabbed from the shelf and flicked through, almost without even seeing them. I ended up buying a historical novel by an unknown author set in the Midlands just because I was attracted by the cover. The woman portrayed was in nineteenth-century clothes and looked a lot like me, she wore a blue dress and held her hair in order not to risk that a gust of wind ruffled it.

I went out with the volume under my arm and in the distance I recognized him as he stood in front of the coffee shop with his head down. He wore a dark hat, one of those he had used in the past when he didn't want to be recognized. But no fake beard this time. Sweater, a light jacket, jeans. He seemed to have lost weight since the last time I met him in person. Even from his last public appearances, which I followed fiercely.

'Hi, Peter...'

He looked up at me and, unwittingly, I felt scrutinized by his eyes, by his way of looking at me. Had I aged? Did I put on weight? No, I didn't think so. But I lived with myself every day, the changes from my point of view could appear unnoticeable. I had worn the same dress as when I had come looking for him the previous week, hoping it would bring me luck, considering he had agreed to see me.

He, in addition to being thinner, didn't seem to have changed much. Of course, I had more chance to check his look over the years. He didn't answer, he simply pointed to the entrance to the coffee shop with a nod.

We entered and stood at the entrance for a few moments. I felt tense as if I was on a first date. No, I had never felt like that, with anyone.

We approached the counter to order. I asked for a simple cappuccino because I didn't have the mental strength to think about other combinations. Peter did the same. He paid for both and then, each of us with our paper cup in hand, walked towards a secluded table. The boy who had served us stared at Peter for a moment, bewildered, but he didn't give any sign of recognizing him.

Sitting in front of him, I dared a smile. My heart was beating wildly, I felt like a girl on the first date with the most handsome boy in the school. Another thing that had never happened to me firsthand. During my adolescence I had never paid attention to the most handsome boy at school, presuming there had been one.

'Thank you for... accepting to see me...'

My voice was also shaking. I managed to look up at him. I noticed his green eyes a little marked, the facial stubble a couple of days old.

'I didn't do it for you.'

Peter gripped the cup in his hands and leaned back in his chair.

'Yes, I understand that.' I sipped my cappuccino to take my time. But it didn't help, my stomach was completely in a knot. 'I... I'm glad you're back. Peter...'

I couldn't bear this coldness on his part. I couldn't stand it. It was like taking repeated punches to my stomach. I could have accepted such an attitude from anyone, but not from him. I lowered my face and bit my lips to hold back my tears.

'Shall we talk about the reason why we're here, Amantine?'

I didn't find the same emotion in his voice. He didn't feel anything anymore for me.

'Sure...'

I raised my face, wishing that my eyes were not too bright and that tears wouldn't drop, betraying me. I wasn't ashamed to cry for what I felt... but I feared that my emotion so alive, so manifest, would lead him to move away, thinking that I had asked him to grant me an appointment for other reasons. Not to talk about William.

'Fine... did you tell him something?'

His eyes were more and more like two blades that granted me no escape. And his voice was just as cold, distant. I hadn't even seen the shadow of a smile in him.

'I... I live in Haworth, near Leeds, half the time. I hold some writing courses at the university, I'll stay there until the end of the semester...' He certainly didn't want to hear the story of my recent life, but I had to start somewhere. 'Then I decided that I will move to London because William studies here, he started university. I mean, he started it a while back, actually... he studies English Literature, like me. I would have never guessed that... I was convinced that he wanted to follow in the footsteps of my mother, he was interested in astrophysics, but instead... And then Madeline also moved here, she studies Dramatic Art, she would like to work in theatre...'

I stopped, feeling my own voice, more and more uncertain, trembling. And above all because I was afraid of annoying him with all this detailed information. On the contrary, Peter listened to me in silence, attentive to my words. He nodded and gestured for me to continue.

'However... I think William knows.' Here, better go straight to the point, even if, not knowing how to organize the words around the sense of what I wanted to say, the only chance I had left was to tell Peter everything. All my feelings, all my dilemmas, all my fears. As they happened, as they were coming up to the surface and scratching my heart, asking to emerge, to be shared. 'And he despises me quite enough. He has never really had time for me, actually. He had always preferred Geoff, then my parents, his sister... even my brother... in short, anyone but me! I think he blames me for the failure of our family, for the separation from his father, I mean Geoff... He treats me with detachment, almost angrily when I try to get close to talk to him... And I tried Peter, so many times! He rejects me, saying that he doesn't have time when I try to take him aside to tell him the truth. And I still have not managed to impose it on him, to force him. In conclusion, I'm pretty sure that William considers me the root of all evils... And I think he's right. I have been the worst mother he could have had, poor boy...'

'I see. As long as he doesn't allow you to tell him the truth, he can reject it, pretend it doesn't exist. But are you so sure he knows?' Peter's expression was thoughtful, absorbed.

'Yes. I'm afraid Madeline suspects it too, actually... She told me she knew we had a relationship. So for sure William knows it, too. I mean, they are no longer children. Going back to the time when the two of us were together...' I bit my lips, laying a hand on the book I had placed on the table and tormenting the cover. 'Then you... with that CD and the song with my name. And poems and sonnets by William Shakespeare... Madeline knows it. William, as a result of her knowing...'

'I'm sorry, Amantine. I'd be lying if I told you I didn't think about it...' Peter sipped his cappuccino, then sighed deeply. 'I didn't mean any harm, I assure you. But somehow... I had to recover, I seemed to be drowning every day just a bit more. It was a project I already had in mind, you know. But I had to find a way to re-emerge to the surface and I let myself get even more involved. I felt betrayed...'

Finally, I could see an emotion in him, the shadow of a feeling even if not for me. Peter was always Peter, although he tried to hide and barricade himself behind a mask of coldness and indifference.

'You were betrayed, Peter. By me. And William too...' I tried to touch his hand with a finger, but I restrained myself so as not to risk losing that glimmer of hope that I had begun to hold on to. Then I went back to venting my frustration on the cover of the book. 'But it wasn't just for that, for your work on Shakespeare and for our song... Geoff moved to America with his new woman and his new son. William wanted to join him some time ago, to study in America. But Geoff rejected him. I don't know if he would have done the same if the request had come from Madeline... Madeline has always wanted to stay with me. But William... well, he might have thought Geoff's rejection comes from...'

I stopped, noticing Peter blush with anger. 'That damn asshole! He kept you trapped for years and then...'

'Geoff has his faults. But the main culprit was me...' This time I touched Peter's hand. A light, shy touch. I pulled back as soon as his eyes crossed me with an almost furious look. 'I should have left him in spite of everything, I should have told you the truth right away... when the children were still small...'

'It's useless dwelling on the past, Amantine.' His expression became quieter, more relaxed. 'Everyone has their faults, me too. Maybe I should have insisted more with you. Maybe I shouldn't have moved to America. Above all, I shouldn't have stayed there after what you revealed to me. I let other useless years go by, I got lost in meaningless situations... And it's not just about William, even for Matthew I've never been there. I'm almost a stranger to him, he was raised by my mother, as his mother was almost as absent as me. Also, my marriage to Kendra failed because of me... So you see, Amantine, we're both awful at dealing with relationships.'

'We still have something in common then, besides William...' I gave him a bitter smile. I swallowed a sip of my cappuccino,

325

now lukewarm, almost insipid. 'Maybe it was the relationships that were wrong... maybe if it was the two of us...'

No, I had to stop. I couldn't face a conversation about the feelings I still had for him. I wasn't ready to feel rejected and despised by him too.

'Yeah... maybe...' Peter closed his eyes, as if he was meditating on something to say. 'Anyway, I... I didn't tell you I've tried to see William. After you told me everything and even recently. I didn't approach him to talk to him, I just wanted to see him. I don't want to invade his space and impose myself, if he doesn't want to... He could have seen me, though. I'm sorry if I have created problems...'

'No, Peter. You did well. We have to talk to him, find a slot that would suit his schedule...' It was no longer about upsetting William. He almost certainly knew. We had to act calmly and by mutual agreement. 'But we must be aware of the fact that he could reject us both. Or for you, he might believe that you deny him, as Geoff did... I wouldn't want to fail again. I've already collected too many mistakes in my life. Above all, I wouldn't want to fail our son anymore.'

I was clinging with all my strength to that atmosphere of serenity that had been created between us. I needed him, a desperate, almost physical necessity. If not as a lover, partner, at least as a presence. I needed his closeness.

'We'll do our best, don't worry. I'll stay here, at least for a while...'

'I'm glad you're here. That you came back...' I tilted my face, raising a more relaxed smile. 'Your suggestion to meet in a public place surprised me. Don't you fear anymore that people recognize you, does that bother you?'

'I don't have fleets of possessed fans anymore, Amantine. I'm old now. Success is gone, fame as well...' Peter shrugged, indifferently. He didn't seem to care. 'I'm an ordinary man. Like a shooting star that for a brief moment travelled the firmament, and then plunged into oblivion... But I don't care anymore.'

'No. You'll never be any ordinary man, Peter.' I felt a faster beat in my heart. Inevitable, sweet and painful at the same time. 'You will remain the only one for me…'

'Don't bring up this conversation, Amantine, please…'

So he said. So he rejected me and nipped every illusion in the bud. But then why was it that every time he pronounced my name, I identified a sore point in his voice, like a regret he couldn't conceal, to keep unexpressed?

'All right. I'm sorry.'

'Do you know what you are for me instead? Do you really want to know?' He narrowed his eyes, focusing on me even more decisively, incisively, almost challenging me.

I nodded, lowering my face. I didn't want to see him while he was throwing all his contempt at me, all the evil that he thought about me. But I was prepared to receive it anyway.

'You are like... Do you remember cassettes tapes that were used some time ago? That kind of tape you recorded on several times and the new recording erased the previous one?'

I looked up, looking at him, confused. 'I'm an old thing that's not used anymore, in short.'

'No, I don't mean that. You are like the first song I recorded on that tape. Then I recorded more... And again, and again, I kept recording as many times as I could to try to forget, to remove what had been previously recorded... But I never managed to erase you, overwhelm you, because your song always came back destroying the next, it has always found a way to re-emerge through all the others. And the one I was listening to then was always that song, always you. But then... it happened that by continuing to record on it and always listen to the same song... the tape broke. That's what happened with those cassettes, once the tape broke it was useless to try to fix them. There was nothing left to do but throw away everything and resign ourselves to a clean tape, and a definitive cut...'

'Peter...' I understood his analogy. It fit perfectly. Was this what I had done to him? Really? I bit my lips and ran both hands

327

over my face. I wiped away a tear almost with fury. He had destroyed me, he had broken my heart, my soul, without even insulting me or telling me something bad. It wasn't like him, in fact. It had never been. What he didn't know was that it happened the same for me. I had never managed to overwhelm him with another. 'And if... if we bought a new tape... And if... we recorded our song again, without the need anymore to record others on...'

'I knew you'd say something like that, Amantine. You see how well I know you...'

Peter closed his eyes for a moment and fidgeted on his chair. I feared that at any moment he would decide to go and leave me alone in the coffee shop. Alone with my now cold cappuccino and with the book that I kept tormenting. Alone facing for the umpteenth time, the pain of having lost him.

'Great. Because if you know me as well as you say, you'll also know that I'm not going to give up. Neither on you nor on our son... although at the moment I understand that you both hate me...'

'I can't speak for William. But as far as I'm concerned, you're wrong. You have no idea how it is for me... how complicated it is to hate you, Amantine.' He grabbed his glass and squeezed it, then pushed it back and laid his hand on the table.

'Good... at least I can have a little hope.' I couldn't resist. I was no longer able to control my feelings or to appease them. 'Peter, I...'

'No, you can't.' He interrupted me, raising his tone of voice. 'Don't say that.'

'Is there... someone else? Is she at your home? That's why you wanted us to meet here...'

My heart was no longer trained to break and recompose itself in such short periods of time. Sooner or later it would explode in my chest, taking my life right there in a café in Notting Hill, right in front of him.

'No, Amantine. This is the point. There is nobody else... but I know well the effect you have on me and at my place I was afraid of not being able to resist despite my will. After all, it wouldn't be the first time.' He gave me a desolate look, then frowned as if he was regretful about what he had just said. I put my hand on his and this time I held it. But he didn't withdraw his. 'I came back for William and for Matthew. Not for you. And not even for myself.'

'I know, Peter. And if you don't want anything to do with me anymore, I understand... You're not the only one. I was a horrible woman, I hurt you. But I don't want to be one anymore. It's enough for me to know that I can still have a small place in your life. I... I also tried to overwhelm you, to record other songs on that tape, but in the end there was always you, our song... The only real one, for me. The only one to give me the strength to go on, all these years. Despite the distance, despite my mistakes.' Peter suddenly withdrew his hand and I had to go back and cling to the book with the cover of the woman with her hair ruffled by the wind. 'I was there even when you were far away... Your every success, every criticism, every relationship that has been attributed to you, true or presumed. I will always be there for you, Peter. Always. Whatever happens.'

'We must think about William, first of all. Let me know if you can talk to him, if you want me to...' Peter stood up, almost suddenly. 'In any case, even if he won't want to see me or know me.'

'Peter...'

I could have hung on to his arm to hold him back. To avoid it I grabbed the book with both hands, squeezing it tightly. Something that served me well in the end, it had been perfect as a focus to channel my energy on, I had done well to buy it.

'I hope it's not too important...' Peter focused his gaze on my hands. 'You've been slaughtering that poor book for an hour.'

'No, I... I bought it while I was waiting for you. It's not important... I don't even know the author, I don't need it for any literature study or research. I have no idea how it goes.' I stood up and smiled, lifting the book to show it to him. 'You'll never believe it, I bought it just because I liked the cover. I'm no longer a little snob intellectual.'

'Attracted to the outer cover. A bit like you did with me that Sunday morning.' Peter nodded, shrugging, avoiding my look and pointing his eyes towards the door of the coffee shop.

'This is only partly true. Initially, I was attracted to the outer cover, you're right.' I threw the book on the table with a sharp snap and I grabbed him, this time, his arm. Even though Peter had completely turned away from me in the meantime. 'But afterwards it didn't have anything to do with the external appearance. And it doesn't even matter that the outer cover is no longer the same and that obviously with the years it will change again. Because it's the content that I fell in love with, Peter. With you.'

CHAPTER 74

Following my declaration, Peter did nothing but turn to me and give me a smile. A faint smile, a tired smile. A smile a bit incredulous and partly embittered. But it was still a smile.

I could have taken him in my arms, I could have held him to me. I could have repeated to him that I loved him, that I would always love him. I would repeat it until I warmed up his now so silent heart, so cold towards me, so hurt by everything I had concealed from him, by the life I had torn from him. Until our song would re-emerge uncontested, alive, throbbing. Amantine's song wasn't just mine. It was ours. And I would have patience, courage and enough love for both of us.

'I... I have to go...' Peter bit his lips tightly, looking down. 'I have a few gigs and studio sessions going on during these months... They are charitable projects that I care a lot about, even if they make me to collaborate with people I don't admire or respect musically, it's for a good cause. But if you need me for William, I'll be there Amantine. I can move commitments, try to postpone them...'

'Thanks, Peter. I'm sure we'll make it... with him. He's just so bloody stubborn. After all, he's our son.' I smiled, touching his face softly with my fingers, meeting his green eyes. Then I left his arm, which I still held with my other hand.

I understood that for the two of us, I couldn't expect much. I had to heal his heart first, cure the wounds that I had myself inflicted on him. Make sure that he returned to trust me and consequently to love me.

Meanwhile, the days passed. I continued my life away in Yorkshire even if I tended to stay in London as much as possible. We were now in early March. A few more months. Then I didn't know exactly what I would do but I would find a solution. I would ask Marianne and Alain for their hospitality for a while, and then look for a house with Madeline or alone.

I followed Peter's projects, as always, after all. The fact that we had an agreement and communicated lightened my spirits. I felt better from every point of view. I knew he was still angry and didn't forgive me. For that it would take time. But I could finally see hope. With William and for us too.

Several times I recalled the analogy he had given me, the one about the recorded tape. I visualized the scene so much and scrolled it in my mind. He had tried to forget me without succeeding... Did he want to tell me this? He was still angry at me, maybe he wouldn't forgive me easily. But his heart still belonged to me. And I would commit myself to take care of it.

I was also constantly recalling the evening that had split us up. That party. Everything. The dream that turned into a nightmare. We were young, happy, with a future to be lived, with the hope of achieving success and consideration. We were in love, even without knowing it. Then everything had been torn from us. Even because of our fault, for our insecurity, for our fear of being rejected. For those absurd rules that we had imposed on ourselves.

Simon Jennings, Darkest Storm, the Stevensons. They seemed a distant memory now, wrapped in the darkness of a past to be removed from our lives forever. Like a photograph faded by time.

I also removed Raymond Carter, Geoff's father. Left by his second wife, married after the death of Geoff's mother, who in the moment of need had thought well of disappearing with much of his money. Abandoned in a luxury clinic in Paris by his son who had decided to start a new life or maybe to take the one he had never had with me, making up for his lost time. The old Carter, the great scholar, the art and ancient objects collector, the successful entrepreneur, had been entrusted to the care of the nurses and of a distant cousin. To the good heart of my mother, who occasionally went to see him, and to Madeline and William, who visited him when they returned to Paris.

I was not a good-hearted woman, I had never been. I had seen him only once after separating from Geoff. And after knowing what he tried to do to Peter. Maybe I wanted to see with my own eyes, for the last time, the one who had contributed to my unhappiness. He was a finished man, immobilized in his bed and in his silence. Geoff was convinced that he no longer recognized anyone now. Or maybe it was just an excuse to justify his escape to freedom in America.

But I wasn't convinced. I saw a glow of terror in the old manipulator's eyes when I appeared before him. When I told him I knew what he had done that night, that I knew about his agreement with Simon Jennings. And that I would have struggled with all my strength to get back and defend what was mine. That I would have killed him with my own hands if something had happened to Peter. So, no... I wasn't absolutely convinced that Geoff was right. Raymond Carter suffered in forced silence the procession of those who out of duty, good heart, curiosity or resentment marched in front of him, waiting for his end.

I didn't like some of Peter's new projects. Our agreement and our contacts had to be exclusively about William, I was aware of it, but that he had come back to interact with some people who had been part of his past, I didn't like at all, although it was for charity and occasional collaborations for a series of concerts.

Perhaps this was further evidence that I wasn't a good-hearted woman. But I hated the fact that Simon Jennings was trying in every way to get involved in the project with a newly formed band. He was a slimy opportunist, greedy and unscrupulous, ready to worm his way back in and take advantage of anyone. I didn't want him around Peter. And I didn't want Peter's name to be associated with his again. So I had to find a way to prevent that individual from being accepted among collaborators and participants.

I tried to call Peter on the phone, after meditating for a few hours on the news I had found on the internet. No reply. I tried several times during the day.

I knew it wasn't about our son but his private and professional sphere in which I had no right to interfere, however I couldn't help but worry about him. I had a feeling... a very bad feeling. If Jennings had already hurt him once, without scruples, without restraint...

I felt boiling. How could Peter be so naïve? Maybe he hadn't believed my words? Didn't he take me seriously? Maybe he thought he wasn't so serious and was underestimating what Jennings had tried to do to him? Or maybe my next revelation concerning William had upset him to such an extent that it led him to minimize his former manager's faults? And yet he was aware of it, too! No, he couldn't have forgotten.

I wrote him an e-mail begging him to answer me immediately or better, to call me. I kept vague about the reasons for my request, implying it could be William. I waited all day, until evening.

I didn't have much left to do. I could go and look for Simon Jennings and order him to stay away from Peter and his projects, threatening to make his past intentions public. But after more than twenty years, that despicable being would laugh at me and my threats.

I had to stay calm. I didn't have to worry. Yet I couldn't get the idea of that man around Peter out of my mind. Other celebrities were involved, including Steve Woodhouse, a former Darkest Storm member who had embarked on a career as a soap opera actor after the band broke up.

I didn't know that world, I had never really known it. It had never interested me. But that Peter was in danger, I felt it like a shiver under my skin, which destroyed every faculty of judgment and rationality in me, struck in me a fear, or rather a terror, almost uncontrollable. And the awareness that I had to protect him, this time.

Peter, saying goodbye at the end of our conversation in the coffee shop, had mentioned having to work with people he didn't admire. I was trying frantically to find out more without being able to find updates on the initiative that would start between late spring and early summer.

I felt irrational as I had never been, I realized. Almost insane in my search. And the next morning I would have to leave to teach at Leeds, with my mind elsewhere and an uncontrollable panic that broke my breath.

I decided to follow another path. I waited for Madeline to come home and asked her for Geoff's new phone number. I urgently needed to talk to him.

It had to be afternoon in the United States, so no problem. I wouldn't wake him up in the middle of the night.

'Geoff, it's me...' I sighed impatiently. But I had to try to keep calm and not to attack him straight away with my unreasonable and slightly absurd requests. I committed myself to assume a more gentle and conciliatory tone. 'How are you?'

My ex-husband didn't hide his surprise at my call but tried to answer in an equally courteous tone, informing me about his health and his work, leaving out his new partner and his new son.

Probably he feared that I reproached him for not accepting William a few years earlier. It was better to be upfront immediately.

'Listen, Geoff. You know me enough, you know that I would never have phoned you just to ask you how you are doing with your new life. I need important information... and maybe even something more. I would ask your father, but he doesn't seem very cooperative, unfortunately, you know it too.'

'It's Peter Wiles, isn't it?' Yes, definitely Geoff knew me enough. Since I mentioned his father he understood where I was headed. That he was investigating on Peter's projects seemed to me more remote as a possibility.

'I need to know... what's true about Simon Jennings. Are you absolutely sure he tried to kill Peter that night? Did he clearly manifest his intention? Your father...'

'Amy... what I told you is what I know. I don't know to what extent Jennings wanted Peter dead, but... In short, my father wouldn't have gone that far, he was certainly not the type who was impressed by a suspicion over him. Then it didn't happen and the story was archived, as I told you.'

I heard him sigh nervously. I realized that he would rather not know anything, have nothing to do with it. In fact, he would prefer not to have anything to do with me either. If only he had realized it before it was absolutely not worth it to love me, marry me and keep me tied...

'Geoff, would you be willing to witness what you know? Without putting yourself and your father in the middle maybe... In case we could say that you found it out recently, before he had the stroke. Or later, when he could still communicate, he might have confessed it to you...'

'No, Amantine. I'm sorry.' His tone became authoritative. When did he call me by my full name? Almost never. 'I no longer want to have anything to do with that story, never again!'

'Peter could work with that man again. I told him what he tried to do to him. I have to convince him at all costs to exclude him or leave the project, rather. Please... I know you hate me, you hate Peter too, but I'm so worried, I don't want Jennings around him.'

I was begging him. Peter probably wouldn't have listened to him either and would reproach my intrusion. He despised Geoff. But among the various resentments that inevitably existed between the three of us, I remained unmoving in my purpose. My feeling was tremendous, like a sentence. I was afraid.

'If it never happened it would have been much better for everyone.' Geoff's voice suddenly seemed calmer, more relaxed. I didn't understand what he meant exactly. I let him go on. 'All right. If needed I will say what I know. But without blackening the name of my father and mine. I paid enough for my obsession for you and my attempt to keep you tied to me. If in this way I can get rid of the past completely, you will have my testimony against Jennings, as long as it's worth something. In the end, now I'm happy, finally. It's right that you are too.'

CHAPTER 75

I received Peter's call the next morning. He apologized for inadvertently leaving the phone run out and only checking his e-mail just a few minutes before calling me. He was tense and worried.

'It's not about William. And not even about me. It's about you, Peter.' I was getting ready to leave for Leeds, but I was willing to give up, make up an excuse and warn them that the lesson wouldn't take place. 'You can't accept Simon Jennings in the project in which you are involved. Yes, well... I look for news about you on the internet, you know. And so... I read it and I don't want you to, Peter. You don't have to work with him. I don't like it, I don't like it at all! He has already tried to hurt you once, I can find evidence and...'

'And do you think I don't know? I don't want it too, it's not up to me but to the event's organizers. I can't throw him out. But Amantine... don't worry, everything will be fine.' Peter sighed with the typical condescension reserved for a petulant girl. He was actually treating me like a petulant girl.

'No, Peter. Please... I...'

I didn't know how to hold him on the line. All I knew was that I shouldn't let him hang up and dismiss me with a "Don't worry.'

'Amantine... there are many other people involved, it's not just about Simon and his new Darkest Storm. I know what he tried to do to me, and I know what he did to us. But I have to be reasonable and not hold on to what happened so many years ago. I don't want that man to still influence my life. So I will face him and I will not let myself be fooled by influence. Try to do the same too.'

Obvious. Perfectly rational answer, even too much, while everything inside of me was screaming my firm intention to protect the man I loved, and that I had already left alone in the past.

'Forget about it so. I don't want…'

I dropped my bag on the floor and started crying. Softly, without making any noise. Probably Peter could only hear a silence interrupted by some sighs.

'Amantine…'

'I love you, Peter. I know you don't want me to tell you. And that maybe you don't love me anymore. But I love you anyway. And I know it's horrible timing and we're on the phone too, so it sucks even more as a declaration. But I love you and I can no longer hold myself back, especially if I think you could be in contact with that unscrupulous man again. I know I promised you that we would only talk about William. But I'm a selfish woman and I love you, even if I don't deserve you. And I should leave for Leeds now, for the lessons of the course I'm giving, but I won't go. Because I love you and I have to protect you…'

After the pseudo declaration in the coffee shop, this was even worse. I certainly couldn't hope to convince him like that. I could have convinced him to think I should go to hell, once and for all. Most definitely.

'Amantine…' I almost recognized the impatient sigh from him. Here and now I would get the reproach, the rejection and the phone hung up on me. 'I think you said more "I love you's" in a minute than in the whole course of your life. Might be the phone that makes you bold…'

'No, I…'

He wasn't angry, in fact he seemed almost amused, even if I had no way of checking his expression.

'Be a good girl, sweetheart. Go to Leeds for your course. You don't want to disappoint your students, do you? It wouldn't be like you, little egocentric intellectual.'

'Peter…'

He called me "sweetheart". And also "little egocentric intellectual". How long since that happened? I couldn't hold back my sobs. My heart was beating so fast that I was bewildered.

'Amantine, listen to me carefully. What I'm doing is important to me. When I told you that I didn't care about my career anymore, I lied to you.' He spoke to me in the tender and persuasive tone like long ago, but determined. I tried to appease my distress and listen to him calmly. 'I need some time. I would like to try to recover what I was, as much as possible. Not so much the fame and success of my youth. Surely not the fans obsessed with my look. But my good name, my artistic value if it still exists. I want to be worthy of consideration, to be reliable and correct. That's why I won't back down. I don't want to be remembered as the one who got on stage drunk. Because it happened... several times. And I don't want to be remembered as the one who betrayed his wife jumping from one model to another. So in these weeks I will take part in the rehearsals for this series of concerts. I will behave in an irreproachable manner, I will offer the best of me. I want to rebuild a name of prestige for my children, for myself... and for you as well, baby...'

I was almost speechless after listening to him. 'For me as well? I... I'm always here, Peter... I...'

Did he really want to include me as well in his life? In his future? Tears of joy and emotion flowed down my face, flooding it completely until they reached my neck.

'Yes, Amantine. For you as well. That's why I ask you to trust me. And to give me some time.' I heard him sigh again. I just wanted to be there with him, hug him, hold him close to me. Look him in the eye and tell him that I loved him like crazy, even more than ever. 'Then if you want, we will buy a new cassette, with a new tape and we will record our song. Because... I love you too, sweetheart. I've tried many times, but I've never been able to stop loving you. And now I love the beautiful and strong woman you've become even more. It's always been real only with you.'

CHAPTER 76

I had to be patient and give Peter the time he had requested. Let him carry out his commitment to those concerts. Even if they involved Simon Jennings. Even if they kept him away from me.

I tried to reassure myself, obey Peter and go back to Leeds. I had to concentrate on giving my students the best of me. His words had made me as happy as I hadn't been for so long. He still loved me. There would be no more obstacles and impediments between us. I just wanted to love him and make him happy. Together we would be able to recover the relationship with William. It was late, of course. But it wasn't too late for us yet.

I did nothing but listen to our songs, the soundtrack of our lives. We could add some new ones, every day now. We would fill the distance, the lost time, all the years of separation.

A few more days passed. I stayed in Leeds for my classes. I was tempted to call him again, but I didn't want to disturb his work. In the end, I decided to send him an e-mail and he replied a few hours later. I had kept myself vague, I just wanted to know how he was and how the work was going. I was firmly determined to leave him to himself but at the same time I wanted him to know that I would always be there for him. I found reassurance in his words and in the messages we exchanged whenever it was possible to communicate. It was also a relief not to have to look for information on the internet anymore, but instead to find out everything directly from him.

I didn't dare to question him about Simon Jennings's participation or even other artists' in order not to discover something that I wouldn't have liked. For the same reason he didn't mention them to me.

He spoke to me about us mostly, he asked me about my work, my books, William and Madeline too. He hoped both my children would accept him. I asked him about his son Matthew. He told me he was fond of opera music. Unbelievable! Then he told me about the organizations to which the funds would be allocated. And about the new ideas he had planned later. He wanted to continue experimenting with other musical horizons.

I dreamed of our life together. A bit like it had been once, during our early days. When I had chosen, against everything and everyone, to be with him. Without telling him that I loved him, but living with him and for him every day.

I remembered those moments when we both worked, him with his guitar and his notebook in his hands, me with my books and my sheets of notes scattered everywhere. And then when he approached me, he took me in his arms and dragged me over him. His kisses, his caresses. I wanted everything back. All of him and all of me. Our song. All we had before that night, before that party. Before my mad desperation, before his emotional and physical annihilation... all that we had suffered because of others and also because of our emotional fragility and insecurities.

Now we had grown strong. I wouldn't allow anything or anyone to separate us. Nor would Peter allow it, I was sure of that.

My self-confidence wavered when I found out that among the places where the rehearsals were to take place there was also the one that had marked our end. The Stevensons' mansion which now belonged to someone else. It had been bought about ten years ago by an American actor, keen on music, who had formed his own band and was enthusiastic about musical events.

Peter had carefully avoided telling me, I knew from some research on the internet. Despite the exchange of messages with him I hadn't lost certain habits. I wanted to read what was said about it. In turn, I avoided informing him of my discovery so as not to disturb him. But his proximity to that place, as well as to Simon Jennings, made my heart sink.

That feeling of a bad omen accompanied me on my return to London. I was forced to keep my fears to myself. I didn't want to upset Peter and the others couldn't understand what it meant for me to know he was there with that man nearby.

I waited with bated breath for the days to pass, those set for rehearsals in what I still considered the Stevensons' mansion. I wrote to him repeatedly. So much so that Peter understood my state of anxiety. The last night of rehearsals he told me that my fear had been unfounded, everything went well.

The day set for the event I would be by his side. Right there, where our story had taken a dramatic turn. And we would change our perception of that place forever. He, despite everything, kept good memories. Of me on that little bridge. When I turned around and we looked into each other's eyes. When he was about to tell me he loved me and he only wanted me.

We were approaching the middle of the month and the last weeks of rehearsals before the start of the actual concert series. They would start to get serious... and the two of us as well. I was ready, I felt ready for years now. I had to be patient a few more days. Just a few days. My fears, my feelings, had been groundless. I could relax.

That morning I woke up at dawn. Even before six o'clock I could no longer sleep. After turning in bed for half an hour I decided to get up and make some coffee. I had held the last lesson of the first cycle of the course two days before and had assigned a paper to the students. So I had about ten days of freedom that I would take advantage of to spend some time in London. Maybe I could see Peter. Indeed, not "maybe". It was all I had dreamed of for almost three weeks. Stay with him a little, even for just a few hours. In his arms. Finally tell him how much I loved him while looking him in the eyes.

Yes, I dreamed of my happiness. The happiness that I had never been able to achieve completely but that was so close now. The happiness that despite all my mistakes I believed I still deserved.

I dragged myself lazily through the house, inconclusive and a little nervous, waiting for my departure. I had prepared everything the night before and still had about two hours to get to Leeds railway station and get my train to London.

'Love... I'm coming. I'll be in London in the early afternoon.'

Recognizing Madeline's number on the screen of my mobile phone, I replied before giving her time to speak.

'Mom...' I heard her sigh. Not a deep sigh, but a broken, anxious one. 'Mom... you don't know yet...'

'What? Baby, what happened?'

I couldn't understand, I had the feeling of climbing a mirror in search of the drama that afflicted my daughter, but I was always slipping down.

'Hmm... here...' She was out of breath, like after a run. She seemed to struggle, searching for words she couldn't find.

'Did something happen to William?' I raised my voice, almost to stun myself. I shouted to such an extent that I felt my breath break and my vocal cords squeal.

'No, not to him...' Another hesitation. My parents maybe? Alain? Madeline's tone suddenly became more determined. 'Mom, listen. Didn't you turn the TV on this morning? Didn't you watch the news?' I was about to reply but Madeline didn't give me the time. 'There was an accident... a fire during the rehearsals, maybe generated by a short circuit, in a residence in the Reading area, last night...'

'No...'

An accident. A fire. It couldn't mean... I was standing in my room and I didn't know where to hold onto. I grabbed the emptiness, backing up to my bed. But I couldn't sit down and slid to the ground.

'I'm so sorry, Mom...' I sensed Madeline's voice more and more in the distance, like a faint whisper. 'They don't know yet if there are any survivors, but...'

'He can't have left me. No, no, he wouldn't leave me like that... He promised it to me. He can't...'

I turned around and found myself on my knees, with my arms and my face on my bed. I grabbed the sheet with all the strength I had. I felt a strange force emerge in me, as if I was undergoing a transformation. As if I was becoming a creature with an extraordinary power that emerged from my bowels, from my blood. Immediately afterwards I was pervaded by a strange, senseless stillness. And then by an unusual tiredness.

Suddenly I just wanted to rest, just sleep. Sleep and not think about anything anymore. Neither the past nor the present. Neither myself, nor others. Not even about him. What had divided us, what had brought us together. Sleep and not feel anymore, not dream anymore. No more hopes, no more illusions. Nothing could have made sense now. The world could even stop. And there was nothing left for me to do but sleep. Hoping not to have to undergo changes again. Hoping not to have to wake up and be forced to face an existence without my life. Without my song.

CHAPTER 77

No, I didn't need Madeline and Alain to come and pick me up. I could very well go back to London by train. It was already booked and would leave shortly. It would take me less time. I decisively refused any other option.

I was a strong woman. I wasn't before, but I would become one. He had reminded me of it. Beautiful and strong. Beautiful perhaps only in his eyes now. But I would become strong, I would prove to be so. I couldn't collapse while there was still hope.

I stayed in touch with Madeline for the entire length of the journey. I had begged her to keep me updated without hiding anything from me. In the meantime, I was looking for information on my laptop but besides the fact itself, there was no news.

After leaving Madeline, I tenaciously clung to hope. So much I dialled Peter's mobile number in the hope that he answered me. Instead, it rang out. I tried again, several times. I also opened his last e-mail and read it carefully. Everything will be fine. I'll see you soon. We'll be together.

No, I couldn't collapse. Peter needed me. I could still feel him. In the meantime, I could see myself as if from the outside, like someone who wasn't me. Who was that woman who was quietly sitting on a train bound for London, looking out the window, who had embarked on a journey like many others, on a day like many others? So composed, so strict. Almost imperturbable.

It almost didn't seem real. Maybe a part of me still rejected what happened. Or maybe my heart strengthened so much now that it absorbed the news without being torn apart by pain. I had collapsed for a lot less. When the loss could be serious, but not so definitive, so drastic.

I found Marianne waiting for me at King's Cross station. I had expected Madeline or Alain. I questioned her with my eyes, but she shook her head slightly. She stroked my back gently.

'Alain was able to find out which hospital they took him to, St. Thomas. Now he's there with Madeline.'

'Thank you...' Never would I have suspected that the word "hospital" would give me such a comforting feeling. Almost a relief that soothed the pain I had restrained with all the strength I was capable of. Then the reason came back to throb powerfully in my mind and I realized that it could mean all or nothing. 'You know...?'

'No. I haven't received any updates beyond that, but now we'll go there straight away.'

Marianne guided me to her car and I let myself be dragged. Like a helpless child, like a tourist in a foreign country who follows her guide without having the faintest idea of where she is leading her.

'Thank you...'

'We know how important he is to you, Amantine.'

I read in Marianne's gaze the desire to tell me that everything would be fine but the impossibility of doing it.

I continued to let myself be guided by my sister-in-law, who skilfully juggled through traffic, without even following the road she was driving. As if I no longer had the absolute need to be brave, unstoppable and controlled at all costs.

Once we reached the hospital, Marianne parked and we got out of the car. As she was talking on the phone with Alain, I felt that the strength was leaving me, at every step. Drop by drop it dried up in me, leaving my heart tight in a grip of terror and exhaustion at the same time. Nevertheless, I kept walking and walking. I began to fear the moment when I would reach the goal and would necessarily have to stop to face the truth.

Meanwhile, memories flashed in my mind. They were not a succession of images, of scenes of the two of us. It wasn't our story. They were more like momentary glares, which appeared in a flash and then disappeared, plunging into darkness. And they didn't even involve just the two of us. Some were before our first meeting. My childhood. Me and Alain on holiday in Italy. My grandparents. The swing in the garden of my parents' first home in France. Then I passed directly to William's birth. My first kiss with Peter. The first interview that Jacob had given me. My meeting with Professor Frey. And so on.

It was the whole of my life really. Picked at random. Without logical sequence, ideal associations or chronological links. A stream of consciousness in bulk as I walked towards my destiny without knowing yet whether it would be of hope or pain.

'Mom...'

I recognized Madeline's voice without having an exact idea of where we were. Inside the hospital, yes. Following Marianne, I hadn't even checked in which ward, lost as I was in the revival of those brief moments of my past, remote or more recent photographs of myself.

I questioned my daughter with my eyes and was joined by my brother, too.

'We don't know much yet. Only that... Amantine, he seems serious. Really.' Alain was a doctor. Now, I needed it. No minced words. Absolute truth.

I let myself be led by Madeline who took me into a narrow room, with predominant shades of pastel colours. Except for the dark grey upholstered chairs. It almost looked like an airport waiting room. I kept my eyes fixed, absorbed to the point of seeming almost indifferent, while the rundown of scenes of my life continued to flow in front of me.

But something was changing. Him. He was taking up more and more space among those scenes. Our meeting on a Sunday morning. The dress I had worn for the party. The pizza late at night. My attempt to make cookies. The book I had bought while

I was waiting for him, for our last meeting in the coffee shop. What had happened to that book? With that woman on the cover... the one with her hair ruffled by the wind... I had left it in Haworth perhaps. Or it remained in the room I occupied at Alain's house when I returned to London. I hadn't read it yet. I wonder if I would have liked it or if it was really just the cover...

"Attracted to the outer cover. A bit like you did with me that Sunday morning." Those words of his. His body. His eyes. His way of smiling at me, making fun of me.

"It's the content that I fell in love with, Peter. With you." The first time I had really confessed that I loved him, while I clung to him, to his arm. In a Notting Hill café.

'No, no...' I shook my head, murmuring to myself. I felt the sob that was proceeding rapidly from my stomach with the intent of bursting into my throat. I had to hold it back, even though I could risk suffocating. I wouldn't allow it to express my pain. I hadn't lost. Not yet. I shook my head even more, more intensely. I didn't even allow my tears to run down my face. I couldn't be desperate. Not yet.

'Madam...'

A voice in the distance. Was it calling me? I raised my face. It wasn't far, but right in front of me, just a few steps. A woman that looked task-driven, with a light, delicate complexion. Brown hair streaked with grey gathered up on the sides of her face. She had something familiar about her, but I couldn't understand what exactly.

She didn't look like a nurse, she wore a black skirt and a light-green twin-set sweater. I frowned, waiting. I couldn't risk that just one word would unleash the hurricane I was holding inside me.

'My name is Sandra.' The woman seated herself directly beside me. 'I'm Peter's mother.'

She maintained a composed, almost neutral external attitude. Like mine, if not more. What was hidden inside her was unknown to me.

'I... I am Amantine...' I managed to whisper, turning slightly to her, looking for support in her eyes halfway between blue and green.

'I know. I recognized you right away.' She tilted her face slightly as if to better study my appearance, my features. 'I've seen some of your photos. Peter had one that he never let go of when... Many years ago, when he had some problems and he was at home with me for a bit.'

'Yes, he told me.' I bit my lips hard to try to restrain the trembling that was taking hold of me from within, forcing me to lose control. 'How he... how...?'

I found Madeline and Alain only a few steps away, while Peter's mother placed a hand on my fingers, entwined with strength in another vain attempt to restrain.

I hadn't yet asked myself the question of what and how it happened exactly. I had been too busy reassembling those small scattered fragments of my entire life.

'He had a serious cerebral concussion, a hematoma that was pressing on his brain, but for that he has already been operated on and it seems to be resolved. Even the burns are not serious enough to put him in a life-threatening state. But he has... a severely damaged liver...' I felt another trembling in addition to mine. It was that of Peter's mother, who was updating me about her son's condition.

What was her name? She had just told me. Did Peter ever talk to me about her? No, never. Maybe he only mentioned her when we exchanged general information about our families. After all, we were just casual lovers. There had never been a need for official presentations. Suddenly I remembered her name, the moment when she had said it a few minutes before. Sandra.

'He will make it, Sandra. He is strong.'

I released my hands, although with a bit of difficulty. My icy fingers had kind of got stuck together. I took Sandra's hand in mine. She was unknown to me, a stranger. But she was Peter's mother and she could understand me more than anyone else in that moment.

'He needs a liver transplant. My son Harry and my grandson Matthew, Peter's son, are doing the analysis to see if they are compatible for a donation. They don't have a whole one available and there's no time to wait...'

'But if they're blood relatives...' I didn't know anything about it. But if they had the same blood, then...

'They must be considered suitable.' Alain, who like me was listening to Sandra's words, stepped in. I hoped to receive some reassurance from him. 'It's not enough to be blood relatives. That's why they need to be analysed, there are a lot of things to consider to see if a partial transplant is possible or it could be too dangerous for donor and recipient.'

'I have to see him...' I stood up and walked a few steps without even knowing where I was heading. Fragments of my past life, dreams and reality mingled in me, compressing my thoughts. I let Peter's mother and Alain's words slip by on me without oppressing me. 'Where is he? I want to see him.'

I was nobody to him. I wouldn't be allowed to see him without the explicit request of his mother. My firm intention wavered at the room door. I caught a glimpse of him lying, stuck in that small bed that seemed too tight, oppressive and suffocating. With his head bandaged, his face swollen. It didn't even look like him. The liveliness, the soul of the man I loved was completely absent from that motionless body.

It was my heart to approach him, before my body. An instinctive, protective movement.

'My love...' I found myself standing, next to him. 'I'm here, my love.'

I knelt down, grabbing his hand hard, then more gently, fearing I'd hurt him. How many other words I wanted to tell him... Not even one came out from me... His bruised, scratched, marked face was always the same. It was always him. I just regretted that I couldn't see his eyes.

I leaned my head gently into the hollow of his shoulder. As he was when he slept. Here, I could pretend he was asleep or pretended to sleep. That's why he wasn't looking at me. I could look for the tattoo on his shoulder, I could barely see it under the bandage, but it was there. Then that A drawn at the base of his neck. *All of me*, he had said. His first solo album. Amantine. No, I didn't delude myself that he had thought about me.

'I love you... I've loved you for so long that I almost can't remember... I think... I think I loved you from the first moment. I couldn't know what it meant to love before. How could I, without you? Here, that's it. Just like this, Peter. How could I know without you? How can I know?'

I spoke to him like that. One word after another. As if I was telling him a story. While he was still napping and I was starting to wake up. And my voice was no longer blocked by a sob that broke my breath by clenching my throat. It came out loose, fluid though light.

'I haven't read that book yet. I wonder if it's as good as the cover... I don't... I don't even know the name. I don't remember the title. Not even the name of the author... It must be beautiful. Then I met you in the coffee shop. Everything that concerns you is beautiful, so... Maybe I could write a historical novel too. I'll let you read it first, though... And then maybe I could teach a bit more in Leeds. You could stay with me at Haworth, you know it's Brontë sisters' hometown? I told you about it, didn't I? At first they used male pseudonyms, like George Sand. But what little egocentric intellectual talks I'm giving you... Anyway, we could go back to London together then... in your home in Notting Hill. I still have to learn how to cook, this time I promise I will ask Gordon to teach me and I will work hard. I will start with cookies, the other time it was a failed experiment. But I don't know if it's a good idea for me to go back teaching in London, even if I could now, considering that I'm almost a celebrity in my field... I should have to deal with that licker Gregor again and I'm honestly too old now and I don't have the physical condition anymore to kick his ass. I'll let William do it... He's so much better than me, you know? I was just a little snob and egocentric intellectual, but he instead...'

Suddenly I raised my face and found myself with my lips not far from his cheekbone.

'Peter... Peter, I love you. And you love me too. You can't leave me right now. Not now that we're finally free. Not now that I've learned to tell you... and you'll have to hear me say it every day, every moment...' My tears flowed down my face and on his as well. 'What a crazy life... First I tell you somehow in a coffee shop, then by phone... And now that I'm ready, you can't hear me... I'm a mess, isn't it true my love? So please... Be a good boy and don't leave me. I... I don't want anything without you. What can I ever do without you? The world would continue to spin with its usual imperturbable mechanism, but I... We have to write a song, Peter, a new one. We have to buy the cassette with the new tape. Do you remember the cassette you lent me that morning I was late at university? The one to keep me awake after frolicking all night? When you taught me how to love music...'

'Amantine...' My brother had to call me three times before he took me away from my story, from Peter.

I forced myself to turn around and pay attention to him. My voice froze again in a knot between my chest and my throat.

'Hmm…'

'Matthew, Peter's son, unfortunately is not compatible. His blood group doesn't match. Now they're still analysing his brother, but he has had some small heart problems. He wants to try anyway, but it's too risky...'

I didn't like it. I didn't like Alain's story at all, I preferred mine, the one I was telling Peter. Yet my brother always knew how to be so enjoyable and funny. He was the funniest person in my family, why did he have to make me feel so bad?

I pulled away from Peter, from his face. But I stayed on my knees beside him anyway, I grabbed his hand and held it in mine.

Someone could... Maybe me? My eyes narrowed for a moment. I put my hand on my chest, then slowly went down towards my womb. I didn't want to keep that baby. What would I have done? Alone, lost, scared. I had to lose it, let it go. But I couldn't. It was his.

'It was his...' I repeated aloud. It's his. Maybe his blood group... Maybe he could be suitable. 'William...'

CHAPTER 78

'He will never come...' Resignation immediately took the place of hope. I had been forced to leave Peter, to leave him alone in that small, aseptic room, in that small tight bed. 'He won't do it. He hates me... Because of me he will never come.'

They were all around me. Besides my brother, my sister-in-law and my daughter, there was Sandra, Harry, Peter's brother, and Matthew, who looked like a youthful version of Peter. Apart from the blue eyes, he looked impressively like him. Peter's green eyes went to William.

'Yes, he will. I can convince him!' Madeline's firm tone of voice caught everyone's attention. Madeline sighed deeply, frowning. 'William has never refused me anything, not since I was born. If I call him, he will come. At the risk of telling him I'm sick myself, I'll draw him here.'

So part of my family and Peter's family had become aware of a truth that some members probably already knew or suspected anyway. William was Peter's son. Of all the ways and the possible moments in which I had hypothesized the great revelation, I wouldn't have imagined this one, not even remotely.

Madeline disappeared for a period of time that seemed endless to me. The wait was dominated by silence. I was looking pleadingly at the corridor leading into his room. After sitting there for a few minutes, I started to walk back and forth, as if pervaded by a boundless physical energy that I was forced to dispose of at all costs.

'He's coming.' Madeline reappeared with the phone in her hands.

I didn't dare question her about the words she had used to convince William to run to the bedside of an unknown father at the request of a despised mother. Maybe she had used an excuse to get him to rush to rescue the little sister he loved, not the parents he would prefer to keep away from.

Meanwhile, the minutes passed. I felt them flow over me, one after the other. I couldn't resist the wish to go back to him. I waited outside the door instead.

The situation hadn't changed. I remained nobody to Peter Wiles. I wasn't his wife, I wasn't a relative. I was just a woman who was at risk of losing him again, for the last time. An intruder, from the point of view of the nurses passing through the corridor, watching me with malice mixed with curiosity. But maybe it was just my own impression. Maybe I represented, more than anything else, an obstacle to their work, a bit like all the relatives and friends of serious accident victims, waiting for news and comforting answers.

Sandra joined me and nodded to invite me in. We remained silent, looking at him for a long time. I held his hand in mine, stroking it slowly, no more words left.

'He's here.'

The announcement was made by Matthew, overlooking the room from the doorway. It wasn't necessary to specify the name. Everything was happening in a too strange, too quick and too convoluted way together. And much of the fault was mine.

I would hold on to Peter, not leave him alone again. I would ask for his support, his help, instead of going to face the hatred that our son would unleash on me all alone. I was scared and I was a coward. But I had to face him and be overwhelmed. Alone.

I found myself in front of him. In front of his severe, inquiring green eyes. His arms crossed on his chest, defensively. Madeline stood by his side, so it was now clear to him that nothing had happened to his sister.

Strangely, I couldn't see contempt in his eyes. And not even resentment. More than anything else a disconcerting disbelief mixed with expectation. He already knew it. And he also knew that I was aware of it. But probably he too didn't imagine that the confirmation would happen this way.

'Peter Wiles is your father.'

There was no other way to say it. There was no time. And there was no chance of revealing the truth in a more delicate and painless way. As far as I knew my son, I would only unleash the fury that he kept temporarily dormant. Every benevolent word that I could have sprinkled the revelation with would be counterproductive to us. The two of us, more than others, having made words and their significance our profession, knew what effect words can have, and their effect would have been wasted on him.

'I've known it for a while, now.' William replied with equal frankness, keeping a firm, almost unperturbed tone. 'But whatever you mean to ask me... don't do it. The answer would be no.'

I had never felt so fragile and close to the end. Not even in my worst moments. Mine was a moral, physical, emotional end. Not an end, like the other times, and then struggle and be able to be reborn, rise from my own ashes like the phoenix. But the total end. Definitive, irreparable. With no chance of return or salvation. There would be no redemption for me, there would be no forgiveness. Never.

I nodded briefly. The strings that held me up were breaking, one after the next. I could have collapsed, it was time. Yet I still remained there. Firm, motionless. Staring at the son I couldn't ask to put his own life into play to save someone who remained a stranger to him, an inopportune presence in his existence. As was mine, especially in recent years.

I turned around without replying, still remaining motionless in what had become my living space. Nobody there was thinking about me. Nobody cared now. There was only him, in that room. He was all that was left for me, maybe just for a short time. And I could only reach him, lean my head in the hollow of his shoulder, close my eyes and keep talking to him...

'The answer for you would always be no, Mom.' William's voice struck me with a harshness I had never encountered in him, despite our repeated conflicts. 'I'll do it for my sister. I'll do it for that boy who, unlike me, could lose a father he has known. I'll do it for these people who are total strangers to me but apparently I'm related to. Not for you. Because I, Mom, unlike you, have a heart.'

CHAPTER 79

Another thing I would never have thought possible was to find myself one day in the small chapel of a hospital praying to a God I had never believed in. And who I didn't even know how to address. Religion appeared indefinite in my eyes. It had lightly touched me during the education that my parents had given me, but it had never involved me nor convinced me. I had always been a humanist, but with a perfectly and purely rational mind. An atheist, maybe? Maybe not. Agnostic, perhaps? Something or someone must have been there, I was willing to admit it. But I wasn't aware of it, I had never dealt with it, I peacefully stood my distance from it.

The only thing I clearly understood was that that something or someone couldn't tear Peter away from me. I wouldn't permit it. I wouldn't be able to tolerate it. And if I had to beg, pray, kneel or prostrate myself... I would do it. Even if I was a heartless woman, as my son had reminded me before undergoing the analysis that confirmed his suitability as a donor.

"He might not make it anyway." I shook my head firmly, trying to push away the voice of the doctor who described to us the situation and the possible side effects. "He might not survive the surgery or have a rejection crisis. He is very weak and has already undergone another operation, complications could take over."

I was sitting on that wooden bench inside the chapel. The others were waiting in the hospital waiting room. The surgery would last many hours, the doctor had not specified how many. Even so, nobody had moved.

Only me, as a perfect culprit and coward, I had stepped away. I couldn't bear that artificial silence any longer, combined with

360

the glances that were addressed at me. I had the feeling that everyone, inwardly, was subjecting me to a trial from which I would receive an exemplary condemnation. They were right, I couldn't deny it. I preferred, as usual, to run away and go and take refuge in a God I didn't believe in and who I didn't know how to address, rather than let myself be annihilated by human judgment.

Maybe because I couldn't admit that something went wrong. No, it wouldn't make any sense. Life wouldn't leave us unfinished business, pending issues. I didn't care about anything, I didn't care at all about the rest of the world and humanity. But my little universe couldn't break leaving me alone, despite my faults.

Peter had been present for too long inside me. It had little relevance that we had not always been together, that we had spent long periods of distance, even emotional detachment. He was there, a permanent presence in my heart. Every day, every moment. He couldn't leave me alone against the rest of the world, because I would never be able to deal with it.

I would return to be the Amantine Delamar I had been before I met him that Sunday morning. With a precise, well-defined road, with a future designed at a draftsman's table. There was a horizon for me to follow, charting many straight lines that would link one goal reached to another. Without interchanges, without surprises, without upheavals. A bit like in the drawings in which the figure is formed by connecting the various numbered dots. This here, would have been my life without Peter. Perfectly drawn but without emotion, without soul. So it would be, back to being, if he goes. Like before meeting him. With the difference that before, not having had the chance of a comparison, I would have considered my life satisfactory and fulfilled.

So for the moment there was nothing left for me to do but sit down on the wooden bench with joined hands and crossed fingers. Not in prayer. I felt more like a schoolgirl being punished. Intimately infuriated, I suffered the torture of having no other choice besides waiting.

Meanwhile, I wondered... if there was a divine justice for my misdeeds why had it to hit Peter and our son? Why should they be risking their lives in an operating room while I was here, perfectly healthy?

I stamped my foot on the ground, angrily. No, all bullshit! There was not a just and righteous God. Only one that has forever been the cause of wars. Only one who forced me to expiate my guilt in the most subtle way. And I didn't even have the relief of those glimpses of life picked at random that had somehow comforted me on my journey from Leeds to London.

I was trying to direct my thoughts towards Peter, my moments with him. And also towards my children... Positive thinking. Other bullshit to subjugate the crowd, the weak, the inept. Damn it! My rationality knew no reason. Although I was a literary scholar, I had a more analytical, more logical, more scientific mind than my mother and my brother combined!

I stamped my foot on the ground again. There was no relief or peace for someone like me. I was starting to envy those who found comfort in faith. I couldn't, not even committing myself to such a delicate moment. Or perhaps it was faith itself that rejected a heartless woman. So much so that I had lost the ability to find comfort even in tears.

I winced at the touch of a hand laid suddenly on my back. Turning my face slightly, I recognized Peter's mother. She possessed a composure superior to mine considering the situation. I hadn't seen her let go to uncontrolled tension and cry. But I noticed in her a peace, a quiet that I would never be able to find. No, my composure was all appearance, in fact. Inside I felt like a time bomb ready to explode causing devastating effects. Or to implode, more likely.

I questioned her with my eyes. Was it possible that they had already finished? Had I lost track of time?

Sandra shook her head slightly and gave me a slight smile. 'A nurse told us they will still have to continue for a few more hours. You should eat something, dear. Or maybe rest a little...'

'I will have plenty of time to eat and rest. Now the only thing I can do is stay here and feel like the most useless woman in the world. Because it's really what I am...' I sighed, lowering my face. 'Only... I had never been so aware of it...'

'It's not like that...' Sandra whispered, continuing to stroke my back. 'You saved my son, Amantine.'

'The doctor said...' I looked at her, shrugging. I didn't even want to repeat all the side effects that he had explained to us.

'No, I don't mean now. More than twenty years ago, when he was about to fall into the abuse of drugs and alcohol again, after they pushed him back in that direction. He resisted for you. Even when you left without a trace.' Sandra slightly closed her eyes as if to re-emerge in a distant past. 'He fought for you. Hoping that if he proved himself to you, if he became a great artist recognized by all... you would forgive him and come back. He said that in the important moments of his career and his life he wanted you by his side. He said that you promised so and he hoped you would remember.'

'I couldn't come back. The truth is that I never left...' I put my hand on hers, with a sweetness unknown to me. 'From the first moment I met Peter... I never left. It was just my body that took another direction. I shouldn't have allowed them to separate us like that, all this time. I was weak...'

Warm tears flowed down on my face. Searing. I had never left. Never. I couldn't lose him.

'Let's go and have something warm to drink, at least. Peter and your son will need you, in a while. You need to keep your strength up.'

I nodded, just to please her. Sandra got up from the bench and walked towards the chapel's exit. I held back a moment before following her. When I reached the entrance, I turned to the altar and raised my face to a crucifix hanging sideways. I needed to keep my strength up. Strength was one of the components that I had almost never gone without in my life. But I needed it more than ever. It was all I could give of myself. I had nothing else.

I walked a few more steps and saw Sandra standing and talking to a blonde woman, looking pained and tired. Before I could question who the woman was, she shook my hand.

'I'm Mark Wright's mother. The boy Peter saved from the fire in the rehearsal room. If he hadn't come back to try to rescue the boys, my son would have died... like the others.'

March 15th, 2014

CHAPTER 80

Where it all began, in a sense a watershed in my life, between past and present. Absurd that he was buried right nearby. It almost seems like a joke of a perverse destiny. Besides not having great faith in a God who has not saved us, I have little inclination and affinity towards destiny too.

I feel like the protagonist of Anna Akhmatova's poem. The title escapes me... No, I have it, here it is: *Last toast.* I try to avoid it, to distract myself, but I find myself reciting it mentally.

"I drink to a destroyed house,
to my unfortunate life,
to solitudes lived together
and I drink to you too:
to the deception of lips that betrayed,
to the dead frost of your eyes,
to a cruel and crude world,
to a God who has not saved us."

It seems written for me. Maybe I could really find comfort in alcohol.

It is useless to attribute responsibility to some unknown and indifferent divinity. I should have saved him. I should have warned him and intervened. Take out all my anger and my contempt on those who hurt him. I had a feeling that he would do it again, even if I didn't know how, when, where. A sort of omen, of illumination. If I had intervened actively instead of just warning him. If I had reported what I was aware of, somehow...

They talked about an accident. I believe it. But I could have still prevented it from happening. Where it all started, where it all ended. Really ended.

The light touch on my shoulder instils relief in me. Maybe in all these years he has been the only one who never judged me. He caught me in almost all the stages of my life. Egocentric, a bit of a snob, opinionated, amused, melancholic, mad, in love, destroyed...

'Gordon... apparently it's really all over.'

I don't ask him why he bothered to come to Simon Jennings's funeral. After all, the same could also be asked of me. I despised that man. I still despise him, despite his atrocious end. Which coincided with mine, unfortunately.

'No, Mrs. Amantine. Mr. Wiles wouldn't like to hear you talk like that. And I don't like it either.' His tone is firm, resolute. There is still so much energy in this now old man. There has always been more than I ever imagined.

I sigh deeply. 'You're right. But I... I don't know where to go anymore. Maybe that's why I came here. To say goodbye to someone who has ruined my life. However, the truth is that he has only partially contributed. I did everything by myself.'

'It's not true. There were circumstances...' Gordon seems busy selecting the words to address me with. Maybe he believes that I need consolation, but nothing can now ease my pain.

'I'm looking for something to hold on to. A good self-esteem manual would tell me to hold on to myself, to find serenity and peace within myself. But inside me now there is nothing left, just an emptiness that I can't fill. And I... I know I can't talk like that to the others, I know I'd make them suffer with my selfishness. But that's the truth, Gordon. I have always been selfish, a conservative and superficial little woman. I have always put myself first. Not Peter. Not my children. Just myself. And I can tell this to you, because you have always seen me for who I am...'

'Amantine... we are all selfish in this world. But we don't all have the same courage and the same clarity to admit it. Easier to clothe ourselves with do-goodism to turn the tables when dealing with the rest of the world.'

Gordon is not complimenting me. He's not telling me that I was and I am a good person. He doesn't deny my selfishness and doesn't try to comfort me. He is a wise man.

I move slowly toward the exit, nodding to Gordon, who walks beside me. Once I have passed this iron gate, I won't think about Simon Jennings ever again. In his death, he dragged with him the members of the new band he had formed, his new Darkest Storm. Four boys between eighteen and twenty. Except for Mark Wright, who Peter managed to save. There were so many artists ready to rehearse in that room. Why him? Why didn't he run away like everyone else?

My eyes become wet against my will, I sniff. My silly boyfriend. My boyfriend who, unlike me, has always followed his heart in his choices. Gordon hands me a white handkerchief. I accept it by nodding gratefully.

'Thanks, Gordon.'

We are out. Another phase of my life has ended, definitively concluded. I myself abandon it behind that gate. Never more rancour, never more sense of psychological and emotional annihilation, never more fragility. Beautiful and strong. Strong above all, as he told me.

'I saw that letter, Amantine. Your letter.' Gordon stops and forces me to stop as well. For a moment I don't understand what he's talking about. Just for a moment. 'Simon Jennings grabbed it out of my hand. He said he would give it to Peter. I shouldn't have believed him.'

'Maybe not. But what's done is done. Peter never received it. And I should have come back earlier. In fact, I shouldn't have left at all. Gordon... if I think back to this whole story rationally,

I can't even find a real culprit. Me maybe, more than anyone else. Even regarding Simon Jennings... there are moments, as before, when I feel an irrepressible hatred for him. After all, I hated him from the first moment. There is not even death to save him from my anger, from my contempt. But there are moments, because then... I realize that he was just a man. Ambitious, egocentric, tenacious. Up to the excess. But besides, haven't I been the same too? It's not a comic book or a novel in which there are totally good superheroes and totally bad antiheroes. Simon was trying to protect himself... but he went too far. I have also made one mistake after the other. You, Gordon, let him grab the letter that would have taken Peter to me... Sometimes I wonder if we are not all part of a destiny already written, of a design. But I don't want to believe in destiny, destiny horrifies me...'

'Simon Jennings was an avid climber, ready to exploit anyone. Indifferent to Peter's fate.' Gordon puts a hand on my shoulder and looks me straight in the eyes. 'Don't compare yourself with such a man. Neither do I believe in death as redemption of human beings. What Jennings was doesn't change. According to the testimony of the boy who survived, even during the fire, he tried to save himself first, he didn't worry about the boys. You, Amantine, have only made mistakes. You were just too scared.'

'I continued to pursue my world, to look for it, without understanding that I had already found it together with Peter. He was my world, the world where I felt free and happy.' I clasp my hands to my chest, as if to protect my overly oppressed heart. 'The world I lost forever.'

July 2014

CHAPTER 81

The more I think about it, the more I am convinced that I couldn't have chosen another place to move to. And I believe it was the first decision that was completely mine. A bit crazy, totally irrational but dictated by the heart. I perceived a stronger beat as soon as the thought touched me. So maybe I'm starting to have a heart and to feel it, more than anything. Not just as a muscle that is beating regularly, that allows me to continue living. Maybe William would be amazed.

As a refuge I chose the hometown of the one who gave me inspiration for his name. Stratford-upon-Avon. Although I actually live in a smaller, more isolated cottage surrounded by greenery. In the village of Shottery, birthplace of Anne Hathaway, William Shakespeare's wife.

My cottage, small in size, is structured in a very similar way to Anne's. It's also for this reason that I had no doubts, I found it adorable at first glance. In this case as well I was attracted by the outside cover, then I really fell in love with it. Perhaps because of the presence of so much greenery around it I felt reborn here, as if I was allowed to find oxygen, to breathe again. To start living again or at least to try. I live on hold, actually. In constant expectation of hope.

This is my home. Tiny but mine. Not my parents' home, the Parkers' home, the home I had with Geoff in which I felt like a stranger, my brother's home... Even when I was teaching in Leeds, my stay at Haworth was a bit forced by my commitment to the university, it wasn't a real choice, even if I still feel connected to all the Brontë Country because of the sisters, Emily most of all. And then there was that home... Peter's home in Notting Hill, which although I felt like it was, has never been mine. This instead is mine, in all respects. I invested my savings in it. I take care of the garden, as far as I can. In a way it has become the place where I buried the love that I no longer know who to give to.

As Virginia Woolf had her famous room of her own, I no longer have my study. Now I have my lovely little brick-built cottage, with white shutters and a green roof. With the tiny garden that surrounds it, as if in a hug. The rose garden on one side and the walkway leading to the low entrance gate. For me it is a bit of a miniature paradise.

I've been living here for almost two months. I've seen others, more beautiful, more elegant, more spacious. But this one, besides stealing my heart, was immediately available. Inherited by two career Londoners who hoped to get rid of it as soon as possible. I found myself in the right place at the right time.

I take care of the roses above all. And I'm still a mess. I don't know anything about them. I bought some books and got advice from the village florist, a sprightly old man with a pure and sunny soul. I find relief among my roses, even if they have only been mine for such a little time.

I also enquired about who this place belonged to before. It belonged to an old widow who had lived here all her life. Unlike me, who has wandered the world, belonging to many places and to no one. Maybe I need a bit of stability too. Among my roses, my books, my tea at five o'clock in the afternoon. I don't feel English, I've never felt I belonged to any nation, actually. I've never had patriotic ideas, but I'm increasingly part of this world, this place, this way of leading my life and spending my days.

I don't know in what way life has been generous to me. Maybe it was, and the responsibility of not having seized the opportunities was mine. I've lost everything. My story. As if I had been forgotten here, confined to this corner of the world that, despite all, I feel more and more mine. So much so as to assimilate and become part of it.

My research, my photographs and my songs remained with me. Our songs. And that tape recorded on a cassette, for me always intact between my memories. I listened again to that song, mine, ours.

I was the reason, not just an excuse to fill a new successful album. From the start, since he gave another title to that melody, so as not to use my name.

Amantine's song was my story with Peter Wiles, it was my life, for better or for worse, with virtues and vices. Love that went beyond appearances, differences, conventions, the difficulties of making my world coexist with his to create one that was totally ours. Because we really were beyond everything. Beyond life, beyond death. Even beyond pain, or defeat.

I keep waiting. But I don't allow my heart to be annihilated, to let itself die in anticipation. I'm in desperate search for oxygen to keep breathing. I'm looking for a smile among the neighbours, among the passers-by, among the inhabitants of this small village. In what I listen to, in what I write.

I'm designing the plot of a historical novel. I found the one I had bought that day and I felt joy seeing that woman again with ruffled hair on the cover. She looked like me before our meeting, while I was waiting for him. I was wearing a blue dress too. I read it as soon as I moved here. The protagonist, Claire, is too young, sweet and pleasing to really resemble me, but I liked it. It's a love story.

CHAPTER 82

I guess many people pity me. In the last few weeks, mostly, I underwent the parade of all those who feel compassion towards me. Probably during the early days of my transfer to Shottery they hadn't taken me seriously, they hadn't believed that I really meant to take shelter in this quiet corner of the world. As if it wasn't like me, wasn't in my nature. The truth is that even I have never been able to define what exactly my nature is. And at my age I don't see the need now to try to define or to classify myself.

Even my parents came to see me. They appreciated my choice, but my mother told me that she didn't feel elderly enough to take refuge in a village of few souls, in a small cottage surrounded by a garden. I do not think it's a matter of age or place. My parents have become too Parisian to adapt to any other city in the world. They have taken roots, having settled there for so many years now.

Rachel and Trevor approved my choice, however. And Alain and Marianne as well. Marianne, more than anyone. She has a weakness for this area, and she had Alain promise her that they will also take refuge here when they "retire to private life" leaving London and its unstoppable and chaotic movement.

Is this what they see in me? A woman who has now retired to private life, because the public one was too heavy, oppressive? Maybe they do. And it's fine with me.

I received a call from Doris, it was nice to hear from her again. And also, Geoff called me, to show me a sort of friendly solidarity. We talked for almost two hours and it was comforting to me. He told me about his intention to return to England next year. By now he started a new life, it's no longer necessary to keep a distance. And he no longer risks being influenced by his father.

Madeline has decided to stay with me for a whole weekend. I don't dare question her about her feelings for me, I find myself in a situation of great tension and above all of embarrassment. But if she's here and she's going to stay for a while, at least with her I think I have some hope of recovery. Maybe I just deceive myself that it's like this. Madeline has always had a sweet and complacent personality, which somehow partly conceals what really hides deep in her heart.

'William still needs some time...' My daughter also has the extraordinary gift of reading minds. I would have never dared to ask her specifically about William, knowing that he no longer wants to know about me. I would have put her in a difficult situation with my questions, forcing her to answer me. 'Anyway, he's fine, he's in perfect shape by now.'

I nod and stroke her hand after placing the tea tray on the wooden table in the living room. I've learned how to make apple pie and a very simple chocolate cake recipe. Not bad for the cooking disaster that I have always been. Here the rhythms are so slow that I always seem to have all the time in the world available to me.

I feel excluded. In addition to self-exclusion by choice, not to put others in excessive difficulty. I hurt too much. Everyone, including myself.

'He just needs time, Mom...' Madeline repeats. She understands my mood and she would like to comfort and support me, I know. 'You'll see... everything will work out in the end.'

I nod again, biting my lips. I can't help but think about it. I can't.

'I was so wrong, Madeline. But besides repeating it to myself and admitting it to everyone, I don't know what to do. I'm not good with words, even though I work at it as my job. And I'm not good at human relationships. With William too, it seems that I'm totally incapable of expressing myself...'

'William is just like you in this.' Madeline smiles while sipping her tea. 'That's why you've always clashed so much.

You have the same character, even if I believe that he has also taken something from...' She suddenly stops.

Also from him. I know. It's true. Perhaps pride and good heart. But inflexibility and obstinacy I fear come mainly from me. I prefer not to think about it, I prefer to completely remove the idea of us. We had gone so close this time... Although often the thought is created by itself, without my precise choice.

'I was hoping it wasn't too late to fix everything. And I kept hoping, waiting for the right moment until the circumstances took us over.'

'I know, Mom. But why didn't you tell him anything during the first years when you saw each other again? Before it was too late, before William began to suspect it and then find out for himself and confirm it like that...' Madeline sighs. I read reproach mixed with resentment in her eyes. Her habitual tenderness doesn't shelter her real opinion and her judgment towards me. 'There was a moment when I thought as well I was...'

'No, darling. You're not.'

I read that question in her eyes the day she became the only hope of convincing William to undergo the operation. She never asked me specifically. Maybe it would have been easier with her. Maybe she would have understood me as a woman. Or maybe being Madeline, with Madeline's character, Madeline's sweetness, she would have found a better way than mine to handle the situation. But she is Geoff's daughter. The daughter I had for him to thank him for saving me from myself. For saving me and my little William.

Madeline scans me silently, tasting my apple pie.

'I was afraid he wouldn't believe me.' I don't even dare to say his name. I almost forbid myself to even think about him lately. It hurts. 'There was a moment when he asked me to leave everything for him. But I couldn't. You and William were too young. So I told myself that I would wait a bit... then a bit more...'

'You should have listened to him, maybe. Waiting, you did nothing but make things more and more difficult, for everyone.' Madeline tilts her face and sighs. Then she raises a smile, she is still in a reproaching phase but has taken a more indulgent tone and look this time. Her hair surrounds her face in soft waves with golden brown tones. I almost didn't realize how much she's growing. How free, intelligent, independent she is. More than I have ever been, even when I was many years older than she is.

'I was afraid of losing you and William... and eventually...' Eventually I lost them anyway, one way or another.

'Eventually... everything can still be fixed. I'm here... and William just has to make some more peace with himself before he makes peace with you.' Madeline smiles and sticks another piece of cake in her mouth, showing appreciation. 'He cares about you. But at the moment he is rediscovering a part of himself that has been a stranger to him his entire life. I know patience has never been your strong point, Mom, but you don't have any other option for now, you have no choice. If you've learned how to make this delicious cake, you can also learn how to be patient.'

CHAPTER 83

Patience. Patience. Madeline is right. It has never been one of my skills. But it's a bit different from learning to follow the recipe for a cake without getting distracted and forgetting it in the oven.

My daughter's next visit with Matthew doesn't surprise me. Or maybe it does. The truth is that it tears my heart a bit to see a youthful version of him before my eyes. And also of myself. It rips it but doesn't totally break it. Sooner or later I'll have to get used to it. I still feel some deep cracks that I will have to cure. A slight compression in my chest. Yes, it's useless to hide it, it hurts. But, among other things to learn now, is the ability to heal the wounds it causes me to see the sight of his own son, who so resembles him.

Maybe I will need a good infusion for the soul, maybe some book from the series *Chicken Soup for the Soul* that I had always considered with suspicion. Those stories so sweet, so delicate and comforting. In which everything may not end perfectly well, but you still get a kind of consolation and inspiration for the future.

I asked Sandra for some pictures. I realized I didn't even have one, besides those I cut from the newspapers. I didn't have any real, personal ones. I wanted to see him as a child, as a teenager. Look in his eyes for William's, in his face the incredible resemblance to Matthew. Sandra allowed me to take some of them, to make some copies. I didn't want to hide away without him. Actually, I didn't even want to exist without him. He left me. He hadn't kept his promise. I just had to learn to live with that and, among the things to learn, this was the one I rejected most fiercely. Now it's a bit better.

I watch Matthew as I offer him and Madeline the cup of tea and the cake which are for me only a beginning of my new course of study "the perfect housewife". I don't think I'll ever have much success because in terms of lunches and dinners I manage somehow but I'm still a beginner. After all, I based my existence on having lunch and dinner with what I could get when I didn't find something ready.

I don't want to inquire what is going on between them. Whatever it is, I hope they won't make the same mistakes we made in the past. But for this to happen Madeline would have to be similar to her mother. And, besides the physical resemblance, she has got almost nothing from me. She is more mature, wiser, sweeter, more careful.

I suppose Matthew didn't tell my secret to anyone. That night remains between me and him and I hope he'll never reveal it to Madeline. The night when I realized I couldn't make it, I couldn't resist a moment more to such clear and drastic pain and rejection. The night that, leaving Sandra's house with my soul destroyed, I had the intention of walking along the river looking for some relief. Because I could no longer be strong, I was no longer able to be. I lacked energy, I lacked liveliness.

And that water seemed so comforting, relaxing, full of promise. It called me towards it. It attracted me with a persuasive invitation, like a mermaid's song. But instead of a mermaid it was him. I heard his voice deep in those waters, of that river. It would have been so easy to give in, let myself fall softly.

It was night and I was alone in that area of South Bank. The Thames ran beneath me over the parapet and I suddenly didn't want to keep walking without a goal. Nobody really wanted me around. I didn't want myself around, either. I stared at that water that was perhaps the only one to desire my presence.

'If you are thinking of doing something stupid, you can stop it now, because I kind of suck as a swimmer.' His voice had come from behind me. I recognized him immediately.

'You are not forced to dive, kid...' I closed my eyes, hoping the moment would pass. I felt cold shivering running across me from head to toe. He shouldn't be so similar to him even in his tone of voice. It wasn't right.

'Yes, indeed. I saw you now.' He leaned his back against the parapet, positioning himself at my side. 'I'm forced.'

'Matthew... why did you follow me?'

Reopening my eyes, I gave him a stern look. I had no choice but deal with him, but I did it with a resignation mixed with annoyance. I often had him in my way. Every time I went to Sandra's house. Which was also his home, and this justified his presence. But he seemed to be fixated with me in an exaggerated way. Almost as if he feared a reckless act from me, he had turned into a kind of bodyguard.

'You had an expression that didn't bode well when you left. This time worse than the others.' He had shrugged and leaned towards me. 'In fact, I think I'm right. So…'

'Go home, Matthew. Or go have fun somewhere. Dance, go drinking, find yourself a girl...' I was running short on suggestions. 'I feel like living in a movie scene, kid. I don't need either a bodyguard or a guardian angel. I'm perfectly capable of getting by…'

Matthew had pursed his lips, giving me a mocking smile. His resemblance to his dad upset me. It hurt me. It was as if an awl had been implanted in my heart and constantly turning, it forced it to bleed without mercy. A feeling even worse than the nail I had perceived in the early years of distance between us, when I tried to survive without him, carrying on the farce of my marriage.

'Will you drag me as well into your dark destiny, Amantine.' Matthew turned back, watching the river with a furrowed brow. 'The real trouble is that I couldn't even pretend I didn't see you because my guilt would condemn me. I would endure your children's hatred until the end of my days. My grandmother's reproaches. But besides all that, I'm not even twenty, I'm too young to die...'

'I wouldn't be a great loss for my children. I've always been a disaster as a mother.'

I had laid both hands on the parapet. I kept myself still, staring into space. Between me and my end there was only this stubborn boy with such a familiar face and a somewhat irreverent expression, but who knew how to analyse the situation in detail.

'A disaster is better than nothing. After all, I would prefer to confront myself with a disaster like you rather than with an absolute nothing, who, when I was a child reproached me for having ruined her top model's figure forever. She told the babysitters actually and anyone who happened to be in her company, but I understood. I was young, but my hearing was good.'

His statement had forced me to watch him. What did this boy want from me? Was he looking for a mother to replace his own? With me he would hardly have had better luck.

'William wouldn't agree...' Another sore note. Now everything and everyone were sore notes for me.

'William can't make comparisons. William should also calm down, sometimes. By now what has been can't be changed, that stubborn will have to give way sooner or later.' Matthew could face the truth with an enviable lightness. Maybe because he wasn't directly involved. Maybe because between suffering to annihilate himself and continue living he had chosen the second option. 'Then there's him, too. Yes, him. My father would never forgive me if something bad happened to you... And that would be the worst problem for me.'

Yes, that secret will remain between us. He won't tell anyone, not even Madeline. I still read it in his eyes, even now that I resigned myself and sheltered here, but without giving up, clinging undaunted to my hope.

I had embraced him in tears, trying to find in him what William still persisted on denying me. If I had decided to throw myself in that night, Matthew would have saved me, or tried anyway. Maybe for Madeline. Maybe for William, his long-lost brother. Maybe because he saw me as something vaguely similar to a mother, replacing the one who had tolerated him but had never really cared about him.

But surely he would have done it especially for him, his father. He, who still burns in my heart like a living and throbbing flame. He, who I still perceive by my side, every day, every night. Waiting for the moment when we will be together forever. Because that day will come, I'm sure. I just have to be patient and start breathing again. To nourish my hope in our love. The only one real, the only one that will show us the way to find each other again and part no more.

CHAPTER 84

My garden needs constant care. My roses above all. They seem to rebel against me, as if they consider me unworthy of them. They all remind me of the peevish rose in *The Little Prince*. I'm afraid that I have got the most bitchy roses in the country, if not on the entire planet. But following the logic, continuing with that of the Little Prince, they are my roses and I have to keep them.

"It's the time you spent on your rose that makes your rose so important."

This is my world now. I keep repeating it to myself, until I become completely absorbed. Now I'm convinced of it. My world. My roses. A small cottage all of my own. My hair gathered in a soft ponytail, my garden jeans and the pink checked shirt tied on my waist.

Then there are certain moments. But it's normal, certain moments happen to everyone. Patience and hope abandon me and I remain alone, the old, tired, fragile Amantine Delamar of the past. But there are roses, my little bitchy roses that I fear are decidedly laggard compared to all the other roses, the blossomed roses of my neighbours, the roses that I have always observed distractedly in the flower gardens. My roses are a little shy, a little reluctant to bloom.

I suddenly feel a little like Mary in *The Secret Garden*, even though her story has nothing in comparison to mine. Maybe just because she was a selfish, spoiled and problematic girl. These are elements we have in common. I also hum the nursery rhyme, as I remember it, as I try to take care of my garden, not secret but definitely rebellious.

"Mary, Mary,
quite contrary,
How does your garden grow?

With silver bells, and cockle shells,
And marigolds all in a row."

The more they rebel, the more I persist in taking care of them, as if I want to tame them, bend them to my will. I have to do it, some days more than others. I am obliged not to explode, not to go crazy.

Because despite everything there are days that start bad, from the morning they drag to the evening under the banner of a bad mood, although nothing different happens out of the ordinary. There are days when I leave everything and I don't care about the will of others and prefer rather to impose mine. Even though I know I can't. It wouldn't be right. So, I'm condemned to suffer and hope.

I sigh and pass a finger over one of my roses, also running it over the stem. Clearly, my roses, in addition to being displeased, are adverse to me because I inadvertently prick my finger with an almost invisible thorn. Maybe it's because of my precarious emotional stability that they refuse to blossom like they should.

I sniff, too loudly, as soon as I feel tears sting my eyes. I throw a hostile and frustrated gaze at the rose that hurt my finger with its thorn and that impassively caused my pain. I'm humanizing a rose to the point of feeling offended by its disrespectful behaviour.

'Cruel rose, rose without mercy!'

I just can't stop myself. I cry. Not for the rose. I cry for the happiness I lost. I cry for letting love go, stubbornly remaining in a world that never wanted me, that has always rejected me without as much as a scruple. I cry because I was deceiving myself for years, of being brilliant, but I was just normal instead. And I realize only now that there is nothing wrong with being normal, like many other people, but happy. Happy to exist, happy to love. Admit that in life you can make mistakes, but then do your best to understand them and make up for them.

Needless to resist the knot in my throat, fight to restrain. I cry and repeatedly wipe my face with my hands. I don't even care if anyone sees me. I have nothing to lose. I've lost almost everything now, except hope. Except my heart that still doesn't give up, but day after day it constantly calls him back to me.

My heart, yes. Still his. Always his. In spite of everything. I close my eyes, I put my hand on it and feel it beating. His name, again. Always.

'Shall I compare thee to a summer's day?'

His voice comes to me unexpected but strong, clear. Maybe it's not real, maybe it's just my imagination, my fragile illusion of the mind. Shakespeare... one of the sonnets he has put to music. In any case I reply, with the next verse.

'Thou art more lovely and more temperate.'

My voice, on the contrary, is trembling and insecure. I keep my look lowered, my eyes closed. I don't dare to open them and find out that it's only a dream.

'What did that bad rose to you?'

His voice, again. This time closer. I open my eyes and see him. Beyond the little gate. He looks at me like a teenager, a boy, a man now. I see all the phases of life in him.

'It pricked me. But in the end, it's what a rose does...'

I tremble from the cold. We are in mid-July, but I feel frozen to the point that I have to stroke my arms to search for warmth.

'It made you cry so much, though, with a little prick. But yet you took care of it, you protected it.' His voice so sweet, so soothing, is like a balm that relieves my wounds.

'I had no other choice. It's my rose.' I barely whisper, that I doubt he can hear me even if he is just beyond the little garden.

'Do you still love your rose, even if it pricked you, if it hurt you?' He leans against the gate with his hands, standing still in his position.

'It wasn't the rose... it was me. I hurt myself. The prick is nothing compared to...' I sigh deeply to find the strength to resist and continue. 'I lost so much. I lost everything. And I can never be forgiven.'

I realize that he puts a slight pressure on the gate to open it. I approach him a few steps, until I'm almost in front of him. I stop for a moment, open the gate completely but I can't take my eyes off his face. Is it really happening? Am I not dreaming? Won't I wake up desperate for having deceived myself once again?

'You forgive your rose, even if it hurt you. I ask you to forgive yourself.' He reaches out a hand towards me, barely touching my hair. I wouldn't have dared to touch him. 'To forgive me.'

I stroke the back of his hand and close my eyes. I still can't believe he's really in front of me. I remain silent, holding his hand in mine.

'So, you took refuge right here, bright star?' His caress moves from my hair to my face.

'This is my world now.' I keep holding his hand, maybe with excessive strength, fearing that it may suddenly slip away from me.

'It looks like a nice place, very poetic. You have chosen a beautiful world for yourself...' One more step, he keeps his hand on my face, then with his thumb he goes upwards and wipes away my tear.

'It really is. I'm learning to grow the garden but I'm not brilliant. As I've never been in literature. I have to give up... it's not in my destiny to be brilliant.' I sigh, resigned, and bite my lower lip. 'I'm just an ordinary woman, unfortunately.'

'But taking refuge in this corner of the world was a brilliant idea in my opinion...' With his fingers he takes a lock of my hair, placing it behind my ear. 'And tell me... Do you want to be alone in this little world of yours?'

'Not necessarily. But... I was sent away so many times and...' I shrug, finally finding the courage to look him in his eyes. 'Day after day, every word has been against me. Without even looking at me. I am no longer desired nor loved. Until... I have been asked to disappear and never come back... I have understood I cause more pain than relief...'

'I remember those words. But how was it possible to endure... having you next to me and not being able to see you. Not being able to walk, not being able to hold you, not being able to love you. Surviving wouldn't be enough...' Now it's his voice that is shaking, his tears that furrow his face.

'I asked nothing but to be with you, to take care of you... day and night, always... I...'

I take his face in my hands, luring him towards me. I feel him quiver. His pain annihilates me.

'I couldn't see you... How could I bear it? How could I tolerate you standing by a blind man, a man who couldn't even stand up? Who continued to have nightmares about that day when...' he sighs slightly, through tears, kissing my hands. 'Sweetheart... I rejected you because I didn't want to turn you into a nurse who took care of me out of duty... I didn't want your mercy...'

'Peter... didn't you feel my love? Didn't you understand that you broke my heart every time you sent me away? Every time you told me that you would never forgive me? So much so that it seemed to me to just hurt you...' I hold him to me. Now he's here, in my arms. I can't and I don't want to think about anything else. 'My love... I waited for you every day... I never stopped waiting for you to call me back... One word from you would have been enough for me to leave everything...'

Time. Everyone told me that he needed time. But time was passing and I felt useless. The days had become weeks. I was the only one he refused with firmness, the only one he rejected and treated with a coldness that bordered on the contempt, the only one he clearly avoided looking at, keeping his face turned towards that window with the curtains closed in his room in his mother's home.

Did he hate me? Did he hate me because in danger he had finally realized what I really was? A useless woman, a woman who was worthless, a woman who had only caused him pain. I had lived a life of fiction for years. I had hidden the truth from him.

Sandra said she knew her son. He was incapable of hating, especially me, he would never be able to hate me. He would come back, she suggested to me to give him the time he needed to recover, to have faith and not to give up. I wanted to be part of that time. I wanted to be there for him, to take care of him, to comfort him. He accepted anyone's help, except mine.

Then I resigned myself to being there in silence. Not to talk to him, not to force him. Observe his photographs, gently place them in an album after making my copies. His fake photographs printed in the newspapers no longer interested me. I wanted real photographs. I wanted him, as I had always wanted him. Find out how he was as a child, learn about his dreams, his hopes.

While others began to doubt my balance, I clung to hope. I didn't care that he couldn't see me well anymore, that he couldn't stand upright. My heart continued to remain intact and alive only in his presence.

I didn't intend to give up even that evening, along the river. I was just thinking of getting away for a while, giving him time as his mother had suggested to me. To create a world on my own, a heaven of peace.

At that moment Matthew had reached me, worried about a gesture I would never have made. How he looked like him that evening... so much so as to break my heart. I realized that my constant presence hurt him. I realized that I could love him from afar, without oppressing him. Even if after so much detachment I wasn't asking anything but to stand by him. I realized that he wasn't ready. Maybe he never would be. He could decide to continue on his own way without me. And in that case, I had to be prepared to respect his choice.

I had built a world, all for myself. Following my instinct only, from what remained of my desire for life. Not the advice or plans of others or a useless brilliance that had never belonged to me. I wanted to free him from my presence, but I would never, never be free of his. He was everywhere. In everything. I felt him. Maybe so much that my call brought him to here. And I still can't believe it's real. I suddenly remember those words.

"Amantine... do you want to make it real?"

'Peter... do you want to make it real?' It's me now asking him the same question.

He tilts his face and gives a smile. His face is almost the same as before, there are almost no signs of what happened anymore. Although he will probably always carry them in his heart, in his mind.

'I've never had doubts, Amantine. For me it was real even in our worst moments. Most of all in our worst moments. Maybe you've never really been brilliant, little egocentric intellectual. But you took my heart and you held it, you never returned it to me. That's why I'm here... to ask you if there is a bit of space for me as well in your delicious little world. Because it seems to me like a small perfect world to start over again... the best you could choose, my sweetheart. And because I love you... I love you and even if I can't yet offer you the best of me, even if I haven't yet recovered as I would like... I could no longer stay a single moment away from you.'

CHAPTER 85

I don't answer him. Not in words. I kiss him, holding on to him. I kiss him indifferent to the fact that we are in the garden, maybe under the indiscreet look of neighbours or bystanders. I kiss his lips, his face, holding him so tight I almost hurt us. His arms surround my waist and I'm immersed in his scent, in his eyes, in his lips that explore my mouth and run through my cheekbones and cheeks.

'Can I take it as a yes? Can I stay?' He smiles, breaking only a moment from me to look me in the eyes.

'If you've decided I'm good as spare girlfriend...' I laugh, kissing his lips again, stroking his hair. 'But I'm beginning to have aches, especially in the morning. And I haven't learned how to cook yet. I know how to make apple pie and a simple chocolate cake recipe. You are warned!'

'I guess I have no choice now there are no more Lolitas available to me as they once were. And it's a shame because I'll miss the jealous scenes of a certain spare girlfriend.' He gently strokes my back, then he holds me tighter, pulling me to him. I can't hold back a sigh at feeling his body merge with mine. 'However, I'm lucky you have decided to keep me because I've dismissed the car that brought me here. I could play on the street, but I doubt that some beautiful girl would pick me up now...'

'Don't even try! Lolitas or not, the jealous scenes are always available. In this small village there are other women who could throw indecent glances at my boyfriend... And I don't intend to allow it!'

He nods, bending his lips in an almost sarcastic grimace that reminds me of our early times together. 'So you mean it won't be all the same as before, Amantine? What was it like in our fantastic agreement? No questions, no claims.'

'No, it's not good for me...' I lower my head, remaining bound in his arms. 'I want more, much more.'

He lifts my chin with a finger and looks at me with a sweetness and intensity that he had never had before in the course of our story. I felt loved by him in the past. A lot, but never like that. Never as if he had gone through hell to get to me.

'You're mine, Peter. I love you and you are mine.' I run my fingers up his arms to reach his hands to hold in mine, intertwining my fingers with his. 'You are only mine. As you see, I have claims this time, many claims.'

I drag him by the hand towards the front door. He resists for a moment, pointing at the gate with a glance. I realize only now that lying on the ground at the entrance there are a duffle bag and his guitar. While Peter grabs the bag by the handle, I pick up the guitar.

'I hope I can satisfy all these claims... I was left a bit blind in one eye and I still limp.'

Moving towards the entrance I realise that he is right. He can barely walk at all, he must proceed slowly. I put my arm around his waist, allowing him to lean on me. In spite of everything I have never seen him so similar to the boy I met that Sunday morning. I never felt more involved, more attracted to him. Even his clothes are similar, a bit shabby, the irreverent way he scans my face, with sweetness mixed with desire.

'This could make you even sexier...' I giggle as I open the door and lay the guitar in a corner to return to look after him again. 'You look a little like Mr. Rochester at the end, when he...' I close the door, pushing him against it, running my hands over his chest.

'Maybe you're right. But you have very little of that little prude Jane Eyre at this moment...' He grabs me by my waist and furtively glances around, over my head. 'Oh, nice home anyway.

I think I'll see it later, the mistress is too impetuous and busy doing something else right now.'

'It's has been months now, and everyone, really everyone has asked me to be patient...' I unbutton his shirt, kissing his neck. 'I've had enough of it!'

I suddenly detach myself, fearing I'm forcing him. I stroke his face tenderly, losing myself in his eyes. He hasn't recovered yet, I risk hurting him.

Unexpectedly, it's he who takes over me, turning me and making me stick with my back to the door. And with my memory I relive all our past scenes, our passion, our kisses.

'Who told you to stop, sweetheart?'

I smile, clinging to him, and he caresses my hips, coming down with his hands towards my buttocks. He picks me up by taking me in his arms, kisses my neck and then my breast.

'I'll take you to see my bedroom for now, then you'll see the rest of the house. Our bedroom, my love...' I caress his arms, grasping his hands, putting me back on my feet against the door. I know he has not totally recovered yet and I don't want him to push himself too hard.

He nods and follows me diligently. As soon as we enter the room, he grabs me by my waist and kisses me passionately, walking me back towards the bed.

'I'm fine, baby. Now that I'm here with you, I'll be even better...'

I fall back on the bed, drawing him above me. And still I recall the past. The first time with him, when we signed our stupid agreement. Almost twenty-three years have passed, and nothing has changed. At the same time a whole world has changed around us, our lives intertwined from that moment onwards, one around the other. My heart has changed, or maybe it has simply understood that it's able to love beyond all limits, beyond all pain, beyond all trials that fate has confronted us with. To love him and nobody else. Despite everything and everyone, despite myself, my superficiality, my resistances. Despite our pact that I unknowingly transgressed from the beginning. Because, from the first moment, Peter Wiles had captured my body and soul. And he never let me go.

CHAPTER 86

What will become of us now? Will we be together forever? What other obstacles will we still have to overcome? We were excellent at creating one after another. I no longer intend to allow it.

I hold him tight to me. I have no idea what time is it, of how much time has passed. I don't even know whether it's day or night. And I don't mind not knowing it. I stroke his bare chest and gently kiss the tattoo on his shoulder. We are still us. I would have waited for him for the rest of my life. I would have waited for him whatever his choice had been.

I remember the first two days after the operation. The days when I was afraid I had lost him. The days when I could only wait for his awakening and he insisted not to come back to me, to us. The days when I forced myself into trying to pray in that chapel, without succeeding, without being able to. The days when they told me there was a chance he wouldn't regain consciousness again. The days when it seemed that all the side effects hypothesized by that doctor had merged against him and that they brought him back and saved him every time by some miracle.

Then he had stabilized. But he gave no sign of improvement. I had spent the two worst days of my life. The fact that he had stabilized was a huge relief. I kept talking to him, holding his hand in mine. I begged the sky to see his eyes again, which he kept obstinately closed. The others insisted on relieving me, to send me home to rest for a while. But I didn't want to leave him, I couldn't.

That day, that March 15th I will never forget, I let myself be persuaded to leave the hospital for a few hours, at least. But instead of going home I went to unleash all my rage against Simon Jennings. He had died in the accident, Mark Wright's parents had given me all the details about the fact. But I didn't feel mercy. I wouldn't have allowed him to drag my love with him, as if he had the power to do it. I was infuriated beyond all limits. I went to say goodbye to him as if to an evil spirit who abandoned my path forever. I realized that my heart is not good and prone to mercy, to forgiveness. That my love is selfish, exclusive. Jennings had tried to hurt him. Dead or alive, whatever he was, I couldn't help but despise him.

The meeting with Gordon at the cemetery put me at peace with myself. I don't know if he followed me or if he was there by chance, maybe driven by his own intention to purge the bad memories forever. Gordon could understand me, and I respected him. Although he never mentioned it to me, I felt that Peter's faithful butler loved me and had always accepted me as I was, though he understood the fundamental difference between Peter and me. Peter, despite the evil he suffered, remained a good person. I didn't. I can't even pretend to be.

No, I'm not, I'm definitely not a good person. Forgiveness or mercy don't win inside me. Not even resignation. While Peter was poised between life and death, I insisted on not giving in, not letting him go. Cursing Jennings, Geoff's father, Geoff, myself above all. His subsequent refusal hurt me, destroyed me. But I wanted, more than anything else in the world, that he lived. I've always loved him. Maybe in the most wrong, twisted and destructive ways for both. But I've always loved him.

'I've always loved you...' I believe I thought it out loud. I sigh, biting my lips.

'I know. I heard it.' He lays his lips on my temple, he holds me to himself. As often happened, this time as well he wasn't asleep. 'In the hospital... I heard you talking to me, Amantine. You talked about us, about our story, you said you loved me. And you were just like that, like now. With your head resting between my shoulder and my neck... As we have awakened so many times... I couldn't go away. I couldn't leave you. Even if it was painful to stay. My body didn't want to resist, it hurt so much everywhere... an atrocious pain, baby.'

'Did you hear me, Peter? Really?' I slowly raise my face to him and stroke his lips with a finger.

'Your every word. Your every word called me back to life. And it hurt even more than letting myself go... My heart was fighting against the rest of my body, against physical suffering, it didn't want to leave you.' He lifts my chin and kisses my lips. 'I wanted to react against death to hear you repeat again that you loved me...'

'I love you, Peter. After telling you in a coffee shop, on the phone and in a hospital bed, I'm getting better, you see. I declared my love for you in a flowered garden, even if among the bitchy roses... And now again...' I smile, taking his hand and kissing his lips with increasing intensity.

'Your roses look like you, little snob intellectual...' He kisses me back and puts his forehead against mine. 'But I love your each and every delicate petal just like your little thorns. Ready to prick me, to hurt me, then come back to seduce me again... again...'

'Implicitly you're telling me I'm a bitch!' I pull away from him, reoccupying my part of the bed and lifting my back against the pillow, crossing my arms.

'Not even too implicitly.' He leans on his elbow, turning towards me, throwing me one of his typical, ironic, allusive looks. 'You've always been bitchy, Amantine. It's part of you. However...'

I turn towards him, tilting my face, on hold. I arch an eyebrow, trying to keep the offended expression and resist the urge to kiss him again.

'However, you saved my life. During that fire I...'

I understand he's not joking anymore. I get close to him and take him in my arms. 'Love... you don't have to think about it anymore. I know it's hard.'

'No. Now it's much better... but... I wanted to help those boys. I was outside but I couldn't leave them. Amantine... they were like me, like Darkest Storm at the beginning. If I had run away, leaving them there, I...' He bites his lips angrily, his breathing becoming heavy, painful. I hold him tighter, ready to share his intimacies. 'It would have been like dying again, that night when I risked it during the party, you know... I didn't think rationally. The truth is that I was trying to save myself too, not just those boys. I managed to grab one of them, but then... I wanted to do more, sometimes I still can't find peace. They were so young... they were like us...'

'Peter... you couldn't do more.' I stroke his face, cradling him in my arms. I don't know how to comfort his pain. The wounds of his body are almost healed, I wonder if he will ever be able to heal the wounds of his soul. 'You saved a boy. An eighteen year old boy who wouldn't have his whole life ahead of him if you hadn't intervened, if you had run away like others did. Love... you risked your life for them. You can't ask more of yourself.'

'I spend a quiet time, but then sometimes I suddenly dream of them... they look at me and ask for help. Now it's better, though. It's really better. But... they were so similar to us, with Simon Jennings as a manager. He's not to blame for what happened, he was a victim too. But as soon as I met them for the organization of the events, I saw myself so much in them... And Mark Wright above all reminded me of myself at the beginning. Amantine, the truth is that I didn't try to save him. I tried to save myself. I haven't told anyone because I doubt that others can understand. You are the first one I've told. Was it fate that I saved him? I had to choose, of course maybe he was closer, but... this changes things a bit.'

'It doesn't change the fact that you saved the life of an eighteen year old boy who would have died if you had not intervened, Peter.' I take his face in my hands, staring seriously into his eyes. I don't address him with tenderness or compassion. He must understand that he has done something exceptional, extraordinary, risking his own life. The reasons that drove him to do so are of little importance. 'It's not important that you saw yourself in him. You saved a young man who can still live, sing, love, smile. His life will surely be marked by this incident. Just like yours. You couldn't help the others, unfortunately. But Mark is alive, with his family. And this happened thanks to you. Only thanks to you.'

'Thanks to you, Amantine. I went in to help those guys. But you... you helped me out, you dragged me out of that hell. I saw you in those flames... when I couldn't see anything anymore and the ceiling was about to collapse on us. I saw you and I followed you. You were like that night at the party. On the little bridge, when you turned towards me, you smiled at me. When I fell in love with you, even more. And I understood that I wouldn't have wanted anyone else in your place, ever. I followed you through the flames. The fire was all around me. I followed you, dragging Mark behind me as best I could, encouraging him not to give up. I told him... you see my Amantine, you see how beautiful she is... and she loves me, I can't lose her now. I have to follow her. I have to sing her song again...'

I grab his hands as he tries to catch his breath. I don't even have voice to comfort him, I tremble and feel suffocated by tears.

'Yes... I told him so... You walked through the fire, then from time to time you turned to look at me, as if to encourage me to follow you. You were just wearing that dress. And you had that smile, that look. You showed me every step towards the exit, you got me to safety, even if, because of the smoke in my eyes, I couldn't see anything by then... but I saw you...' He wipes away my tears. He suddenly seems more serene, his green eyes resume intensity, while I feel annihilated by the desperation of both, I take his pain on myself. 'Then, once I got out, I was hit on the head by something that fell on me. I don't remember anything else.'

'Peter... in those days I did nothing but think about you, when we could finally be together. So you came back to me following my image of that evening. Now we just have to try and be happy.'

There is nothing left that can separate us from our happiness. Nothing except... I sigh, bending my head. Except for him.

'You don't have to have any more secrets with me, sweetheart.' Peter immediately catches my concern. I can't escape him. He knows every one of my most intimate turmoil now.

'I don't. It's about William. He recovered very quickly after the operation, but he competed with you in not wanting to know about me as soon as he woke up. I was calm because I knew he was fine, he's a strong boy, but...'

'He came to know the truth in the worst way. Even if he already knew about it.' He strokes my hair and then my face. 'After you left, William came to me. He came back to see me almost every day, especially in the last month we spent a lot of time together.'

Nobody informed me about it. It doesn't matter. It's a bit as if I had been excluded and sent into exile, even if voluntary.

Peter goes on, continuing to caress me gently. 'Don't feel bad, Amantine. William and I had a lot to talk about. We needed to get to know each other, even if we are only at the beginning.'

'The truth is that I feel a bit excluded. But I'm glad he came to talk to you. In fact, at this point I did well to be away to give you the opportunity to get closer. I'm just sorry that now he will avoid you as well if you stay with me. William hates me, he will never forgive me.'

'It's not true. William loves you. He is disappointed with you. I believe you are the most important person in his life. He's also following the same career path as you.' Peter grabs me onto his chest and gently strokes my head, to comfort me. 'We spent a few days in Brighton. Me, William and Matthew. It was strange... even with Matthew I had never spent a lot of time, so initially we were a bit like three strangers sharing a temporary accommodation. But William immediately accepted the proposal to come with us, then things went very well. We talked a lot. He's not the introverted and hostile boy I imagined…'

'No, not with the people he appreciates. He's introverted and hostile just with me, in fact!' I raise my face to look at him. 'Because you're a darling when you want… and Matthew is adorable! I am… Amantine Delamar, the bitch par excellence who also bitchifies the roses in her garden!'

He tries to hold himself back, then bursts out laughing at me. 'You are a delicious bitch, though!' He kisses my forehead and sighs, looking at me with the expression a serious talk coming on. 'William is very stubborn and obstinate, just like you. He knows I was willing to stay here with you, I decided it during that week in Brighton with the two boys. I know you can't bear being told again, but you have to be patient with him.'

'I've been mean to him, since he was a child.' I bite my lips, caressing the arm with which Peter holds me tight against his chest. 'When he was three, he wanted a small toy guitar he had seen in a shop. My parents gave it to him as a present, but I didn't agree. He reminded me of you… he reminded me of you so much that it tore my heart. William, as soon as he received it, was enthusiastic about it. He never parted from it. He sat on the couch, poor little boy, with his toy guitar. And he started strumming it. He had a focused, absorbed expression, like you when you're playing and writing… So I ripped it out of his hands, angrily. I remember his expression, he looked at me with his big green eyes, full of tears… I was bad, and it was unfair to him. My poor little boy, he was so sweet and I…'

'I'm sorry, love. Amantine… I would have taken care of you and William. I would have done anything to make you happy. But don't suffer any more about the past. Think about what we have now. Even if…' He frowns and bites his lips and I notice a veil of tension crossing his gaze. 'In that time we spent in Brighton, along with William, I realized another truth that in all these years I couldn't admit, I didn't dare to confess even to myself. He already knew that before he was my son, he escaped you because he feared a confirmation from you. And he feared that I would refuse him accordingly. The truth... Amantine, my truth is that, unlike William, I feared a denial.'

I look at him, perplexed, disoriented. I can't understand what he's trying to tell me. I hold his hands to make him continue.

'Do you remember when we first met again, after a few years? When I asked you the names of your children? There, I... As soon as you pronounced his name, I felt... I wanted to ask you if by chance... It was only a moment that then I forced myself to erase from my mind forever. I didn't want to know. I didn't want your denial, or rather your confirmation that he wasn't mine. I didn't want the certainty that you had given that name to the son of another man, because William Shakespeare had tied you to me...' He shrugs, lets my hands go to hold me to himself. He sighs, averting his gaze from me, and then returns to stare at me with shining eyes in which I read a sort of remorse, of repentance. 'Do you understand, Amantine? I preferred not to know. I also feared the truth, because I wanted it to be mine and I feared I had deceived myself. Your fault was also mine... I attacked you and made you suffer unjustly. Forgive me, Amantine. William will have to understand, I will make sure that he understands that the responsibility was not yours alone.'

'Peter... of course I forgive you. I confess that a part of me had deluded myself that you understood that day. That you knew me enough. And indeed, you had understood. I would never have given that name to another man's child. I'm glad that William is tying himself, to get to know you. I can wait...' I nod and smile. The awareness of my son's contempt for me hurts. But it makes me happy that he is building a relationship with his father. If he decides to avoid me, I will accept it, I don't want to force him. 'Don't try to intervene in my favour. You would risk ruining everything with him and I don't want you to. If you want to spend time with William without me, don't worry. I'll stay here waiting, like a good girl.'

'Don't worry. Now I'm here and I intend to stay. Then we can stay a while in our house in Notting Hill as well... We can stay anywhere we want, but I won't leave you alone anymore.' He lifts me up and makes me turn towards him to stare seriously at me, stroking my face down to my shoulders. 'I've spent too much time without you. William will understand... You're just... here, you two are very similar, honey. Obstinate, stubborn, with that vaguely bitchy component that makes you unique.'

'I always thought he chose the same career as me, to challenge me... But who knows, maybe he was born to follow yours and I prevented him.' I smile, shrugging.

'Better this way. Matthew has got it into his head to become an opera singer. He continues to study and is doing auditions to sing in musicals in the meantime. Do you understand? I wanted to be a rock legend!' Peter shakes his head and gives me a frowned grimace, showing a terribly offended look. 'I don't dare to think of what William could do with his mother's temper! Maybe he can decide to become a conductor...'

'Who knows... Given the fact that we'll have some free time, I don't work at the university anymore and you're resting for now... you could teach me to play too.'

'Do you want to compete with me? Do you want to become a little egocentric musician?' He laughs and kisses me on my lips. Then he starts to tickle me and while I try to free myself, he manages to lie me down on the bed and get on top of me.

'Of course... but no opera for me. I intend to become a real rock star and have so many fans going crazy for me and waiting for me out of my home with love letters, presents and indecent proposals!' I laugh too and caress his hips, and his back.

I'm happy. After so many years I finally feel happy. I don't know if I deserve it, but it is so. I don't know if I deserve Peter's love, if one day I'll be able to deserve our son's forgiveness. My life is not perfect. It never has been. I lost a lot of time trying to conform to a world that wasn't mine, to an existence and a destiny outlined by me but to which I never felt I belonged.

I belong to Peter Wiles, to his world. To our children. To the world we will build together from today onwards. I can only regret my mistakes and the lost moments, those that we haven't lived together and we can't get back. But we have today. We have tomorrow. And above all we finally have our forever.

September 2016

CHAPTER 87

We live between our lovely cottage in Shottery and the Notting Hill home. In over two years of life together we have also enjoyed some holidays.

Peter has recovered completely. Sometimes he is troubled by some bad dreams, but it happens more and more rarely. In the morning, as soon as I wake up, I cling to him while he sleeps or pretends to sleep, I listen to his breath, keeping my eyes closed. It's one of the moments that I love most in our days. So that I can be convinced, that finally I have him all to myself.

He taught me how to play the guitar. Or at least he tried. I think that my furious strumming, as Peter calls it, has caused him more than a few headaches. But he is a patient and determined teacher, at least as much as I am a hysterical and prickly pupil. We also tried to compose some songs together. He mainly dealt with music, I helped him with words. However, "Amantine's Song" still remains our best collaboration. The song is his, actually, I just made sure that he didn't lose that melody.

Madeline continues her theatrical experiences and improves with each performance. When she informed me of her desire to study dramatic art a few years ago I took her intention as a whim.

I was wrong. Now she is letting herself get involved with Matthew to deepen the singing study as well and to collaborate in the company where he works too. Peter had to surrender to the fact that his son chose, at least momentarily, a different genre from his own.

So in addition to the soundtrack of our lives, our unbridled pop, rock and hardcore dances, we also gave some space to classical music, opera and musicals to encourage the kids. We are becoming romantic in a disturbing way, especially me. Old age is playing a bad joke on me.

I encouraged Peter to resume his career, however, only carrying out the projects he really cares about. The project of charity events has been carried out and completed, moving the dates scheduled for almost a year. It wasn't easy to get back into it, especially from the emotional and psychological point of view, but none of the participants wanted it to be lost. Peter also sang with young Mark Wright, during all the stages of the concerts. It was moving to see them together. They have been wonderful and are planning to record some pieces in collaboration. I hope that the boy has a bright future ahead of him.

One of the dates took place in the former Stevensons' mansion, as it had been previously planned. Peter and I walked together in the garden, then crossed that little bridge, holding hands. So it had to be. So it had to be since that night. But as Peter also says, I try not to regret too much from the past, I think about the present and the future. How happy he makes me now. And I do my best to make him happy.

'Amantine...' Peter, sitting on the sofa in the Notting Hill home, lays down his guitar for a moment and puts aside his notebook too.

'Hmm...'

I have just finished reviewing my book on Anne Hathaway for the last time, collecting everything I could find about her, her cottage, the environment she grew up in. Now it's ready to print.

I'm pondering on whether to start a research on the Brontë sisters, starting with Emily. I realize that maybe enough has been written about them, so it should be something innovative, I'm thinking of some sort of novel. Meanwhile, however, I am also tempted to try to write a real novel, starting from a completely original idea of mine. I alternate the writing from my PC to that by hand on a little notebook that I call "notebook of ideas". All the notes for my original novel end up in the notebook of ideas.

'Sweetheart…' Peter bends over to me and points his eyes at me. He sighs deeply to get my attention.

'Hmm…' I finish beating the keys on the PC keyboard, put it aside and continue to write in the notebook, I have an idea in embryo to be developed.

'My love...' I know him. When he acts like that, he's not willing to surrender.

'Peter, if you want the cookies stand up and go get them in the kitchen. Gordon has also left the delicious cream and dark chocolate cake made by his wife...' I smile and send him a kiss. 'While you're there bring me a piece of it and make some tea, maybe. In mine, don't overdo the milk. Thanks, love.'

'No, greedy girl. I don't want the cookies or the cake.' He shakes his head and crosses his arms over his chest with a piqued expression. 'I wanted to ask you something else.'

I lift my face and look at him. Now he has suddenly become very serious. I stop taking notes and close the notebook.

'Okay, you have my full attention. What do you have to ask me, Peter?'

'A very simple thing.' He sighs and moves towards me. He frowns, hesitant, purses his lips. I don't understand why he's so tense.

I raise my shoulders impatiently. 'So? Do I have to prepare some jealous scenes or what else? I'm out of practice, but...'

'Marry me, Amantine.' His eyes scan me, doubtful but determined. 'I love you and I want to marry you. Here's what I wanted to ask you, not the cookies or the cake... even if you might have preferred them.'

'Peter, but...' Is he serious? Getting married now?

'It's not a difficult question. Yes or no?' He's talking seriously.

'Love, but... get married now, at our age...' I sigh and reach out to stroke his face. He frowns and pulls back. 'And then hadn't we already been married enough?'

'Sure, with other people!' He acts offended and resumes his guitar and notebook, ignoring me.

I drag myself next to him, resting my head on his arm. Then I lift my face, kiss his shoulder and neck.

'You twice...' I point to him with my fingers.

'You for longer!' He gives me another sulky look.

'I love you so much, Peter, you know. But we didn't have much luck with the marriage history...' I take the guitar from his hands and lay it behind me, so that he can't reach it without crossing me.

'It wasn't us, Amantine. But I understand if you don't want to... I give up.'

'Peter... I want to stay with you forever. For all of my life. Of this I'm absolutely sure.' I kiss his cheek and then his lips. 'You think if we get married...'

'We've been together for more than two years, not counting what happened between us all the previous years, before we could really be together. We have already exceeded the standard duration of my relationships by at least three times. I don't think the problem was in marriage, Amantine, but in the people we married.' He gently strokes my cheek with his thumb. 'I'm sure it would have worked between us twenty-five years ago... just like now. We have been together for quite some time, I hope to get the approval of your relatives and friends. It seems that they have accepted me this time, they no longer see me as the damned and cursed pop star. I'm officially your boyfriend, at least I believe so...'

'I've never been in favour of marriage, Peter. But...' I sigh and bite my lips and feel myself blushing. It hasn't happened to me for a long time. 'I would have said yes to you twenty-five years ago. Not giving a damn about relatives and friends and their opinions. But now...'

'Now?' Peter grabs my waist and pulls me towards him. But at the same time, he gets off the sofa and kneels in front of me. He looks for something in his jeans pocket. 'I know you hate very official situations, sweetheart. I have to take you in good times, when you lower your guard for a moment...'

'You already had a ring in your pocket, Peter...' I point at him in disbelief. 'Then you had everything planned! You're setting me up, naughty boy!'

'Yes, I would say it looks like a ring. And usually the girl would get excited, cry for joy, say yes all moved... Things like that, as far as I can remember having seen it in the movies and in my previous experiences.'

'As a third experience, I don't think I live up to your expectations, Peter.' I sigh and look at my hands, free of rings. 'It must be said that I'm certainly not a marriageable girl. I've never been, in fact. I've always been a too busy and too demanding woman to be moved sitting in front of the movies. But... Peter, do you think it will work between us? As married, I mean. I realize that it won't be very different from now, at least I hope not...'

'Amantine, you are definitely demanding. I've been aware of this for a long time.' He takes my hand, gripping it in his. 'Listen to me, my sweetheart... The two of us could split up, it might not work between us. I know that I love you and I know that I want to be with you all my life. I've known it for almost twenty-five years. Of course, it could end tomorrow or in ten years. I could have died in that fire or long before, during the party many years ago. You could have thrown away the note I left you through Jacob and so you'd never really know me. I know that I want to take that risk with you, I know that I want to spend the rest of my life with you. I've never been more certain of anything in my life. We don't have absolute security, we will never have it, like everything else in life, after all. It could go wrong between us, as it went wrong between other people, but I'm ready to take risks with you now, exactly as I was twenty-five years ago. As I would have proposed to you twenty-five years ago, because I loved you. Regardless of whether you were pregnant, Amantine. Because I have never loved a woman as I have loved you, as I love you now, in these last years we spent together. Because I have never found in another woman what I have found in you, little intellectual snob. I have wanted you from the first moment, I looked for you in every woman I met in my life. You're not perfect, Amantine, far from it. Most of the time you're a mess and you're incredibly snobbish and egocentric. You made me suffer as I didn't believe was possible, you left me too many times, you hid the truth from me about our son. But you also saved my life, more than once over a long time. I clung to life thanks to you. With your strength, with your fragility, with your mistakes, with your fears... You are always there, you have always been there. And you've never shown yourself different from the way you are. You don't pretend to be better than you are. You tried to deny your feelings, but it's a mistake I made too. And if I can... if I really want to give all of myself to somebody, it's to you that I want to give myself. Because you, Amantine Delamar, have never asked me to change. You have always accepted me as I am, you love me as I am. I've never been Peter Wiles with you. With you I'm still an ordinary boy. An ordinary man.'

'Peter...' Nobody in the world has ever told me anything so beautiful, so true. He doesn't see me as a pure and wonderful being, indeed. He knows I'm not an angel. He's perfectly aware of all my faults, he has a very clear vision of them. And he loves me anyway. This I find extraordinary and unique in Peter Wiles. He loves me as I am. He has always loved me without trying to change me or to improve the slightly edgy and harsh aspects of my character, my ways sometimes a bit too rough. I had never cried before meeting him, I always believed it was a sign of weakness. With him I've learnt to cry when I feel the need. Above all, I've learnt to be moved without feeling ashamed. 'Stay with me forever, Peter. Be part of my world forever, even if maybe I don't even deserve a man like you. You are better and sweeter than me. But I'm lucky to be loved by you. In all that has happened to me in these years, since we met for the first time, I felt happy and free only with you. This is because you are my world, nobody else, nothing else. So yes, Peter. Let's get married, I want to be your wife. As soon as possible!'

I smile as he puts his ring on my finger. It's a simple and delicate engagement ring. He knows how much I hate appearances. He kisses my hand and my fingers, hugging me. He takes me in his arms on the sofa.

'Yes, baby. We will certainly do it quickly, before you change your mind.'

'I will never change my mind, Peter!' I kiss him repeatedly on his lips. 'You've convinced me now, you'll have to keep me! I don't believe in marriage at all...' I look him in the eyes, then I slowly lean my forehead against his. 'I believe in us. I believe that between us it will really work. Because I believe in you. And more than anything else, I believe in the two of us together.'

November 2016

CHAPTER 88

We get married in the very month of our first meeting, twenty-five years ago. Almost the same day. Peter took me at my word when I said, "As soon as possible!"

After the proposal we ordered pizza and danced all night. Our romanticism is always very atypical, the difference this time is that Peter had created a compilation of very romantic songs for the occasion, even if he wasn't entirely certain that I would accept the proposal to marry him.

I focused on the words of "Starting over again" by Natalie Cole and I promoted it to "our song". Not written by us, but that describes our story.

"And now we're starting over again
It's not the easiest thing to do
I'm feeling inside again
'Cause every time I look at you
I know we're starting over again
This time we'll love all the pain away
Welcome home my lover and friend
We are starting over, over again."

Even if I have to admit that our life is filling up every day with more of our songs, our books, our authors... our desserts that I commit myself not to let the oven burn anymore.

For the wedding we organized a private ceremony, very simple. Peter is relatively famous, although he doesn't have fans who obsessively follow him now. I'm only known in the publishing environment, but not even excessively. We have avoided spreading the news as much as we could, however we don't believe there is too much interest around our private life. Or maybe we only hope so. We don't want to attract attention, we never wanted it. There will only be the closest relatives, the closest friends, some of Peter's colleagues and collaborators.

I've never believed in the tradition that requires you not to spend the night together before the wedding, but Madeline, Marianne and even my mother insisted and didn't want to hear reasons, so I withdrew to the Shottery cottage where the girls organized for me a sort of bridal shower involving Sandra, Rachel and some other friends as well.

I suppose the boys organized the same thing for Peter, who remained in the Notting Hill house. They are all nonsense for me, I had suffered the same fate even on the occasion of my first marriage. In that case in Paris a rather stylish ceremony was organized but it was deliberately hastened by me and Geoff, because of my pregnancy.

This time everything is different. This time, even if we are slightly out of time, I really want it. And I bear little of anything that causes me to be without Peter to respect a stupid tradition. But I promised to be good and I don't want to upset those who have self-appointed themselves as my bridesmaids.

While, during the previous weeks, my daughter and Marianne had fun in proposing dress patterns of wedding dresses, I already had a very clear vision of what kind of dress I would choose for my wedding. I had it since the day of the proposal.

All I had left at Peter's house long ago had remained exactly where it was. Although he had ordered me to get rid of my things from his closet, his house, his sight, Peter had never put into practice the threat of throwing everything away. He couldn't get rid of it, he told me. Despite our detachment, they would occupy those spaces forever.

Among the other things, that dress was still there too, hanging in the closet. As soon as we got back to the Notting Hill house, I saw it, recognized it, softly touched it with my fingers. While I struggled to hold back, I couldn't resist. I burst into tears, seeing it again, remembering my despair that night. But also, the love I had realized I felt for Peter. Mine was a liberating cry. He hugged me from behind, holding me to comfort my tears. Turning around I met his green eyes, bright and moved.

So the day has come. I should feel excited, like all the brides, but the truth is that marrying Peter Wiles seems to me the most natural and spontaneous thing in the world. Maybe because our situation won't actually change. The fact of calling us husband and wife won't add or take anything away from our love. We have been many things during these years: we have been accomplices, we have been friends, we have been lovers, we have been in love against everything and everyone. Even against our will, against life and against death. We really have been everything to each other.

The ceremony has been prepared in a private hall that we rented in Stratford-upon-Avon. Among the choices available we jointly decided to avoid London by preferring a more secluded place.

I'm lying to myself. It's not true that I don't feel any emotion. The closer the moment comes, the more I feel the tension seizing me. Sitting in front of the mirror in the room where they helped to give me the last touch-up before the ceremony began, I watch my hands shake. I lift my face to look at myself. I watch my reflection carefully, wondering if he will like how I look. I'm afraid of disappointing his expectations. I pass my fingers over my temples, descending to my cheekbones and cheeks. I'm still the same, but at the same time I'm no longer the girl of that time. My skin is still quite fresh and my eyes are a little marked, especially from tension. I didn't sleep much last night. I hope the make-up and the hairdo stand up against my emotionality.

I stand up to look at myself completely. My dress is simple, of a light blue-green tone. I have delegated the organization of most of the marriage to Madeline, Marianne, my mother and Sandra. The preparation of the room, the choice of the cake and everything else.

My only real commitment was to track down the tailoring that had sewn that dress. I couldn't and I didn't want to wear the original model again, not even with the necessary adjustments. It belongs to the past. It wasn't even the fact that Peter had already seen it on me that disturbed me, I don't give a damn about traditions. I could even wear it again one day. For our wedding, I wanted something new, but that at the same time it symbolically recalled our past, all the years that, even apart, we have been together. I wanted him to see again in me the woman he had fallen in love with that night. The woman who had saved his life. As he saved mine loving me in such a unique, exclusive way.

Madeline looks inside the door and points at me with a gesture that the moment has come. They are all ready, they are waiting for me. She is so beautiful with her lavender dress, her long golden brown hair loose on her shoulders. She looks like an improved version of a past me. Improved in every sense, also temperamentally.

'I'm ready...' I join my hands and intertwine my fingers. I close my eyes for a moment and breathe deeply. I open my eyes again, look at my daughter and smile. 'I hope I won't cause any trouble.'

'Don't worry, Mom. The people here are used to it by now.' She laughs and holds out her hand. 'If you don't run away and don't kidnap the groom before the wedding, you'll see that everything will be all right.'

I reach the main door of the room that has been reserved for me. It's not very big, so just as I enter I immediately see Peter waiting for me in front of the small altar that was set up for us.

I tilt my head slightly as I meet his eyes. I see his expression change gradually from when he turned to when his gaze rested on me. My fear was unfounded. He looks at me exactly as he did then. With that love, that passion in the eyes. The only difference is that now we no longer feel constrained, forced to restrain it.

He tries to recover and reaches for me. I nod, keeping my gaze fixed on him, I begin to move to reach him, while Matthew hints at the melody of "Amantine's Song" at the piano. I feel my heart beating in my chest at a faster pace. I can handle all this, of course I can.

As we had established, there are not many guests, but the people who have been close to us for years. I greet Gordon with a smile, he is sitting next to his wife Annie. How much this man has done for us, with his discreet but important, indispensable presence.

Then I recognize young Mark Wright with his parents who regard Peter as a saving angel to be forever indebted to.

On the other side Doris with her husband Rupert. I remember the video seen at their house one afternoon, while Doris and I were having tea. A television appearance of Peter Wiles, when I still didn't realize who he was and considered only an ordinary boy I met on the street.

Rachel and Trevor, who remained my friends despite my divorce from Geoff. Rachel smiles and winks at me, waving her blonde bob.

Alain and Marianne with their three kids. My brother and his wife have supported all my craziness during these years. And they are, themselves, the demonstration that between two totally different people it can work if the feeling is authentic.

Sandra looks at me with tears in her eyes. She seems enchanted looking at me. I don't know what she thought about Peter's previous marriages, but since I met her that day in the hospital, she has been a constant presence in my life, sweet and reassuring. I also greet Harry's wife, Peter's brother, and their two kids.

I see my parents. My mother gives me a glance of encouragement that knowing her also indicates a warning to behave myself and don't get into trouble. My father extends his hand, accompanying me for a few steps until we reach Peter. This is not a church and I'm not a sweet, helpless girl to lead to the altar. It's just a civil wedding, but I make him happy and I let him accompany me.

Next to Peter is his brother, whom Peter has chosen as a best man. Madeline will be my bridesmaid, along with Marianne, and also my maid of honour.

He alone, is missing. It doesn't hurt me much anymore thinking about it. Also because in these two years we have had the opportunity to see each other and spend some time together. But I always had the feeling that it was Peter he wanted to see, not me. In a sense, I felt more like his father's partner than his mother.

It's all right. He established an excellent relationship with Peter and also with Matthew. He learned how to play the guitar. He had started taking lessons years ago, without my knowledge. He has always had a more stubborn and combative character than mine, he will never give up and he will succeed in achieving all his goals. I have always made "much ado about nothing", to put it in a Shakespeare way.

Now he has moved to America for a year, to deepen his studies of American literature. So I can... Here, I can pretend he is not present at our wedding just because he couldn't return, not because...

I put my hand on my chest. It hurts but I have to accept it. Everything is all right. Peter is here, in front of me. He holds my hand in his, smiles and nods. He still looks at me as if I was the most beautiful woman in the world. So I feel, through his eyes. In him I still see my boyfriend, the only one I have ever loved in my whole life. I have to bite my lip to resist, not to cry. I'm not so good at controlling myself anymore. But I mean, it wouldn't be like me, in front of all these people who have accompanied me throughout my life. They deserve a balanced and peaceful Amantine Delamar. Then no tears for the moment. Absolutely no tears, Amantine!

'Sweetheart... you're so beautiful.' Peter brings my hand to his lips. 'You're really here...'

'Did you fear me running away, Peter? It's all real though, we're here.' I smile and lean towards him to kiss him on his lips, stroking his face.

I hear coughing behind me. Am I subverting the traditions?

'The kiss usually comes later, Amantine... And it's the groom who kisses the bride...'

I accept my brother's suggestion and detach myself from Peter, shrugging. The celebrant in front of us smiles. I think he considers me an atypical and definitely rebellious bride. He glances at Peter as if waiting for directions from him to get started.

'I'd like to say something...' Peter sighs, taking up my hand. 'Amantine, there have been words between us that will remain ours only. They have been the words of our life, words that we have repeated over the years. Words that I also wrote in a song dedicated to you. First obligatorily concealed, then manifested openly. Now, in front of these people, I use the words of a poet that you love so much and on whom, under the suggestion of someone we both loved, you wrote your first successful book. I dedicate these words of John Keats to Jacob, who somehow put us together many years ago and we both miss today. And above all, I dedicate them to you, my love, because they clearly express what I've felt for you during these years. If I hadn't been there that Sunday morning... I wouldn't have met you. My life would have been completely different. Maybe happy somehow. But I would have never known what it means to love. Because to love for me means to love you, Amantine.'

John Keats. I wonder if he chose the same poem that I would dedicate to him... I close my eyes, waiting.

"I cannot exist without you.

I am forgetful of everything but seeing you again:

my life seems to stop there,

I see no further.

You have absorb'd me.

I have a sensation at the present moment as though I was dissolving:

I should be exquisitely miserable without the hope of soon seeing you.

I should be afraid to separate myself far from you.

You have ravish'd me away by a power I cannot resist;

and yet I could resist till I saw you;

and even since I have seen I have endeavoured often to reason against the reasons of my love..."

Peter stops, he seems to hesitate. He looks at me as if Keats's words came to life through him. I grab his hand and weave our fingers together. I decide to conclude with him.

"I can do that no more.

The pain would be so great.

My love is selfish.

I cannot breathe without you."

'I have a little surprise too...' I smile holding Peter's hand in mine. 'I hope that my surprise is not too devastating for you... and for everybody, I mean. I have been very attentive to your music lessons, my love... Even if it didn't seem like, I've learnt something.' I nod to Matthew to play the melody I composed on the piano. Matthew nods and executes. I look closely at Peter's expression as the notes played by Matthew spread into the atmosphere. 'I realize that it is very simple, elementary, but working on it perhaps... You know, I would like to complete it with you, I would like this time to write the words together. Because "Amantine's Song" is part of the past. This new melody

416

is for our present and for our future, a new story for us, all ready to be written. I've called it, "It will always be real". '

Our worlds have merged to the point of becoming blended. Peter wanted to dedicate to me a poem by John Keats. I, with the collaboration of Madeline and Matthew, tried to compose a piece of music for him. Peter has invaded my field, more than once already. Now I've tried to invade his too.

'We will write it, baby. I can't wait. I've already found the title track of my next album, apparently.'

At this point we have to start. I made my little surprise to Peter and I wanted to make our day special and unique, within the limits of my possibilities. But now I can't wait for everything to end so that I can finally free myself from the tension. Also, because this situation of bride in the centre of general attention, it's not for me. The usual Amantine shouts to return to herself.

'Can we begin, then?' The celebrant asks for our consent and Peter nods. 'The best man has the rings, hasn't he?'

Peter turns to Harry and I follow his look. Harry checks his jacket pockets with hasty touches. His expression is halfway between bewildered and sorry. No, it's not possible! It just can't happen to me!

Harry glances at Alain, across the small aisle that separates the two rows of guests' chairs. He too feels the pockets of his jacket but shakes his head in dismay. Matthew gets up from the piano and performs the same gesture. My father, Gordon and all the other men in the hall do the same.

No, I don't believe it! What are they doing? Are they all crazy? Are they making fun of me? They can't do this! Not to me!

'You have chosen truly unreliable best men.'

Having turned to observe the guests, I find him right in front of me. At the main door from where I entered myself.

I turn to Peter for a moment, then I go back to look at him. Am I dreaming? I cover my mouth with one hand, trying to hold back a sob.

'William...'

He's really here. Peter had told me that he wouldn't come, that he was too busy, that...

'You're not the only one to organize surprises, Amantine.' Peter strokes my back as William walks towards me and the tears begin to flow, streaking my cheeks.

'Mom... don't cry, it should be the best day of your life.' William comes in front of me and smiles, stroking my face. 'I haven't crossed the ocean to see you cry.'

'Love... you're here...' I hold him close to me. My baby. My little William, whom I have made suffer so much during these years, for a fault that wasn't his. For my despair. For my lost love. For his green eyes so similar to his father's. So similar, that it was to wear my soul out, to break my heart. 'Forgive me, forgive me, my little one...'

'I'm not so little, Mom...' he whispers in my ear, returning my hug. 'As for forgiveness, you and I still have to work on it. But we have time. Meanwhile, be good, wipe away your tears and get married. I brought the rings. I'm here to be my father's best man. You didn't make me waste a journey, did you?'

I pull away from him, smile and shake my head. 'No, love, you didn't waste a journey. I'm ready to live the best day of my life.'

William places himself next to Peter, who gives me his angelic and provocative smile at the same time.

'You really are a terrible boy!' I sigh, drawing him to me. 'You made me cry in front of everyone... How could you? I'll take revenge tonight, you're warned!'

'I know, sweetheart... but this is what you have always liked in me. I'm looking forward to tonight's revenge...' He kisses my lips, indifferent to those present, to the tradition, to this marriage that only awaits being celebrated. 'The surprise was specially designed by me and our son, with the collaboration of the guests, to move a little snob and egocentric intellectual that I've loved for twenty-five years. You'll still say yes, won't you, Amantine? Will you stop being my girl to become my wife?'

'I said yes to you from the first moment, Peter. Since I decided to stop that Sunday morning. I kept saying yes to you over the years. I will become your wife now, but I will never stop being your girl...' I hold his hand tight in mine, we intertwine our fingers in a gesture that is habitual for us, common but intimate at the same time. Our moment has come. I'm happy, completely happy as I have never been before in my life. 'The girl in love who that night would have replied to you that she wished with all her heart that it was real... that it was real forever. The girl who loves you and will love you for the rest of her life. And for all eternity.'

This is our love story. Long, intricate, tormented. Dotted with mistakes, resentment, pain, regrets, obstacles, misunderstandings, setbacks, wrong choices. But also with so much love, joy, sweetness, passion, complicity. And finally, with redemption and forgiveness. Yes, this is really our story. The story of Amantine Delamar and Peter Wiles, who met and stopped, being an ambitious university researcher of English literature and a singer in a successful band. But they have become two imperfect people who together have achieved perfection.

QUOTES

John Keats: "Bright star", "La belle dame sans merci", "I cannot exist without you"

William Shakespeare: "Romeo and Juliet", "Then hate me when thou wilt", "Shall I compare thee to a summer's day?"

Alessandro Manzoni: "The betrothed"

Anna Akhmatova: "Last toast"

Antoine de Saint-Exupéry: "The little prince"

English Nursery Rhyme: "Mary, Mary, quite contrary"

PLAYLIST

Nirvana: "Smells like teen spirit"

Madonna: "Material girl"

The Supremes – Phil Collins: "You can't hurry love"

Blondie: "Call me"

Simple Minds: "Don't you (forget about me)"

Queen: "The show must go on"

Cyndi Lauper: "Girls just want to have fun"

Natalie Cole: "Starting over again"

ACKNOWLEDGEMENTS

Strangely, this part is always the most complicated for me to write, so I won't go on much. The story itself has already been long and hard-fought. Yes, I had to fight above all, against Amantine, against her not so easy to manage personality, her contradictory and often twisted thoughts, her internal struggles, her wrong choices, her dramas and the streams of consciousness that always carried her too far away from the achievement of happiness, the fulfilment of her destiny. With her heart that didn't want to give up, with her fears, and her frustrations that have become partly mine too. With her reason that didn't give in and accept, to leave room for feelings, love, sweetness.

However I thank, as always, you readers who have come this far. My intent, this time, was to write the story of a love that goes beyond and oversteps reason, a love that also unites two universes and two opposing personalities. Amantine and Peter, belonging to two different worlds, meet by chance. Apparently, they have nothing in common, however over the years, even against their own will, their paths continue to intertwine. They are guided and linked by a love that overcomes every barrier: personal, cultural, social. A love that in the end, despite adversity and despite contrasts, ends up triumphing.

I thank the people, the places, the emotions that have influenced the drafting of a story that has distant roots and is inspired, a bit like most of my stories, by my personal experience.

I thank the literature and the music that accompanied me in writing this story, as well as having accompanied me through my life.

I'd really like to thank Sheryl Lee, my proof-reader.

I thank Ghostly Whisper Ltd.

I thank Joseph, for being so supportive and sweet. You'll be in my heart, forever.

I thank the "real people" behind this story.

I thank my family for being so supportive to me since I started writing, all my life basically.

As I promised, I won't go much further. But after many pages, many words, many emotions, I confess that I feel a certain sadness leaving Amantine to her happy destiny together with Peter and with the people who are part of her life.

Is there the chance I'll come back to her in the future? I really think so.

About the author:

Website: https://www.barbara-morgan.com

Facebook: https://www.facebook.com/BarbaraMorganAuthor/

Instagram: https://www.instagram.com/barbaramorganbooks/

Twitter: https://twitter.com/BabsiMorgan

www.ingramcontent.com/pod-product-compliance
Lightning Source LLC
Chambersburg PA
CBHW030759260626
47169CB00001B/119